He didn't want to play it safe now.

Dave slipped his arms around Kara and drew her to him ever so carefully, a nurseryman with a new cactus he was still trying to determine how best to handle without getting pierced.

"I remember," he replied, his voice low, his mind already trying to figure out how to survive the turbulent ride looming ahead.

Part of him was fervently hoping that the impact of that first kiss was, for some unknown reason, all in his imagination.

Part of him was hoping it hadn't been.

Dearest Reader,

People are always asking me where I get my ideas for stories. Most of the time, they are knitted together from bits and pieces that come from newspapers, magazine interviews, TV shows and conversations around me. It's usually hard to trace back an idea to its origin. That's not the case this time. This story has its roots in handwritten letters, then typed ones and finally, e-mails, all of which have spanned over the last thirty-plus years.

I first met Nancy, my oldest young friend, in third grade. She was poised and pretty and I idolised her. Slowly, because I was shy back then, we became friends. We never stopped. I moved to California, she remained in New York. We wrote sporadically. And then we both became mothers at the same time. She had a son, I had a daughter. Hers was born in April, mine in July. And over the years, one or the other of us has wistfully said, "What if…?" Luckily, from our kids' point of view, there is not a chance in the world that our wistfulness will bear fruit since there's three thousand miles between the two homes. So, I did the next best thing. I imagined it on paper. And hopefully, you will be entertained (and for the record, if you're wondering, neither one of us is going to tell our kids about this book).

Thank you for reading and, as ever, I wish you someone to love who loves you back.

Best,

Marie Ferrarella

THE LAST
FIRST KISS

BY
MARIE FERRARELLA

MILLS & BOON®

First published in Great Britain 2012
by Mills & Boon, an imprint of Harlequin (UK) Limited,
Eton House, 18-24 Paradise Road, Richmond, Surrey TW9 1SR

© Marie Rydzynski-Ferrarella 2012

2in1 ISBN: 978 0 263 89421 9

23-0412

Harlequin (UK) policy is to use papers that are natural, renewable and recyclable products and made from wood grown in sustainable forests. The logging and manufacturing processes conform to the legal environmental regulations of the country of origin.

Printed and bound in Spain
by Blackprint CPI, Barcelona

USA TODAY bestselling and RITA® Award-winning author **Marie Ferrarella** has written more than two hundred books, some under the name Marie Nicole. Her romances are beloved by fans worldwide. Visit her website, www.marieferrarella.com.

To
Nancy Parodi Neubert,
My Youngest Oldest Friend

Chapter One

"Oh, c'mon, Lisa, think about it. What have we got to lose?"

Maturity, for the most part, had been kind to Paulette Calhoun, leaving few of the customary telltale age lines on her face. Closing in on sixty, the tastefully dressed strawberry blonde with deep blue eyes leaned her still very trim body in, as if the proximity would add more weight to her urgings and win the other woman over.

Lisa Scarlatti, younger by three months, sat facing her lifelong friend across a black lacquer-top table for two. She held a cup of tea between her hands, the warmth just beginning to fade.

"Well, offhand, I'd say our kids. If Dave so much as smells a romantic setup, quiet though he normally is, he'll read me the riot act. And, if memory serves, I'm pretty sure that goes double for your independent, out-spoken Kara."

Laughter sparkled in Paulette's eyes. "They won't smell a setup because they know that *we* know better than to try one, which is the beauty of all this."

Lisa frowned. Her heart fought with her brain. Since they lived a good sixty miles apart, she and Paulette got together for lunch several times a year. More often now that they both found themselves unavoidably and sadly unattached. Paulette's husband had died almost thirteen years ago, while Lisa's had passed away after an accident eight years ago.

"I never thought of alienating my child as having anything to do with beauty," she told Paulette. "For heaven's sake, Thomas and I put that boy through medical school. I'm finally coming out from under that staggering debt. Let me enjoy Dave for five minutes before I do something that will have him renouncing me in the public square."

Paulette rolled her eyes. "And here I thought I was the dramatic one. Dave's not going to renounce you," she insisted. The subject of setting up their children had been on her mind ever since she'd heard about her second cousin's overwhelming success in playing matchmaker for not just her daughter, but her friends' daughters—and son—as well. Hell, if Maizie could do it, she could, too. And so could Lisa.

"Listen, this plan is perfect," Paulette enthused. "You said your niece's little boy has a birthday coming up, right?"

There was a trap here somewhere. Lisa knew Paulette too well for there not to be. "Right," she replied cautiously.

"And what, according to you, does Melissa's adorable son, Ryan, want more than anything in the whole world for his birthday?"

Lisa sighed. She saw where this was going.

"'The Kalico Kid' video game," Lisa finally said because Paulette was obviously waiting.

Nodding, Paulette asked, "And what is impossible to get?"

Why were they playing this game? "'The Kalico Kid' video game."

Paulette's wide smile grew wider. "And where does my daughter work?"

Lisa closed her eyes. She was being sucked into this, but there was no other course open to her. "At the video game company that puts out 'The Kalico Kid.'"

"Exactly," Paulette declared with feeling, warming to her subject. "So, since Dave is a softhearted sweetheart who likes making his cousin's little boy happy, and Kara has access to copies of the all-but-impossible-to-get game, it's all very simple." She paused for a moment for effect, then delivered her plan's grand finale. "I ask Kara to get a copy and deliver it to Dave when he's volunteering at that free clinic near where Kara works—"

"And just like that—" Lisa snapped her fingers, a touch of uncustomary sarcasm in her voice "—they'll see each other, and angels will sing while the sound of heavenly music echoes everywhere."

"No." Paulette dismissed her friend's convoluted scenario. "Dave'll be grateful and offer to take Kara out to dinner to repay her for her kindness. You raised a very polite son, Lisa." Paulette folded her hands before the still half-full teacup. "And then they can take it from there."

"Maybe there'll be no place to take it," Lisa suggested.

She knew how stubborn her son could be. He hadn't told her anything close to personal in more than ten years. The only way she deduced that he was unattached was that he kept coming back to his childhood home on his days off. Much as she loved seeing him, she wanted him to spend his days off with a woman worthy of him, nurturing a relationship.

"At least we would have tried," Paulette insisted. She attempted another tactic. Putting her hand on top of her friend's, she peered up at her, a silent plea in her eyes. "Don't you remember how we used to all go on family vacations together when our husbands were alive, just the six of us? And you and I used to watch the kids play and dream about Dave and Kara getting married?"

"We used to watch them fight," Lisa corrected. "And anyway, that was a long time ago. It hasn't been the six of us for a while now," she reminded Paulette. "Thomas and Neil aren't around any longer." The words weighed heavily on her tongue. All these years later, she still missed Thomas as if he'd died yesterday. She doubted that the ache would ever really go away.

"All the more reason to get our kids together," Paulette pressed. "Neither one of them is getting any younger, you know."

Lisa pointed out one glaring fact. "It's not like we haven't tried before."

More than once they had attempted to get their grown offspring together, but something always came up at the last minute, preventing it. It had been *years* since Kara and Dave were even close to being in the same room at the same time.

Paulette waved her hand, dismissing the argument as not worth her time or effort to get into.

"That was for occasions—Christmas, Thanksgiving," she specified. "One or the other always begged off, saying they had to work. I swear Kara logs in more overtime than any other human being on the face of the earth, with the possible exception of Dave. You ask me, they're perfect for each other. All we need to do is get them to see that."

Paulette beamed at her friend. "There was no pressure before. We kept it light. But this time, I mean business," she announced. "This is going to be more like a sneak attack." Her eyes glowed with anticipation. "They'll never know what hit them."

Lisa still didn't like it. She enjoyed the relationship she had with her son. They didn't speak as much as she'd like, but he did call her and he appeared on her doorstep on many of his days off, which were rare. She treasured that and didn't want anything to jeopardize their relationship.

"But we'll definitely know what hit us," she countered.

Paulette stared at the friend she'd had for more than five decades. "Since when have you gotten so negative?"

Lisa shrugged. Then, because once again Paulette was waiting for an answer, she tried to explain.

"If we don't try to get Dave and Kara together, I can always hope that someday it'll happen. If we do get them together and it blows up in our faces, then it's all over. The dream is gone. For good. I'd rather have a piece of a warm, fuzzy dream than a chunk of stone-cold negative reality."

Paulette summoned a look of complete disappointment. "The Lisa I knew and went to school with was absolutely fearless. Where did she go? What happened to her?"

"The Lisa you knew was a lot younger. I like peace and quiet these days. And a son who calls his mother once in a while."

The sigh that escaped Paulette's lips could have rivaled a Louisiana hurricane. "So you're not going to ask Kara if she can get that game from her company for Dave so that he can give it to Ryan?"

Lisa's frown deepened several degrees. She knew when she was outmatched. Paulette could wield guilt like a finely honed weapon. "I hate it when you put on that long face."

The long face was instantly gone, replaced by a wide smile of satisfaction. "I know."

It was Lisa's turn to sigh. "I think if anyone should do the asking, it should be you. Otherwise, Kara's going to be suspicious. I don't call her," she pointed out. "So getting a call from me might alert her that we're up to something. In any event, this'll make it your fault when Dave and Kara decide to put us out to sea on a tiny ice floe."

"They'll have to interact with each other in order to do that," Paulette concluded, grinning. "So, either way, it's a win-win scenario. Okay, that's settled," she declared happily, adding, "Suddenly, I feel very hungry." She picked up the menu.

Lisa's eyes narrowed as she looked at her best friend. She'd walked right into that one, she thought. "Suddenly," she countered, "I'm not."

Paulette raised her blue eyes to Lisa's face. "Eat. You're going to need your strength."

Which was exactly what Lisa was afraid of.

Something was off in the universe. She could just *feel* it.

Closing her eyes and taking a five-second break, Kara Calhoun, senior quality assurance engineer for Dynamic Video Games, tried to tell herself that she was allowing the game she'd been assigned to crack to get to her.

After working on this particular version, with its wizards, warriors and spell-casting witches, for close to twenty days straight—not counting the overtime she'd been forced to amass—Kara was beginning to feel as if she had become one with the game. Not exactly something she'd recommend to anyone wanting to maintain their hold on reality.

Luckily, her hold on reality was stronger than most. She'd loved video games ever since she'd wandered into her very first arcade at the age of four, when she'd become hooked on the whirling lights and noises. But most of all, she loved the challenge of defeating whatever adversary she found herself pitted against.

Even so, she was careful to keep it all in perspective. These were games she was working with and playing with, nothing more. In no manner, shape or form did they remotely represent real life.

Definitely not hers.

There was no way she was going to allow what happened to her coworker Jeffrey Allen to happen to her. He began believing that the people within his game were communicating with him, warning him of some imminent disaster. He'd clearly lost his grip on reality.

That being said, she couldn't shake the feeling that there really was something off. That some sort of pending doom was shimmering on the horizon and it had her name written all over it.

Maybe she needed a vacation, Kara thought.

She began to play again and immediately discovered another glitch in the program. The Black Knight was not supposed to be able to ride his equally dark steed into the ocean, much less have the horse gallop *across* the waves.

Kara shook her head. It seemed that every time she pointed out one error and the programmers fixed it, two more errors would pop up, tossing another wrench into the works. To make matters worse, the company's deadline was swiftly approaching, and she was beginning to have serious doubts that the game would be ready to hit the stores as had been promised.

But, ready or not, here it came, Kara thought, knowing how the market operated. Games were often sent out without having all their programming problems and bugs addressed with the fervent hope that the buyers wouldn't find the glitches. Right. And maybe pigs would fly.

When the phone rang on her desk, Kara debated

simply ignoring it. After all, she was deeply involved in trying to figure out exactly why the knight's horse was veering off its path. Preferably before six o'clock tonight. The idea of actually getting home by something resembling normal time for a change seemed like a borderline miracle to her.

The phone continued to ring. Kara shot it a dirty look and sighed. With her luck, it was probably someone from Corporate calling, and she knew they would only go on calling until she finally picked up.

Might as well stop putting off the inevitable, she thought. Muttering an oath, she yanked the receiver from its cradle. "This is Kara. Speak."

"My God, is that the way you answer the phone at work?"

"Hello, Mother." Kara immediately thought of her feeling that something was off. Maybe there was something to this intuition stuff after all. "What can I do for you? Speak fast, I'm up against a deadline."

She heard her mother make a noise and could just envision the disapproving look that came over the woman's heart-shaped face.

"You're always up against deadlines. That's all I ever hear. I never see you anymore, Kara," her mother complained.

Pointing out that, yes, she did, would do her no good and Kara knew it. "Get out the pictures you insisted on taking at Easter and look at them, Mom. I haven't changed any since then."

"You still haven't gained any weight?" Paulette lamented.

Trust her mother to turn her remark against her. "That's a good thing, Mother."

Unable to concentrate on two things at once when one of those things involved her mother, Kara stopped working on the game and turned away from the monitor. She lowered her voice. This was not a conversation she wanted anyone in one of the other cubicles to overhear.

"Are you actually calling me to find out if I'm eating?"

"No, I'm calling to ask you a favor. Your company puts out that 'Kalico Kid' video game, doesn't it?"

This was a trap of some sort, she could smell it. "You know we do," Kara answered cautiously. She'd mentioned how hard her team had worked on getting the game out on time. What was her mother up to?

"Can you get a copy?"

The company store had several copies set aside. "I probably can," she allowed, "seeing as how I worked on it for six months." Kara sat up, her body at attention. "Don't tell me you've suddenly decided to play video games." Mentally, she crossed her fingers. It would be nice if her mother found another hobby other than watching over her life, Kara thought. She also knew that the chances of that happening were as unlikely as her striking gold in the company's first-floor ladies' room.

"Lisa's son, Dave, needs to get his hands on a copy for his cousin's little boy. It's a birthday party and Ryan, Melissa's son—Melissa is his—"

"I get it, Mom, I get it," Kara protested, trying to

stop her mother before the woman verbally drew an elaborate family tree for her.

"Anyway, Ryan has his little heart set on getting that game. Can you come through with one, or is he going to be heartbroken for his birthday?" her mother asked her bluntly.

No doubt about it, when it came to wielding guilt, her mother knew no equal. "Stop, Mom," Kara pleaded, holding the receiver away from her ear. "I'll see what I can do." Pulling her calendar over, she picked up a pen, intending to mark the date. "When do you need it by?"

"Tomorrow."

"Tomorrow?" Kara echoed. Talk about being last minute. "Mother, that's—" She stopped herself. She knew better than to attempt to argue with the woman who'd made it into an art form. Instead, she said, "I'll see what I can do, Mom."

"That's my girl." Warmth radiated from the phrase. "I told Lisa you'd come through. By the way, would you mind dropping it off with Dave when you get it? Tomorrow is his day to work at the Seventeenth Street Clinic. He volunteers there, you know."

As if her mother hadn't already told her that little tidbit countless number of times. "You don't say."

"The clinic isn't all that far from you," Paulette went on, ignoring the sarcasm in her daughter's voice.

Kara suppressed a sigh. If she sighed too often, she was going to wind up hyperventilating. Worse, she'd have her mother fussing over her, which was the last thing she needed.

"I know where Seventeenth Street is, Mother." This time, a hint of impatience came through.

Sadly, it appeared that her mother hadn't perceived it. "Wonderful, then we're all set. Dave'll be there all day," Paulette stressed. "That young man is positively selfless, never takes any time off for himself," Paulette marveled.

This was getting a little too thick. Kara smelled a rat—the kind that wore high heels and was given to being sneaky.

"Mother—"

"Oops," Paulette exclaimed abruptly. "I've got to go. Talk to you later, Kara. Bye!"

Her mother's flood of words came at her fast and furious—just before the receiver on the other end went "click."

She'd been right, Kara thought as she leaned forward and replaced the receiver into its cradle. The universe was out of whack today. Now all she had to do was figure out why.

There were times, like today, when Dr. David Scarlatti wished he'd been blessed with an extra set of hands. Either that, or had learned to increase his energy level and work twice as fast as he normally did. There just never seemed to be enough hours in the day for him to do everything he needed to.

That was especially true whenever he volunteered at the free clinic. He'd been here since seven and he didn't feel as if he was making a dent. For every patient he saw, two more seemed to pop up to take his or her place. After six hours straight, the waiting room was *still* jammed. So much so that some of the patients were sitting cross-legged on the floor.

Nobody was here for something as mundane as a routine checkup. Everyone had something wrong, usually something that they had been enduring for at least several weeks before grudgingly swallowing their pride and making the pilgrimage to the clinic.

It was one o'clock. Typically, most doctors' offices were closed for lunch at this hour. But for him, lunch was only a faraway dream. Other than a candy bar, he hadn't had anything to eat—nor the time to consume it if he'd thought to bring something with him.

He didn't like being hungry, but they were down one doctor today, which made him not low man on the totem pole but *sole* man on the totem pole. Added to that, one of the nurses didn't show and the one who did looked as if she were running on empty. Clarice, a normally no-nonsense nurse whose age he wouldn't dare attempt to guess—he knew she had grandchildren— had been out sick for a week, and it was rather obvious to him that she needed a couple more days.

Too bad neither he nor the clinic had that kind of luxury. There were patients to attend to, and there was no putting that on hold.

As Dave walked out Mrs. Rayburn and her allergy-challenged twins, Megan and Moira, he paused by the reception desk to pick up the next file. There had to be a break coming soon, right?

"How many more, Clarice?" he asked the full-figured dynamo, who was, among other things, his first line of defense.

"You don't want to know," the woman informed him darkly.

Since the clinic had originally opened its doors, Clarice Sanchez had seen doctors come, burn out and go. For reasons he wasn't quite sure of but was eternally grateful for, after an initial butting of heads, the somber nurse had taken him under her large, protective wing. Clarice was the one who kept things moving, even when she was operating at less than her usual maximum efficiency.

Dave read the side of the folder and was about to call the name of his next patient when suddenly, someone was calling out his instead.

"Dave!"

Caught off guard, he momentarily forgot about Ramon Mendoza and glanced about the waiting area to see who had just addressed him by his first name. No one did that around here. It was disrespectful. If they spoke to him, they always invoked his title in a grateful voice.

He didn't have far to look. His line of sight was immediately engaged by a vaguely familiar, rather sexy-looking blonde. She was striding across the packed room, heading toward him as if she were the bullet and he was the bull's-eye. From the expression on her face, he could see that she seemed agitated.

One thing was for damn sure. She certainly didn't look as if she belonged here. It was like a lily suddenly sprouting in the middle of a field of weeds.

Before he could acknowledge the woman—God, that face looked familiar—Clarice stepped in. "I already told you," she snapped at the blonde, giving her a withering look, "you're gonna have to wait your turn, lady."

"I just need to see the doctor for a minute," the blonde insisted.

"That's what everyone says," Clarice told her coldly. "Now either sit down and wait your turn or I'm going to get someone to escort you out of here."

Kara decided that she was going to give this one more try and then leave. Lunch was almost over and she was hungry. More to the point, she really didn't need this kind of abuse.

"Dave," she called to him again, deliberately ignoring his guard dragon. "It's Kara Calhoun. Your mother sent me."

Chapter Two

Dave found himself staring at the blonde, stunned. While the face was vaguely familiar in a distant sort of way, the name was familiar in a far more vivid, in-your-face kind of fashion.

He knew only one Kara, God help him.

That would be the only daughter of his mother's oldest friend, Paulette Calhoun. Every single memory associated with Kara Calhoun was fraught with either embarrassment or frustrated annoyance—or both. He didn't even try to remember one good moment spent in her company. There weren't any.

Back when he was a little boy, his parents and hers would get together frequently. All the summer vacation memories of his childhood had Kara in them. Kara and turmoil. He'd been rather shy and introverted. Two years younger, Kara had been the exact opposite, as wild as a hurricane, and just as fearless. He'd felt inadequate.

And then mercifully, just before he turned thirteen, his father's company began moving him, and thus them, from location to location. They traversed the Northwest and then the Southwest. Changing addresses so frequently made it hard for him to make any friends, but the upside was that at least during the rest of the year, he didn't have to spend time confined in some remote summerhouse with the wild tomboy, counting the hours until September and the beginning of school.

If, after all these years, this gorgeous woman really *was* Kara Calhoun, then God, he couldn't help thinking, had a very macabre and somewhat sadistic sense of humor.

Despite the pressures generated by an incredibly hectic morning stapled to the makings of an equally insane afternoon, Dave stopped what he was doing and waved his next patient into the first open room.

"Be right there, Mr. Mendoza," he promised.

Then, instead of following the man, Dave rounded the reception desk and walked toward the sexy-looking blonde with the long legs.

That just *couldn't* be Kara.

Still, why would she say she was if she wasn't? He wasn't going to have any peace until he found out for certain one way or the other, so, warily, he asked, "Kara?"

"Yes," she cried with the same sort of feeling a contestant might display when their partner finally guessed the right answer after being supplied with countless clues.

He still couldn't get himself to believe it. Why, after all these years, would she suddenly appear here, in a place where she was clearly out of her element? Her shoes alone looked as if they might equal a week's salary for one of his patients—the ones who actually *had* a job.

"Kara Calhoun," he said, trying to reconcile the image of a bratty, skinny girl with pigtails and a nasty sense of humor with the clearly gorgeous young woman who was standing in the packed waiting room. Obviously nature could work miracles.

Why all the drama? Kara wondered. The Dave she remembered had been a super-brainy geek. Had he been forced to trade in his brains for looks? Was that how it worked?

"Want to see my driver's license?" she offered, wondering what it would take to convince this man who she was.

The touch of sarcasm in her voice was all he needed to convince him. "It's you, all right. Still have the sunny disposition of an armadillo, I see."

She stretched her lips back in an obviously forced smile. "You've filled out since I last saw you." Which, she added silently, was putting it mildly. If the way his lab coat fit was any indication, the man now had muscles instead of arms that could have doubled for toothpicks. "Too bad your personality didn't want to keep up."

He would have liked nothing better than to turn his back on her and walk away, but she hadn't just appeared here like some directionally challenged genie out of a bottle. There was a reason Kara had sought him out after all these years and he had just enough curiosity to wonder why.

He made it simple for her. He asked. "What are you doing here?"

"I was wondering the same thing myself," she cracked. But then, as he apparently lost patience and began to turn on his heel to walk away, she relented. There was no point in coming all the way over here and *not* giving him the game. "I brought you a copy of the latest version of 'The Kalico Kid' video game. Your mother told mine that your cousin's little boy's birthday is coming up and he's dying to get his hands on one."

If this were anyone else, he would have expressed his gratitude, paid for the game and taken it. But this was Kara, and the ordinary rules didn't apply here. His memory was crowded with a host of different sneaky tricks that a gangly ten-year-old played on his trusting twelve-year-old body. Spending summers trapped in her company had taught him to hold everything she was involved in suspect.

His eyes narrowed as he looked at her. Motioning her closer to create at least a semblance of privacy, he asked, "What's the catch?"

"Catch?" Boy, talk about not being trusting. But then, looking back, maybe she couldn't quite blame him. She had been pretty hard on Dave when they were kids. "The catch is you have to spin a room full of straw into gold by morning."

"You can do that?" a small voice directly behind her piped up. Despite the distance, her voice had carried enough so that the only child in the room heard, and he was clearly awestruck.

Kara turned around to see a little boy of about eight or ten. He looked rather small and fragile, so he might have even been older. She couldn't tell for sure. But she did know that he had the widest smile she'd ever seen.

He also, she noted, had an extremely pale complexion and, despite the fact that it was unseasonably hot outside, he was wearing a bright blue wool cap pulled down low on his head. She suspected that the boy's mother, sitting behind him, had put it on him to keep people from staring. The stigma of a bald head on one so young was difficult to cope with.

"She was making a joke, Gary," Dave told the boy. "She does that kind of thing."

Or did, he added silently. The truth was that he had no way of knowing what Kara was like these days, but he suspected she was still true to form—even if her outer form had turned out incredibly well.

He got back to business. "How much do I owe you for 'The Kalico Kid' game?"

But Kara was no longer paying attention to him. Her attention was now completely focused on the little boy. Even if he hadn't been the only child in the room, he would have stood out because of his near-ghostly pallor.

"You really have 'The Kalico Kid' game?" Gary asked. She would have had to be blind not to notice the wistful gleam that came into his brown eyes.

She smiled at him, blocking out everyone else, especially Dave. "Yes, I do."

Reaching into her shapeless, oversize purse, Kara felt around until she located what she was looking for. Instead of the boxed game she'd brought for Dave, she pulled out a handheld gaming system that had become all but standard issue for every bored kid sitting in the backseat of his or her parents' car, forced to endure yet another cross-country family vacation.

She guessed by the way the little boy's eyes lit up that not only did he not have a copy of the new version—only a few had hit the stores—but he didn't have a handheld set, either.

"Want to play the game?" she offered, holding the gaming system out to him.

"Can I?" he breathed almost reverently. His smile was the closest to beatific she'd ever seen.

She had to restrain herself from hugging the boy. Hugging was something she did when she became emotional. Instead, she nodded and choked out the word "Sure."

"Gary, you'd better not," his mother chided. The woman looked as worn-out as her son. "I don't want to risk having him break it. I can't afford to replace it," she explained.

Her eyes went from the boy to his mother. There was no way she was going to separate Gary from the gaming system. That hadn't been her intent when she'd handed it to him. "I take it he doesn't have one."

Pride entered the woman's face as she squared her shoulders. "We manage just fine."

"I'm sure you do," Kara quickly agreed. "I didn't mean to suggest you didn't." She looked back at the boy. "Would you like to keep that, Gary?"

Gary looked as if he'd suddenly stumbled into paradise. "Can I?" he cried in absolute disbelief.

"No, you can't," his mother told him firmly, even though it clearly hurt her to have to deny him.

Prepared, Kara was quick with her assurances. "It's okay. I work for the company that produces the game. We're giving out a few handheld systems as a way of promoting this latest version."

The boy's mother looked doubtful. Gary looked ecstatic.

"Really?" he cried excitedly, his eyes now bright and as large as proverbial saucers.

Kara had to struggle to contain her own smile. She nodded. "Really."

Gary clutched the system, fully equipped with this newest version of "The Kalico Kid," to his chest. "Thanks, lady!"

Kara solemnly put her hand out to him as if he were a short adult. "My name is Kara—and you're very welcome, Gary."

Gary quickly took her hand and tried to look serious as he shook it, but his grin kept insisting on breaking through.

Kara raised her eyes to look at Gary's mother, half expecting the woman to voice some kind of objection. Instead, she saw tears gathering in the woman's soft brown eyes. Gary's mother mouthed, "Thank you," over the boy's head.

Her mouth curving just a hint, Kara nodded in response.

Behind her, Dave was busy instructing Clarice, telling her to send another one of the patients to the second newly vacated exam room. Done, he turned his attention to Kara.

"I'd like to see you in my office," he told the specter from his childhood.

Kara couldn't help grinning as she followed him around the reception desk, then toward the back of the office. "Bet you've been waiting years to be able to say that line to me."

He bit off his initial response to her flippant remark. After all, she'd just been very kind to one of his regulars. Instead, he waited until Kara had walked into the closet-size office, and then closed the door behind him.

The scarred, faux-mahogany desk listed a little to the right. It and the two chairs, one in front of the desk, one behind it, took up most of the available space. He didn't bother trying to angle his way behind the desk. He anticipated that this was going to be short.

"You're not really having some promotional give-away, are you?" It wasn't a question.

She would have played this out a little longer just to see how far she could take it, but she was running out of time. As senior quality assurance engineer, she was supposed to set an example for the others when it came to keeping decent hours. "No."

"Didn't think so. That was rather a nice thing you just did." He didn't bother going into any details about how very strapped Gary's mother was, or what a brave little person the boy was. That was the kind of stuff that violins were made for and he had a feeling it would be wasted on Kara anyway. It definitely would be on the Kara he remembered.

Or thought he remembered, he amended.

Getting what sounded like a compliment from Dave felt awkward to Kara somehow. Not to mention unsettling. She shrugged, dismissing the words. "Well, I make it a rule not to eat children on Wednesdays."

And then she sobered. Raising her eyes to Dave's green ones, she started to ask, "Does he have—?"

He cut her off, sensing that talking about the disease that had ultimately claimed her father was difficult for her. "It's in remission, but I'm not all that hopeful," he confided.

"That was always your problem," she recalled, not entirely critically. To her, that was just the way things were and she viewed it as something that needed improvement. "Not enough hope, too much practicality."

"You were just the opposite." Almost to the point where she'd stick her head in the ground, he recalled.

She flashed him an irritating smile. "And pleasingly so."

He needed to get back to work before they were literally drowning in patients, and he knew from experience that Kara could keep up the bantering responses all afternoon.

"So, you didn't tell me," he reminded her, taking out his wallet. "How much do I owe you?"

Right, the game. She still hadn't given it to him. Kara dug into her purse again. This time, she pulled out the copy of the video game she'd brought for him. The cellophane around it crinkled as she said, "Your immortal soul."

He pinned her with a look. "Exactly how much is that in cash?"

"I'll let you know." She had no intentions of selling him the game. That made her too much like a lackey. Giving it to him was far better. Besides, she liked the idea of having him indebted to her. "Maybe I'll take it out in trade sometime. I might need something stitched up someday."

He suddenly had an image of her sitting on a rock by the lake, blood running down her leg. The wound had appeared a lot worse than it actually was. That was the summer he'd made up his mind to become a doctor. "You mean like that time at the lake?"

She knew he was referring to that last summer at the lake before he and his family had moved away. She'd been eleven at the time and had slipped on the rocks, trying to elude him after playing some prank. She'd gotten a huge cut on her knee and it wouldn't stop bleeding. She'd valiantly struggled not to cry.

"Those weren't stitches. That was a butterfly bandage you put on it."

The point was that it had done the trick and had held until her father could get her to the emergency room. "Would you have let me come at you with a needle?" he asked.

A rueful smile curved one corner of her mouth. "Point taken, Davy."

He stopped the cringe before it could surface. "No one's called me that in years." She had been the only one to ever do it. Dave looked at her pointedly. "I hate being called Davy."

She grinned, her eyes laughing at him. "I know." She had to get going, and from the sound of the noise in the next room, so did he. "Forget about owing me anything for the game," she told him. "It's on the house. For old times' sake," Kara added.

If she was making restitution for things she'd done to him all those years, this didn't begin to make a dent.

But he saw no point in saying anything. After all, Ryan really wanted the game, and she had been nice to Gary, who had enough hard knocks against him. Besides, saying anything remotely adversarial to Kara would only embroil him in another no-win verbal match. She was probably still a master at that and he wasn't up to one at the moment.

"Thanks." As he said the word, his stomach growled, as if adding a coda.

She stared at him. He couldn't begin to read her expression. Some things never changed, he thought.

"I had no idea you were a ventriloquist."

His stomach growled again, a little softer this time. This was getting embarrassing. "I am on the days I don't get to eat breakfast—or lunch."

She cocked her head, as if she found the information fascinating. "You haven't eaten yet?"

He knew her well enough to wonder what she was up to now. "No."

"But you will."

What kind of a question was that? Everyone had to eat—or expire. "Eventually." He could feel her eyes delving into his skin. Just what did she expect him to say? "Someday," he allowed, then amended his answer to, "Yes," as he brushed past her to get back into the tiny hallway that was desperately in need of a paint job. "Right now there's no time to go get something."

She could see how he couldn't leave, but that didn't mean he had to go hungry. "Why don't you send out Ms. Personality?" When Dave looked at her blankly, she nodded toward the reception room. "The anaconda at the front desk."

"We're shorthanded. Clarice's my backup nurse—and the only one manning the front desk. I can't spare her, either."

Dave always did make things more complicated than they were, she recalled. Resigned, she dug into her purse yet a third time. "In that case, take this."

Though he would have preferred not to admit it, Dave stared in fascination as the woman from his past pulled out what appeared to be an entire foot-long sandwich from her purse. It was cut into two equal halves.

What else did she have in there?

"Is that your equivalent to a clown car?" he asked. "Do you just put your hand in, then pluck an endless amount of things out?"

She didn't feel like being on the receiving end of what he might call wit. She had traffic to face and a game with her name on it waiting to be further deconstructed. Holding it out to him, she asked, "You want this roast beef sandwich or not?"

He'd always thought of her as being rather unusual, but he had a feeling she wasn't given to arbitrarily carrying food in her purse. There was only one other explanation for it. "Isn't that your lunch?"

"Well, if you take it, it becomes yours," she pointed out with a trace of impatience. And then she sighed. "Look, it's not like I can't buy myself another one on my way back to the office. You, on the other hand, look like you haven't a prayer of making it out the door without that gestapo agent throwing a net over you and stopping you before you take three steps."

He felt honor bound to defend the woman working with him. "Clarice's okay."

"I'm sure. For a gargoyle," Kara agreed. She raised the sandwich a little higher, into his line of vision. "You want this or not?"

She might be annoying, but that was no reason to deprive himself in order to show her he didn't need her help. "I'll take it."

She placed the wax-paper-wrapped sandwich into his hand. "Very kind of you." With that, she turned on her heel to leave.

"Kara?" he called after her.

Pausing, she looked expectantly at Dave over her shoulder. "Yes?"

He still really hadn't thanked her—and found that it was difficult to form the words where she was involved. He settled for: "Tell your mom I said thanks."

Amused, Kara inclined her head and said, "Sure."

That, he knew, was a cop-out on his part. He was better than that, Dave reminded himself. Just because this was Kara shouldn't mean that he reverted back to behaving like an adolescent. "And thanks for bringing it by."

She gave him a quick two-finger salute. "I live to serve."

Same old Kara, same old sarcastic remarks, he thought as he walked out behind her.

"You look good."

The words had slipped out without his permission, going directly from his gut to his tongue without pausing to clear it with his brain. His brain would have definitely vetoed having the words said aloud.

Surprised, Kara stopped abruptly and turned around,

causing a near collision between them. He immediately took a step back.

"Are you addressing that assessment to me in general or just to the back of me?" she asked, an amused smile on her lips.

She could still fluster him, Dave thought. He'd assumed that reaction was years behind him. After all, he'd graduated at the top of his class, been voted into all sorts of positions of honor and had, in general, become confident in not just his abilities but in himself, as well.

Five minutes around Kara and he turned into that gangly, tongue-tied geek whose physique was all but concave the last summer their families had vacationed together.

"Let me think about it," he said evasively.

She nodded. "Thought so."

As she walked out, Gary rose to his feet. "Thank you," he called after her.

She spared the boy a wide smile. This made everything worthwhile. "My pleasure, Gary. All my pleasure."

With that, she was gone.

But not, Dave thought as he turned away to see the patient in room one, forgotten.

Chapter Three

Kara barely had time to run to the sandwich shop to purchase another roast beef sandwich for herself and get back to her desk before her lunch hour was officially over. Just when she'd managed to finally catch her breath, the phone on her desk rang.

Picking it up, she cradled it against her neck and ear. She needed her hands free for the control pad. The newest version of the game still had the pesky Black Knight's horse water surfing.

"Hello?" Kara said absently, guiding the horse and rider over the water to see just how far this glitch extended.

The voice on the other end of the line responded with a single word. "So?"

Kara came to attention as she recognized her mother's voice. The Black Knight and his horse were temporarily forgotten.

"So?" she repeated, having no clue what her mother was asking or saying.

She heard her mother sigh on the other end of the line, then carefully enunciate her question. "Did you bring the game to Dave?"

The question irritated her. Why wouldn't she take the game if she'd already told her mother that she would? "I said I would." She picked up the control pad again. The horse resumed galloping erratically. "Yes, I brought the game to Dave."

"And?"

Kara frowned. Just what was that supposed to mean? "And what?"

A note of frustration entered her mother's voice. "How did he look?"

Damn, the horse just rode off the edge of the earth. This was *not* good. "Like a maniacal serial killer. What do you mean, how did he look? He looked like Dave. Only taller." She paused for a moment, then added, "And handsomer."

"Aha."

"Aha?" Kara repeated, confused. Okay, just where was this conversation headed?

"Never mind," her mother said quickly. "Sorry, I need to go."

Her mother definitely had too much time on her hands. "What you need, Mom, is a hobby." *Other than me,* she added silently. Kara paused to make a notation about the game on the pad she kept by the computer.

"Agreed. Maybe someday you'll give me one," she

thought she heard her mother say. The next moment, the line went dead.

Kara looked thoughtfully at the receiver in her hand. *Maybe someday you'll give me one.* Under ordinary circumstances the most logical "hobby" would be one involving playing on a gaming system. But she had a feeling that her mother was *not* referring to anything as run of the mill as a video game.

And then, just like that, that strange, unsettling feeling that the universe was tilting began to come into focus for her.

The "hobby" her mother was referring to was a grandchild. Her mother wanted a grandchild. And the only way to get one of those, according to her mother, was to get her married and pregnant.

The woman was actually trying to play matchmaker. Damn. Ordinarily, her radar was better than this. How had she missed it?

For the time being, the black stallion was on its own. His aquatic adventures were definitely the last thing on her mind now.

Kara looked at the framed photo on her desk of her mother, her late father and her, taken when she was seventeen. It was the last family photo she had. Looking at her mother now, she shook her head.

"Why, you little sneak. I know what you've been up to. I'm really disappointed in you, Mom," she murmured.

Jake Storm, the man occupying the cubicle next to her, rolled his chair back a little in order to catch a glimpse of her. He had hair and eyebrows that made him look like an affable sheepdog. One shaggy eyebrow arched in amusement now.

"Talking to yourself, Kara?"

She glanced to her right. "No," she told him. "To my mother."

Jake rolled his chair out a little farther, allowing him a clearer view of her space, which was, due to her position in the hierarchy, twice the size of his.

"That would be your invisible mother?" he asked.

"No," she answered. "That would be the meddling mother on the other end of this now defunct phone call." Putting the receiver down, she pushed the offending instrument back on her desk.

"Ah, meddling mothers. Tell me about it. Mine isn't going to be happy until I chuck this game-testing job to the winds, get a degree in something she can brag about, marry the perfect girl and give her three and a half grandchildren—none of which is really doable," he said with a heartfelt sigh, then brightened as he looked at her again. "Unless you're free tonight to drive to Vegas and become Mrs. Jake Storm."

She knew he was kidding. They were friends—without benefits. "And the three and a half kids?" she asked, mildly curious.

"We could rent them." He grinned. "I think a month of endless babysitting might teach my mother a valuable lesson, as in 'careful what you wish for.' Might even be worth the effort," he said wistfully.

However unintentionally, Jake had just given her an idea. A very good idea. She looked at him sharply. "Jake, that's brilliant."

"Clever, maybe," he allowed, "but not brilliant. By

the way—" he leaned in closer "—what clever thing
did I just say?"

"Something," Kara told him as she shifted over to
the other monitor on her desk, the one directly hooked
up to the internet, "that just might get my beloved
mother to back off."

"Well, I'm all for that," Jake declared with feeling. Anyone who knew him knew that to be true. His
mother was forever trying to set him up with the offspring of her friends. "Let me know how it goes." He
nodded toward his own area. "Gotta get back to that
crazy horse. He's still walking on water."

"Tell me about it," she murmured under her breath
as Jake moved back into his cubicle.

She had no idea what Dave's number was, but she assumed that, as an M.D., he had to be listed *somewhere*.
Starting out in the most obvious place, she did a people
search through the white pages. The effort took several
tries, but ultimately, she came away a winner.

Dialing the phone quickly, she was connected to
Dave's office in less than a minute. And then she got
to listen to an answering machine. He wasn't in, which
only made sense since she'd just seen him at the clinic.
His message said his office was closed today.

"Better than nothing," she murmured under her
breath with far less enthusiasm than usual as she waited
for the outgoing message to end.

If Dave didn't call her back by tonight, she was fairly
sure she could find his private number using some creative methods on her laptop at home.

The beep sounded in her ear and she started talking. "Hi, Dave, it's Kara. Remember I said that I'd take

that favor out in trade? Well, trading time just arrived. We need to talk. Call me." She rattled off both her cell phone number and the number to her landline in her apartment.

Hanging up, Kara smiled to herself, relishing her plan. Once it got rolling, it would be just what the doctor ordered, she thought, feeling very confident about the outcome. This was going to teach her mother—and possibly Dave's—never to even think about matchmaking again.

Dave was more than a little surprised, when he picked up his messages that evening, to find Kara's among them. Not only was it the only phone message that didn't describe some symptom in depth, but he and she hadn't had any contact in—what, eighteen?—years, and now twice in one day?

Exactly what was up and why did he feel so uneasy about it?

Dropping his mail onto the coffee table, Dave made his way over to the phone on the kitchen wall.

"Only one way to find out," he said aloud. But even so, he didn't begin dialing immediately.

It wasn't that he wanted to renege on the unofficial agreement to reciprocate when she asked. After all, Kara had produced the much sought after game. Then again, how hard could it be for her? She did work for the company that put it out.

Still, she didn't have to deliver it herself—or even give him the game in the first place. Once upon a time, he would have bet his last dime that she wouldn't have given him the time of day, much less gone out of her way, to bring him something he needed.

He also wouldn't have thought that there was a kind bone in her excessively skinny little body. But her treatment of Gary in the waiting room showed him he'd been wrong in his assessment of her. Or at least the "new" her.

No, none of that was holding him back from immediately keeping his word. What *was* stopping him was the hour. He'd just walked in and it was after eleven. Added to that, he was bone tired.

He had no one to blame for that but himself, he thought. Himself and the endless line of sick people who just kept on coming. Clarice had finally closed the doors two hours later than the clinic's official closing time. And he'd gone on treating patients until there was no one left in the stale-smelling waiting room.

Now, two steps beyond dead tired, he was too exhausted to even get anything to eat out of the refrigerator. One way to lose weight, he mused. That sandwich Kara had pulled out of her magic bag was practically the only solid thing he had to eat all day until Clarice had called her grandson to bring some food from the Thai takeout place in her neighborhood. He hadn't really recognized what he'd eaten, but whatever it was had substance to it and ultimately had helped to keep him going, which was what counted.

His mind came back full circle to Kara. Okay, she'd given him a game and her sandwich. If nothing else, that meant he needed to return her phone call.

And if, God willing, she didn't answer, well, at least he was on record for trying. Recorded record. He punched out her numbers on the keypad and crossed his fingers that she didn't answer, but he might as well have saved himself the trouble. Kara picked up her phone on the second ring.

"Hello?"

Her voice sounded a bit sleepy, he thought. An image of Kara in bed, wearing nothing but the moonlight breaking through her window, suddenly popped up in his head.

He really needed that social life he was sorely missing out on.

"Hello?" he heard her say again.

He dove in. "Kara, it's Dave. You called."

At the sound of his voice, Kara dragged herself up into a sitting position. She'd fallen asleep on her sofa, playing a portable version of the game that was bedeviling her and the staff she supervised. She struggled to clear the fog from her brain. She didn't even remember shutting her eyes.

Squinting, she tried to make out the time on the cable box across the room. The numbers swam around, and she gave up.

"Right. I called," she murmured, dragging her hand through her hair, trying to figuratively drag her thoughts together at the same time.

"About anything in particular?" Dave pressed. She sounded sluggish. He thought back and couldn't remember a time when she wasn't going ninety miles an hour. "Because if this can wait, or you just called to yank my chain, it's been a really long day and I've got an early call tomorrow in the hospital—"

She wasn't about to give him a chance to hang up.

From the sound of it, she was going to have to make an appointment to talk to him on the phone if she didn't speak up quickly. So she did. "Our mothers are trying to set us up."

"What? With who?" he asked incredulously.

Was he kidding? "What do you mean, with who? With each other. At least," she amended, backtracking just a step, "I know mine is, and whatever mine does, yours usually does, too."

When did this happen? It wasn't making any sense. She must have made a mistake. "What are you talking about?" he demanded.

She took a breath and explained how she'd come to this conclusion. "After I came back from your clinic, my mother called me at work to see if I'd given you the game."

"She obviously knows how dependable you are," he observed dryly.

Her back instantly went up. "I'll have you know that I am— Never mind."

This wasn't the time to allow herself to get into an argument with him. They were both tired. Things could be said that couldn't be retracted. The best way to prevent that was not to start anything at all. Besides, she had a far more important point to get to. She couldn't allow herself to get sidetracked.

"Anyway, she wanted to know how you looked. More accurately, she wanted to know what *I* thought of the way you looked."

So far, he wasn't hearing anything that should have set off any whirling red lights for her. "Natural question," he commented. "We haven't seen each other in almost two decades."

She stopped her narrative, struggling with her temper. Was he for real? Or was he just baiting her? If it was the latter, maybe he'd learned a thing or two since they'd last seen each other. But somehow, she doubted that. He'd always been too upstanding to stoop to anything.

"Were you always this naive, or did you just suddenly decide to go back to your childhood?"

He really wasn't in the mood for this. "If you're going to insult me—"

"Tempting, but I'll save that for some other time. Right now, hard as it is for me, I need to ask you for your help."

Dave interpreted her question the only way he knew how. "You have a medical question?"

"No, I have a mother question. Or rather, a solution to a meddling-mother situation." He was very quiet on the other end. Was that a good sign, or had he fallen asleep? "Our mothers want to get us together. I never told you," she segued quickly, "but I once overheard them talking about how terrific it would be if, when you and I grew up, we'd get married."

His voice was stripped of all emotion as he said, "No, you never told me that."

"At the time I heard it, I thought it was too gross to repeat," she explained. "But it obviously has never stopped being on their minds."

He was trying to follow her logic and found that there were gaping holes in it. "And you think that your mother calling you to see if you delivered the game to me is actually some kind of a confession on her part that she's trying to get us to the altar?"

She knew he was mocking her and forced herself to swallow a few choice words. "Her asking me what I think of your looks is pretty transparent."

Where was all this going, anyway? "So you called to warn me?"

She shifted the phone to her other ear. "No, I called to get you to cooperate with an idea I have."

He *really* didn't like the sound of that. "This never turned out well for any of the characters in those sitcoms you always liked so much," Dave pointed out.

That he remembered she used to watch them astonished her. She told herself it meant nothing and kept talking. "What if you and I pretend to go out together? Pretend to, you know, like each other."

It sounded as if she were forcing herself to endure a fate worse than death. "Assuming I've had my rabies shots," he said sarcastically, "how is this going to teach our mothers a lesson? This is what they want—according to you."

Kara sighed. "You really don't have an imagination, do you?"

"I have one," he told her. "I just don't let it go off on wild tangents."

She took offense and shot back through gritted teeth, "Okay, *Davy,* let me spell it out for you. We go out. We pretend to fall in love, and then we have one hell of an argument, making sure that we have this fight where our mothers can hear us. After the argument, we go through the throes of an agonizing 'breakup.' A devastating breakup," she specified, really throwing herself into the role, "where we both act as if there's no tomorrow—"

"Being just a little melodramatic, don't you think?" he interjected.

He really was spoiling for a fight, wasn't he? Not that she was intimidated, but she wanted this to get under way quickly. The sooner the better.

"Maybe. We'll have to play it by ear. But they'll be so upset that we're upset, I guarantee that it'll cure them once and for all from trying to play matchmaker with us on any level—separately or together." She paused to take a breath. "What do you think? You game?"

If he said no, he had a feeling she'd keep calling and badgering him until he agreed. Still, throwing his lot in with Kara made him uneasy.

"Why do I get the feeling that I'm about to sign my own death warrant?"

What was it about him that set her off like this? Eighteen years and nothing had changed. Except that he was better looking, but that had no bearing here.

"Because you're running on next to no sleep, you have no imagination and you don't know a good plan when you hear one. Shall I go on?"

He laughed shortly. "Not that I have the slightest doubt that you could, but please don't."

She was still waiting for an answer. "Does that mean no?"

This was the moment of truth. He could still walk away. But he had a feeling that she had a point. Though he loved his mother dearly, he could think of nothing he wanted less than to have her playing matchmaker on his behalf.

"That means that I'm probably going to really regret this, but you do have a point."

Yes! "Glad you recognize that."

He wanted to move this along while he still had a prayer of getting some sleep. "All right, mastermind, so what's our next move?" he asked her.

She would have thought that was self-evident. "We pretend to go out."

"And what, notify the press first? How are our mothers going to know we're going out? I think they'd be suspicious if either one of us just picked up the phone and called to tell them."

She smiled. He was almost cute when he tried to be flippant. The key word here was *almost*.

"Ah, there is more than just space between those manly ears. You're absolutely right. How about that birthday for your cousin's son?" she asked. "The one I got you the video game for."

"Ryan," he supplied.

"Ryan," she repeated. "Ryan's going to have a birthday party, right?"

"Yes—" He got no further.

Kara pounced on the next question. "Is your mother going to be there?"

Okay, so now it was all crystal clear to him. Not bad, he acknowledged, albeit silently. Saying it out loud would just give her a bigger head. "Yes."

"Okay, then we will be, too. All we need is one eye-witnessing mother to spread the news to the other."

"Eyewitnessing," he echoed. "Is that even a word?"

"It is for this purpose," she said glibly. "Anyway,

they'll think their plan is working—until we show them otherwise. So, are you in?"

"I'm in," he answered even as part of him had the sinking feeling that by agreeing, life as he knew it would never be the same again. This very well could be a huge mistake.

Joining forces with Kara was always dangerous. It was a known fact that she possessed a golden tongue. It was also a known fact that she could abruptly leave him holding the bag if it suited her purposes.

He had no reason to believe that eighteen years had changed anything, her greatly improved figure notwithstanding.

Chapter Four

The phone rang just as Paulette walked past it. On her way out, she debated just letting the answering machine pick it up. But there was something about a ringing phone that always captured her attention to the exclusion of everything else. It was irresistible.

Pausing, she lifted the receiver from the cradle and brought it to her ear. "Hello?"

"I thought you'd want to be the first to know—well, not really first, but close," the voice on the other end said.

Lisa. Paulette dropped her purse to the floor, kicked off the high heels she'd just slipped on and deposited her body into the overstuffed chair in her living room. There was no such thing as a quick exchange of words between her and Lisa.

"Almost the first to know what?" Paulette asked.

Even as she did so, she mentally crossed her fingers, hoping that her little plan had succeeded in its next stage.

"That Dave called Melissa and asked her if she'd mind if he brought someone to Ryan's birthday party."

Paulette could hear the smile in her friend's voice. It mirrored the one on her own face. "And this friend wouldn't be Kara, by any chance, would it?"

At this point, it was a rhetorical question. She sincerely doubted that Lisa would be calling her to say that her son was bringing someone else to the little boy's party.

And then Lisa confirmed all her hopes by saying, "Yes, it would."

Paulette would have clapped her hands together with glee if both of them had been free. "See, I told you so. All it took was for the two of them to be in the same place at the same time." And just like that, she was flying high on confidence. "The rest will soon be history."

"Don't start sending out the wedding invitations just yet," Lisa cautioned. "I mean, it's not like Dave hasn't dated before. And you've told me that Kara has gone out with a few guys from time to time. Wasn't there that guy, Alex something-or-other, she was seeing pretty regularly a while back?"

The name instantly brought a wave of anger. "You mean the bigamist?"

"He was *married?*" Lisa asked, horrified.

"Well, not exactly," Paulette backtracked. "But he *was* seeing several women at the same time, including a live-in girlfriend who just *happened* to be the mother of his little boy. Kara was devastated when she accidentally found out—devastated and furious. He's the one who made her swear off having anything to do with men."

At the time that it happened, she'd kept the news to herself in deference to Kara's wishes. But in her opinion enough time had passed for the truth to finally come out. Besides, she wanted Lisa to know that her daughter wasn't a wallflower because no one was interested. She was one by choice.

"I don't think you realize what this actually means," Paulette continued.

"Enlighten me," Lisa urged.

"If Kara actually agreed to go out with Dave, it means she's ready to get back into life. This is a really big deal," Paulette enthused. "Why don't we get together at the end of this week and celebrate?"

As ever, Paulette was getting ahead of herself, Lisa thought. "A family gathering for a child's birthday doesn't exactly fall into the same parameters as a date," Lisa pointed out.

"Walking down the block holding hands is a date," Paulette insisted. "Anything involving two consenting people is considered a *date*. C'mon, Lis, don't rain on my parade."

It wasn't that she wasn't as hopeful about the outcome of all this as Paulette was, it was just that she was a little more grounded than her friend. And yes, a little more pessimistic.

"I'm not raining on it, Paulette, I just want you to have an umbrella handy—just in case," Lisa explained.

"By the way, about Ryan's party… There's always room for one more. Would you like to come?"

"You know I would, but…"

Lisa thought that Paulette would have jumped at the chance to be there to watch over her daughter interacting with Dave. "But?" she questioned.

"If I'm there, Kara might feel self-conscious and not be herself." Her daughter also might think she was being spied on, Paulette thought.

Lisa sighed, considering Paulette's reasoning. "I suppose you have a point."

Paulette paused, chewing on her lower lip. "On the other hand, I also have an insatiable desire to see them finally come together." She weighed the two sides for a moment, thinking. Desire won out over sensibility. "Oh, what the hell? Count me in."

Lisa laughed. As if there was ever any real doubt, she thought. "Consider it done. I'll call Melissa right now," she said, ending their phone call.

This was taking way too long. By all rights, it should have been a snap, Kara told herself as she took yet another outfit out of her closet and looked it over carefully.

Ordinarily, she'd reach into her closet and throw just about anything on. Or, at the very least, she wouldn't regard everything she'd taken out with such a critical eye.

Why did how she looked matter so much? She upbraided herself.

The problem was that she worked for a company that had no dress code—beyond requiring that their employees show up at work clothed. During the summer she went in wearing a tank top and shorts half the time. And since she hadn't had a date since the Alex fiasco had burned her so badly, all of the things she might normally wear for any sort of actual occasion had been pushed to the back of her closet. Now, as she pulled them out, she kept finding something wrong with each outfit.

What was the matter with her? This was just Davy she was going with. Comfortable, old stick-in-the-mud Davy. And this was all pretend, anyway. There was no need to fuss like this.

"Damn it," she said to her reflection in the wardrobe mirror. "It's a kid's party. A stained T-shirt and dirty jeans would probably blend right in."

Even so, she took out yet another garment, this time a light blue sundress with white piping along the edges of the skirt, spaghetti straps and bodice. Holding it up against herself, she decided that it was as good as anything she'd pulled out so far. Maybe a tad better than most. For one thing, the color brought out her eyes and the dress's waistline brought out her own.

Finally.

Or maybe—

Kara glanced at her watch. How had it gotten to be so late? This was supposed to take her only ten minutes, not an hour. The party was beginning in less than half an hour.

"Sundress, it is," she declared.

She'd no sooner shed her tank top and shorts and put the sundress on than her doorbell rang.

Now what? she wondered. She wasn't expecting anyone.

Maybe it was the new gaming system she'd ordered, Kara thought hopefully. It wasn't scheduled to be delivered until next week, but you never knew. Once in a blue moon the mail actually arrived before it was supposed to.

Leaving the dress unzipped in the back—she wasn't planning on walking away from the mailman—Kara hurried to the door.

"Coming!" she called out, hoping the mail carrier wouldn't leave before she got there.

She yanked the door open, and disappointment descended swiftly. "You're not the mail carrier."

"Very observant," Dave commented. "Were you expecting him?"

"Well, I wasn't expecting you," she informed him crisply.

Since she wasn't inviting him in, Dave took hold of her shoulders, moved her slightly to one side and walked into the apartment on his own.

"Correct me if I'm wrong, but weren't you the one who said we're supposed to be 'pretending' to be on a date while attending Ryan's birthday party?"

God, but he irritated her, she thought. There was no reason to talk down to her like this. "Yes, but I thought we were meeting there—at Melissa's house."

"It occurred to me while driving to the party that arriving in separate cars didn't seem very datelike," he pointed out. "Is that how all your dates go? Because if so, I might have the answer as to why you're still unattached."

Maybe she should just kill him here now and be done with it. The idea had definite appeal.

"You could have called and given me a warning. And never mind how my dates go," Kara snapped, closing the door he'd left open. She frowned, then shrugged. "Well, since you're here, I guess we can go to the birth-day party together. But I'm not ready yet," she informed him. When he raised a quizzical eyebrow she explained, "I don't have my shoes on."

"I thought you looked shorter." And then his mouth curved in a half-amused smile as she moved away. "You don't exactly have your dress on yet, either."

She turned back and looked at him sharply. "What are you talking about?" she demanded.

Rather than answer her, he turned her around and then zipped up her dress, his knuckles lightly skimming along her bare skin.

Something warm and shivery shimmied up and down her spine, discharging tiny zaps of electricity as it went. Kara struggled not to let the tingling sensation get to her.

"There," Dave pronounced. "You're decent. It's a kid's party. Ryan's precocious for his age, but he's a little too young to see his first half-naked woman, no matter how tempting the sight might be."

Her temper flared. "I'm not—" The rest of his state-ment suddenly hit. "Wait, did you say 'tempting'?"

That had been a careless slip on his part. He had to remember that Kara pounced on the least little thing. "Just a general observation," he said mildly. Shoving his hands into the pockets of his slacks, he deliberately moved away from her and looked around the room.

"Nice place," he commented. "A little claustrophobic for my taste, but nice."

She'd forgotten about that. Dave had been claustrophobic as a kid. The second she'd found out, she'd taken every opportunity to put him to the test. She herself was fearless and couldn't fathom anyone breaking into a sweat just because they were confined to a tiny little space.

"Thanks," Kara responded.

Preoccupied, she was still mulling over his "tempting" remark. Had that been a slip of the tongue or just a word he'd used carelessly? There was nothing in his tone or his facial expression that gave her the slightest clue.

Most likely, she decided, he was setting up a joke at her expense. There was no reason to believe just because he'd become a doctor who volunteered at a free clinic once a week that he'd suddenly become a noble specimen of manhood. At least, not as far as she was concerned, anyway.

Getting her shoes, Kara stepped into them and then grabbed her purse from the coffee table before pausing to pick up a large shopping bag next to the sofa.

With a toss of her head, she announced, "Okay, I'm ready."

Dave began to walk out. Noticing the shopping bag, he nodded at it. "What's that?"

"A present for Ryan. You didn't expect me to go to this party empty-handed, did you?"

When it came to Kara, he really didn't know what to expect. He never had. The logic he cherished had no place in her life.

"I thought 'The Kalico Kid' game was from both of us," he admitted. "Reinforces this dating thing you're trying to sell everyone on."

"Not *everyone*," she corrected. "Just our mothers, remember? And as far as *reinforcing* anything, coming with one video game between the two of us only reinforces the idea that we're cheap since I do work for a video game company."

"Ryan doesn't know that," he pointed out. "And I suggest that if you don't want to find yourself under attack from a whole bunch of kids, you might think twice before making that little fact public knowledge at the party."

She looked at him in silence for a moment, then smiled. "If I didn't know better, Davy, I'd say you were being thoughtful."

"I was being practical," he corrected. "And I've asked you before, don't call me Davy," he added with feeling.

They walked out the door, and he waited until she locked up, then led the way to his car. "So what are you giving him?"

The company was releasing two new games at the beginning of the month. Senior engineers were allowed to get the first copies. She was passing hers on to Ryan but she didn't want to say as much to Dave, so all she said was, "You'll see."

When they came to a stop before a gleaming red sports car in the guest parking, she looked at him incredulously. This did *not* go with his usual image. "This isn't your car, is it?"

He might have known she'd have some kind of crack

about it. Admittedly, it was an indulgence. He'd just gotten rid of the secondhand car he'd been driving since his senior year of college. Since it had been so reliable, he hadn't wanted to give it up until it wasn't functioning anymore.

Dave braced himself for a punch line. "Why wouldn't this be mine?"

"Because it's sleek and powerful with a hell of a lot of horsepower." *And a damn beautiful vehicle,* she added silently, then raised her eyes to his. "Everything you're supposedly not."

"You have no idea what I am, Kara," he informed her coolly. Hitting the security release on his keychain, he unlocked the car doors, then nodded toward the passenger side. "Get in."

Kara opened the car door and looked inside. There was still the faint new-car smell. The interior was utterly pristine. No junk, no crumbs, not a single thing to testify that anyone had even ridden in the car. Her own car looked as if she were living out of it. She was glad he hadn't seen it. It would only give him added ammunition to make fun of her.

Getting in and buckling her seat belt, she said, "You just had this detailed, didn't you?"

"Detailed?" he repeated as he did the same, his eyebrows drawing together over a nose that would make sculptors and plastic surgeons alike weak with envy. "What do you mean by 'detailed'?"

He watched as a smile unfurled on her lips. If it hadn't been at his expense, he would have enjoyed the sight.

"I forgot. You're not a car person."

"I think the word you're looking for is *fanatic*. Car *fanatic*," he said pointedly.

She knew he was just saying that because he felt lacking in that department—and embarrassed about it. She doubted if the E.R. doctor knew very much beyond where the key went and where he put the gas. Still, she couldn't help bristling at the put-down.

"There's nothing fanatical about knowing how a car works or where the dipstick goes," she informed him haughtily.

"I have a suggestion where to put the dipstick," he muttered under his breath. "And if you really want to convince anyone that I'd actually voluntarily spend time with you, I suggest you stop being so damn antagonistic and taking apart everything I say."

Instantly, Kara felt her back go up. "I don't—"

She got no further. Inserting the key into the ignition, Dave gave her a look that said, "Yes, you do." The awful part was that she knew she really couldn't argue with him. She was being antagonistic, but only because she felt he was being condescending.

The reason didn't matter, she told herself. She had to work on her attitude, work on her delivery. Neither of their mothers were going to be taken in by this charade if they saw her with her hands wrapped around Dave's throat, choking the life out of him.

She paused to pull herself together before saying anything. Two deep breaths later, she finally murmured, "Sorry." Another fortifying deep breath came and went before she added, "I'll try to act like I think you're the greatest thing since sliced bread."

"Don't go overboard," he cautioned. "Neither of our

mothers is going to buy into that. If you ask me, they're not even going to buy that we're dating."

He was wrong there and she really wanted to say it that way, but she settled for a more diplomatic delivery. "They'll buy into it because that's what they were hoping for by sending me to you bearing a video game, remember?" She thought for a moment, searching for a plausible excuse as to why they initially got together. "We can tell them, if they ask why we're seeing each other, that we're catching up on the years since we last saw each other. Since that covers about eighteen years, it should take us a bit."

"Sounds reasonable enough, I guess," he conceded. "But to make that work, you realize we're actually going to have to exchange some information."

He sounded as if he was putting her on notice, she thought. She had nothing to hide. Her only problem was going to be staying awake to listen to eighteen years of his life.

"I'm game," she told him.

Dave pressed down on the accelerator, making it through the light at the crosswalk just before it turned red.

"Okay, what have you been doing these last eighteen years—in fifty words or less?" he qualified as she opened her mouth.

This, Kara thought darkly, was definitely not going to be a walk in the park. Why in heaven's name would her mother think she would *ever* want to become romantically involved with this man? Other than his looks and maybe his selflessness, he had nothing going for him.

She reminded herself that this was to teach her mother a lesson. Eventually, it would all be worth it. If she survived.

Chapter Five

"I take it your cousin likes balloons," Kara observed, an amused smile curving her lips.

There'd been three balloons, one blue, one white, one yellow, attached to the sign right outside his cousin's residential development along with an arrow pointing the way to the party. Another three balloons, comprised of the same colors, and another arrow were on the street sign at the first corner. Three more balloons again at the next turn and so on until they had reached the block—a cul-de-sac—where the party was taking place and, if parked cars and noise level were any indication, was currently in full swing.

She could see that the mailbox of a two-story house in the center of the block had not just three but six balloons, again comprised of the same three colors, indicating journey's end. As if that were actually necessary.

"Melissa just didn't want to take the chance that anyone would go the wrong way," Dave told her as they entered the cul-de-sac.

He pulled up into the first available parking space he saw. It was also the *last* available parking space on either side of the street. A convention of SUVs hugged every available inch of curb space not only along both sides of the block, but trickling down toward the next block, as well.

Dave unbuckled his seat belt. But as he started to get out, Kara put her hand on his wrist, stopping him. Puzzled, he looked at her. "Change your mind?"

Having gotten him to play along, there was no way she was going to abandon her plan now. That was the whole point.

"No, I just want to remind you that we're supposed to be into each other. That means you're going to have to hold my hand and not look at me as if you'd really rather be attending my vivisection."

He deliberately looked intrigued. "You're having a vivisection?"

"Don't get cute. You know what I mean. Just act as if you actually like me."

He shook his head, a dubious expression on his face. "That's an awful lot of acting you're asking for," he cracked. "I don't know if I'm up to it.

Her eyes held his, trying to determine if he was being flippant or if there was more than a small vein of truth to his words. Maybe it was time to have it out in the open.

"You hate me that much?" she wanted to know.

He thought he heard a hint of vulnerability in her

voice. Probably just his imagination. He really doubted that Kara had had a vulnerable moment in her life. But on the outside chance that her question was actually serious—and that his answer mattered—he told her the truth.

"I never hated you—well, almost never," he amended, remembering a couple of incidents that involved purple paint and a great many showers afterward. He'd lost count just how many it had taken to get the hue off his skin the second time. "It was more that I was very leery of you. I never knew what you were going to pull next."

Okay, maybe she had been a little hard on him, but it wasn't as if he was an innocent in all this. "Maybe if you hadn't treated me like I was contagious, stupid and beneath you, I wouldn't have pulled anything." He looked at her for a long moment without saying a word. But she could read his expression. "Okay," she relented, amending her initial statement. "Maybe a few things, but you would have never had to submit yourself to being scrubbed down with nail polish remover."

He'd forgotten about that. The distance of time allowed him to laugh at the memory. "I guess I should count myself lucky that I even survived my childhood with you around."

"That goes double for me," she countered.

He looked at her incredulously. Was she kidding? Or did she think he had amnesia? There were times she'd made his life a living hell.

"You? Ha!"

"What do you mean, 'ha'?" she challenged, ready to

go a few rounds with him right now, the party and her mother notwithstanding.

"You were Kara Calhoun. You were invincible. As invincible," he recalled, "as the comic-book heroine your dad named you after."

He'd thought that? Somehow, she found it difficult to believe. But then, if he didn't believe it, why had he just said it? Agreeing to her fallibility would have been more in keeping with his regular behavior, at least as it applied to her.

Something to puzzle over later, Kara told herself. Right now, they had mothers to fool.

"All water under the bridge," she said with a shrug, getting out of his car.

Rising, he closed the door on his side. "Gee, that's a clever saying. Mind if I use it sometime?"

"And we're back," she commented. But rather than being cryptic, she coupled the comment with a grin that she flashed at him.

A grin, Dave thought, that was oddly and perversely appealing. Which only meant that he needed to get in out of the sun before his brain was completely fried, he decided as he rounded the back of his vehicle and stepped onto the sidewalk next to Kara.

"All right, let's get this over with." Then, pausing to brace himself—an exaggerated moment for her benefit—he took Kara's hand in his.

She leaned her head slightly into his and whispered, "It'd be a bit more romantic if your teeth weren't clenched."

"Baby steps, Kara. Baby steps," he replied as he walked toward the house.

Kara did her best not to notice that when his hand enveloped hers, a strange feeling of well-being, of protection, washed over her. It was almost as if something inside her felt that all was well in heaven and God was in His kingdom.

She would have philosophically chalked it up to pre-performance jitters, except that she'd never had any, not even when she'd taken to the actual stage in elementary school. She was a ham and loved the spotlight, loved being the focus of attention. This, however, felt different somehow. She decided now wasn't the time to explore why.

"Showtime," she murmured to Dave as they stood on the front porch, which was completely festooned with balloons.

Dave said nothing as he rang the doorbell. A moment later, the door opened. Dave's cousin Melissa was a tall, willowy, dark-haired woman with an easy, welcoming smile. A smile, Kara realized, that resembled Dave's a great deal.

Not that it mattered.

"Kara," she greeted her warmly. "Dave said he'd be bringing you." Taking Kara's free hand in both of hers, Melissa lowered her voice before continuing, "I can't thank you enough for getting that game for Ryan. He's talked about nothing else since he saw the first commercial for it two months ago. Every place I tried was sold out and told me they would be for weeks. My husband, Simon, and I really hated knowing he was going to be disappointed, but now because of you, he isn't going to be." Dave's cousin underscored her statement by giving Kara a fierce hug.

She was surprised that Dave had actually given her credit in this matter. Maybe he wasn't as easy to read as she'd initially thought.

Released from the bear hug, Kara brushed off the woman's thanks quickly. "Part of the perks for working at a company that pays dirt," she confided flippantly. "I brought Ryan a few other games," she added, raising the shopping bag in her hand. "They're all age-appropriate," she assured Melissa.

"I may never get Ryan to go to bed again." Melissa laughed. "Just leave it on the birthday pile over there." She pointed out a card table that had been set up on the side. Someone was calling her name and she was already withdrawing. "There are beverages in the kitchen and snacks all over the place. Please help yourself to anything you want."

Pointedly, if perhaps a beat belatedly, Kara looked at Dave and told his cousin, "I already have everything I want."

She hoped it wasn't obvious that the words had stuck in her throat and had to be forced out. Dave, to his credit, didn't look surprised. He remembered the plan. When she slanted a glance toward his cousin, Melissa was beaming, as if she was genuinely thrilled for them.

Obviously everyone in his family had, until now, just assumed Dave was going to remain a grumpy, unattached bachelor for the rest of his life, Kara thought. Apparently she was regarded as the answer to their prayers.

"Your mom's already here," Melissa told Dave, then glanced back at Kara. "Yours, too."

Kara stretched her lips back in a smile that Dave

found unreadable—but he could make an educated guess as to the feeling behind it.

"Wonderful," Kara commented. Looking at Dave, she said, "Let's put the gifts on the table, Dave." At the last minute, she stopped herself from adding the *y*, managing to stretch out his name instead.

"Sure, Kara."

"Try not to sound so stilted," she whispered as they walked away, taking care that Melissa didn't overhear them.

"That's my everyday voice," he told her, irritated. Was there anything she didn't feel compelled to edit?

"I know."

Dave let out a long breath but said nothing.

Leading the way to the growing pile of birthday gifts, Kara took the games she'd wrapped less than an hour ago and deposited them on top. Dave waited until she was finished, then added his to the stack.

"Laying it on a little thick back there, weren't you?" he asked her.

"Melissa obviously didn't think so," Kara pointed out. "She looked happy."

If that made her feel guilty, she was determined not to dwell on it. The old saying about breaking eggs and making omelets echoed in her brain.

"Besides," she continued, also keeping her voice low, "the more in love everyone thinks we are, the more impact the breakup will have. My mother—and yours—will feel just awful that their misguided match-making efforts brought us nothing but pain. In the end, that should keep them from ever attempting anything like this again. I figure that's a good thing—unless you actually like being set up on blind dates."

Dave shivered at the mere suggestion of it. "God, no."

"Okay, then we're agreed." She looked around but didn't see her mother or his. Maybe their "audience" was out back with the children, she thought. "Could you get me something to drink?" she said to Dave.

Instead of doing as she asked, Dave physically turned her toward the kitchen and pointed. "Kitchen's right through there. You can get it yourself."

That wasn't the point. No wonder he was still unattached, she thought. "You're supposed to be willing to slay dragons for me," she told him. "You can't get a simple can of soda?"

"I'm saving my strength for the dragons," he answered. "Besides, I figured you'd be insulted if I usurped your right to choose your own beverage. Trampling on your independence and all that sort of thing," he elaborated when she looked at him quizzically.

Did he think she was that neurotic and insecure? "My independence is alive and well, thank you." Well, they were supposed to be inseparable at this stage in their relationship, she thought. At least, so she'd heard. "Tell you what," she proposed, taking his hand and lacing her fingers through his, "we'll both go. I mean, since we're in the beginning stages of euphoric infatuation. It only stands to reason that we'd want to spend every minute we can together, right?"

He looked at her, a little stunned. "You really plotted all this out, didn't you?"

Kara raised her eyebrows until they disappeared beneath her feathery bangs. "And this surprises you?"

He thought back to all the elaborate tricks she'd played on him those summers he was forced to endure her company. Now that he reexamined them, a lot of planning must have gone into those tricks. She'd been a mini-Napoleon. Obviously, she still was.

"No, not really," he conceded. And then a thought struck him. "This isn't going to involve one of us getting left at the altar, is it?" Because if it did, he had a sinking feeling it would be him. He saw no reason for him to have to endure any sort of humiliation in this little charade of hers.

She stopped abruptly and looked at him. She hadn't thought of that before. "No, but that's not a bad idea," she said as she turned it over in her head.

"Yes, it is," he contradicted firmly. "A very bad idea."

"Okay, I'll shelve it," she said agreeably as she resumed walking. "Temporarily." She sidestepped another couple, flashing an absent smile at them even though she had no idea who they were.

Dave nodded at the couple. "You'll shelve it permanently," he snarled between clenched teeth, "or this stops right here."

"Down, boy," she soothed, placing a calming hand on his chest—which only irritated him further. "We're not up to the part where we have public tiffs yet." He made no response but his glare was boring a hole right through her. "Okay, you win," she surrendered. "No getting left at the altar." Kara cocked her head, giving it one last try. "Not even if it's me?"

Dave's one-word answer came quickly and firmly. "No."

She thought that her being the one would have changed everything in his eyes. She was convinced the man would have enjoyed having a front-row seat to her humiliation, especially if it was in public. "Just curious. Why?"

"Because bailing out at the last minute and leaving you standing alone at the altar just isn't something I'd do, and everyone knows it." Because there were people within earshot, he lowered his head and his voice, talking into her ear. "Besides, that would put people in a really awkward position—not to mention there's also the expense of getting a sitter for the afternoon, buying a wedding gift, maybe buying new clothes for the occasion, all for ultimately no reason." There was more but he stopped abruptly because she was staring at him in amazement. "What?" he demanded.

It was a struggle for her to ignore the effect of his warm breath along not just her neck but other parts of her body, as well. Instead, she forced herself to focus on what he'd just said. "I forgot how you could over-think things."

"The other side of that is that you *under*-think them," he pointed out.

"There's no such word," she pointed out, the wide smile on her lips for everyone else's benefit so that the people at the party would think they were just indulging in lovers' talk.

Dave snorted. "Maybe not, but in your world, there should be."

Reaching the kitchen, she crossed to the refrigerator

and opened it. The beverages she was interested in—diet soda—were lined up on the bottom shelf. She bent over to look at the various labels.

"What's your pleasure?" she asked, turning around various cans and bottles to examine their names.

Dave watched, almost against his will, as the back of the narrow skirt of her sundress hiked up to a new, mesmerizing height, stopping just at the tops of the back of her thighs and managing to tantalize him.

You.

The word flashed through his mind in response to her question, surprising him probably more than it would her had he said it out loud.

Dave smothered both the word and the feeling as quickly as if it were a sudden spark in a tinder-dry forest.

Hearing no answer, Kara, still bent over the shelf, looked at him over her shoulder. "Dave?" she prodded.

"Anything," he said quickly, looking away as if someone had called to him. "I don't care."

"Okay." Taking a can of a popular brand of diet cola in each hand, she stood up, turned around and handed one to him. "Anything, it is."

The paper cups were on the counter directly behind Dave, and Kara brushed against him as she reached for one for herself. The unexpected jolt of electricity that raced through him had him convinced that this, coming here with her, was a bad idea. Definitely a very bad idea.

Served him right for listening to her, he upbraided himself.

As he heard several people enter the room, he saw

Kara tense ever so slightly. He didn't have to turn around to know why, but he did anyway. Just in time to see Kara's mother crossing to them. Or perhaps it was the refrigerator that was the object of her focus.

Rather than greet her daughter, the petite woman turned her attention and remarkable blue eyes exclusively on him. The smile on her lips lit up her whole face, and her eyes crinkled as she took his hand and shook it.

"Dave," she cried warmly. "It's so nice to see you again. Your mother's been telling me all good things about you."

He knew how much his mother liked to brag about him. Though he loved her dearly, it made him uncomfortable. Dave shrugged in response. "She likes to exaggerate."

"Oh, I doubt that, Dave," Paulette assured him, still not looking at Kara. "I've known your mother a very long time. Exaggeration isn't in her nature. Why, thank you," she said as he handed her the can of soda Kara had just given him a moment earlier. Briefly, her eyes shifted toward Kara, then back to him. Popping the top of the can, she picked up a paper cup and filled it halfway before asking, "Who's your friend?"

This, Kara knew, was a not-too-veiled comment on the fact that, according to her mother, they didn't see each other nearly enough. Working overtime at the company meant she had enough time to go to and from work, then crash as she tried to eat a very late dinner. It left no time for visiting.

"Very funny, Mom."

"Mom," Paulette repeated as if she were tasting the

word for flavor and then turning it over in her mind. "I seem to remember knowing someone who used to call me that," she told Dave. "But for the life of me, I can't seem to recall who. I just have this vague feeling that I haven't seen that person in ages."

"And you might not," Kara warned, "if you keep this up. And you—" she turned toward Dave "—stop smirking. It's only encouraging her, and God knows she doesn't need any encouragement."

Paulette patted Dave's arm and offered him a very conspiratorial smile. "Her bark has always been worse than her bite, Dave," she assured him. "Kara might seem rather prickly, but on the inside, she's really a softie. You just have to be patient. Sometimes it takes longer to surface."

He doubted if there was that much patience in the world, but he kept that to himself. Instead, he said dutifully, "Yes, ma'am."

Paulette smiled. It was obvious that she was allowing herself a moment to dream. And by her expression, Kara had a sneaking suspicion she knew exactly what her mother was dreaming.

Not in a million years, Mom. Sorry.

"I always liked you, Dave," Paulette told him with feeling. She sifted her eyes toward her daughter. The smile cooled a little. "You, I'm not so sure about." Picking up both the paper cup and the can of soda, her eyes swept over both of them. "Carry on, you two," she urged as she left the room. "And I mean that from the bottom of my heart."

Kara rolled her eyes, refusing to look in Dave's direction. There had been train wrecks that were subtler than her mother, she thought in dismay.

Chapter Six

Despite the carefully mapped-out placement of the balloons and the elaborately decorated patio and family room, which fairly sang of Ryan's affection for all things Kalico Kid, the party was really a rather informal one. There were a number of adults milling around, either catching up with one another or exchanging the kind of pleasantries that were involved when strangers attempted to become acquaintances. All the voices were raised in varying degrees in order to compete with the joyful din created by approximately ten children, each of whom sounded not unlike a small army of his or her own.

Consequently, midway through the celebration, Kara found herself the less-than-proud owner of a really raw throat. This was more shouting than she was used to, even though the people she worked with had a tendency to yell across the room to communicate.

By the time she joined in singing "Happy Birthday" with the others, she felt as if she were literally gargling with sand. Once the off-key rendition of the traditional birthday song was mercifully put out of its misery, Ryan got to make the first cut on his cake. With an eye toward saving all ten of his digits—and the fingers of those close to him—his mother quickly took over. She deftly sliced the cake, which she'd baked in the shape of the aforementioned Kalico Kid.

"Lucky thing I could get my hands on the game," Kara commented to Dave's back. Since he'd somehow managed to get in front of her and stood between her and the cake, she was about to ask him to pass her a slice when he turned around and handed her the paper plate he'd picked up.

Stunned at his thoughtfulness, she discovered that she'd temporarily lost the ability to speak. Instead, she stared. At the cake, at him.

Amused, he bent over and whispered into her ear, "Took your thunder away, didn't I?"

She wished either that he'd stop doing that, or, at the very least, that the sensation of his warm breath gliding along her skin would stop affecting her this way. "Something like that," she finally murmured.

He hadn't moved back yet. His face remained just inches away, and looking into his eyes was doing some very unexpected things to her. Things she was having a great deal of difficulty reconciling with the all-but-glaring fact that this was *Davy,* someone she'd once found irritating and annoying. Someone she'd enjoyed torturing whenever the opportunity arose—which had been often.

Unable to hear her because of the noise level, he cocked his head, pretended to cup his ear for her benefit and said, "What?"

Kara began to repeat her answer, but then, not trusting her voice to remain intact if she allowed herself to utter more than a single word, she finally gave up and merely said, "Yes."

Just then, Ryan drew all attention in his direction when, untouched cake plate in hand, he looked up plaintively toward his parents, specifically toward his mother, who, Kara had already assessed, was clearly the reigning disciplinarian of the duo.

Ryan's appeal confirmed it the next moment. "Please, Mom?"

It was obvious that Melissa had wanted to establish a little order within the chaos, or at least generate a small eye within the hurricane that was her son's birthday party. But it was equally obvious that Ryan had been drooling over his pile of gifts and wanted only to tear into the wrapping paper to unearth the treasures hidden beneath.

Melissa sighed. Her ultimate decision was never in doubt. "Okay, you can open your presents. But remember to go easy."

Kara laughed, shaking her head. "He probably didn't hear a single word she said after 'okay.'"

Kara had half expected Dave not to hear, but the look he gave her as he glanced over his shoulder was almost conspiratorial and showed her that he had and was in agreement.

Now, there's a first, she couldn't help thinking. She and Dave in agreement—and there'd been no choking involved. Would wonders never cease?

"I think he was off and running when she started to nod her head." A great deal of fondness flooded his eyes as he glanced back at Ryan. "You're only eight once."

Something in his voice piqued her interest. Kara slanted a glance toward Dave even as she watched Ryan tearing into his gifts with the innocent gusto only an eight-year-old could display.

"You actually remember being eight?" she asked him, curious.

"Vaguely," he admitted. Then he looked at her, his expression becoming more animated. "I remember you at eight."

She wasn't expecting that. Surprised, she asked, "You do? Why?"

That, as he recalled, was the year she really went to town on him. The year that she seemed determined to drive him insane. "Because you made my life a living hell that year."

Maybe she had been a little too forceful, but only because he seemed so intent on ignoring her. She'd already felt like an ugly duckling, and his treatment of her—acting as if she were invisible—was the precursor to her exacting revenge on him.

She'd implemented a lot of pranks that year. And he'd deserved every one of them, she added silently. Out loud, she apologized. But the words lacked heart.

"Sorry about that."

"No, you're not," he told her, turning to face her now. "You're grinning."

She did her best to dial it back a little, but she could feel that she was still grinning. And really enjoying herself. Her mind cast about for a good cover—and she found one.

"Just happy to be here, watching what is actually my core audience getting ecstatic over the games the company's been producing this last year," she said. To prove her point, she motioned toward Ryan.

When Dave turned around to look, he saw that his cousin's son was surrounded by a flurry of wrapping paper. The expression on the boy's face could only be described as pure rapture. The object of all this unbound excitement was now in his hands, and, Kara noted with deep satisfaction, it was the game that had initially started this particular complex ball rolling.

"Looks like our game is a hit," she murmured more to herself than to Dave.

But Dave did manage to hear her. Moreover, he looked very pleased, whether with her or himself, it wasn't clear. But he gave her shoulder a quick, reinforcing squeeze, saying, "Thanks for getting it. The look on his face is absolutely priceless."

His cousin was in obvious agreement because she seemed to be in her element, filming her son and his joyous unwrapping frenzy.

Glancing over toward him and Kara, Melissa mouthed, "Thank you," to both of them.

Kara suddenly realized that Dave had misunderstood her use of the word *our*. She'd said it referring to herself and the team she'd headed up that had done the testing and retesting of the game until they all but hated the mere mention of the title. He, obviously, had taken it on a far more personal level, which was fine for the charade they were undertaking, but not so fine if he began to believe it.

It was a problem inasmuch as she had no plans of ever being attached to anyone. She'd learned early on that the consequences of using her heart for anything other than pumping blood were daunting and came with a dark promise of being hurtful somewhere down the line. She didn't need that. *Ever.*

So instead, she concentrated strictly on Dave's cousin and smiled in response to the silent thanks, mouthing back, "Don't mention it."

Melissa's happiness at her son's joy was utterly obvious. Kara couldn't help wondering, just for a second, what that had to feel like. What was it like, having someone you'd given birth to, someone created out of a surge of love, and then nurturing that little being until it was all knees and elbows and someone you would gladly give your life for?

No point wondering, Kara told herself sternly.

Sorry, Mom, she thought, glancing in her mother's direction. *No kids for me, no grandkids for you.* She felt guilty that her mother, suddenly aware of the eye contact, smiled at her.

"Thank you, Uncle Dave!" Ryan cried as the last of the wrapping paper fell away. He dashed over and, still clutching the prized video game, threw his arms around Dave's waist.

Dave put his arms around the boy, momentarily relishing the hug before saying, "Don't thank me, Ryan.

Kara's the one who actually got her hands on the video game to bring it to you."

The fact that he was actually willing to share the glory surprised Kara. But the fact that, within less than a heartbeat, Ryan shifted his assault and threw his arms around her waist, crying, "Thank you, Aunt Kara!" surprised her even more.

She assumed that Ryan called Dave "Uncle" as a term of endearment and because there was no official title to describe their actual relationship. But calling her "Aunt" had a whole different meaning in this context. It bound her to Dave. Her natural reaction was quick and firm: deny.

"I'm not—" she began to protest, but her voice was partially drowned out by the excited squeals of Ryan's friends, who were dying to try out the game with Ryan, and partially cut off because, for such a little guy, Ryan squeezed as tightly as any metal-shop vise. He completely stole her breath away.

"Ryan, there's more," Dave coaxed, peeling back the boy's arms from around Kara's waist.

Kara tried not to be too obvious as she sucked in her first lungful of air. Dave's grin didn't help matters too much.

"Not as super as this!" the boy cried with the unabashed certainty of the very young.

"I wouldn't go betting on that, big guy," Dave warned him, a secretive smile on his face.

She looked at Dave, puzzled. Leaning into him so he could hear her, she asked Dave, "How do you know that he'll think they're cool? I mean, I know, but you don't even know what I brought," she pointed out.

He looked at her as if he was just humoring her by answering. "You work for Dynamic Video Games, don't you?" It was a rhetorical question. Or at least, it would have been, had it come from anyone but Dave.

"Yes, but how would you know if he'll even like the video games I picked for him? I mean, like I said, I know," she repeated with a casual certainty, "but isn't this a little out of your sphere of knowledge?"

Not in her wildest dreams would she have ever imagined Dave even knowing how to take a video game out of its box, much less playing one or knowing which game was the current rage. Not without help.

"Why?" he wanted to know. "Doctors play video games, too, Kara." He saw the dubious look on her face. "What, you think all I do is go to the hospital and then come home? I work in the E.R., which means that my shift can either be incredibly boring or so tense and frantic I don't get a chance to draw two breaths in succession and hope to God I made the right judgment call in a time frame where most people just have lunch." A smile played on his lips. "After a day like that, how do you think I unwind?"

"By lying in your crypt and having electrodes recharge you?" she asked innocently, keeping a straight face.

He disregarded her sarcastic reply. "I play video games."

He was serious. This was going to require a little bit of mental readjusting on her part, she decided. Kara looked at him as if she'd never met him before. Because, she thought as she took the first bite of the birthday cake he'd handed her previously, maybe she really hadn't. Apparently some people could change if they wanted to.

He could feel her eyes scrutinizing him. Delving into him as if to burrow down beneath his top layers. "Something wrong?" he wanted to know.

She shook her head, lowering her eyes back to the quickly disappearing piece of cake. "Nothing's wrong. Just trying to figure out if you're pulling my leg or not."

He took his time responding, choosing instead to let his eyes do the initial talking for him. He knew that silence, that pretending to study her, would drive her crazy.

Finally he said, "Don't worry, when I'm misaligning any part of your body, I promise that you'll be the first to know it." And then his smile widened. "Or maybe the second, but definitely one of those two numbers."

Why did that sound more like foreshadowing than a glib comment? she wondered. And why did she feel as if she'd just been placed on notice? Something hot jumped over her spine. She congratulated herself for not reacting, at least not noticeably.

Rather than answer him, she pretended to be utterly taken with the last of her slice of birthday cake and also with Ryan's revelry. He was still ripping the wrapping paper off the video games she'd bought at the company store at the last minute.

His friends cheered with each unveiling. The discovery of the Holy Grail could not have been greeted with more enthusiasm than this pint-size crowd had for these games. The shouts of encouragement and urgings to "play one of them already" were all but deafening.

Almost loud enough to drown out the special feeling growing inside of her. Unfortunately, the latter was rather overwhelming and all her attempts to ignore it were proving to be futile and useless. But she went on trying nonetheless, giving it her best shot.

Her best didn't feel nearly good enough.

Several hours later, the party began to peter out and guests left with thanks ringing in their ears and doggie bags comprised of warm leftovers placed in their hands. Kara had been elected to safeguard theirs.

Something had been weaving its way in and out of Dave's thoughts for a good part of the evening, plaguing him. He found that the answer wasn't easy and it had pushed him to teeter on a fence.

He looked at Kara somewhat uneasily as they walked down the darkened block toward his car. Unlike when they'd first arrived, there were now a great many parking spaces available. The car that had been parked behind him as well as the one that had been parked in front were gone. Pulling out was going to be easy.

Other situations remained a bit more complex.

"This isn't a real date," Dave said to her, wanting to both get her reassurance and place her on notice in case there was any sort of doubt as to what he'd signed on for. To be honest, when he'd said yes to her plan, he'd felt as if he'd been backed up against a wall. In theory, it had sounded like a good idea. In action, he wasn't so sure. Not the part about deceiving his mother—at this point she should know better than to feel a need to play covert matchmaker. What he wasn't sure about was being thrown into Kara's company time and again. It was asking for trouble.

Kara rolled her eyes. "Oh God, no. If it was a date, there'd be that first-kiss syndrome hovering over us in the background. Making us edgy."

He had no idea what she was talking about, but that was becoming par for the course. "First-kiss syndrome?" he asked. Ordinarily, he wouldn't have, feeling that by asking, he was only encouraging her. But this, he had to admit, had stirred up his curiosity. He knew he wasn't going to have any peace until she explained.

"Yes." She looked at him as they walked by a street-lamp. She couldn't believe he was actually asking. Was the man sheltered, or made out of iron? "You know what I'm talking about."

"If I did, I wouldn't be asking," he pointed out, trying to be patient.

She sighed and began to explain. "It comes packaged in a box filled with a whole bunch of anticipation. You always imagine that first kiss is going to be far better than it could possibly be so that when it finally does happen, well—" she shrugged "—it never lives up to all the preperformance hype." A glib smile played on her lips. "Kind of like most movie trailers. Anticipation embodies the very best, reality turns out to be, well—" she shrugged again, a bit more helplessly this time "—disappointing."

In his opinion, the whole process sounded much too complex and draining. For once she was the one over-thinking something. A kiss should just be spontaneous. "And this is what you go through?"

He made it sound as if he'd never experienced that first-kiss anticipation. Still, she gave him the benefit of the doubt. "Don't men go through the same thing?"

They were still within the scope of the streetlamp, not to mention that there was a full moon. Both illuminated her. His eyes swept over Kara.

For just a lingering moment, he could see himself anticipating sampling the taste of her mouth—purely on an experimental level, of course. For scientific purposes. "Well, I can't speak for most of the species, but I know I don't."

Was he that jaded? Or that innocent? It was a hard call, but with a face that Michelangelo would have been thrilled to have before him as a model, Kara had a strong feeling that it wasn't the latter.

"That's because you obviously haven't held anything in your hands that can't be found in a medical supply closet."

His mouth curved. He was not about to rise up to the bait and start citing what he *had* held that was *not* found in a medical supply closet. But he couldn't just let her challenge go completely unanswered, either. "You'd be surprised."

Her eyes met his. What would it be like to— Nope, she wasn't going to go there. She didn't care what kissing him felt like, she told herself firmly.

"Yes," she told him. "I would be."

"What do you say," he proposed, pushing a strand of hair off her forehead and tucking it behind her ear, "just for the sake of this charade, and to get it out of the way, we go through the motions of this first-kiss thing?"

She tossed her head, freeing the newly tucked strand of hair. "Syndrome."

He gave a careless, impatient shrug. "Yes, that."

"Well—" she pretended to consider "—I guess there

won't be any disappointment involved, seeing as how I'm not anticipating anything."

"A win-win situation," he replied.

She was about to ask exactly what he meant by that when he leaned in, took her face in his hands and then pressed his lips against hers.

She was expecting something simple and braced herself for the usual disappointment. Though what came next was anything but disappointing.

Chapter Seven

Her skin on fire, her mind gone, Kara could feel herself free-falling.

Or was she actually just leaning into him as she desperately attempted to absorb every beat, every nuance of whatever this was that was happening?

And all because Dave had upped the ante, increasing the depth and scope of what had been, up until this very moment, a cherished if somewhat disappointing ritual.

This wasn't even a real date, for pity's sake. The realization drummed through her head and then vanished.

Maybe, Dave thought, he was just trying to get this over with. Or maybe, his ego battered, he was attempting to teach the brat from his childhood a lesson not to write him off so cavalierly.

It might have started out being a little bit of both.

He really didn't know, couldn't remember. What he did know was that he could almost literally *feel* his blood rushing madly through his body. Could feel a cache of needs suddenly come spilling out, tumbling to the foreground. All while his head was spinning like an old-fashioned top, snatching away his breath, not to mention his better judgment. Hell, snatching away any kind of judgment at all. Because if he'd had a shred of that left, he would have backed away.

Instead, rather than fleeing, he was moving forward, reaching out for the mind-scrambling experience—and for her—so that he could continue this. Whatever the hell *this* was.

The closest thing he could liken it to was being drunk. He'd been in that state only once before and had vowed never to be like that again. He didn't enjoy the feeling nor the fact that he was not in control of his own actions.

Just the way, Dave realized with a start, he wasn't in control now. And though that deeply offended his sense of order, the rush kissing this woman created was instantly, incredibly, completely addictive.

All he could think of was getting more. And that there had to be a way to make it never stop.

Those desires and passions that had risen up within him were demanding he do something about them. Demanding that he explore exactly what it was that this otherwise exceedingly irritating woman with a face like a mischievous angel and a body that could lead a man happily to sin was doing to him. Then do it back to her. In spades.

But the edge of his cousin's block was not the place to find out, his common sense insisted.

And so, even though his body was begging for satisfaction, Dave summoned every ounce of strength within him and abruptly pulled his head back. He was surprised that his neck didn't snap.

He saw confusion and wonder in Kara's bright blue eyes—why hadn't he ever noticed how blue her eyes were before? They seemed to delve into him and go beneath all the layers he'd carefully placed between himself and the world, leaving him not just naked but in the state he hated most of all.

Vulnerable.

He did his best to sound nonchalant, as if his insides were not still on fire. "Well, we got that out of the way."

The words hit her like a water balloon, and it took Kara a second to find her tongue. And then another second more to remember words and how to form them.

"Yes," she agreed, her throat so tight it was almost choking her, "we did."

Didn't you feel *anything, you bum?* her mind screamed.

She felt as if she'd been fried to an absolute crisp, and he looked as if he'd endured something necessary, but annoying, like an inoculation against the flu.

Because she had a very uneasy feeling that she might fall over and pass out if she didn't get in more than a trickle of oxygen, Kara drew in a deep breath as covertly as possible. It helped.

A little.

Stealing a look at Dave to see if he was the *least* bit rattled, she felt the bitter bite of disappointment.

And then she thought she saw a bead of sweat at his temple. Unless the man had suddenly come down with a fever—and even that could act in her favor—the bead of sweat meant that she had gotten to him.

It seemed only fair since he had gotten to her. Big-time. Not that she was ever, *ever* going to admit that to him. Not even under penalty of death, she tacked on silently.

If she did, she *knew* it would lead to her undoing because the man would take to crowing about it and he would be utterly insufferable. Even more than he was right now, Kara added.

And then he completely blew her away by asking, "Want to test-drive another one, in case the first kiss was just a fluke?"

He asked the question with no more emotion than if he were inquiring how she liked her eggs.

What she didn't realize was that he was trying his very best to sound as nonchalant as possible. In reality, he was anything but. So much so that he doubted if he was actually fooling her.

She saw the uneasiness in his eyes. That trumped anything he had to say. It was at that moment that she knew she'd gotten to him.

Lifting her face up to his, a grin played along her lips as another, stronger dose of anticipation—this time fueled by knowledge—raced through her.

"I was always game for anything," Kara reminded him, her eyes dancing.

That she was, he recalled. But he hadn't been, especially not back then. He'd played it safe.

He didn't want to play it safe now.

Dave slipped his arms around her and drew her to him ever so carefully. "I remember," he replied, his voice low, his mind already trying to figure out how to survive the turbulent ride looming ahead.

Part of him was fervently hoping that the impact of that first kiss was, for some unknown reason, all in his imagination.

Part of him was hoping it hadn't been.

Back away. Now! something in his head screamed, and maybe he would have, except for the fact that the smile on her lips was daring him. Silently issuing a challenge.

God help him, he could never walk away from one of her challenges, even when he knew it was going to turn out badly for him. It was as if he was determined to prove something. Back then it was that he was at least as manly as she was, if not more. Now it was…

It was…

Hell, he didn't know what it was or why he was doing this, only that he *had* to.

He had no choice.

It wasn't a mistake, wasn't a temporary foray into insanity, Kara thought as the impact of his mouth on hers hit her with the force of an exploding grenade. The next moment, she was lamenting the very same thing she'd just been glorying in. Because a tiny drop of common sense had returned and found her.

Why, of all the times she'd been in this situation, anticipating a first kiss and being so sadly disappointed moments later when there was no magic, did she have to feel it now?

Why *this* man of all men, for heaven's sake?

Maybe because secretly, I always had a crush on him. Maybe, all this time, I've known that was the case and tucked it away in my heart.

Or maybe I'm just a glutton for punishment.

And the next moment, she didn't know anything—except that this kiss was even better than the first one. That was something she would have said was utterly impossible—if she weren't in the midst of experiencing it right now.

Every fiber of her being was melting into a puddle at his feet.

"Hey, you two, get a room!"

The glib comment, coming out of nowhere and followed by a chuckle, made Kara's heart slam against her rib cage as she all but leaped away from Dave.

She was behaving like some inexperienced adolescent who was guilty of misconduct. Behaving like someone she didn't know.

A lot of that going around, Kara thought, upbraiding herself.

She was extremely annoyed, though more with herself than with Dave. But he wasn't blameless in this, she thought, upset.

As her mental fog began to clear, Kara found herself looking up into the face of one of the party guests—a friend of Ryan's father. If it wasn't bad enough that he'd stumbled upon them in this compromising situation, the man was a priest to boot.

Despite the situation—or maybe because of it—there was a genial expression on the man's face.

"Just so you know," he told them, claiming the last car, located at the end of the block, "I'm available for impromptu weddings." He punctuated his offer with a broad wink.

"We'll keep that in mind," Dave replied a little stiffly.

Now *that* was the Dave she remembered and knew, Kara thought. The one who acted as if he had a pointy stick strategically positioned where the sun didn't shine. Not the one who brought her blood up past the boiling point without even trying.

Forcing a smile to her lips, Kara tried to look relaxed.

"Nice to have met you, Father," she said, referring to earlier at the party, hoping to get the focus off the present and the fact that he had found them hermetically sealed to one another.

"Same here," he told her, taking her hand in both of his and shaking it. There was a definite twinkle in his eyes, visible even in the limited light. "I look forward to seeing you again," he added, then his eyes shifted to include Dave. "Both of you."

Dave had no choice but to nod. After all, the priest had just stumbled across them bringing new meaning to the term *kissing*.

"See you around, Father Jack," Dave said, hoping to urge the man along his way.

"I can only hope." Father Jack chuckled as he got into his vehicle and then closed the door.

The moment mercifully interrupted, Dave did his best to view it as a last-minute reprieve. With that in mind, he shoved the incident behind him and out of sight.

"C'mon," he said to Kara gruffly, "I'll take you home."

Home.

Kara nodded, deciding it was best if she didn't speak just yet. Everything inside of her was still trembling, and she wanted to wait until it calmed down a little before trying to form words that made sense.

Because right now, she was feeling anything but sensible.

If she had been, she wouldn't have been hoping that by taking her "home" Dave had meant he intended to continue what had been so suddenly interrupted.

Because she wanted to make love with him.

She upbraided herself again. What the hell was wrong with her, anyway? This was Dave. Dave, who had been as squeamish as she had been reckless and brave, handling the slimy critters he wouldn't pick up and then finding ways to torture him with them.

Kara stared straight ahead into the night, concentrating on getting herself under control. Beside her, she heard Dave put his key into the ignition and assumed they would be on their way in a moment.

The moment came and went, but they didn't.

She looked at him. His profile was rigid. Now what? "Something wrong?" she asked.

Dave didn't answer her. Instead, he turned his key again—and received the same exact results.

Nothing.

She heard him let out a long, deep, frustrated sigh. She waited for the obligatory curse words, but there were none. Impressed, she watched him in silence.

He gave starting the car a third try, this time with his

foot on the accelerator, pressing down hard. A horrible sound pierced the night air, but his attempt made no difference. The vehicle wasn't moving and had slipped into silence.

Her first thought was that Dave had run out of gas, and she glanced at the dashboard just in case. But the gauge claimed that there was over three-quarters of a tank still available.

Dave saw where she was looking and said with barely reined-in irritation, "No, I didn't forget to put gas in."

"Never hurts to check," she told him cheerfully. She unbuckled her seat belt and got out of the car.

"Where are you going?" he asked.

"Nowhere, apparently," she commented, frowning at the front of his sports car. "Pop the hood." Her instruction was accompanied by a hand gesture aimed upward.

She was nothing if not animated, Dave thought. But instead of doing as she said, he started to get out of the car. Maybe he could help.

"No." The single word snapped out of her mouth, sounding far too much like an order to please him. "Stay inside the car," she told him. "I need you to pop the hood and then turn the key for me."

Dave bristled. This wasn't the way it was supposed to be, he thought, annoyed not so much with her as with his own lack of expertise when it came to things with engines and tires. He was the guy, damn it. He was supposed to be the one standing out there, issuing orders to her as he tried to diagnose what was wrong with the damn car. Their relationship was too new to be behaving like this.

He bit off a couple of words, swallowing them instead. When it came to cars, he had never had either the time or the interest to learn what it was that made them tick.

Or not tick.

"Pop the hood," she instructed again, looking at him expectantly. When he didn't comply, she came back to the driver's side and peered into the car. "What's the matter? Why aren't you popping the hood like I told you to?"

He would, if he knew where the hood release was. The fact that he didn't just served to make him feel even more inept. Ordinarily his lack of experience in these matters didn't bother him, but it did this time. Because this was Kara.

"Um…"

Kara realized what the problem was. She moved closer to the driver's side, opened the door and leaned in to feel around the area beneath and to the left of the steering wheel. Per force she had to brush up against his leg. When she made contact, she flashed him a grin.

"I'm not getting fresh," she told him innocently. "Your knee's in the same area as the hood release." Feeling around for the lever as Dave tried to shift his knee away from her, she finally located it. "Ah, here it is," she declared with triumph.

She pulled the lever, then returned to the front of the car, where she lifted and secured the hood.

"Okay," she called out. "Turn the key for me. Please."

He did, and this time he thought he heard what sounded like a slight cough coming from his engine. Praying that it had caught, Dave began to pump the pedal, giving the engine what he thought it needed: more gas.

"Stop!" Kara cried. "You'll flood the engine." Peering around the side of the car, she asked him, "Do you have a flashlight in the glove compartment? I think I know the problem. If I'm right, we can be on the road in about fifteen minutes."

"Sounds good to me," he said, his voice somewhat wooden. The moment was long gone. Just as well. He opened up his glove compartment and took out a small, sleek flashlight. Shifting, he leaned over in his seat and offered it to Kara.

"Okay, let's see if I can get us rolling," she murmured, getting down to business.

He knew he should be relieved, for a number of reasons, that they'd be parting ways soon.

But he wasn't.

Chapter Eight

"Where did you learn how to fix cars?"

Dave's question surprised her as it broke the silence that had filled the interior of his car. She had all but given up hope that he'd utter a single word before dropping her off at her apartment, and she'd be damned if she was going to be the first one to say anything. It wasn't her fault that she knew how to fix cars and he didn't. It wasn't in her nature to play the helpless female when she wasn't any such thing.

"So you *can* talk." Kara shifted in her seat to look at him. "I thought that maybe you'd suddenly been struck mute. To answer your question," she continued, "my dad was a car enthusiast. He loved taking engines apart, restoring old cars. He was never happier than when he was fixing some kind of engine problem, getting it to run more efficiently," she recalled fondly.

It seemed like a million years ago now. Neil Calhoun had been gone for thirteen years, succumbing to the disease that had ravaged him the summer she turned seventeen. She still missed him like crazy. Especially whenever she tinkered with a car.

"When my dad wasn't at work, he was in the garage, working on a car. I wanted to spend time with him, so I pretended to be interested in cars." Her mouth curved. "After a while, I didn't have to pretend."

Dave wondered if she was aware of the irony of what she'd just said—that she'd gone through the motions of a pretense until it no longer was a pretense.

Not wanting to get embroiled in a potential argument—he knew when he was outmatched—he decided not to bring it up. Instead, he focused on Kara's initial glib comment regarding his silence.

"I wasn't struck mute," Dave informed her grudgingly. "It's just that…" His voice trailed off as he realized that there was no ego-saving way to finish his sentence.

"Having me fix the car when you didn't have a clue what was wrong made you feel less than a man?" Kara supplied.

Dave was prepared to go one round with her, expecting some sarcastic comment about his manhood or lack thereof, but again, just like with the kiss and with Gary at the free clinic, she surprised him. This time by not trying to humiliate him the way she would have done when they were kids. Reluctantly, he nodded.

"It shouldn't have," she said. He continued waiting for the punch line. There wasn't any. "Lots of guys don't know their way around a car. And everybody has their strengths and weaknesses. Yours is fixing people. Me, I can generally figure out what's wrong with a car. In the grand scheme of things, yours is the more important skill."

For a second, he was tempted to ask to see some identification. This was *not* the Kara Calhoun he'd known. That one would have filleted him with her razor-sharp tongue before he could even think of a way to defend himself.

Still not completely at ease, Dave did begin to relax just a little more. Enough to ask, "What's your weakness?"

The question caught her off guard. Kara blinked. "Excuse me?"

"You just said that everyone's got a weakness," he reminded her. She had succeeded in arousing his curiosity. "So what's yours?"

"I should have said everybody *but* me." She could feel him waiting for her to give a real answer. After a moment, she shrugged. Still looking out through the front windshield, she said, "I can't cook."

"I can." It would have been difficult, growing up in an Italian home, not picking up a few pointers. His mother, perhaps because he was an only child and she had no daughter to share things with, had made sure he knew all the basics when it came to finding his way around the kitchen.

She heard him laugh shortly to himself. "What?"

"Nothing." But then he went on to say, "It's just that I'd say we complement each other."

"Not without some severe arm twisting," Kara countered. But her mouth was soft as she said it, giving way to a smile at the end.

He spared her a look just as he made a right turn and approached her apartment complex. She'd changed, he thought. She had never smiled like that when she was younger. It was a warm, inviting smile. Made a man let his guard down.

"Maybe not so severe," he commented.

She wanted to deny his assumption, but she couldn't manage to do it. Lost for a retort, she fell back on another shrug.

"Anyway," she began, shifting topics, "I think we pulled off the first leg of our plan pretty well. Both your mother and mine looked as if they bought into our fledgling romance."

For a moment back there, under the streetlamp, so had he. The power of suggestion was a dangerous, scary thing, Dave thought.

"First leg," he repeated, turning his car into her complex. He headed for guest parking. Kara really had put a lot of planning into this, he thought. "Are we talking about a two-legged creature, a four-legged one, an octopus or a centipede?"

Knowing it was going to take more than just one more shot, she went with the second choice. "The four-legged kind," she said.

Okay, he supposed that sounded reasonable. He'd been worried that she'd want to go on with this charade for several months. "And the second leg is?"

"Just letting our mothers see us out and about." They were going to have to be noticeable, but not obvious, which was tricky. Too obvious and her mother would definitely see through the plan, ruining everything. Not obvious enough and what was the point? "I'll see about coming up with a list of places and activities where one or both of the dynamic duo would be sure to see us."

"'Dynamic duo'?" he repeated, confused. "What do Batman and Robin have to do with all this?"

"Nothing." She saw the confusion on his face. Kara sighed. "I forgot how literal you could be."

How the hell else was he supposed to take her comment? "And I forgot how you hardly ever made any sense."

"To *you*," she emphasized. "Nobody else ever has trouble getting my meaning."

He highly doubted that. "Do you visit an alternate universe often?"

"A joke." Kara splayed her hand across her chest, as if to press back a heart attack brought on by shock. "Wow, maybe there is hope for you yet," she said with an easy smile. "And for the record, the dynamic duo in this case refers to—"

"—our mothers, yes. I get it."

She patted him on the shoulder, a teacher proud of her slow but determined student.

"Doesn't matter how slow your mind works, Dave, as long as it eventually comes through." She was surprised when he started to get out on his side. "Where are you going?" she asked with just the slightest hint of wariness in her voice.

Slight or not, Dave picked up on it and it changed all the ground rules. She'd looked flustered for that one unguarded second. She was afraid, he realized. Afraid that he was inviting himself over. It wasn't hard to figure out what she was thinking after that. That, once inside her apartment, he'd try to press his advantage.

The thought placed the ball back in his court, making him far less leery and a great deal more relaxed. "Your father taught you how to work on cars, mine taught me that you always walk a lady to her door after a date." A smile played along his lips. "I guess that would apply to you, too."

"Very funny," she answered. "So about our next 'date,' I think I've got the perfect place. Our mothers have a standing date for the Orange County fair each year—the first Saturday the fair's open. That's this coming Saturday." Her grin was wide. "I thought we'd join them." Then it faded a little as she said, "It'll require lots of hand holding. Are you up to it?"

He wasn't twelve anymore. There was no stigma attached to holding a girl's hand. Even hers.

"If I have to, I have to," he replied, trying to sound convincingly put out.

But the parameters had changed suddenly and drastically with that experimental "first-kiss syndrome" she'd sprung on him. He knew now that he never should have proposed "getting it out of the way." It was far better to be attracted to her and wonder if there was anything to the attraction than to actually go through the steps and find out.

Because now there was no room for doubt. He *was* attracted to her. A great deal.

And that, he knew, was definitely going to be a problem, at least for one of them.

"I'll get my shots," he said as they came to a stop before her front door.

"You do that," she told him. Getting her key out, she paused before putting it into the lock. "You don't want to come inside, do you?"

Actually, he did. Very much so. Which was why he couldn't.

"I'd better be getting back," he told her evasively, not answering outright. "I've got an early shift tomorrow," he tacked on for good measure.

She nodded. Relieved.

And yet…

There is no "yet," Kara silently argued. If she was feeling anything, it was just her, throwing herself into this part. There was nothing between them and there wasn't going to be. If she was lucky, she would get through this charade intact without giving in to the temptation of killing the man. She knew it was just a matter of time before the desire to put him out of her misery returned to tempt her mercilessly.

"Okay, then, I'll be in touch." She saw the look of surprise on his face. "About the fair," she prompted. Had he forgotten already?

"Oh, right. Okay."

It was time for him to get moving, Dave told himself. Time to point his feet toward his car and start walking back to guest parking. Why he felt as if he'd just stepped into glue that was holding him fast was something he didn't quite understand. It couldn't be because he wanted to remain in her company for a couple more minutes, that would be too ridiculous for words.

So why was there no other part of him moving except for his lips? "Um, thanks again for getting that game for Ryan."

"You don't have to thank me," she told him, and she meant it. Then, before Dave could respond, she added, "The look on Ryan's face was thanks enough."

Goose bumps were beginning to claim her flesh, traveling up and down the length of her bare arms. She blamed it on the night air, although it really wasn't all that cool.

"See you," she said cheerfully, then launched herself into her apartment and shut the door behind her before she did something stupid, like pull him in after her. Or kiss him again.

Dave stood there on her doorstep, looking at the closed door for several moments. For a split second, he contemplated knocking and asking to come in under some pretext or other. But then decided against it.

He'd been up too long and sleep deprivation was making his mind wander into strange, incomprehensible areas, tempting him to go against his own better instincts. Never mind that while in medical school and then during residency, he'd pulled back-to-back-to-back shifts that would have worn out the average robot. This was his excuse and he was sticking to it.

"See you around," he said to the door and then turned and walked away.

Kara had remained on the other side of the door, torn. Listening. Aware that he hadn't walked away and struggling with the very strong temptation of opening the door and pulling him in. Only the realization that it would have been a very huge mistake kept her from doing it.

The future, from where she stood, looked a little rocky. Of course, she could just decide to abandon this whole charade, but she knew that her mother was not about to give up now that she'd gotten her toes wet in matchmaking waters.

She might not be aware of any biological clock ticking, but apparently her mother, somehow newly equipped with super-hearing, was. And if her mother wasn't stopped in her tracks now, who knew who the next candidate she came up with might be? Better to nip this in the bud now.

All of this angst would be moot if only kissing Dave had been like rubbing her lips along a dead fish. Then all her problems would have been solved and she wouldn't be feeling as attracted to him as she was.

"Oh well, like the flu, this too shall pass," she told herself out loud.

For the time being, though, she forced herself to put it out of her mind.

"So it's working," Lisa declared.

The minute she'd walked into her house, the phone had started ringing. It was no surprise that Paulette was on the other end of the line. Paulette always did have timing down to a science, and this time she was calling, Lisa assumed, to crow about how successful her plan to get their children together had turned out.

"Of course it's working," Paulette answered with no small display of confidence. "I knew it would. Kara wants to teach me a lesson. I mean, teach *us* a lesson."

This, Lisa thought, had to be the fastest that Paulette had ever lost her. "Excuse me?"

Paulette laughed and proceeded to explain. "I know my daughter. She has this radar that puts her on the alert if something is a little off. In this case, the request for that game tipped her off."

"But Ryan really wanted it," Lisa pointed out. That hadn't been a ruse. "You saw his reaction at the party when he unwrapped it. He was overjoyed."

"Yes, but you have to admit that my coming out and asking Kara to deliver the game to Dave at the clinic because it was closer for her than for me was rather obvious."

Lisa had thought that herself initially, but her friend's enthusiasm had made her overlook that point. "If it was that obvious and you knew that she was going to see right through it, why did you do it?"

"Because I knew she'd react this way."

She could hear the smile in Paulette's voice. "What way?" she asked, frustrated. "You know, until this minute, I didn't think I was in jeopardy of coming down with Alzheimer's so early, but now I'm not so sure I'm not already mired in it." Drawing in a long breath, Lisa braced herself. "Paulette, what are you talking about? I'm not following you."

"I know it sounds kind of involved," Paulette allowed patiently, "but neither one of us has simple kids. Consequently, we're engaged in a mental chess game. The only way to get Kara and Dave together is to make them want to outsmart us. Challenge them. Especially Kara. And I was right."

If you say so, Lisa thought. Out loud she asked, "Okay, so do you have any idea what they think they're doing?"

"Does spring follow winter?" Paulette asked.

"With you I wouldn't bet on it," Lisa answered.

Paulette laughed. "Our kids are pretending to hit it off so that eventually they can break up dramatically—undoubtedly somewhere within our hearing range. The thought behind that—I'd stake my life on it—is that we will feel so bad that things didn't work out between them and that they wound up in emotional pain because of us, we'll swear off meddling in their affairs for the rest of their lives."

"In other words, once this little three-act play is over, we'll be back to square one and they'll be no closer to a relationship with each other—or anyone else—than they were when we started," Lisa concluded glumly.

She was about to ask what the point of going through these paces was if that was to be the outcome, but she never got the chance.

Paulette laughed quietly at the summation. "Not if I'm right."

Lisa sighed. "Okay, I admit it. I'm the slow one," she said, not believing it for a minute. "You're going to have to explain what you mean by that."

"What I'm counting on is that they're both going to get so involved in pretending to fall in love, they won't see it coming."

Exasperated, Lisa enunciated each word slowly. "See *what* coming?"

"That they really are falling in love."

Paulette was taking a great deal for granted here, Lisa thought. She wasn't nearly as confident about the outcome as her best friend seemed to be. "And you think this is a sure thing."

"Yes," Paulette cried with feeling. "They're perfect for each other. We both know they are. Besides, I saw the way they looked at each other when one thought that the other wasn't looking. There's definite electricity going on there."

"Hopefully not enough to kill them," Lisa murmured under her breath.

"Okay, I can see you definitely need convincing. I was saving this for last." She paused for effect, then delivered her crowning glory. "Father Jack saw them."

It was, Lisa decided, like pulling teeth. Except that Paulette really seemed to be enjoying this. "Saw them what, Paulette? Saw them what?"

"He saw them kissing. Your son was kissing my daughter. Or my daughter was kissing your son. Either way, lips were locked, and there was no one around to serve as an audience. Which meant they were acting on their feelings, not putting on a show for us."

Lisa wasn't so quick to celebrate. She'd always been the more practical one in their friendship. "Maybe they thought there was an audience. Or maybe they were practicing."

It was obvious that Paulette didn't think either point was valid, but she let them slide, saying, "I don't care what the excuse is, as long as they wind up in love. You look best in green, by the way."

That had come out of nowhere. "Thank you, but why are you telling me this?"

"So that you know what color dress to wear for the wedding," Paulette explained cheerfully. "A mint-green dress. Cocktail length," she added. "I'll wear baby blue."

Lisa could only laugh. There was no arguing with Paulette when she got like this. All she could do was go along with it and fervently pray that her friend was ultimately right. Because she really did want to see Dave and Kara together.

Chapter Nine

The doorbell rang.

Damn it, he's early. Figures.

Luckily, this time so was she.

Nonetheless, Kara felt her pulse flutter a beat before she opened her front door. She told herself she was being stupid. This was Dave, someone she'd technically known for most of her life. When she got right down to it, she couldn't remember *not* knowing him.

Nothing had changed, she argued silently, except maybe that he'd gotten taller, but then, so had she. Increased height was absolutely no reason for her pulse to skip a beat.

Stepping back, she opened the door wider. Dave was on her doorstep, looking ruggedly handsome in jeans and a Wedgwood-blue T-shirt—did he know that was her favorite color?

Oh, c'mon, Kara, how could he know that?

There was also an odd expression on his face as he looked at her. Was it just her, or was it getting warmer? The weatherman hadn't said anything about breaking records today. But there was no denying that she certainly felt hot.

"You're staring," she admonished.

Damn it, he was, Dave upbraided himself. But she was wearing denim shorts. Incredibly short denim shorts—and had somehow managed to grow several more inches of leg than he remembered her having. The icy-blue halter top that accented her taut midriff and small waist didn't exactly help keep his body temperature down any, either. Where was it written that skinny little brats could grow up to be sexy as hell?

Dave blinked to clear his head and refocus his eyes. "Sorry," he murmured, "didn't realize I was staring. I didn't get much sleep last night."

"Anticipating our date?" Kara asked cheerfully, tongue-in-cheek.

Or, at least, she meant for him to *think* she was being flippant. Truth was, she'd had less than her usual amount of sleep herself for that very reason. She told herself it was because she wanted to pull this off properly in order to ultimately teach her mother and his a lesson, but there was a part of her that wasn't really buying her own excuse. There was something about Dave, this new, improved model, that was definitely getting to her. Especially after she'd made the mistake of locking lips with him. Now all she seemed to do was think about that kiss. It was definitely getting in the way of her being her blasé self.

"Extra shift at the E.R.," he told her. It was a white lie, but there was no way for her to check that out and it was a handy enough excuse to hide behind. He hadn't counted on her reacting with concern.

"You want to reschedule?" Kara asked him. He expected her to say something like "Gotcha!" but she looked dead serious. "The fair's here for another twenty-eight days."

No, he didn't want to reschedule. For a number of reasons. Not the least of which was that he'd psyched himself up to spend the afternoon and possibly the evening as well in her company.

He had no idea how she would react if he admitted that to her—most likely it would result in her torturing him one way or another—so instead he said crisply, "Don't want it hanging over my head."

Her smile slipped away. "Fine," she retorted.

Served her right for trying to be thoughtful and put his needs first. Things like that were just wasted on someone like Dave. "By all means, let's get this over with."

She grabbed her oversize purse and walked out in front of him.

Giving him what amounted to the best view he'd had in a very long while.

Half an hour later, thanks to a decrease in morning traffic, they were meeting both their mothers at the entrance to the fairgrounds.

The two women were already there, waiting for them, which came as no surprise to Kara. She'd expected as much. Her mother waved with the enthusiasm of an Indy 500 starter signaling the beginning of the famous race.

May the better side win, Kara said to herself, smiling at the two women.

"Lisa and I talked about it, and we don't want you two to hang back just for us. Enjoy yourselves," she urged with feeling. "Take in some of the rides. You'll make more progress without us tagging along, dragging you down. We can all meet for lunch," Paulette suggested, going on to name one of the booths specializing in barbecued spare ribs and a few other things guaranteed to make a cardiologist weep. "Say about one?" She looked over her shoulder at Lisa for confirmation.

"One's fine with me," Lisa responded, picking up her cue. She smiled at Kara, then at her son. "How about you two?"

"Whatever you want, Mom," Dave replied. The easygoing response had Paulette smiling as she looked back at her best friend.

"I always thought he was such a good boy."

Kara felt herself bristling. "Mom, in case you haven't noticed, Dave's not a little boy anymore. He's grown up. We both have," she emphasized. That she was suddenly championing Dave surprised even her.

Her mother looked completely unfazed by her argument. "Doesn't matter how old you get," the woman maintained. "You'll always be my kid."

Kara rolled her eyes, then turned toward Dave, who was acting like a spectator rather than a participant, she thought irritably. She took his side, why wasn't he taking hers?

"Why do I feel as if I've just had a curse placed on me?" she asked wryly.

Her mother seemed to take no offense. "Because you're as rebellious as I was at your age. Takes standing on this side of parenthood to understand what I'm feeling." There was deep affection in her eyes as she ran her hand along her daughter's cheek. "You will someday," she predicted. Then, reverting back to her bubbly self, she concluded, "Until then, go, have fun."

"You're being kind of hard on her, don't you think?" Dave asked once they were walking away from their mothers.

She didn't like him pointing out her faults, especially when it seemed as if he was taking her mother's side. "Did it ever occur to you that I might have to be? If I'm not, she'll have me in a bib, a bonnet and a high chair in under an hour."

He moved slightly to the side to avoid a group of five heading in another direction. The fairgrounds were already fairly crowded, he noted. "If that were the case," he pointed out, "she wouldn't be trying to get us together for the purpose of marriage, now, would she?"

Kara frowned. She might have known that Dave would be perverse. "Well, I can see why she likes you so much. I'm surprised my mother thinks that I'm good enough for you."

He moved behind her, taking her arm to avoid walking into two teens busy texting, their eyes glued to their cell phone screens. Electronics should be banned in certain places, he thought.

"And I can see why you have trouble getting dates with that winning personality of yours."

Her back went up instantly. "I get asked out plenty, thank you."

"So why aren't you with someone?" His eyes pinned her. "You're certainly attractive enough."

"I could ask you the same thing," she declared tersely, then did a mental double take as Dave's second sentence registered in her head. "What did you just say?"

Dave obliged and repeated, "Why aren't you with someone?"

Kara shook her head. "No, not that. The other part."

He knew what she was referring to the first time around, but decided to draw this out, curious to see her response. "You have a mirror, you know what you look like."

This caught her completely off guard. "You think I'm attractive?"

The last time he'd said anything about her looks, he'd said she had a face that not even a frog would want. He'd been eleven at the time and she'd just put a red-striped ribbon snake on his shoulder. He didn't know they were harmless and it had scared the hell out of him until he heard her laughing. He'd been furious.

Maybe he'd said too much, he thought. Still, she really was a knockout. Especially in that outfit. "What I think doesn't matter. Certain things are just self-evident."

What did she say to something like that? If she thanked him, she might discover that it was all a gag. But if he was serious, then shouldn't she say something?

Kara shook her head. "I have no idea what to make of you."

She saw the corners of his mouth curve. "Good. It goes both ways." Dave looked out on the fairgrounds. "So, what do you want to go on first? How about the Ferris wheel?" he suggested since they were standing only a few feet away from the ride.

She didn't answer him immediately, which was highly unusual for her. Ordinarily, no one could get her to stop talking. At least, that was the case with the Kara he remembered.

Looking at her more closely, he noticed that she seemed uncomfortable. What was that all about? he wondered.

"What?" he prodded. "You don't like riding on Ferris wheels?"

"They're fine," she retorted a little too quickly and a little too forcefully. "C'mon," she declared, looking for all the world like someone who had made up her mind to face a firing squad with bravado. "Let's go."

"Wait a second." Grabbing her arm, he pulled her back and held her in place. He knew that look in her eyes. That was definitely fear. He put two and two together. "Are you afraid of heights?"

"No!" she cried angrily.

"You are, aren't you?" It seemed incredible. She'd always been fearless to the point of being reckless. He tried to make sense of it. "But you used to climb trees like a monkey."

She frowned, turning away. When he looked at her, she felt as if he could see right into her. "Very flattering image."

She wasn't denying it, which meant he'd guessed right. "What happened to change that?"

She shrugged, still avoiding his eyes. "I found out I can't fly."

The woman had to learn how not to talk in code. "Care to explain that?"

She looked at him resentfully. Why was he poking at her sore points? She hated admitting a weakness. Hated being shackled by fears. "I fell out of a tree, okay? I've been a little leery of high places ever since then. Satisfied?" she challenged.

"Okay, we don't have to go on the Ferris wheel."

Oh no, she wasn't falling for that trap. "What? And have you hold it over me? No, thank you. We *are* going on the Ferris wheel." Grabbing his hand, she pulled him after her as she deliberately walked toward the end of the line for the ride.

She didn't get very far because he wasn't about to allow himself to be dragged along. "What are you, twelve? If you're afraid to go on, we don't have to go on. Plenty of other things to do here. It's not like it's the only ride."

She was not going to wimp out. Kara was determined to be brave.

"I'm facing my fears," she announced between clenched teeth. But despite her yanking at his arm, he wasn't budging. "Now what?" she demanded.

"I changed my mind." His tone was simple, but anyone could see he was not a man who was about to be budged. "I don't want to go on the Ferris wheel."

She began to say something terse, then relented.

Maybe this was his way of giving her a way out. She let go of his arm and stepped back to look at him.

"You know," she began slowly, almost shyly, "if I didn't know any better, I'd say you were being nice."

Dave looked at her, and the moment felt strung out in time, moving toward infinity. It didn't help. All he could think about was her. About the way her lips had felt beneath his. The way her body, all soft curves, had yielded against his.

Damn if he didn't feel a pull within him. With effort, Dave shut out the surge of desire that threatened to overrun him.

"But you know better, don't you?" he asked quietly.

Before she could answer, they heard someone screaming for help. Turning, they saw a distraught-looking woman running in their general direction with a child in her arms. The little boy—he couldn't have been any older than six—was bleeding from a gash on his forehead. His eyes, usually the liveliest part of a boy's face, were shut.

"Help me!" the woman cried desperately as she ran, looking around wildly. "Someone please help me!"

Before Kara could do anything, Dave quickly moved in front of the woman, causing her to stop in her tracks.

"I'm a doctor," he told her, his eyes never leaving hers. "Can you tell me what happened?" His voice was calm, soothing, in order to pull the woman back from the brink of hysteria.

Suddenly, the woman all but melted before him, her legs giving way as if they couldn't support her any longer. Dave caught the little boy before she could drop him. At the same time, Kara grabbed the woman, keeping her reasonably upright.

"It's okay, I've got you," she told the woman, doing her best to mimic Dave's tone. "Tell us what happened," she repeated.

By now people were beginning to gather around them, drawn by the woman's cries and the drama that was unfolding.

The woman looked at them, wild-eyed, as if she couldn't believe what was happening herself. "He was running ahead of me and he tripped and hit his head on the side of a cart. I told him not to run, I *told* him," she insisted frantically.

"Kids don't always listen," Dave assured her, his voice still low. He needed to keep her talking. "Go on," he urged while he continued working on the boy, pressing a clean handkerchief against the gash on his forehead.

The woman swallowed. She was beginning to shake. She was going into shock, Dave thought.

"There was so much blood." Her eyes filled with tears. "When I got to him, he wasn't moving. I can't get him to open his eyes. Why can't I get him to open his eyes?" she demanded hysterically, her voice cracking as she looked to Dave for an answer.

But it was Kara who answered her. "It's going to be all right." She continued holding on to the woman. Her voice was low, comforting. Unshakable. "Don't worry, he's in very good hands."

As she said it, she looked at Dave, silently raising an eyebrow, waiting for him to say something. He'd placed the boy down on the grass on his back and was checking him for a pulse. The slight nod told Kara he'd found it.

Glancing up at the woman, he asked, "What's your son's name, ma'am?"

It took her a moment to pull her thoughts together. "Um, Kyle. His name's Kyle. Kyle Taylor." Her breathing was growing erratic. "Is he going to be all right?"

"He's going to be fine," Kara assured her, cutting in, afraid that Dave would say something practical and conservative, hedging his bets. It wasn't something the woman was up to hearing. "You have to calm down," she told her. "He's going to need his mom to be there for him when he opens his eyes."

The woman hiccuped, as if repressing a flood of tears, then nodded.

"All right," she murmured. "All right." Her eyes never left her son's inert body on the ground.

Dave pulled out his cell phone. Tucking it against his shoulder and neck, he quickly placed a call for an ambulance while he worked to stop the blood from oozing out of the boy's head wound.

"Wake up, baby, please wake up," the woman begged her unconscious son. The boy's eyes remained closed, and the woman's panic grew.

The paramedics arrived within minutes. In short order, the boy was strapped onto a gurney and placed inside the rear of the ambulance, his mother beside him.

"Maybe you'd better come along with us, Doc," one of the paramedics suggested. It was obvious from his manner that he knew Dave. "We're short an EMT this run."

Under normal circumstances, Dave would have complied without hesitation. But he wasn't alone today. He couldn't just leave Kara behind without a second thought. Dave looked at her quizzically now.

She knew what he was asking and had to admit, if only to herself, that she was pleasantly surprised at this unexpected act of thoughtfulness. He really wasn't such a bad guy after all.

"Go," she told him, her gesture reinforcing her words. "Don't worry about me."

Nodding, Dave climbed aboard and took a seat beside Kyle's distraught mother. When the ambulance doors closed, the last thing he saw was Kara, standing where he'd left her, watching the ambulance as it pulled away from the fairgrounds.

He had no idea why that struck him as so melancholy. With a shake of his head, he turned his attention to his patient.

It took a while to stabilize the boy and to stop the bleeding. When Kyle Taylor finally opened his eyes, several hours had passed. Dave had ordered a C.T. scan of his head to confirm that he'd sustained only a minor concussion and that there was no brain damage, minimal or otherwise. In between, he found himself reassuring the boy's mother and wishing that Kara was around. She seemed to be able to handle the woman better.

It wasn't exactly the way he'd intended on spending his day off. When he was finally finished, Dave walked out into the parking lot toward where he usually parked his car. And then he remembered. His car wasn't here. It was still parked at the fair.

At least, that was where he'd left it. Which was why

he was surprised to actually see it parked in the lot near the E.R. exit. And even more surprised to see Kara leaning against the hood like a model waiting for the photographer to get busy and earn his keep.

Curiosity had Dave picking up his pace as he crossed to his car. And her.

"What's up, Doc?" Kara grinned. "Sorry. I always wanted to say that." Straightening, she stood back from the vehicle. "I was beginning to give up hope that they'd ever let you out. The boy okay?" she asked.

"He's asking for ice cream and saying he wants to go back to the fair, so yes, he's okay. I'm not so sure about his mother. I'm keeping him overnight for observation. His mother's staying with him." He couldn't hold it back any longer. "What are you doing here?"

"Talking to you," she answered innocently, then said more seriously, "And I thought you might want your car. I was pretty sure they weren't going to bring you back in that ambulance."

"Good call." He frowned, still mystified. "I didn't give you the keys." As if to prove it to himself, he felt his pockets—and found the outline of his car keys.

"No," she agreed, "you didn't."

She knew what he was asking her, he thought, but he put it into words anyway. "Then how did you get the car here?"

The grin on her lips was pure mischief, he couldn't help noting. And damn if it wasn't getting to him. Bigtime.

"How to change the oil and jump-start a car weren't the only things my dad taught me," she told him, her eyes shining.

Chapter Ten

Dave would have been the first to admit that his memory of Kara's father was rather vague at this point, but he was pretty sure he remembered the man being easygoing and likable. Neil Calhoun hadn't struck him as the kind of man who would have passed on this sort of larcenous knowledge to his daughter.

"Your father taught you how to break into a car and hot-wire it?" he asked incredulously.

"That's all a matter of your point of view," she replied. "What my dad taught me was how to get into my car and start it if for some reason I lost my car keys and found myself stranded somewhere. As it happens, the procedure is pretty much the same for all standard cars."

He supposed her explanation sounded a bit more plausible, as well as in keeping with what he remembered of her father's character. But he was also having a little trouble accepting another piece of this puzzle that was Kara Calhoun.

"And you've been waiting here all this time for me to come out?" He found that really hard to believe, given how much they rubbed each other the wrong way.

"Had to," she told him innocently.

"You had to," he repeated incredulously. This he had to hear, Dave thought. "Why?"

"Because you're my ride home," she answered with a straight face. "A girl always goes home with the guy who brought her."

That sounded like something his mother would say. Or hers. Which brought him to another question.

"What about our mothers?" Because everything happened so abruptly, he'd left the park without letting his mother know he wouldn't be there to have lunch with her. It hadn't even occurred to him until now—and he knew his mother had a tendency to worry.

"I found them and let them know what happened— not that I had to," Kara told him. She saw him raise a quizzical eyebrow, debated stringing it out, then took pity on him and explained, "Story's already spreading around the fairgrounds. 'Local Doctor Saves Kid.' Our mothers put two and two together before I ever found them to say that you were off being super-doctor."

He supposed his stepping up as the situation occurred had ruined what she'd had in mind. But for someone who'd suffered a setback, she certainly looked pretty chipper about it.

"What about your great plan to teach them a lesson?" he asked.

Oddly enough, that was going perfectly. "Oh, as far as they're concerned, that's still moving forward," she assured him. "I told them I was coming to bring you your car and that I was going to wait for you until you finished taking care of the boy. Your mother wanted me to tell you that she's very proud of you."

Kara opened the car door on the passenger side, but instead of getting in, she asked him, "Are you hungry?"

Breakfast was a misty memory. He didn't even remember what he'd had. Then he'd been too busy with the boy from the fairgrounds to stop for lunch and now it was close to dinnertime. He saw no reason to pretend that he wasn't close to starving.

"I could eat," he allowed.

"Good." She bent over and reached into the passenger side. Straightening, she emerged with a foam container, the kind restaurant leftovers were usually packed in.

The instant he smelled food, his stomach began to cramp up, protesting its empty state. Nodding at the container, he asked her, "What's that?"

"Food," she answered simply. "I figured even heroes have to eat."

Opening the lid, he saw that she'd brought him one of those fast-food chain specialty burgers that were a limited-time offer. Currently out, this one threatened to disappear from the menu in the next thirty days. Somehow, that was supposed to make it more desirable to the consumer, and right now it was working.

"I'm not a hero," Dave told her, rejecting the label she'd just awarded him.

Kara smiled. He was surprised at how sunny that smile seemed. "You are to Kyle's mother."

Dave shrugged, unfazed. Turning sideways, he sat down in the passenger seat. As he bit into the cheeseburger, a look of sheer contentment came over his face.

Watching him, amused, Kara asked, "Tastes damn good, huh?"

As a doctor, he should know better. After all, this came under the heading of junk food, but right now he didn't care.

"When you're really hungry, there's nothing better," he confessed, taking another bite. For a second, he closed his eyes, relishing the taste.

Kara smiled, watching him eat for a moment. He really seemed to be enjoying that. She was glad she'd thought to stop and get him something.

"You know," she told him genially, "you're not as much of a dork as I thought you were."

She'd almost kept that to herself, thinking it might give him something to use against her, to poke fun at her. But then she told herself she couldn't go through life being paranoid, and besides, maybe it was time to hold out an olive branch to Dave. One of them had to be the bigger person and take the first step. And, after all, he *had* done a pretty selfless thing.

Dave slanted a glance toward her. "Thanks. I think."

"Hey, I don't mind giving credit where it's deserved," she told him. She had a hunch he'd be expecting a *little* of the "old" Kara to remain within the new, updated version. "Why don't you get in and I'll drive so you can finish eating your cheeseburger?" she suggested.

He was tempted, but it still didn't seem fair. "What about you? Aren't you hungry?"

"I ate waiting for you," she told him, which was partially true. Although she hadn't been hungry when she got his food, that changed as she waited. So she'd had a candy bar that she'd found at the bottom of her purse, vintage unknown. It was a wee bit stale. "Go on, get in," she coaxed. "Unless, of course, you're afraid to let me drive."

"Well, you got here in one piece without the keys. Which reminds me—take the keys." Digging into his pocket, Dave retrieved his car keys and held them out to her. "I'll feel better if you do it the conventional way."

"Spoilsport." She laughed. But she took the keys from him and got back in on the driver's side. She buckled up then waited for him to swing his legs inside the car and secure his seat belt. "Here, I'll hold your cheeseburger," she offered.

He surrendered the cheeseburger, placing it back into the box on top of the now-spilled French fries and handing that to her while he slid the metal tongue of his seat belt into place.

"Thanks," he told her, taking the meal back.

The slight movement of her shoulders in a careless shrug blended in with her verbal response. "Don't mention it."

"I mean for everything," he emphasized, his eyes holding hers. "Bringing the car, bringing food. I get caught up in a patient's care, and I tend to forget everything else," he confessed.

"Well, that's a good thing, isn't it? Aren't all doctors

supposed to be that selfless? Oh God," she groaned, as if suddenly becoming aware of something.

When she didn't follow it up with an attempt at an explanation, he looked at her. "Oh God what?" he prodded.

"I keep saying these good things about you. If I'm not careful, somebody overhearing us might think that we're actually friends," she told him flippantly.

He knew what she was doing. She was trying to make him think that she was still the old Kara with the flinty tongue. But she wasn't. She was caring despite her attempts to seem otherwise. His thoughts went to Gary that morning in the clinic. She had a good heart, as well. That went a long way to balancing things out in his book.

"Heaven forbid," he said, just before taking another bite of his cheeseburger.

"Yeah," she agreed, backing the car out of the parking space. "That's what I say."

She wove her way across the hospital grounds until she came to the exit. Within a few minutes, they were on the main thoroughfare, heading for the freeway.

Time for directions, she thought. "Okay, how do you want to do this?"

"Do what?" he asked.

She gave him his options. "Shall I drive to my place so you can drop me off and then drive yourself to your house, or do you want to stop by your place first and then take me to my apartment?"

The second choice seemed to be rather convoluted, but he kept that to himself. Instead, he said simply, "I pick option number one."

"You know, if you're not careful, you're going to have me thinking that you're actually a real person instead of this plaster saint I always believed that you were."

"Why on earth would you think I was a plaster saint?" he asked, completely mystified.

She looked at him, stunned. He didn't remember? It hardly seemed possible. She remembered perfectly. "Because that's the way you used to behave. As if you were holier than thou—or at least holier than me."

Was that it? Dave laughed quietly, shaking his head. "As I recall, it wouldn't exactly have taken much to be holier than you. You were hell on heels back then."

She was about to get slightly defensive of the girl she'd once been—the woman she still believed herself to be—but what he said next completely took the wind out of her sails.

"I really envied you that freedom."

Her eyes narrowed. "Freedom?" Kara echoed, a little confused.

"My father had certain expectations of his offspring," Dave confided.

Having made short work of his cheeseburger, he crumpled up the paper it had been wrapped in within the container and turned his attention to the French fries. They had long since ceased to be warm but they still tasted good. He couldn't remember when he'd last had fries. He allowed himself to savor the first one before continuing what he was saying.

"When you came right down to it, my dad expected me to be mature by the time I took my first step."

That didn't jibe with the man Kara remembered from those summer vacations.

"Your dad was a lovely man who was always a lot of fun," she protested, remembering the tall, robust man fondly.

Now that she thought about it, Dave looked a great deal like his late father. The same thick, dark hair, the same green eyes and broad shoulders. The only difference was that Dave's hair was a bit unruly while his father's had always appeared to be perfect.

"With you," Dave agreed readily. "Because you were a girl. Had I had a sister, I don't doubt he would have been more or less the same with her. I guess in his own way, he was a chauvinist," Dave theorized. "He didn't expect nearly as much from 'the softer sex,' as he liked to call them, as he did from the male of the species, namely me." He spared her a look. "I have no doubt that you and he would have probably gone a few rounds once you got older," he told her with certainty.

She felt for him. Your father was the parent you were supposed to bond with if you were a boy. How awful for Dave if his father had gotten so caught up in rigid expectations that there was no place for the more memorable moments. She had a boatload of the latter not just with her mother but with her father, as well.

She began to see Dave in a whole different light. "Was he hard on you?" she asked.

Was that pity in her voice? Or sympathy? Either way, it surprised him. He hadn't thought her capable of that sentiment, at least not where he was concerned. But then, he wouldn't have expected her to be thoughtful, either, and he was obviously wrong in that department.

In response to her question, he shrugged. "No more than was necessary, I suppose. He told me there were no do-overs in life and that I had to get it right the first time because the world had no patience for the losers and the inept." The corners of his mouth twisted in a mirthless smile. "God knew that he didn't," he added almost under his breath.

She thought how his relationship with his father had differed from hers with her own father. She worshipped the ground her father had walked on, and he had always made her feel secure in his love. She'd wanted to please her father, to reward him for his faith in her, but he'd never asked anything more of her than that she be a good person and that she be happy.

Because of him—and her mother—she was.

Kara took a breath. Dave probably didn't want to hear this, but she needed to say it anyway. "I'm sorry you had a rough time of it."

The French fry he'd just popped into his mouth went down the wrong way. He coughed, his eyes beginning to water. One hand on the wheel, Kara reached for her soda. Pulling it out of the cup holder, she held it up to him. He took it without offering a protest and drank deeply. The coughing subsided.

"Thanks," he said, finally catching his breath. And then he looked at her as he wiped away the dampness from the corners of his eyes. "You keep sounding like that and I'm going to ask to see some ID pretty soon. Either that or we need to swing by your mother's garage to check for a pod."

"Invasion of the Body Snatchers." She laughed. "Who *are* you and what have you done with Dave?

Talk about pod checking, I should be looking in *your* garage for one." And then she grinned. "You really are getting to be a revelation. I didn't picture you as someone who was a movie buff."

"I'm not," he told her honestly.

The hell he wasn't. "Then how do you explain all the movie references? The *accurate* movie references," she emphasized.

That was simple enough to explain. "I remember everything I read or see, even just in passing. And as for having a rough time of it—" he got back to her initial question "—I didn't. Living up to my father's high standards helped me achieve as much as I did. There are easier things than getting through medical school," he told her.

She was certain that it had been hard. But she was just as certain that he was capable of it. "You would have done that on your own. Don't look so surprised. Just because I gave you a hard time when we were kids doesn't mean I didn't think you were smart or capable of making something of yourself. Young as I was, I always *knew* you'd be somebody when you grew up. Truth was, you made me feel a little inadequate. That was part of the reason I gave you such a hard time," she confided.

"And what was the rest of the reason for giving me such a hard time? Why *did* you give me a such hard time, Kara?"

"I already told you," she answered, looking back at the road. Glancing at the speedometer, she realized that she was pressing down too hard on the gas. The needle was nosing its way past the sixty mark. She eased back.

The subject was getting her too agitated. *He* was getting her too agitated.

Dave did a quick mental review. No, he hadn't missed anything. "No, you didn't."

"Well, okay, maybe not in so many words," she allowed. Maybe the man didn't take behaving "holier than thou" as a reason to get her back up. "Because you looked down on me."

"No, I didn't," he protested. He'd thought of her as annoying, a brat and, at times, skillfully humiliating, especially for her age. But he'd never thought himself better than her. Just nicer.

She knew what she knew. "Yeah, you did. There was a two-year age difference between us, but it might as well have been twenty. Those two years made you act as if I were beneath you. Insignificant," Kara added for good measure, vividly remembering those years and how it felt.

Dave stuck to his guns. "That's not what I thought. You were so fearless, you made me feel self-conscious. And there was that incident with the snake," he reminded her pointedly. "You didn't exactly endear yourself to me with that."

Handling snakes had never bothered her. But she knew it bothered him and she'd acted on it. "That only happened later. After you—" She sighed, stopping herself. "Never mind, there's no point in rehashing all this old stuff. Just water under the bridge," she told him.

She didn't want to open up any old wounds and make them fresh. That could all be pushed into the background. She had a mother to ease into her place and so did he. That was far more important than renewing any

old squabbles with him that she knew were not about
to be won today.

Kara spared a glance in his direction. "Any fries
left?"

He hadn't realized that he'd been eating all this time.
The fries were almost all gone. But there were still a
few stragglers left.

Dave raised his brow. "Want one?"

"No, I'm taking inventory," she answered sarcastically, then stopped herself. Maybe that sounded a little
too sharp. She laughed a bit self-consciously. "Sorry,
old habits die hard. Yes, I want one."

Since her hands were on the wheel, he decided just
to put a French fry in her mouth. Taking the largest one
that was left, he held it up to her lips and said, "I know
I'm going to regret saying this, but open your mouth."

She turned her head slightly toward him. Even so,
Dave saw that her eyes were laughing at him as she
complied. When she closed her lips again, they brushed
against his fingers.

Or perhaps his fingers brushed against her lips. In
whatever order it happened, the effect was still the
same. An electrical surge, quick and jolting, passed
through both of them at the same time.

Chapter Eleven

Kara's skin felt hot and her heart suddenly leaped without warning, pounding madly like some impromptu marching-band drum soloist.

Belatedly, she shifted her eyes back to the road and realized she was about to go right through a red light. Alarmed, she slammed on the brakes.

Kara felt the back end of the vehicle fishtailing first to the right, then to the left as she attempted to compensate for the sickening lunge by turning the steering wheel quickly in the opposite direction.

The front tires had gone well over the intersection's white line before she finally managed to get the car to stop. Fortunately for them, there was no through traffic.

Her heart was pounding so hard that it hurt. She told herself it was because of the near miss, but it had begun beating erratically before she ever had to slam on her brakes and she knew it.

Her heart was pounding because of him. How dumb was that? she asked herself.

Beside her, Dave had both of his hands braced against the dashboard, anticipating a traumatic collision at the very least.

When there wasn't one, he blew out a breath and tried to relax. His neck and shoulders felt as stiff as if they'd suddenly been turned to iron.

"You charge extra for that?" he cracked, attempting to make light of the near-overwhelming moment.

Who *was* this man beside her? The Dave she remembered hadn't had a sense of humor—possibly because she hadn't really given him anything to laugh about, she thought now ruefully. But he would have definitely read her the riot act at being this careless—all but flying through a red light and then almost sending them both through the windshield in her attempt to stop the car.

Letting out a long, shaky breath, she shook her head in response to his question. "The first one's on the house," she told him.

Dave looked at the traffic light and then back at her. She wasn't moving.

"Light's green," he prompted and then leaned forward, peering closer at her. "And so are you," he observed.

"There's a reason for that," she murmured, moving her foot back to the gas pedal. Her stomach had tied itself up in a knot.

She wasn't used to doing stupid things like that. Granted, there were times when she drove fast, maybe a wee bit faster than the speed limit, but she was *never* reckless or preoccupied.

Until just this moment.

Once is all it takes, Kara reminded herself ruefully.

"You want to pull over for a minute?" Dave suggested. "We could switch places and I could take over. After all, it is my car and I've finished eating," he added.

She didn't want to surrender the driver's seat. If she did, she knew that she'd never hear the end of it from him. As it was, she probably wouldn't anyway, Kara thought.

Never hear the end of it? Listen to yourself, the little voice in her head silently mocked. *Like you're going to keep seeing him or running into him once this charade is over? C'mon, Kara. This is all temporary. You know that. What's wrong with you?*

She had no answer to that, no idea why she was behaving the way she was. She felt restless and unsettled, as if she was waiting for something to happen without really knowing what—or why.

"Kara, are you okay?" Dave was asking her. When she looked in his direction, she saw concern in his eyes.

"I'm fine," she snapped out a little too forcefully, ashamed of herself the moment she did. "Just can't seem to be able to eat and drive at the same time," she added a bit stiffly.

"Yeah, that must be it," he agreed for the sake of peace. But he didn't believe it for a second. Kara could easily do five things at once and keep track of each; she always had. Something else was going on here.

Most likely, he judged, the same "something" he'd felt himself.

"Sorry if I scared you," she said in a smaller voice that sounded completely unlike her usual one.

"Ditto."

It felt as if every single nerve she possessed had gone on red alert and no matter how she tried to talk herself out of it, they all refused to stand down.

She spared him a glance now and even though part of her understood what he was saying—that he'd sensed her reaction to him, to being fed by him—she asked sharply, "Excuse me?"

He knew that telling her to relax would only fall on deaf ears. Kara was the most contrary person he'd ever known, always ready to do the exact opposite of whatever she was told. The only way out of the situation—and an argument—was to make this about him, as well. It would keep this from escalating or becoming some kind of battle of wits, neither of which he wanted. And, he suspected, if really pressed for an honest answer, neither did she.

"I felt it, too," he told her quietly.

He might as well have shouted it. She could feel every vein in her body pulsing, making her grow extremely hot in the space of what felt like a nanosecond.

Still, being Kara, she felt compelled to deny the obvious. So she feigned ignorance. "Felt what?"

He wasn't exactly certain how to describe it. "That electrical spark," he finally said. "You know, when your lips brushed against my fingers."

Her back went up almost instantly. "You mean when *your* fingers brushed against *my* lips."

"Really?" he asked, his voice as quiet as hers was intense. "You're going to break this down into who did what to whom first? You really want to go that route?"

He didn't say it, but his tone indicated that she was being juvenile. And she supposed she was. But that was only because this reaction she'd just experienced— desire? Longing?—was very, very new to her. She supposed it was something that teens went through, but she'd never felt connected like this to anyone before, never felt herself growing hot with anticipation before. Imagined it, maybe, wondered about it, sure, but never actually experienced it. Not until just this moment.

"No," she answered with what she could only hope looked like a careless shrug. "Um, what was it that you think you felt?"

He knew exactly what she was doing. She wanted him to say it first. "I'll show you mine if you show me yours?" he guessed. With a laugh couched in disbelief, he shook his head. "Okay, I'll go first." He looked at her profile as they drove. Damn but it was near perfect, he thought. Why, after all this time, especially with their history, was she getting to him like this? "God help me, I felt something. And—" he took a breath, as if to fortify himself before continuing "—not for the first time."

Kara gripped the steering wheel harder. Her chin went up in unconscious defense. "This isn't my first time, either."

He realized that she'd misunderstood him. "I meant with you. Not my first time *with you*," he emphasized, trying to get his feelings across.

With her?

That completely threw her. Her eyes darted toward Dave quickly. Her heart decided to relocate back up into her throat, possibly permanently this time.

"Really?" Did that sound as breathless and tinny to him as it did to her? Her nerves were all over the place and she damned herself for it.

This is Dave, damn it. Nothing-special Dave. Don't act stupid.

"Really," Dave said. "Face it, Kara," he went on. "For whatever reason, there's an attraction between us."

She didn't want to face it. Didn't want to admit it or lower her defenses. She was actually *afraid* to lower her defenses. The only way to take the edge off this was to be flippant. So Dave would think that this was business as usual for her instead of completely uncharted territory.

"You probably have some kind of a scientific name for all this," Kara said.

Why in heaven's name would she think that? But then, the way her mind worked had always been a huge mystery to him and, he suspected, most likely to anyone else dealing with her.

"No," he told her simply.

He wasn't helping, Kara thought. If she wasn't careful, she'd find herself slipping into a vortex, one from which she didn't think she would ever emerge.

"Okay," she said gamely, "how about if we call it 'Albert'?"

It was official, he thought. He really hadn't a clue what went on in that head of hers. "'Albert'?" he questioned.

"Yes, Albert. As in Albert Einstein." Kara didn't

have to look at him to know that he was staring at her as if she'd lost her mind. Maybe she had, but this tiny tidbit actually did make sense. "According to one of the latest biographers, it seems that Albert Einstein had one heck of a raging libido."

That might or might not be true, he didn't know. But there was one thing he did know. "You're driving past your development," he told her.

Kara did a double take.

Damn it, he was right. She *was* driving past the entrance to her development. Pressing her lips together, she refrained from saying anything as she made her way to the next light that, fortunately, allowed for U-turns.

"I guess the conversation with you is so scintillating," she cracked dryly, "I didn't notice the entrance."

"I like you better without the sarcasm," Dave told her quietly.

Kara was grateful that they were inside his car so he couldn't tell she was blushing. Because of her fair skin, she was probably an embarrassing shade of pink right now.

Why his comment should do that to her was something she didn't completely grasp and refused to explore at the moment. The less she thought about him—or "them"—the better, she decided.

"I'll make a note of that when I get a chance," she promised flippantly.

"Right." He reminded himself that Kara *had* brought his car to him and that she had brought him something to eat, as well. She was under no obligation to do either, so beneath the bravado, there really was a very decent, kind person.

One who, for some unknown reason that pointed to the fact that God *had* to have a sense of humor, stirred him the way he really had never been stirred before.

Every single woman he had ever been out with—women he felt were close to perfect in temperament, women who'd matched his own personality and intellect—almost immediately left him restless, eager to be on his way. Bored. Every woman he thought he should be attracted to, he really wasn't.

And the one woman he would have bet his soul that he *wasn't* attracted to, he was. How was that for a cosmic joke at his expense? Dave thought darkly.

Kara drove into her development, but rather than take the first available space in guest parking, she continued driving until she came to a second set of guest parking spaces. He hadn't even noticed them when he came to pick her up.

She finally picked a space, parking in the last empty one that was closest to her apartment.

"Less distance to walk," she explained when she saw him looking at her quizzically.

Taking a breath, as if bracing herself, Kara unbuckled her seat belt and opened the driver's-side door, then got out.

Dave quickly followed suit on his side, emerging from the vehicle at the same time she did.

Time to beat a hasty retreat, she thought nervously, feeling disgusted with herself at the same time for her reaction. Just what was it that she was afraid of? She'd always been so fearless around Dave, had always en-

joyed being able to tease him. Since when did she sub-
scribe to the better-safe-than-sorry school of thought?
And exactly what was she being "safe" from?

Still, she heard herself saying, "Well, I'll give you a
call when I figure out the next phase of Operation Meddling Mothers."

To her surprise, rather than agree or just say goodbye
the way she expected him to, Dave looked at her over
the hood of his car and said, "The world won't end if
you invite me in, you know."

Stunned, she was certain she hadn't heard him correctly. And if she had, then he needed to explain why
he'd just said what he had. "What?"

His eyes held hers as he began to repeat his statement. "The world won't—"

"No, I heard you. I heard you," she cried, holding
up her hand to stop him from going on. "And you're
wrong," she told him. There went her pulse again. What
was *wrong* with her, anyway? "It just might. Why
throw the whole universe off just to continue with an
experiment named Albert—?"

It was the last thing she said.

Dave had rounded the back of his car while she was
talking and, right when she'd started to voice her last
question, he'd framed her face with his hands, drew her
to him and kissed her.

He kissed her not as if it were some sort of an experiment, but as if he'd been restraining himself from
reaching over while they were still on the road and kissing her right then and there.

There was enough energy and passion within the
kiss to completely take her breath away—as well as,

in her opinion, to supply enough electricity to light up Las Vegas for a week.

Part of her, for just a split second, wanted to flee. To run and save herself before it was too late. But that survival instinct died quickly. Survival was the last thing on her mind. Enjoyment coupled with eagerness and excitement took center stage, wiping everything else from her brain cells.

Her knees went weak, as did the pit of her stomach. To steady herself—or perhaps to anchor Dave into place—she put her arms around his neck, holding him closer to her. Savoring the taste of him as her head continued to spin madly around.

He wanted her too much.

The way Dave saw it, while he was still capable of coherent thought, was that he had one of two options. He could either run like hell and find himself fighting off this urge time and again, even when she wasn't anywhere around. Perpetually wondering if he was missing out on something.

Or, he could just follow his instincts, make love with this one-time harpy from his past and most likely discover that the expectations ricocheting through him right now were far too high. Then, once again, he would find himself being greatly disappointed in the person he'd selected because she wasn't what he'd hoped she was—someone who actually made him feel alive and grateful to be so.

Still, he couldn't very well force himself on Kara. She needed to make her own choice.

Drawing back, Dave looked at her. He pulled in a

somewhat ragged breath before he asked, "So, are you going to invite me in?"

Shell-shocked, Kara looked around, more than half expecting that civilization as she knew it had self-destructed.

Apparently, it hadn't. She had no idea why everything was still intact. God knew she wasn't.

"You mean you're not in yet?" she murmured, her voice low and husky.

She looked so dazed. Dave bit his lower lip to keep from laughing at the confusion in her eyes. There was almost something endearingly sweet about her expression, even though he knew better than to comment on that or point it out to her. If he did, it would probably be the last thing he'd get to say on this earth.

So instead, he gave her a serious answer and said, "No, not yet. We're still standing out here in guest parking."

"Not for long," she assured him. Taking his hand in hers, she pulled him along in her wake. Looking over her shoulder, she told him, "I have no intentions of remaining in 'Park' any longer than I really have to."

Ignoring the warmth that anticipation was spreading through his limbs—hadn't he been disappointed enough times to know that this was all eventually leading nowhere?—Dave laughed.

"You never struck me as someone who could keep from moving around for long."

She looked at him over her shoulder again as she dug through her purse, searching for her keys. "I guess we're about to find out a lot of things, aren't we?"

Yes, he thought, *I guess we are.*

Chapter Twelve

As he walked across the threshold into Kara's apartment, Dave waited for his common sense to prevail. At that moment, he had every intention of stalling, of giving them both time to think through what seemed to be on the verge of happening.

Those were his intentions.

But then Kara turned around and looked at him with those incredible blue eyes of hers. And just like that, all the air around him evaporated, making it almost impossible for him to catch his breath.

Impossible to do anything but focus on her and this sudden, intense and overwhelming need he felt raging inside of him.

What the hell was going on with him anyway?

This wasn't him, he argued. He wasn't given to feeling these kinds of passions and desires. He was far more sedate than that.

Yet here he was, his mouth sealed to hers, his body heated in anticipation of what was to come.

Maybe if she hadn't kissed him back the way she had, his ardor might have dampened slightly and his mind would have been able to prevail, to take control. But the moment they came together, Dave could feel her responding to him, could taste the desire on her lips. In less time than it took to draw in a breath, all bets were off and sanity went straight out the window.

Dave was only vaguely aware of moving into Kara's living room, but he was acutely aware of her. The way her curves fit into the spaces of his body. The way her skin felt like the softest newly spun silk. And the way her mouth worked over his, fueling his passion and moving it up to the next level. Had he been a lit torch instead of a man, he would have burned so brightly that no one within miles could miss it.

His downfall, he knew, was inevitable.

Kara was in trouble and she knew it. This was no longer pretending, going through the motions for the benefit of their mothers. *This* was something that was happening in the privacy of her apartment with no one to see what was going on but the two of them. There was no excuse for this, no reason for it to be happening.

None except that she was going to self-destruct if it didn't. If he didn't make love to her soon and thus uncork the volatile forces that threatened to implode her if they weren't released, she was certain her minutes were numbered.

Survival meant only one thing. She needed to make love with this man.

Now.

With her hands amazingly a great deal more steady than what was going on inside of her, Kara began to peel Dave's T-shirt away from his rock-hard chest. She dragged it up over his head and threw it on the floor without missing a beat. Her lips were hardly separated from his.

When she began to uncinch his belt, Dave reached behind her, found the knot holding together her halter and started to untie it. For a second, she felt him fumbling as the knot initially gave him trouble, but finally the ties fluttered apart, one to either side of her, leaving her exposed.

She could have sworn she felt a hot breeze pass over her bare skin as she anticipated what was to come next.

She felt him catch his breath as his hands passed over her breasts lightly, reverently, as if she were breakable and required the utmost care.

Her heart began to hammer so hard, Kara was certain it was going to crack a rib.

She didn't care. It was worth it.

Reacting to the way his fingers caressed her, she kissed him harder. His touch was gentle, soft, but there was no question. At this singular moment in time, Dave owned her. She was his without a word needing to be uttered.

Kara drew in a fortifying breath, then began undressing him again. With less-than-certain moves, she pushed his jeans down over his hips. The moment he was left wearing only his underwear, it was as if Dave suddenly snapped to attention and got busy. Within the next two heartbeats, she was no longer in her denim short-shorts. One more heartbeat and the white thong she'd had on beneath them became history, as well.

A slight groan escaped her lips. Trying her best to keep her wits about her, Kara returned the compliment in kind. She hooked her thumbs beneath each side of his underwear and pulled it down with one quick snap of her wrists.

Their bodies hot, their desire hotter, they came together like the opposite fields of a magnet, sealed against one another, their mouths still questing, still devouring.

And then she was on the floor with Dave's body over hers.

Breaking contact, his mouth moved from hers. But there was no respite in the offing. His lips were already moving along the sensitive side of her neck, driving her absolutely crazy as desires she'd never felt before suddenly came to life within her core. Kara arched her body into his, trying to capture this sensation he was creating inside her.

As his mouth slid down, bringing havoc to everywhere his lips and tongue touched, it stoked an urgency within her that was threatening to explode. Kara found herself in the throes of a sweet agony she'd never even suspected could exist.

And then stars exploded as his tongue found what was to her a brand-new pressure point. Next to no extra contact was required before bursting rockets joined the stars, obliterating her sky, utterly and completely disorienting her.

As she fell back, gasping, her eyes reduced to small slits, she could still make out his expression. Dave wasn't smug, but there was a smile curving his mouth. A definite smile that denoted triumph.

Seeing it caused her to rally, to somehow find a second wind and to silently vow that she was not the only one who was going to undergo this kind of wondrous torture.

With a quick movement, she caught him off guard and managed to flip their positions. Within a blink of an eye, she was over him.

Taking her time, teasing, moving forward and then back, she swept the tip of her tongue over him. With that one weapon, she successfully brought him to the brink, only to retreat again.

Once.

Twice.

As she ventured toward a third time, Dave caught her wrists, tugged her over to one side and was on top of her again. No more games, he thought. He could only hold himself in check for so long before it all slipped beyond his control.

His eyes on hers, vaguely mystified how he and the person he'd thought of as his mortal enemy close to twenty years ago had gotten to this place, he brought his mouth down on hers. Completely lost in her, he kissed her over and over again until they were both in danger of simply dissolving in a puff of steam.

Parting her legs with his knee, the warmth of her core guiding him, Dave began to enter her slowly.

And then stopped.

His eyes widened and he looked at her, dumbfounded.

He saw her looking back at him, something almost defiant in her crystal-blue orbs.

Drawing back, he managed to form the words, "Are you—?"

She threw the word "yes" back at him, thrust her hips upward and the discussion-that-wasn't became a moot point.

They were one now.

Her hips moved in tandem with his, initially setting a pace until he took over. And then she mimicked him, not just echoing his movements but actually anticipating them. It seemed almost impossible for him to believe that this was their first time, they were that in sync.

And yet, it was. It was their first time together.

And it was hers, as well.

His arms tightened around her protectively as the last moment seized him, bringing him to the mind-numbing, heart-pounding climax he sought. For a frozen moment in time, it held on to him as tightly as he held on to her. And then, the effects began to loosen, to recede, until he was left with a semi-racing pulse and encroaching confusion mingled with guilt.

The euphoria disappeared.

The guilt didn't.

Shifting, he dropped down rather than simply lay down beside her, his heart rate slowly returning to normal.

"You're a virgin," he said hoarsely.

"Not anymore," she corrected, a wide, satisfied grin on her lips.

He was completely mystified. Gathering together

what little strength he had left, Dave propped himself up on one elbow and fixed her with an unwavering gaze, trying to sort things out. And failing miserably.

"How is that possible?" he wanted to know.

"Well, you see," she began calmly, "when little girls are born…"

Holding on to his temper, Dave let out an impatient breath. "I know how it's possible," he bit off. "I'm asking you how the hell you got to be one."

"I'm trying to tell you," she answered innocently, "I started out that way."

Damn it, she knew what he meant, he insisted silently. It didn't make any sense to him. "But you're thirty."

"Nothing gets by you."

"You might have a disposition like a viper, but you *are* beautiful. There had to be all sorts of guys who could put up with that tongue of yours for a little while," he theorized, then came to the crux of his question. "How the hell did you stay a virgin?"

"Clean living?" she offered, widening her eyes innocently.

He was really losing his temper now. She was jerking him around, the way she used to when they were forced to spend their summers together. The memories it brought back were far from sweet.

"Damn it, Kara," he snapped. "I'm dealing with monumental guilt here. The least you can do is give me a serious answer to my question."

In all the ways she'd pictured him, she'd never envisioned him feeling guilty. It made him seem all too human to her. She felt something beginning to stir inside. Again.

"There's nothing to feel guilty about," she assured him calmly. "In case you didn't notice, this wasn't exactly one-sided." She punctuated her statement with another wide grin.

Dave let out a ragged breath, then slowly took one in, trying his best to center himself. He didn't believe in things like Zen, but he knew the merit of breathing correctly. And slowly.

It helped. A little.

Okay, he was going to ask one more time. He *needed* to know and he wanted a straight answer from her. "Why didn't you ever sleep with anyone before now?"

Her eyes danced with humor as she looked at him. "If this is what you call *sleeping,* you must be hell on wheels when you're awake."

Okay, he'd had enough. He'd tried but there was just no winning with this woman. "Damn it, Kara—"

She held up one hand, the other holding the blanket she'd had across the back of the sofa that was now pressed against her. "Okay, okay, you want an answer, I'll give you an answer. Because I decided long ago that I wasn't going to do it just to do it."

Her decision, she didn't tell him, had been arrived at shortly after her father had died. Shortly after her mother's heart had been broken into so many pieces she'd been afraid it would *never* work right again. It was also at that time when she'd sworn off getting serious with the male of the species. Ever. And she'd kept her word. Until just now.

"That the only way I was ever going to wind up

naked and spread-eagle with a guy was if my emotions were engaged. So far, they never had been." She saw the alerted expression on his face and laughed shortly. Just as she'd thought. "Oh, don't look like Bambi caught in the headlights. Relax, you don't have anything to worry about. I figured it was high time for me to finally do it, so I decided to do it with someone I'd known forever." It was a desperate lie, but, she judged, a believable one. "You happened to fall into that category, that's all. It's that simple. Scout's honor," she added, forming what she hoped was the scout pledge salute.

Well, it sure as hell didn't feel simple, not to him, Dave thought. Maybe he was old-fashioned, but he still believed that a girl's first time was supposed to be something she would remember forever, not something that happened on the spur of the moment on the floor of her apartment.

"You should have let me know," he insisted, his voice accusing.

"I would have, but I must have misplaced my business cards. It's printed right under my name," she told him, her face deadly serious. "'Kara Calhoun, Resident Virgin. Approach at your own risk,'" she concluded with a wicked grin.

"Can you stop being flippant for one damn minute? Do you think you can do that for me?" he demanded.

Where did he get off talking to her like that? she thought, annoyed. "I'm not sure. I can try," she said, acting as if she were as dumb as a proverbial post.

Dave surprised her by looking at her seriously. "Are you all right with this?" he wanted to know. "I mean…"

She put her finger to his lips, knowing that he could

probably go on and on and say nothing and still feel tortured while he was doing it.

"I know what you mean," she assured him, "and I think it's actually kind of sweet. Yes," she told him in reply, "I'm all right with this. I would have told you to stop if I'd wanted you to, or if I had a change of heart. That's *why* it was all right."

He shook his head, slipping his arm back around her and lying down again. "You know I'm never going to understand you."

She grinned. "Luckily for you, you don't have to. Hey, since you broke me in—"

"Oh God," he groaned, hating the way that sounded. How could she be so cavalier about something so intimate as making love?

"Can we do it again?" she continued, looking at him to gauge his response. "I mean, it was nice and— Oh, unless you can't do it again," she said suddenly, realizing she might be asking for more than he could deliver at the moment. "I heard that some guys can only do it once, and then they need to recharge. Kind of like a cell phone that loses all its power after a series of calls."

He rose on his elbow again to look at her. Dave shook his head. Damn but he should run for the hills before he slipped any further into this field of quicksand he'd wandered into.

He felt it was a dangerous sign that he really didn't want to flee. That he wasn't at least *trying* to make a run for it. But he didn't want to. He wanted to be exactly where he was. Here, with her. About to make love with her all over again.

"You're insane," he told her, peering at her face. "You know that, right?"

"So you keep telling me," she said with a sigh. "So I take it that's a no?"

Curious as to how her brain actually worked, he asked, "Why would you think that would automatically be a no?"

"Because—" She stopped suddenly, her eyes widening in surprise. And then pleasure. Dave was leaning against her, his still very naked, very rugged body touching hers. In all the right places. Grinning wickedly, she laughed. "Oh, wait, maybe you *do* want to do it again."

The woman would have been downright embarrassing if he wasn't mercifully past that point with her. "Kara?"

Settling in against him, anticipation humming through her veins, she turned her face up to his. "What?" she asked, her voice almost melodic.

The order was short and to the point. "Shut up."

She grinned. Dave was so predictable. In an odd sort of way, she found that comforting. "Okay, I can do that."

"I sincerely doubt it," he replied.

There was no such thing as true silence with Kara, only less talking. And then, to keep her from saying another word, he did the only thing he could. He effectively sealed his mouth to hers.

And with that, they began the sultry, stimulating dance all over again.

Chapter Thirteen

Sleep slowly peeled away from Kara's brain one layer at a time.

When she finally opened her eyes to the intrusive early-dawn light, she discovered that she was curled up against Dave with her arm splayed possessively across his chest.

Startled, shaken, she nearly bolted upright and pulled her arm away. At the last minute, she managed to stop herself.

Kara slowly exhaled a sigh of relief. She was certain that the sudden movement would have woken Dave up, and she wasn't ready for that yet. She had no idea what to say. She'd never had a "morning after" conversation, mainly because she'd never had a "morning after"—or "a night before" for that matter.

And even if she'd had one of those nights in her past,

it definitely wouldn't have prepared her for this, for waking up and finding herself next to Dave, still apparently as naked as the day she was born.

And so, from what she could detect, was he.

What the hell had she been thinking? How in heaven's name had she allowed this whole situation to get so far out of control?

She knew the story that she'd given Dave, one she'd made up on the spur of the moment, but it had been a lie. She had no overwhelming desire to join the huge ranks of the nonvirgins. Old-fashioned though it might sound, she actually—until last night—had felt that lovemaking was supposed to happen with someone who meant something to her. With someone who meant *everything* to her, not someone with whom she engaged in frequent verbal sparring matches.

Damn it, what *had* she been thinking? Or, more to the point, *why* hadn't she been thinking? What was it about her childhood arch enemy, her irritating-as-hell adolescent nemesis, that turned her into an eager participant in the lovemaking game?

And why the hell was she smiling like the Cheshire cat?

Despite her mental upbraiding, Kara could still feel her lips curving. Amid the nerve endings that were standing at attention, all on high alert, she could feel an unaccountable surge of, well, *happiness* for lack of a better word.

Damn it, she didn't want to be happy about this, *couldn't* be happy about this. She and Dave didn't have a relationship, not the kind that didn't require sharpened tongues at ten paces, at any rate. There was no future in this—not a single chance in hell. It would be like allowing herself to fall in love with a fictional character, someone like Shakespeare's Romeo.

No, not Romeo, she amended. There was no way anyone would ever mistake the very precise, exceedingly straitlaced and orderly Dr. Dave Scarlatti for the impetuously passionate character Shakespeare had penned. If she had to compare him to a fictional character, Dave was more like the stern, honorable Atticus Finch from *To Kill A Mockingbird,* more prone to loving principles than a flesh-and-blood woman.

No, not him, either, she thought in the next moment, rejecting that image. God, but she felt confused.

There was a headache growing between her eyes.

"A penny for your thoughts."

Her heart slammed into her rib cage at the sound of his voice. Kara clamped her lips together to keep from uttering a gasp. She'd thought he was still asleep.

Recovering, she took a breath to steady her nerves. "Sorry, at this point my thoughts are up to at least five-fifty."

"Five-fifty? Inflation's a bear," he commented with a laugh. He studied her face for a moment, making a judgment call. "Okay, I'm good for it. What are you thinking about?"

There was no time to be creative, or even make up a last-minute lie. That left her no choice but to go with the truth, odd though it might sound. "What fictional character you're most like."

"And?" he asked. "What conclusion did you come to?" *This should be interesting,* he couldn't help thinking, bracing himself.

She shrugged, her blond hair brushing along her bare shoulder. "I can't come up with anyone."

"That means I'm either very unique, or so nondescript I don't even leave an impression," he theorized, amused. His eyes on hers, he asked, "Which is it?"

She sighed again. Why did he scramble her insides this way? Why, with all the men she interacted with— her field was still dominated by mostly males of all ages—did *he* turn out to be the one who lit her fire?

"I'll let you know when I figure it out. So, until then—"

She was about to wiggle her way out of bed, taking the blanket with her to cover up, when her phone rang. Now what?

Nobody ever called her at this hour in the morning, not if they didn't want their head taken off. They knew better.

Kara was tempted not to answer it, but one glance at caller ID told her that her mother was on the other end. She had a better chance of growing six inches in the next half hour than she did of avoiding her mother. There was no escaping the woman. Paulette Calhoun would just keep calling and calling all day long, not leaving any messages, until the receiver was finally picked up.

Better to face the music now than listen to the intro all day long, anticipating some kind of dire repercussions, coming up with scenarios in her head that were probably way off.

Exhaling loudly, she silently counted to ten and then yanked the receiver off its cradle, pressing it against her ear. "Good morning, Mother. My, you're up early," she noted with sarcasm.

"Couldn't sleep," her mother confessed, as if imparting some sort of dark secret.

Tell me about it. Kara could remember being grilled by her mother as a teenager—where she went, who she went with, all the typical mother questions. These days she understood better why her mother had done it, but at the time, it seemed like a huge invasion of privacy.

Right now, of course, it still was.

"They have pills for that, Mother. Pop two and sleep until morning," she recommended cheerfully.

Since her daughter wasn't asking her what was keeping her up, Paulette volunteered the information. "I kept thinking about you and Dave."

Kara's eyes narrowed. There wasn't even an attempt at subtlety on her mother's part. "They have pills for that, too. You can find them in the reality section of your local pharmacy."

It was obvious to Kara that her mother had no intentions of allowing herself to be drawn into a verbal sparring match. "Did you bring Dave's car to him?"

Here came the headache, full force, Kara thought. "That I did."

"And?" Her mother made no attempt to hide the eagerness in her voice.

"And he took it, just as you might have suspected, Mother." What did the woman want from her? A blow-by-blow statement written in blood?

She could almost see her mother shaking her head. "How did you ever get so sarcastic?"

"It's a gift," Kara quipped. "Did you call for something specific, Mother? Or just to harass me in general?"

"I just wanted to know if you saw Dave last night after you took off from the fair, that's all," her mother answered.

"I gave him his car, so I pretty much would have had to see him, now, wouldn't I, Mother?" Out of the corner of her eye, she could see Dave taking this all in. And grinning, damn him.

"If you gave him the car, how did you get home, dear?" her mother asked innocently.

She was fishing, Kara thought. And being painfully obvious about it. "He drove me, Mother."

"And let you off at your door?" her mother guessed innocently.

It was official. The headache had exploded all over her forehead. "Instead of playing twenty questions, Mom, why don't you just invest in a surveillance camera so you can have all your questions answered before you even have to ask them."

Her mother absolutely refused to get angry and hang up. "Then what would we have to talk about?" she asked innocently.

"Normal things," Kara shot back.

"Asking about my daughter's social life *is* a normal thing, dear," her mother pointed out. "At least, it is to everyone but you."

Completely distracted by her mother, Kara wasn't prepared to suddenly feel Dave's hand brush up against her inner thigh and *definitely* wasn't prepared to feel that immediate, intense reaction to him that was now ripping through her like a tornado. She let out a gasp.

"Did you just yelp?" Paulette asked, picking up on the sudden sound.

Kara swallowed a curse. That was a dirty trick, she thought angrily.

"No," Kara denied with feeling, batting away Dave's hand and glaring at him. What had gotten into him? "No, I didn't yelp. Must be something wrong with the connection."

She didn't like the long, drawn-out pause on the other end of the line. She could only surmise that her mother must be thinking, and that was never a good thing. Her mother possessed far too fertile an imagination.

"Kara, is he there with you right now?" her mother asked suddenly.

She was right. This wasn't good. Rather than just wasting her breath with a denial, Kara turned the tables and asked *her* a question. "What makes you think that, Mother?"

The answer came with no hesitation. "Because I can hear him breathing."

That was absurd. Kara couldn't even hear him breathing. She could, however, much to her downfall, *feel* him breathing, because his breath was trailing along her neck and upper torso and swiftly undoing her.

"No, you can't," Kara insisted.

"Aha, so he *is* there." Her mother sounded imminently pleased with herself. Too late Kara realized that she'd fallen for the trap. "Give him the phone, Kara."

Kara blew out an annoyed breath, knowing it was utterly useless to argue with her mother. So far, the woman was winning all the points.

"Here," she muttered, holding out the receiver to Dave. "My mother wants to talk to you."

If he was surprised, he didn't show it. Dave took the phone from her and put it to his ear. "Hello, Mrs. Calhoun, how are you?"

Kara closed her eyes. This whole scenario was just too bizarre for words.

"I'm fine, Dave, thank you. Tell me, how did that little emergency of yours go yesterday? Is the little boy all right?"

Dave was surprised at the show of concern. But then, as he recalled, Kara's mother had always been a very caring person. As had her father. "He's fine, thanks for asking."

And then Paulette Calhoun got down to business. "Listen, Dave, would you and my daughter be free for dinner next Saturday, say about six?"

"Let me find out," he told her. Cradling the receiver against his ear, he asked Kara, "Are you free next Saturday for dinner at six?"

Other than work, she had no set schedule, and as far as she knew, there was no overtime in her immediate future. But the invitation wasn't coming from him, it was coming from her mother.

This is all supposed to be part of your plan, dummy. Why is there this enormous pit in the middle of your stomach?

Maybe it had something to do with making wild, passionate love all over her apartment, culminating in her bedroom, and then waking up to find Dave in her bed—the very last place she would have *ever* rationally thought to find him. But then last night hadn't been very rational, had it?

She shrugged, and the blanket she had wrapped around her torso sank a little. She tugged it back into place. "I guess so."

Putting the receiver back up against his ear, Dave told her mother, "Kara says yes."

"Wonderful," Paulette cried with enthusiasm. "Then I'll see you both here next Saturday at six. Oh, by the way, you've probably already surmised this, but your mother will be here, as well. We're having a few friends over. Tell my daughter to wear something sensible."

Kara overheard that and the directive struck a nerve. She felt compelled to call out, "I'm coming in a bikini, Mother."

Paulette sighed audibly. "As long as all the important places are covered, dear, I suppose it's all right." And then she added, "Good luck, Dave."

He didn't bother to try to stifle the laugh that came to his lips. "Thank you, Mrs. Calhoun. I think I'll need it. We'll see you and my mother next week."

Deliberately leaning over Kara, he reached over to the nightstand and hung up the phone. As he drew back again, his chest brushed against hers. "Are you hungry?" he asked as if a jolt of electricity hadn't just traveled between them.

"Yes." But she wasn't as hungry for food as she was for something else.

Was this normal? she couldn't help wondering. After all, they wound up making love a total of three times last night. Any curiosity about the act of lovemaking and the sensations that were involved with it should have all been laid to rest by now, not wildly stirred up the way they felt right at this moment. But that, she knew, was because his body, naked beneath that section of sheet he had over his hips, had come in contact with her equally naked body.

It would help, she upbraided herself sternly, if she stopped fantasizing about him.

Something in her voice caught his attention and he gave up the idea of getting out of bed and cooking, at least for the moment. Still, he kept up the pretense—wasn't that what this was all ultimately about? Pretending?

Or maybe, he amended, in light of things that seemed to be happening, about pretending to pretend?

His eyes delved into hers. "What are you in the mood for?" he asked.

Kara had to suppress a groan. Oh God, he'd fed her such a straight line. It took everything she had not to give voice to the answer that had instantly sprung to her lips: *You.*

Instead, with effort, she told him, "Surprise me."

"Tall order," he commented, his eyes slowly caressing her face.

Even first thing in the morning, Kara was still beautiful. Maybe, Dave amended, even *more* beautiful than she'd been last night.

Just his luck, he thought with an inward sigh. He was falling for her. All the intelligent, poised, even-tempered, clear-thinking women in the world and *he* had to fall for the one emotional, volatile, outspoken harpy in the lot.

"Oh, you're up to it," she replied with confidence,

her voice so low it felt as if it were rumbling along his naked skin.

This was where he got up and marched off to the kitchen, dressed in confidence if nothing else, he told himself, because what was unfolding between them was way too hot to indulge in.

This was where he got up from the bed and put some distance between them.

Quickly.

This was where he—

Oh damn, he knew exactly where "this" was all leading him: to hell in a handbasket.

In one swift movement, he went from being next to her to looming directly over her. Bracketing her face with his hands, he paused for a moment, looking at her as if he'd never seen her before. And maybe he hadn't, at least, not *this* version of Kara, the one who seemed to so effortlessly fire up his soul.

He finally gave voice to what he was thinking. "You just might single-handedly set the course of cosmetics back half a century."

She wasn't altogether sure she understood where he was going with this.

"And why is that?" she wanted to know, waiting for a punch line she could rip apart. Secretly *hoping* for a put-down so that this feeling inside of her, this caramel center, melting feeling would finally go away instead of undoing her.

"Because you're beautiful without it. *More* beautiful without it," he corrected himself.

Still ready and waiting to read him the riot act, Kara came to a skidding halt before she was able to utter a single word. As his words sank in, she looked at him, utterly stunned and speechless. And confused.

What the hell was he up to? Was this some kind of bait and switch?

Mentally, she threw up her hands as his began to roam over her body, discovering her pressure points all over again.

"You don't play fair," she accused, the words scraping out of her dry mouth. The rest of her, however, was all but salivating with anticipation.

"Maybe," he told her slowly, his warm breath creating havoc everywhere it touched, "that's because I'm not playing at all."

Okay, now he really had her confused. "What are you saying?" she asked with effort, unable to draw in a complete sustaining breath.

"You're a bright woman," he told her, his lips beginning to unravel her again as they proceeded to tease all the different parts of her body. "You can figure it out."

Maybe she could. But that was for later.

Much later, she told herself, slipping her arms around Dave's neck. She planned to be far too busy right now to think at all.

Chapter Fourteen

This was crazy, Dave thought.

It was nearly a month later, and rather than winding down, the way both he—and, he was certain, Kara—had expected, things were only becoming more intense, more complex and, consequently, more confusing.

He knew he sure as hell was confused by this unexpected turn his life had taken. A month ago, he would have never seen this coming. And yet, here it was, confounding him even as it mocked him.

Damn it all, anyway.

It didn't make any sense to him. The only woman he'd ever actually felt as if he'd made a connection with was the one woman he never thought he'd *want* to make a connection with.

Somewhere in the universe, something was either seriously off-kilter, or God had the kind of twisted sense of humor none of the nuns ever publicized in the parochial school he'd attended.

And the really weird thing about all of this was that the further away their "breakup" was pushed back—as it had been twice already—the more he secretly found himself *wanting* to have it pushed back.

Something else he would have never expected.

It was as if he was in on the planning of his own self-destruction.

And he was *smiling* about it, Dave thought darkly, catching a glimpse of himself in the shiny surface of a stainless-steel cabinet door in the tiny room where he kept all the free clinic's medications locked up.

He thought back to the beginning, which now seemed like eons ago. Back then, this charade of falling for one another was to last only a week. Ten days, tops. Kara was supposed to have picked a fight with him at her mother's house the first Saturday they had been invited over for diner.

That had fallen through by mutual consent when Paulette Calhoun surprised them by inviting a few other people to dinner, as well. People, as it turned out, who came equipped with deep pockets and even deeper hearts. Over dinner Kara's mother had talked up the free clinic where he volunteered, praising all the good it was doing for the destitute people in that neighborhood.

Conversationally, she let it drop that the clinic was facing a funding shortage and she lamented the possibility that it might have to close its doors. She added that it would be morally criminal if that did happen, because all the children in that neighborhood would have nowhere to go if they became ill. Her guests, parents all, could readily identify with the angst of parents who had to stand by and watch their children suffer.

There was no question about it. The woman was good. He began to see where Kara got her craftiness and her stubbornness.

He vividly remembered how surprised—and, damn it, how relieved—he was that evening when Kara had drawn him aside and said in a hushed voice, "We can't get into a fight in front of these people now. They might think you're unstable and change their minds about those checks they've promised to send you for the clinic."

He'd wanted to point out that since she was the one who was to start the argument, most likely her mother's guests would think *she* was the unstable one. But he bit his tongue and merely nodded.

And just like that, there was a stay of execution. A stay that per force wound up extending his time in purgatory—or hell, depending on the point of view. Except that, even though he told himself that was what pretending to be romantically involved with Kara was supposed to feel like, being forced to spend time with her, presumably where her mother or his would be able to cross their paths, didn't feel like either hell or purgatory to him.

What he *did* feel like was, well, *alive*. Whether it was his anger that she periodically managed to arouse, or something else, there was no denying that the bottom line was that she did arouse him.

Very much so.

And even when he wasn't around her, she was haunting his thoughts as well as his dreams. There seemed to be no getting away from Kara. His head was utterly filled with visions of her that popped into his brain unprovoked, unannounced and utterly unbidden.

The woman had definitely cast some kind of spell over him, and while he didn't actually believe in things like voodoo, *something* had to be at play here that wasn't readily explainable.

Why else would he be thinking of her so much? Why else would he be looking forward to getting together with her, even if it was just to argue, the way they seemed to do about half the time that they were together? There was no denying that she was an infuriating, utterly perverse person.

The other half of the time, he'd already noted more than once, somehow managed to find them winding up in bed, whether it was after coming home from dinner at her mother's, or after a quick visit to his mother's place, or just after a long, hard day's work.

The charade—and their lovemaking—had fallen into almost a pattern. Chaotic, but nonetheless still a pattern.

When he felt dead tired after a day in the E.R., she would turn up in the parking lot, waiting for him, the scent of a hot pizza emanating from inside her car. And the times that his shift actually ended on a quiet note and *she* had put in copious amounts of overtime on some kind of save-the-world video game that was overdue for production, he'd invite her to his place, where he proceeded to whip up something seductively appetizing to romance her mouth. And then he'd proceed, after dinner, to do the same to the rest of her. It all seemed to follow so naturally.

In short, he thought as he made some quick notations to the file of the patient he'd just seen, he was enjoying himself. For the first time in his life, there was something beyond his work that he found himself looking forward to.

Even arguing with the woman was enjoyable, because somewhere amid the words that threatened to grow more and more heated, he'd either find himself filled with a passion that could be sated only by her, or she would seal away the words about to come pouring out of his mouth with her lips.

And then nothing else mattered but her.

God help him but he was in a bad way. Especially since he caught himself hoping more and more frequently that this pretense he found himself involved with would continue indefinitely—or at least until such time as he could figure out what was going on with him.

Closing the file, Dave looked at his watch. Damn it, it was getting late.

Ordinarily, the doors to the clinic would be closed by now and the number of people in the waiting area would be at least beginning to dwindle. But there was a new strain of flu making the rounds in Southern California. Children under ten seemed to be particularly susceptible to it, and it looked as if half the felled population were in the clinic's waiting room, most of them crying and growing more irritable.

Tonight was the night he'd told Kara he would take her out to that Chinese restaurant she liked in order to celebrate the donations her mother had rounded up. At first the invitation had been extended to her mother as well, but Paulette had demurred, saying three was a crowd.

"I will, however, let you bring back some of their absolutely fabulous shrimp lo mein for me," Paulette had told him.

"She wants proof we went" was Kara's cynical way of interpreting her mother's request.

He would have pointed out that it was a simple matter for him just to swing by the restaurant and get takeout without having to take her anywhere, but he knew when to keep things to himself. These days he picked his arguments, usually with an eye out for making up with her.

Now, from the looks of it, he was either going to have to give Kara a rain check on that dinner or wind up turning away at least half a dozen small, suffering patients and their equally suffering—although for an entirely different reason—mothers.

He made his choice. He was staying. But his nurse didn't have to, he thought. Approaching her, he said, "You can go home, Clarice."

The ebony-eyed, heavyset woman gave him one of her sterner looks and shook her head. "Don't go telling me what to do, Doctor Boy." She'd awarded him that affectionate nickname the first week he came and had been inundated with patients. She'd been forced to marvel at his staying power and had told him that he looked younger than her grandson, hence the nickname. "I can stick it out if you can."

He should have known better than to try to get her

to leave. "Thanks, Clarice. Tell the patient's mother in room two I'll be right there. I have to make a call first."

Clarice raised an eyebrow. "Canceling a date?" she asked.

He didn't ask her how she knew.

"Just canceling an obligation," he told her, deliberately avoiding a direct answer.

Clarice looked at him as if she saw right through his evasive maneuver. "It's a date. Tell that pushy woman I said hi."

Someday, he thought as he pressed numbers on the keypad, there was going to have to be a whole branch of science devoted to the study of the female mind so men like him had a prayer of understanding it.

He counted the number of rings. On the fourth one, he heard Kara pick up. "Hello?"

She sounded confused, he thought. Had she forgotten about tonight? "Kara, this is Dave."

"I figured it would be—that's what it says on my caller ID. What's up?"

He heard noise in the background. Where was she? "I'm running late. Actually, I'm not sure if I can make it tonight. The waiting room's packed and I can't turn them away. There's no place else in the area they can go where they can be treated for free," he explained.

Rather than comment on his possible no-show for their date, she said, "Sounds like you're having a revolt in your waiting room."

He supposed that was probably what it had to sound like to her. "It's full of kids." It was a given that young patients didn't do well confined to one room for hours at a time.

"You really should have something to keep them occupied while they're waiting. It would be a lot easier on their parents, and it would also go a long way toward reducing the level of your noise pollution."

She had a point, he thought. He was here only one day a week and tended not to occupy his mind with what was or wasn't out in the waiting room. His only concern was the patient. "Maybe I'll use a small portion of those donations your mother managed to raise for the clinic to buy some toys."

He heard her laugh. Three weeks ago, he would have bristled at the sound, offended that she was laughing at him. Now, although it still might be what was happening, he no longer took offense so easily.

"Toys?" she echoed. He could envision her wide smile. Even seeing it in his mind's eye had an effect on his gut. It hit him dead center, creating its own little tidal wave. "You really are old-fashioned, aren't you?"

"What's so funny?" he wanted to know, and then, before she could answer, he stopped to listen more closely to the sound he was picking up. "What's all that noise I hear in the background?" Dave asked. If he didn't know any better, he would have said she was somewhere surrounded by kids. But she worked with adults, or at least overgrown kids in adult clothing. "Where are you?"

"Someplace where I can implement a solution for your problem."

He didn't have time for riddles. He had to get back to his patients—and then it hit him.

On a hunch, still holding the cell phone in his hand, Dave came out of the closet-size office he shared with the other doctors who volunteered their services the other days of the week. Walking into the waiting room, he discovered that Kara was there—had they arranged to meet at the clinic? He didn't think so. He was almost certain they'd agreed that he would pick her up at her apartment. But if that was the case...

Dave looked at Clarice, but the nurse just shrugged her very wide shoulders, silently conveying that she hadn't a clue what was happening out here.

Kara was surrounded by an army of short people, all eagerly watching her every move. That included dropping to her knees beside an orange plastic chair that appeared to be bolted onto the floor.

"What are you doing here?" he wanted to know. And why was she now snaking her way under that chair?

"In a minute," he heard her mumble in response.

Then he heard her grunt as she struggled to push a plug into the electrical outlet directly in front of the bolted chair. When she snaked her way back out again, Kara brushed off a layer of dust bunnies from the front of her tank top before she stood up.

Only then did he notice the gaming system on the magazine table—now completely devoid of any magazines—standing beside the orange chair. Above the system was a twenty-inch monitor. That was new. He looked from it to Kara, momentarily too stunned to adequately form his question.

"Okay," Kara announced. He was about to ask her, "Okay, what?" when he realized she wasn't talking to him. She was talking to the squadron of pint-size patients who were still in the waiting room. "This is up and running," she told the children. Pointing to the four control pads, each in a different color, she said, "Four of you can play the game at the same time." She raised her eyes to Dave. "That should take care of your noise problem," she told him cheerfully.

That was when he saw that there was a different system hooked up across the room from the first one. The four hand controllers attached to that system were quickly claimed and four patients began their mighty adventure, all struggling to keep their colorful vehicles on the track while they raced toward a virtual finish line. The children not fast enough to grab a controller gathered around them, watching and waiting for their turn at the game.

Satisfied that the children were all occupied and no longer restless, bored and whiny, Kara finally turned around to face Dave. "I think I just might have found a solution to your noise-level problem *and* your restless-child syndrome," she told him with a very pleased grin on her lips.

"Good thing your mother secured those donations when she did," he commented. He knew that gaming systems didn't come cheaply. When he saw the way Kara frowned, he hadn't a clue what he could have said to bring that on. Or why the frown intensified when he asked, "So how much will I owe you?"

Forcing a smile back on her lips, she quipped. "Oh, so much more than you will ever be able to repay in one lifetime."

He hated being in anyone's debt—for any reason. "Seriously," he prodded.

Kara's smile was deliberately wide, deliberately innocent and deliberately bright. "Seriously," she echoed.

He tried again. "No, what do you want me to write on the check?"

"To Kara with love?" It was half a question, half a suggestion. The little girl standing beside her giggled and covered her mouth up with both hands. She muffled the sound but giggled again, her bright blue eyes dancing.

"Besides that," Dave said patiently, his pen poised over the checkbook he'd taken out of his back pocket.

"Be right back," she told the little girl she had begun tutoring on the game's finer points.

Taking Dave by the arm, she turned him around so that he was facing away from the people sitting out in the waiting room.

"Put your checkbook away," she ordered.

"But—" he began to protest. That was when he discovered that he really needed to talk quickly to get anything said around Kara when she was on a roll.

"Did I ask you for money?" she wanted to know, her eyes all but pinning him in place.

He was determined to get his piece out. "No, but this had to cost more than just two box tops and a stamp."

"I can see why you're regarded so highly in your profession. Nothing gets past you." She took a breath and he saw that she was not just looking for the right phrase, she was gathering herself together, as well. "Let me explain it to you so that even someone as removed from the lowly, common, everyday world as you obviously are can understand this. You did not ask me to bring any of these systems, thus you do not owe me anything for their sudden appearance at the clinic. You do *not* have to worry about footing this bill or any bill that has anything to do with video games."

She could see that his integrity was making him resist. Kara put her arm around his shoulders, or at least as high up as she could reach.

"The company I work for is producing video games for a certain target audience. Namely kids under fourteen. Once in a while, it's nice to come out into the real world and see that 'audience' play the games I've been slaving over. As a side benefit," she pointed out, gesturing toward first one group of kids, then the other, "it keeps them quiet for you." Stepping back, she smiled. "Consider it my contribution toward achieving world peace."

It wasn't that he wasn't grateful. It was just that he felt as if he'd been taken by storm. This was the way people in the path of a hurricane had to feel once it was over.

Dave shook his head. "Like I said, I'm never going to understand you."

She smiled broadly at him, obviously tickled by his admission. "It's what I'm counting on." She saw the puzzled look in his eyes. "Every woman likes to be considered mysterious," she explained, then winked.

There was mysterious, and then there was dealing with a complete enigma, he thought. Kara definitely fell into that second category. But he didn't have time to ponder over that. He had patients to see. Patients who, if he didn't start seeing them, were liable to be here all night, as would he.

And now that Kara was here, organizing his patients into two teams, he really didn't want to be here the rest of the night. There was dedication and then there was behavior bordering on the fanatical.

Maybe he would have slipped into that niche before, but now he had someone waiting for him who didn't need him to put a thermometer under her tongue. This might not actually be his life, but while it lasted it made one hell of a diversion.

Picking up a chart, he went to see his patient in the first exam room, already anticipating the light at the end of the tunnel. And, oddly enough, he knew that Kara would be standing there.

At least for now.

Chapter Fifteen

The end finally had a date pinned to it. It was coming tonight. At her mother's house right after dinner. Maybe even before.

She didn't much feel like eating. Kara wiped the sweat from her forehead with the back of her wrist. She was going to have to change clothes, she thought listlessly. She was practically soggy.

That's what happens when you sweat all day, she thought sarcastically. This had to be connected to her telling Dave that they were giving their final "lovebird" performance tonight. Her stomach had been in knots when she'd told him that last night, and he hadn't received the news very well.

Undoubtedly because he wanted to be the one to call the shots, she thought.

But this needed to happen. Now. It certainly couldn't

continue like this indefinitely. She needed to wrap this up, to bring it home.

Because the longer she put it off, the longer she waited before bringing an end to this mythical romance she and Dave were supposedly involved in, the harder that outcome was going to be to take. For her mother, for his mother and, damn it all to hell, for her, too, Kara thought irritably.

Feeling oddly woozy, she stopped getting ready for the fateful dinner and sat down on the edge of her bed. It was Friday night and she'd gotten home about half an hour ago. Usually that was enough time for her to get ready with time to spare, but tonight she was moving as if there were molasses in her veins. When she'd gotten up this morning, she'd felt off, and it had only worsened as the day progressed.

Damn Dave, anyway.

Against her own advice, against all reason, like a careless spider, she had gotten caught in her own web. And it didn't look as if she could work her way free without causing some damage.

What had possessed her to begin this stupid charade, anyway? If she'd held her peace, put up with her mother's annoying but heart-in-the-right-place, less-than-veiled hints and attempts to get her to jump into the dating field with both feet, then she would have never known that there was actually someone out there capable of rattling the very foundations of her world.

She also, Kara quietly reminded herself, wouldn't have gotten to know the teeth-jarring ecstasy Dave had introduced her to.

Makes it that much harder to do without it, she

thought, unable to shake the aura of sadness that insisted on descending over her.

"And next week's going to be harder than this week, Kara," she said aloud. "C'mon, you knew what you were getting into when you started all this. Don't get cold feet on me now."

The problem was that she *hadn't* known what she was getting into, not really. And right now, her feet were far from cold. They were hot.

All of her was hot.

Last night, she'd been so wrapped up in how and when to end this make-believe romance, she hadn't really paid attention to the fact that she was feeling progressively weaker and was now as energetic as a raccoon that'd been run over by a truck.

Flattened out and close to dead, she thought cynically.

Again she ran the back of her wrist along her forehead to wipe away fresh perspiration. Had she caught something the last time she'd gone to the clinic? On a generous roll, she'd gone to the clinic to bring a third gaming system and had stayed to hook it up. Her thought had been to minimize the possibility of squabbling children. This time, she'd noted, Clarice had actually smiled at her when she'd gotten the system up and running. The longtime nurse had given her personal seal of approval. It shouldn't have meant anything to her, Kara thought.

But it did.

Looking back, this was obviously a case of no good deed going unpunished because she *really* felt icky, not to mention dizzy.

When she heard a bell ringing, it took Kara a couple of moments to realize that the sound was coming from her own doorbell.

At least her ears weren't ringing, she thought.

Every bone in her body ached in protest as she got to her feet and dragged herself across the seemingly long distance from the foot of her bed to her front door.

Taking a deep breath, doing her best to pull herself together, she opened it. Dave was standing on the other side, looking far from happy, she noted dully.

He'd spent all day telling himself that he was going to welcome getting back to his usual routine. Welcome not seeing her anymore after tonight. And all the while, his mood kept darkening.

About to grumble a perfunctory greeting, the words died unspoken on his lips as Dave took a good look at the woman who had turned his world on its ear and was threatening now to drop-kick it to the curb.

Walking in, he told her, "You look like hell."

She left the door open and ambled into the living room, dropping onto the sofa. Her knees felt like rubber bands. *Used* rubber bands.

"Hello to you, too."

He doubled back to close the door, then crossed over to her. She really did look pretty awful. "What's going on?" he wanted to know.

Kara tried to shrug, but her shoulders suddenly weighed too much for her to complete the movement. Instead, she tried to content herself with giving him an accusing glare.

It was a feeble attempt.

She was definitely *not* comfortable in her own skin

tonight. It felt as if she were inhabiting someone else's body. And that body was sick.

"I think I caught something from one of your patients the last time I came to the clinic." Her breathing was growing progressively labored. "How come you don't come down with anything?"

Oh, but I have, Dave thought. *And for me, there's no medicine, no cure.*

But that wasn't anything he was about to share with her since she'd nonchalantly told him last night that it was time to finally put this little performance of theirs to bed. She'd undoubtedly have a sarcastic quip for him or, worse, laugh that he could have been dumb enough to get caught up in all this while she was only playacting.

So he merely cracked, "I don't know. Clean living, I guess." Concerned, he tried to put his hand to her forehead but she jerked her head back and almost fell over on the sofa as she did so. "Hold still," he ordered gruffly.

"Sorry, didn't mean to interfere with the latest scientific breakthrough for gauging a person's body temperature—or are you just trying to get fresh and working your way down?" Each word cost her a little and it took a great deal of effort to remain coherent. She didn't like this. She was hardly *ever* sick and she had no patience with her own weakness.

"Well, there's obviously nothing wrong with that rapier tongue of yours," he observed. "That still seems to be working just fine." He'd barely touched her forehead, but what he'd felt told him she was burning up. Her eyes appeared almost hollow with dark circles under them while the rest of her was very flushed. "You need to get into bed."

She lifted her chin, or thought she did. One hand on the sofa's arm for support, she pushed herself up to her feet, the picture of unsteady defiance. "Not even going to buy me dinner first?"

"I'm serious, Kara," he said sternly. "You're burning up. I don't know how you're managing to even stand." Although, he added silently, she was weaving in place a bit.

"Grit," she answered between clenched teeth. At this point, she could have sworn that the perspiration was pouring out of her.

"Either that, or you've glued yourself upright." Okay, enough was enough, he thought. Time to be her doctor and not her rejected would-be lover. He had an oath to follow. "In any case, you're going to bed."

"No, I'm not," she argued, although not with anywhere near the verve she'd intended. "We have a fight to get into, remember?" she protested. That *was* what they'd agreed to, wasn't it? To go to her mother's for dinner and then pick a ridiculous fight with one another that would escalate into a shouting match.

Oh God, her throat felt raw. How was she going to hurl accusations at him with a raw throat?

"I'd say we're already into it," he pointed out coolly. "Now, are you going to listen to me and go to bed, or are you going to force me to take drastic measures with you?"

"Sounds kinky," she quipped, doing her best to ignore the fact that her head was spinning at a progressively faster and faster speed. This didn't happen to her, she insisted. At least, it didn't happen without a soul-draining kiss from Dave to start her off.

She blinked, trying desperately to cast off the encroaching fog consuming her brain.

"You are the most infuriating woman," he complained. The next second, he scooped her up into his arms. Turning, he began to carry her into the bedroom.

"Where did the floor go?" she asked weakly. She was still trying to focus, though it was growing more and more difficult.

Beneath the barrage of sarcastic remarks was one very sick young woman, Dave thought. Her whole body felt hot in his arms, right through her clothing. That wasn't a good sign.

"How long have you been like this?" he asked her gruffly.

"About thirty years," she answered, pushing each word out. It took a great deal of effort. "My mother said I started talking when I was less than a year old."

He could readily believe that. And obviously, she hadn't learned how to stop since. "I mean, how long have you had this fever?"

She felt like she had been this way forever. She paused, trying to think.

"I woke up with it," she recalled. Lately, she'd been waking up with him beside her. But last night, after she'd told him about what they were going to do tonight, Dave had opted to leave. He didn't even bother making an excuse.

Oh well, that was something she was going to have to get used to from here on in, she'd told herself. She'd hated being alone in her bed, but that wasn't up for discussion. Ever. Though the fact remained that before this fever hit with full force she'd begun feeling remarkably empty and disconnected.

She knew it had to do with the fact that she was missing him—how stupid was that? How could she have gotten so used to having him there for her when she'd spent most of her life *not* having him there?

It made no sense.

Nothing made sense anymore. They were breaking up, she thought sadly.

"And you went to work?" It was more of an accusation than a question.

"It's what I do." The answer came out breathlessly. "Don't walk so fast," she ordered, doing her best to sound authoritative. The words came out in a raspy whisper. "You're making the room spin."

He was walking slow and in a straight line that couldn't be responsible for making *anything* spin. "What are you taking for your fever?" he asked, reaching her bedroom.

"I don't know." She pressed her cheek against his chest, seeking the comfort of hearing his heart beat. "What'll you give me?"

Well, at least her mind was still functioning, he consoled himself, even if it was an old joke.

With the side of his shoulder, he pushed the door open all the way and crossed to her bed. A bed, he couldn't help thinking, where so much had happened. A bed that, for a little while, had belonged to both of them.

Laying her down as gently as possible, Dave began to remove her tank top. It was soaking wet.

"No foreplay?" her voice croaked.

"I'll give you a rain check for the foreplay," he answered. "Right now I want you in bed, drinking lots of fluids. I'm also going to give you a shot of acetaminophen."

Every time she closed her eyes, the world kept insisting on fading and swirling around her. She was going to be sick.

She *was* sick, a little voice in her head reminded her. "I don't like the sound of that," she protested weakly.

It was a common enough medication, present in a weakened form in so many over-the-counter drugs. "It's to lower your fever," he told her. "It's faster than ingesting it."

She could barely make him out. The overhead lights kept blurring his features. "You just want an excuse to stick pins into me."

"Yeah, there's that, too." He knew that protesting or arguing with her would be extremely futile and get him nowhere except aggravated. "Stay here," he ordered. "I'll be right back."

She tried to prop herself up on her elbow and discovered that she barely had the strength to do so. Instead, she fell back, flat on her back. What was going on?

"Where…are…you…going?"

"To get my medical bag," he told her. "It's in the car."

"Oh." It took her a moment to process the information. "Are…we…going…to…play…doctor?"

"Something like that," he told her.

He really didn't like the way she looked. Up until now, this strain of flu attacked predominantly children and the elderly. But that didn't mean that everyone in between was safe. She obviously wasn't.

He returned in less than three minutes to find Kara exactly where he'd left her. That in itself wasn't a good sign. When had he ever known her to listen to common sense?

Worried, he quickly swabbed an area on her hip and then sank the needle completely into her flesh, dispensing the medication. He knew it was going to be painful.

Sure enough, her eyes flew open, a cry of protest rising to her lips.

"The fever should start going down soon," he promised her. Sitting on the edge of the bed, he took out his cell phone.

"Calling...for...backup?" she asked breathlessly.

"I'm calling your mother to tell her that we won't be there." He didn't want the woman worrying when they didn't show up.

Her eyes felt as if they were on fire. She closed them, unable to look at anything. "Don't...tell...her... I'm...sick," Kara begged weakly. "She'll...be...here with...chicken...soup." Struggling to stay conscious, she added, "She'll...worry... I...don't...want...her... to..." Her breathing was growing increasingly labored. Kara struggled to open her eyes again, but all she could manage were narrow slits. They shifted accusingly at him. "You...put...something...in...that...shot."

He *had* put in a little something extra. It was intended to make her sleep. "Only way I can have my way with you," he told her.

It was the last thing she heard before everything faded to black.

* * *

It figured, Dave thought as light slowly began to slip into Kara's bedroom, dutifully chasing away the shadows and sending night packing. Even a predominantly unconscious Kara was a handful to deal with.

She'd opened her eyes several times during the night, plying him with questions and heaping accusations on his head that told him she was hallucinating, skipping around in time.

And then there was that one instance…

Oh, he didn't doubt that her mind had been wandering then, and that her hold on reality had been weak. But hearing her, someone else would have sworn that she was at least *relatively* lucid.

He argued with himself, saying that she was ill and didn't really mean what had come out of her mouth at that point. But even so, he *really* had wanted Kara to mean it.

Delusional or not, he committed every word she'd uttered to memory. Because he wanted it to be true.

In the middle of tossing and turning on the bed, her eyes had suddenly flown open as her mouth was simultaneously engaged.

"I should have never started this. No, never started this," she told him with such feeling, for a second he thought she'd made some kind of miraculous recovery.

But then he realized that she was having a conversation she'd begun in her head. With him? With someone else? He had no way of knowing. But he intended to try to get as much as he could out of her.

"Started what?" he prodded. Exhausted, he'd stretched out on top of the covers and was lying next to her on the bed. He leaned in a little closer. Her voice was barely audible.

"This pretending thing with Dave. It's not pretending anymore," she admitted with a heartfelt sigh that went right through him.

Holding his breath, Dave asked, "Why not?"

"Because."

"Because why?" he pressed.

"Because I love him," she blurted out almost accusingly. Certainly not happily.

Hearing her, it was, he thought, not unlike the sensation a soldier might feel throwing himself on a grenade that was about to detonate and blow his buddies to kingdom come.

Dave could have sworn he felt the rumble going right through his entire body, mushrooming out from the center of his chest and reaching his fingertips and toes. Did she actually mean—?

Cautioning himself against getting caught up in all this, he broke in to say, "You what?"

"Love him," she repeated with effort, her voice fading even more. "I…love…Dave… And…he…hates me."

Busted! he thought, more pleased than he could recall ever being in his lifetime.

Out loud he did the best he could to comfort the young woman who'd once taken such glee in showing him that she was the "better man."

"No, he doesn't," he told her.

But his words, he saw, fell on deaf ears. She'd lapsed into unconsciousness again.

Up until that point, he'd grabbed only the slightest

of cat naps. After Kara had said what she had, unconscious or not, Dave found that he couldn't sleep at all.

So he lay beside her as dawn turned into morning, replaying her words over and over again in his head.

She loved him. She'd said so. Drifting in and out of consciousness, devoid of any inhibitions, she'd professed her feelings. That was good enough for him.

Now, as he sat up, he looked at the still-sleeping Kara and then slowly shook his head. Who would have thought that he and Kara would *ever* be anything other than a couple of squabbling acquaintances?

Rousing himself, he moved to the edge of the bed and then came around to her side. She'd slept fitfully for the most part, but even without a fever, she had a tendency to move about the bed restlessly.

A moving target whether she was awake or asleep, he thought, his mouth curving slightly.

She was right about the charade. If she'd never made up her mind to undertake this fabricated romance to teach their mothers a lesson, he might not have ever discovered that he could be moved to such heights, never discovered that he had the capacity to feel so deeply. In essence, being with Kara, making love with her, had taken his black-and-white life and enhanced it with a whole rainbow of colors.

So much so that he didn't think he could ever go back to black and white again. He'd come too far.

In that respect, he thought as he got up and ran his hand through his hair, she'd ruined him. Taken his life and turned it upside down as well as inside out. The tranquility he'd once treasured was no longer golden. It was boring. Everything was boring without Kara in it.

Who would have ever thought he'd be this happy about being ruined? Certainly not him.

And now, he knew, he was going to have to do something about it.

Chapter Sixteen

Her eyelids felt like lead.

Kara had been struggling to open her eyes for what felt like forever. It had really been only ten minutes, according to the clock on her nightstand, since she'd first pried them open only to have them shut on her immediately. But now she was really awake.

Or at least getting there.

It took her several seconds to orient herself and realize that she was in her bed in her room. She needed another couple of seconds to realize that it was daylight, which meant that she must have been out for a long time. The last thing she remembered was sitting on her sofa, feeling like death warmed over, and it had been evening.

She didn't exactly feel much stronger now, but at

least her brain was returning to the land of the living and actually working.

The first thing her brain did was let her know that she wasn't alone. Startled, it took her exactly one erratic heartbeat to recognize the owner of the back she was looking at.

Dave.

What was he doing here?

She vaguely remembered that he had come to pick her up last night. Hadn't he gone home? For the life of her, she couldn't remember if he did or not. Couldn't really remember much of anything beyond opening the door to let him in. Details after that felt as if they were lost in a fog.

"Don't you have a home to go to?" she asked, her voice sounding really raspy to her ear.

Surprised, Dave swung around. For a second, she thought she saw relief wash over his features, but then it was gone and he looked austere again. Or maybe still.

"Apparently I seem to like yours better." Crossing back to her, he put his hand to her forehead. It was cool for the first time since he'd arrived. The worst of it seemed to be over, he thought. Even her cheeks weren't as pink as they had been. "Looks as if your fever finally broke."

A few vague memories floated through the back edges of her mind. She remembered he'd looked concerned. "Have you been here the whole time?"

"Yes."

Hadn't they agreed to stage the breakup last night? He was supposed to be out of her life, not hovering over her. She didn't get it. "Why?"

Feelings, especially his own, had never been something he could easily talk about. Dave shrugged. "I had nothing else scheduled after you canceled on dinner at your mother's."

She recalled being dizzy and feeling hot all over. "I didn't exactly cancel," she protested.

"No," he agreed. "You're right. What you did was pass out." A small smile curved his mouth.

"My mother," she remembered suddenly, replaying some of his words in her head.

He was way ahead of her. "Was duly notified and gently instructed to refrain from arriving here with a pot of chicken soup."

Kara's eyebrows drew together in a confused line. "Why would you do that?"

She really had no recollection of last night, did she? "Because you asked me to."

She shook her head. Nothing was really coming together in her mind yet. It was all just disjoined pieces bobbing up and down. "I don't remember saying that to you."

He looked at her for a long moment. A semismile barely passed over his lips and then receded as if it had never been there at all.

"You probably don't remember saying a lot of things to me."

Kara stiffened. There was something about the way he said that that made the hairs on the back of her neck stand up. The rest of her felt as if it had just been put on red alert.

"Like what?" she asked in a hushed tone.

"Things," he replied vaguely. "No need to go into them now."

Just the way he said it, she knew she needed to find out what she'd said.

"Tell me," she insisted.

His eyes held hers for a moment, and she felt her stomach take a dive off the high board. "You really want to go into this now?"

Oh God, he was daring her to ask. This had to be worse than she thought. But what could she have told him and not remembered? She would have happily believed he was bluffing just to get under her skin, but she knew him. He didn't bluff. There wasn't going to be any peace for her until she knew what he *thought* he knew.

"Yes," she breathed. "Tell me. Now. Please," she added in case he was waiting for her to humble herself.

The smile on his lips went clear down to her bones. She braced herself.

"You told me you loved me."

She wasn't braced nearly enough, she realized as every system within her screamed, *Mayday! Mayday! Damage control!*

She grabbed at the first excuse she could. "I was delirious," she pointed out so quickly, he almost got whiplash.

The smile on his lips told her he knew better. "You were uninhibited," he corrected. Before she could protest, he put the tip of his finger to her lips to still them and made his case. "To the casual observer, you don't seem to be uptight and repressed, but it turns out that you really are. At least as far as your feelings are concerned." And he, Dave thought, could fully relate to that.

The best defense, her father had always told her, was a good offense. So she forged ahead, although not nearly with as much verve as she would have liked. "I wouldn't throw rocks if I were you."

"No rock throwing," Dave assured her. "I'm just making a very logical observation. Why is that, do you think?"

"That you think you're being logical?" she asked him with a dismissive sniff. "I'm sure I haven't the faintest idea."

"No," he said patiently, "I'm asking you why you're afraid to let your feelings out, afraid to let anyone know that you even *can* feel." He took his best guess. "Someone walk out on you, Kara?"

She resented his probing. Resented, even more, his hitting so close to the truth. "Since when did you become a shrink?"

"Since when did you become afraid of a straight answer?" he countered.

She'd had enough of this. Throwing back the covers, she was about to storm out of bed and the room, praying her knees wouldn't buckle under her, when her plan was instantly aborted.

She had nothing on beneath the blanket.

Stunned, she threw the blanket back into place, anchoring it down with her arms, and glared at him accusingly. "You took off my clothes."

There was a reason for that. "You were sopping wet," he explained.

Why would she be sopping wet? "What did you do to me?" she demanded.

He gave her a quick summary. "I gave you an injection to break the fever. You were perspiring so much your clothes were almost soaked right through. All I did was get you out of your wet clothes."

He made it sound completely altruistic. "And nothing else?" she asked suspiciously.

"I applied a few wet compresses to your forehead, but the shot did most of the work. And as for what you're implying, tempting though you might look to me, I prefer you awake if I'm going to be doing anything that requires tacit consent."

Her heart believed him. Her mind was having trouble. Especially in light of the expression on his face. "You're smirking," she accused.

It was always going to be like this, he thought. A constant battle, heated or otherwise. And now he understood what had been missing from those other relationships that never went beyond a few steps. Passion. Passion had been missing. All those other women had been too much like him, too orderly, too blandly agreeable. They were black-and-white, and Kara, incessantly argumentative Kara, was the rainbow that he subconsciously craved.

"No, I'm not. That's called a smile," he informed her.

A smile at her expense, Kara thought. Because, temporarily out of her head, she'd blurted out her true feelings.

She tried another approach. "I can't be held responsible for anything I said when I was ill," she protested.

When he said nothing, some of her ardor slipped away. "You were really here the whole night?"

He nodded. "Yes, I was." And then he added, "And the next day, as well."

She stared at him, utterly stunned. "The next— How long have I been out?"

He looked at his watch before answering, "A little less than thirty-six hours."

"Thirty—six—" No, that had to be wrong. "You're just making that up," she protested.

"I could carry you into the living room, put on the news channel. They always run the time and the date in the lower right-hand corner of their broadcast." He rose to his feet as if he was going to pick her up and make good on his suggestion. Upset over losing a day, Kara waved him back. She couldn't remember when she'd ever slept so long.

"I believe you."

He laughed shortly. "Nice to hear you're that trusting."

She wasn't accustomed to his sounding like that. "Sarcasm doesn't become you."

"Sorry." He inclined his head. "Didn't mean to invade your home territory."

She deserved that, she supposed. He'd been nothing but kind and obviously caring even if she'd been out for most of it, and as a reward for his behavior, she was being combative.

But, in her defense, she wasn't used to being the one who needed help. "Why did you do it, Dave?" she asked.

He wasn't sure exactly what part she was referring to. "Do what?"

"Why did you stay here with me? You could have just put me into bed and left me there."

Did she really think that? "You were sick, I'm a doctor. It's kind of self-explanatory." Not to mention that she had "thoughtfully" gotten sick on a Friday night. That afforded him the weekend to watch over her.

"No, it's not. Most doctors would have called a family member, or, if the person was really sick, they would have called an ambulance and had the person taken to a hospital." This was definitely above and beyond the call of duty.

This, she realized, was something a friend did for another friend. *Or a lover,* a little voice whispered in her head.

"I'd rather not have you haunting my hospital," he quipped.

That was the kind of flippant thing she would have said to him. Kara picked at the sheet, pulling it in tighter around herself. She kept her eyes down as she asked, "I really said…you know?"

"Yes, you really said 'you know,'" he confirmed, amused.

Kara blew out a breath. "I'm surprised you're still here, then." He looked at her, puzzled. "Hearing something like that from me, I would have expected you to run for the hills."

"Why?" he asked. "Love shouldn't make a man run. Your mouth, on the other hand, well, that's another story." He paused for a moment. He had nothing to lose by pushing this and hopefully everything to gain if she stopped playing games and told him the truth. "Why are you so afraid of love, Kara?"

"I'm not afraid of love," she denied indignantly with a toss of her head. She instantly regretted the latter.

"You're also not much of a liar," he observed. "I'm waiting."

It was on the tip of her tongue to tell him he could wait until hell froze over, but she knew him well enough to know he would. And besides, he didn't deserve that. Not after he'd been so selfless.

So, with a sigh, she answered his question. It wasn't easy. "When my father died, I saw my mother all but completely fall apart. I was never so scared in my life."

He could well imagine. "But she didn't, did she?" he pointed out.

"No, but—" That wasn't the point. The point was the horror her mother had felt. The horror of being left behind to live, to take one step after the other, in a world that no longer contained the man she loved. The *only* man she'd ever love.

"And she has her memories of life with your father, doesn't she?" Dave continued.

"Yes," she grudgingly admitted. And then her eyes widened as she looked at him. "Are you going to tell me that 'it's better to have loved and lost than never to have loved at all'?" He wouldn't even dare think about that now, she silently threatened.

His broad shoulders rose and fell in a careless shrug. "Alfred, Lord Tennyson seemed to think so," he told her. "Who are we to disagree?"

That was all well and good in poetry, but this was

real life. And real life brought with it scars. "I don't want to ache the way my mother ached."

"She ached because she'd loved. There are far worse things than death," he told her.

She couldn't imagine there being something worse to endure than the death of a loved one. "Such as?" she challenged.

"Being alone," he told her simply. Being alone the way he'd been alone—until she returned to his life. That was when he came to understand what he'd been missing all along. Her. "There are no guarantees in life, and no one lives forever." He looked at her and knew that there was only one way to play this. It was all or nothing. He didn't usually take risks, but then that was why his life was all but flat-lining. It was time to take that risk. "All I can do is promise to love you for the rest of my life."

She had to be hearing things. "You love me?" Kara asked incredulously.

Why did she look so surprised? He would have thought that she at least suspected as much. "That didn't occur to you? Say, around the second time we made love?"

Why would she have thought that? Unless, of course, he thought she was that naive. "Men don't have to *be* in love to *make* love," she told him.

"Granted. And God knows I didn't want to be, not with you," he told her honestly. "But I don't seem to have a choice in this."

She was still very much stuck in first gear—afraid to believe what her heart *wanted* to believe. "You love me?" she repeated, mystified.

"I thought we already established that." He smiled. Okay, this was for the record. "Yes, I love you. And I'd like to keep on loving you. I stopped pretending two days into this charade and finally admitted that little fact to myself. Now, you can take your time making up your mind how you feel—"

It was beginning to sink in, but she was still afraid to embrace the thought. "Hey, with medical care costing what it does these days, I'd be a fool to turn down the opportunity to have my very own doctor on call 24/7."

His eyes pinned her down. "And that's the only reason?"

"No, it's not the only reason." She sighed. "You already know I love you," she said, staring down at the comforter. She felt more naked than she had when she'd thrown the comforter back. This admission left her completely exposed. It wasn't a position she relished.

He ran his fingertips along her cheek, sending butterflies into both their stomachs. "I'm going to need you to convince me a little more when you're feeling stronger."

"Whoa, feel that?" she cried.

"Feel what?" he asked, puzzled.

Her eyes teased his. "My strength. That was my strength, coming back." She put her arms out to him, and he took her into his own. "You know what this means, don't you?"

He was a little wary of giving her an answer. With Kara he never knew what was safe and what played right into her hands. "What?"

"That our mothers were right. About matching us

up." She rolled her eyes. "They're going to be impossible to live with from now on."

He grinned, brushing a strand of hair back from her face. "I wasn't planning on living with them."

The way he left that open had her asking, "Who are you planning on living with?"

He looked into her eyes and wondered why he hadn't seen this before. But then, maybe he had. Maybe he'd been aware of this all along and that was why he never became involved with anyone else.

"You."

There went her heart again. Going off like fireworks on the Fourth of July. "You want to move in together?" she questioned, surprised. "Isn't that a big step for you?" She knew how cautious he was, how much he liked his own space. And here he was, asking her to share that space with him. Did it get any better than this?

"That's the usual step two people take after getting married."

"Married?" It did, it really did get better than this, she thought—provided she wasn't hallucinating. "I think my fever's back."

"Well, then I'll just have to nurse you back to health again." He brushed his lips against her forehead. Just as he thought. It was cool.

Kara was staring at him, wide-eyed. Trying to absorb what he was saying to her. Afraid to take it to heart and yet, she knew she already had. "You're serious."

"I'm a doctor," he told her innocently. "Making people healthy is what I do."

"Idiot," she cried. He knew perfectly well what she was referring to. "I'm talking about asking me to marry you." She pinned him down in earnest, putting the question to him. "You're asking me?"

He nodded. "I'm asking you."

She didn't want him parroting her. "I want the words, Dave. I want to hear the words. The official words." She held her breath, her eyes on his lips.

"Kara Calhoun, will you marry me and keep turning my boring life upside down?" His eyes crinkled at the very end.

Oh God, he was really asking her. *Really* asking her. It was all she could do to keep from screaming out the single word. Her eyes danced as she said, "Well, if you put it that way—yes!"

He let go of the breath he'd been holding. Kara was nothing if not unpredictable.

"We're going to have to tell our mothers," he reminded her.

"I know. How about right after the first baby?" she suggested, entwining her arms around his neck. "Until then, we can just keep it a secret."

He knew she didn't mean it, or at least *thought* she didn't mean it. But it cost him nothing to go along with it.

"Works for me," he murmured just before they sealed the bargain with a very long kiss.

It occurred to Kara, just before she sank into the kiss, that she'd had her last first kiss that evening right after the birthday party.

Her feeling of contentment and joy knew no bounds. She was counting on it remaining that way for the next fifty years or so.

Epilogue

"So was I right, or was I right?" Paulette Calhoun asked smugly as she adjusted her baby-blue dress, her eyes meeting her best friend's in the mirror.

Lisa Scarlatti shifted slightly in the limited space right outside the room where the bride was getting ready. Technically this was a room, too, but someone was going to have to show her the floor plans before she was convinced of that.

She paused, allowing her best friend to have her moment. After all, it *had* been her idea that had started this wonderful ball rolling. "Doesn't leave me much of a choice, does it, Mother of the Bride?"

Paulette turned, her blue dress brushing against the mint-green one Lisa had on. "There doesn't really need to be a choice, Mother of the Groom, does there?"

"Go ahead, gloat." Lisa laughed softly. "You have every right to."

Paulette inclined her head. "Thank you. I fully intend to, and yes, I know." She took a deep breath after glancing in the narrow mirror one last time. "Well, I'm ready—how about you?"

Lisa's smile was radiant. "I've been ready for this for the last thirty years."

"Thirty?" Paulette echoed. "Dave's thirty-two."

"I decided not to push the first two years," Lisa deadpanned.

"Very understanding of you."

They entered the next room together, and the moment Paulette saw her daughter, she felt her eyes begin to sting. Kara was in her wedding dress and had just put on her veil.

"Oh God," Paulette moaned, taking out her handkerchief, "I told myself I wasn't going to cry."

"Mother, don't you dare." The words were half a warning, half a plea. It wasn't as if her mother hadn't seen the dress on her before. She'd been there for the last fitting and had helped her with it just this morning.

"She's right," Lisa told her best friend. "Tears are contagious." As if to prove it, she dabbed at her own eyes, which had become moist. "So don't cry."

"I won't," Paulette promised, even as another tear spilled onto her cheek.

Kara shook her head, then readjusted her veil. "You're hopeless, Mother."

Paulette came closer. *It was happening. It was* finally *happening.* "And you are the most beautiful sight I have ever seen."

"Think Dave will think so?" Kara asked as she examined her reflection in the mirror one last time. Her floor-length gown nipped in at the waist, then flowed out with yards of satin and lace. The strapless bodice had delicate beadwork woven all through it.

"If he doesn't, he's no son of mine," Lisa assured her.

Just then, there was a knock on the door, followed by a deep voice asking. "Everything all right in there? It's almost time to make this official."

"Dave!" Kara cried, pleasure and relief in her voice. There was a small part of her that had been afraid he'd change his mind at the very last minute and make his escape, taking off for parts unknown. But he hadn't. He was here. Her smile widened.

Horrified that her son might come in, Lisa quickly opened the door a crack and angled her body through the space. Once outside, she firmly shut the door again, blocking access with her own slender body.

"Dave, don't take this the wrong way, but go away!" she ordered. She tugged on her son's arm to lead him away from the door. "It's bad luck for the groom to see the bride before the wedding."

His smile was tolerant as he looked at his mother. He owed her a lot and he knew it. "Then I'll just go to the altar and wait for her there." He raised his voice so that Kara could hear him through the door. "I'll be the impatient guy in the black tuxedo next to the priest."

"I'll be sure to look for you," Kara called out.

A moment later, strains of the wedding march began to filter into the small room.

"They're playing your song, darling," Paulette told her daughter.

Kara took a deep breath. "Okay, here we go," she murmured, suddenly feeling butterflies in her stomach. "Just promise me something, Mother."

Paulette squeezed her daughter's hand as more tears slid down her cheeks. "Anything."

Kara opened the door. The music swelled. "Promise me that you two won't start playing matchmakers with your grandchildren until they're at least in their twenties."

"Well, I won't," Paulette promised solemnly as they left the little room. "But I'm afraid I really can't speak for Lisa...."

* * * * *

"I'm going to ask you out on a date." Cole said.

"I'm a little afraid, though," he continued. "My last few dates were…"

"Interesting?"

"Disasters."

Lauren laughed and turned her head. Their lips brushed, met, settled together for a kiss that rocked him to the core.

She took her lips from his and whispered. "Let's not over-think this. If we do we might end up talking ourselves out of something good."

"You don't strike me as a 'go with the flow' kinda girl."

"I'm usually not. For you I'll make an exception." She tilted her head, touched her lips to his.

Before the kiss had a chance to grow into more, a sharp crash from next door—too close—interrupted.

"I have to go," he said, reluctantly stepping away.

Lauren nodded. "If you ask me on a date," she said, "I think I'll say yes and take my chances."

Dear Reader,

You never know where inspiration will come from, when or where characters will come to life—and then refuse to let go. I've recently started following baseball rather fanatically, thanks to a nephew's success in that sport. When you watch every game of the season, when you get to know the players, you see well beyond the games. You begin to get a small glimpse of their lives. These very talented ballplayers travel all the time, during the long season. Their families make a big sacrifice. And there was my "what if?" What if a father was suddenly left to raise three kids on his own? It would be a sacrifice to walk away from a lucrative career in order to be a single parent, but that's what Cole Donovan did, and that shaped his character for me.

Having three kids of my own, I know what a rowdy household can be like.

Lauren Russell comes from a world I know well. The South. Her grandmother was a big influence on her, and is still around to help shape her life. Cooking is at the center of Lauren's world. She's also organised to a fault and she has plans for her life, personal and professional. Plans thrown into chaos by a handsome man and three adorable (if occasionally unmanageable) children who move into the house next door and turn her neat life upside down.

Sometimes chaos is a good thing. Sometimes it's the *un*planned that shapes us.

I hope you enjoy their story!

Linda

THE HUSBAND RECIPE

BY
LINDA WINSTEAD JONES

First published in Great Britain 2012
by Mills & Boon, an imprint of Harlequin (UK) Limited,
Eton House, 18-24 Paradise Road, Richmond, Surrey TW9 1SR

© Linda Winstead Jones 2012

2in1 ISBN: 978 0 263 89421 9

23-0412

Harlequin (UK) policy is to use papers that are natural, renewable and recyclable products and made from wood grown in sustainable forests. The logging and manufacturing processes conform to the legal environmental regulations of the country of origin.

Printed and bound in Spain
by Blackprint CPI, Barcelona

Linda Winstead Jones is a bestselling author of more than fifty romance books in several subgenres—historical, fairy tale, paranormal and, of course, romantic suspense. She's won a Colorado Romance Writers Award of Excellence twice. She is also a three-time RITA® Award finalist and (writing as Linda Fallon) winner of the 2004 RITA® Award for paranormal romance.

Linda lives in north Alabama with her husband of thirty-seven years. She can be reached via www.lindawinstead jones.com.

With special thanks to The Cooking Women, Doris and Joyce. Fried chicken, pinto beans and cornbread, sweet potatoes, coleslaw, fried squash, seven-layer cake, peach cobbler...and that's just a part of one meal. Y'all have inspired me to go back to my grandmother's cookbooks and give some of those recipes a whirl. And of course a thanks to Benny as well. Because when I'm not around *someone* has to take care of the eating.

Chapter One

B*lam!*

Something hit the side of her house, right outside her office. Lauren Russell jumped half out of her skin, jarring against the desk and sending hot tea sloshing over the edge of the cup and running under the stack of articles she'd printed out, as well as coming dangerously close to her optical mouse.

"Damn it!"

She leaped up and grabbed her napkin—high quality linen, of course—and swabbed at the spill. When she'd rescued the mouse, she left the rest for a moment and hot-footed it over to the window to see what the heck had happened. She was just in time to spot a little boy pick up a baseball and hurl it to his sister in the yard next door, then race back into his own territory.

She should have known. The monsters were loose again.

Lauren immediately felt guilty, because in general she liked children. Maybe the pertinent phrase was *in general,* because these particular children were driving her nuts.

Going back to her desk, she finished mopping up, drying off the papers as best she could, then taking them into the bathroom and using her blow dryer to finish the job. They were crisp and wrinkly, but readable. She didn't like the fact that they were now less than perfect, but it would take too much time to go to each and every website and reprint everything. Later, maybe.

She sat at her desk again and did her best to tune out the happy screams and shrieks of what sounded like fifty children romping around a sprinkler on a hot summer day, as well as the occasional thump of a ball hitting the side of her house. Every time it hit, she jumped. How could three kids make so much noise? Weren't children supposed to spend hours indoors playing video games these days? How was she supposed to work with this going on?

She had a deadline, an article to finish and send off by noon. The first thump had alarmed her, but now that she knew what was going on she should be able to dismiss the noise and concentrate on her work. Though it was tempting, she didn't march outside to tell the kids to take it easy. Yesterday she'd had to tell them not to tramp in her flower bed, and last week she'd had a talk with them about Frisbees in her tomato garden. She didn't want to be *that* neighbor, the grumpy woman all the neighborhood children were afraid of, the witch who did her best to squelch the kids' fun. Might as well get herself a pointy hat and construct her house out of candy. No, thanks.

Still, a very tall privacy fence was looking more and

more like a necessary investment. That would ruin the ambience of her carefully landscaped backyard, but if this continued she might have no choice. Her office was on the newly noisy side of the house, as was the spare bedroom. Unless she wanted to try to move her bedroom furniture into these rooms and convert the master suite into a large office, she was out of luck. Yeah, like she wanted to try to sleep on this side of the house.

The Garrisons had been such good, quiet neighbors! Why had they moved? Lauren was happy that the older couple now lived closer to their eldest daughter and their two grandchildren, but why couldn't the daughter have moved here? Why did being close to family mean going to Arizona, of all places? Maybe Alabama was hot in the summertime, even if Huntsville was about as far north as you could get and still be in the state, but it couldn't be any hotter than Arizona. Worse, the Garrisons had sold their house to a family with three children. At least, she'd seen three so far—two boys and a girl. Good Lord, she hoped there weren't more.

Lauren stared at the computer screen, concentrating diligently in an effort to mentally block the noises from next door. Naturally, trying so hard only made her more aware of every sound. A piercing squeal. A shouted taunt. Laughter. She just had a couple of hours to finish this piece for the local paper, and then she needed to tackle the edits on her book. They were due back in three days, and she was hoping to make quick work of them this afternoon and evening, and then tomorrow morning overnight the changes so they'd be there a day early. It was her first book, a collection of recipes and household tips—many of which had come from her weekly newspaper articles—and she was certainly hoping there would be other books to follow. Being late wouldn't endear her to her editor. Besides, Lauren hated to be late, almost as much as she hated it when others were late. It was a… well, a *thing* she had. Everyone was allowed a *thing* or two, in her opinion.

As she was attempting to place herself in a magic bubble of silence, a loud crash jerked her back to reality. A loud crash accompanied by shards of glass that flew into her office, landing on the area rug and her grandmother's occasional table and into the vase of fresh flowers there. Lauren's heart almost jumped out of her chest. She screamed—just a little—and then, a split second later, she realized that all screams and laughter from next door had gone silent.

When she'd gathered her composure she stood carefully, stepping over the pieces of glass on the floor, glad that she wasn't working barefoot as she often did. And there, on top of her edits, sat a baseball. The offending, intruding, destructive and *muddy* baseball, which was now perched on top of the once-pristine top page of a once-perfectly-aligned stack.

Lauren had heard the term *her blood boiled,* and now she knew exactly what that felt like. She experienced an intense physical response to the sight of that baseball on her work, to the broken glass and the ruined papers. That was it. She literally couldn't take any more.

She snatched up the baseball and stalked to the back door, bursting onto her small stone patio like a woman on a mission. In her fury she noted—not for the first time—the crushed flowers and the broken tomato stalk. The trampled grass and the discarded juice box. The juice box was new, tossed into her backyard as if this were the city dump. Like her office, the backyard had been in perfect condition before the new family next door had moved in and disrupted her life.

In the neighboring yard—where the recently added trampoline and soccer net marred the landscape—the sprinkler continued to spurt a jerking stream of water this way and that, but the children were nowhere to be seen. For once, all was quiet. Lauren cut in between the two houses, glancing at her broken window as she walked by on her way to the front door. She'd never before really noticed how close the two houses were. Little more than an alleyway separated her home from the one next door.

The Garrison house, which wasn't the Garrison house any longer, was larger than her own. Some years ago, long before Lauren had bought her home, Mr. Garrison had built an addition that consisted of two bedrooms and another bath. At one time he'd had children of his own living there, and they'd needed the space. Once the children moved out, that extra space had been unnecessary. Helen Garrison had happily told Lauren all about the small condo they'd bought in Phoenix. The older woman was thrilled to have less house to clean, no yard to tend.

Ringing the doorbell would be too passive for Lauren's mood, so she knocked soundly on the front door. She knocked so hard her knuckles stung. As she waited for an answer she shook out her hand and studied the mess on the small porch. A baseball glove, Frisbees, a Barbie doll with one leg and a frighteningly original haircut, and a skateboard. It could be such a cute porch, with a couple of white wicker chairs and a pair of hanging ferns, but instead the space was messy, untended and chaotic. She imagined whatever lay beyond the door was no better.

No one immediately answered her knock, so she rang the doorbell. Twice. Inside she heard whispering. The heathens were ignoring her. Heaven above, surely those kids weren't in there alone! No, the family car, a white minivan that had seen better days, was parked in the driveway. It was the only vehicle she'd seen in front of the house since the new family had moved in, not that she spent her time watching the neighbors. She couldn't help but notice a few details, as she collected the mail or drove into her own driveway. For all she knew there was another vehicle parked in the one-car garage.

All was quiet now. She didn't even hear whispering. She rang the doorbell for the third time and then lifted her hand to knock once more. Harder this time around.

The door swung open on a very tall, broad-shouldered man who held a cell phone to his ear. Obviously distracted, and also obviously not in a good mood, he held up one finger to indicate that he needed another minute.

The heathens' father needed a lesson in manners as much as his children did. It was all she could do not to snatch the cell phone out of his hand! What she really wanted to do was grab the offending finger and bend it back. *That* would get his attention.

But of course, she did no such thing. The hand holding the offending baseball dropped, and some of the wind went out of her sails. She'd never been very good when it came time to confront a man—especially a good-looking one. In most situations she was confident and in command, but most situations didn't require her to look up quite so far.

He who had spawned three little devils was much too tall for her tastes, which didn't help matters at all since Lauren was barely five foot three. Her new neighbor was six feet tall, at least, which meant she was at a serious disadvantage when it came to talking to him face-to-face. A step stool would come in handy right about now. The man needed a shave; he didn't have a beard, but that face hadn't seen a razor in a day or two. He had shaggy-ish dark brown hair which wasn't long but wasn't freshly cut either, fabulous bone structure, a perfect nose—Lauren always noticed noses—and big hands with long fingers. Dressed in jeans and a plain, faded gray T-shirt, he still managed to give off an "I'm in charge" vibe.

Great. Maybe she should've tacked a scathing note to the front door.

"Look, I'll have to call you back." For the first time, the man who'd shaken his finger at Lauren really looked at her. And he smiled. "A woman in bunny slippers and her pj's is on my doorstep holding a muddy baseball and looking like someone spit in her Cheerios this morning, so she must be here about something important."

Lauren tried not to be obvious about turning her gaze downward, but yes—she *was* still in her pajamas. Long, soft cotton pants and a matching tank just a touch too thin for someone who wore no bra. Not for the first time, she thanked her lucky stars that she didn't have much to brag about in that department.

But still…she loses her temper in the first time in *forever,* and this is where it gets her. Embarrassed. No, mortified.

And she was still holding the damn baseball.

Her new neighbor, the father of the heathens who were tearing Lauren's neat schedule to pieces, ended his phone call and looked at her. He really looked at her, his gaze cutting to the bone. He had blue eyes. Not just a little blue, either, but wowza blue. Cut-to-the-bone blue. His eyes were the color of a perfectly clear spring sky shot with disturbingly piercing shards of ice. Lauren shifted her own gaze down and stared at his chin, which was perfectly normal and not at all eye-catching like his nose or his eyes or any of the rest of him. It was just a stubbly chin, thank goodness, not at all out of the ordinary.

Lauren handed over the baseball, which he took, then she crossed her arms over her chest in a too-late attempt at modesty. She had quite a few things to say, and she'd played a few of them through her mind as she'd waited. But suddenly she lost her nerve. "Is your wife at home?"

Cole had been amused, but with a few words that amusement died entirely. He should be used to the question by now, but he wasn't. He'd given up beating around the bush long ago. "She's dead. You'll have to deal with me. Sorry."

He was accustomed to the change in expression, the shift from annoyance to pity.

"I didn't mean to… I apologize." The pity turned to confusion. "I saw a woman carrying in suitcases when you moved in, and I just assumed…"

"That was my sister-in-law. She helped us move." Grudgingly, yes, but Janet *had* helped.

Cole recognized his neighbor. He'd seen her a few times, working in her garden or collecting her mail. That was about it, since her garage wasn't filled with unpacked boxes—like his—and she could actually park in it. He'd noted from a distance that she was cute, but up close she was more than cute. Not gorgeous, but interesting. Pretty. She had honey-blond hair caught in a ponytail, hazel-green eyes, nicely shaped lips, petite build…. Yeah, she was definitely interesting.

It was easy enough to guess that the muddy baseball had either gone into her garden or through a window. No wonder the kids had come running inside and dashed straight to their rooms.

She took a step back. "I shouldn't have bothered you with this. Just forget it. I'll…"

Cole turned and yelled. "Get in here, every one of you!" After a moment of strained silence, the three kids came creeping into the room. Heads down, bare feet shuffling, they were all soaking wet and chagrined. Cole asked, in a calmer voice, "What happened?"

After a moment of complete silence—a rarity in this house—all three started talking at once, each trying to outdo the other in pitch and storytelling. It was a window after all. Just what he needed. A damaged garden would be easier to fix. A little dirt, a new plant or two, and it was done. Windows were more complicated. He tried to make sense of the story. Apparently Justin had thrown the ball, but it was Hank who'd missed it. And as the oldest, Meredith should've stopped them from playing ball in the first place.

Cole had to work hard to disguise his fatherly pride. Justin was just five. It had to have been a helluva hard pitch to break a window. He kept his pride to himself. What kind of parent would he be if he gave his son a pat on the back for breaking the neighbor's window?

"Y'all apologize to…" He looked over his shoulder to the pretty neighbor who'd taken yet another step back. "I'm sorry, I don't know your name."

"Lauren Russell," she said.

He stepped forward and offered his hand. "Cole Donovan. These rug rats, in order of appearance, are Meredith, Hank and Justin." She took his hand for a quick shake that was firm enough but not long-lasting, then quickly resumed the position meant to protect her from showing too much boob but that actually pushed them up and out a bit. Something he really shouldn't be noticing. "Kids, apologize to Ms. Russell. Then everyone gets a time-out."

The kids apologized without much sincerity, then complained about their punishment. Cole turned to look at them. "No one came to me and told me about the broken window. Accidents happen, but trying to pretend they didn't isn't acceptable."

"Would you like me to make you some coffee, Dad?" Meredith asked sweetly. Almost thirteen—and wasn't he terrified by that fact—she was sometimes the spitting image of her mother. Long blond hair, deep brown eyes, high cheekbones and long legs. Why couldn't she stay twelve forever? Awhile longer, at least.

He maintained a stern expression. "Coffee isn't going to fix this."

Cole could practically see Hank's mind spinning. Great. His middle child, the budding wizard who was currently without front teeth, would probably be in the kitchen this afternoon whipping up yet another potion designed to improve his father's mood. If coffee wouldn't work, surely magic would. The boy was seven; when was he going to outgrow this phase? Why couldn't he be into baseball or football or soccer? No, he had to be into dragons and spells and magic wands. As always, Justin, the wizard's apprentice, would help with the process when Hank went to work. Leftovers, half-filled boxes of juice, whatever they could find in the pantry—anything was fair game when it came to their concoctions. Cole would drink at least a sip of the potion, no matter what it contained. The boys hadn't killed him with their experiments yet.

He never should've let the kids watch those movies....

Chastised, all three shuffled off to their rooms. He

wouldn't make them stay there long. Just long enough to realize they'd made mistakes.

Cole turned back to Lauren. "I'll fix your window."

She was already making her escape. "Don't worry about it."

Cole stepped onto the front porch, but stopped short of following his neighbor into the yard. She was most definitely a woman making a getaway. "Nope. My kids broke it, I'll fix it."

"Whatever." She waved, but her back was to him by then so he didn't get another nice view. Too bad. Though he had to admit, the rear view wasn't too shabby. Lauren Russell walked like a woman, with a hint of sashay as she hurried home.

Like he had time for a woman, pretty or otherwise.

"Hang on a minute," he said, ignoring his initial instinct and following in Lauren's footsteps. She stopped, waited a couple of seconds longer than was necessary, and turned around slowly. Her chin was up, her eyes... defiant. He just wanted to talk to her, smooth the rough way they'd been introduced. After all, they were going to be neighbors, probably for a good long while. But the way she looked at him... Maybe this wasn't such a good idea....

"Yes?" she prodded when he just stood there too long like an idiot, saying nothing.

"Sorry we got off to a bad start." He tried to think of a couple of neighborly questions he could ask. *Where's the best shopping, what about the other neighbors, what are the best movie theaters... Can I borrow a cup of sugar?* Yeah, right, that would go over well. Judging by the look on her face, the woman just wanted peace and quiet, she wanted to be left alone. He couldn't blame her. "I'll try to keep the kids out of your hair."

Her expression softened. "I'm sorry I overreacted." She was trying to very casually cover her breasts, which only drew his attention to her gentle curves. "Kids will be kids, I suppose, and it's not like I think they broke the window on purpose."

Cole rocked back slightly and shoved his hands in his pockets. He shouldn't have followed her. What the hell had he been thinking? Oh, yeah, he'd been thinking that Lauren Russell was cute and interesting and he hadn't talked to an adult face-to-face in days. Fortunately he knew how to undo his awkward mistake. He knew how to end this conversation here and now. "So if I ever need a babysitter…"

The horrified expression on Lauren's face was priceless, and Cole couldn't help but grin widely. "Just kidding."

She nodded her head, muttered a polite goodbye and made her final escape. This time, he didn't bother to follow.

Chapter Two

Lauren leaned into the computer. Her stomach was telling her that it was time for lunch, and she had leftovers in the fridge. Vegetable lasagna, one of her favorites. But her growling stomach could wait. Her article was finished and off by email, the broken glass had been swept and picked up from the floor and carpet, and she'd taped a piece of cardboard to the broken window. She'd decided to take a break before she got to lunch and then to the edits on her book. Google was a wonderful invention. Not only did it lead people searching for recipes right to her website, it was great for checking out new neighbors.

She'd been prepared to search for the correct Cole Donovan for a while. Neither Cole nor Donovan were unusual names. It wasn't like his name was Rumpelstiltskin. She hadn't started with a lot of hope; she was prepared to find next to nothing. It didn't hurt to try, she supposed. Surprisingly, he came up first on the list. She knew without doubt that it was him because there was a picture.

Baseball. Huh. She'd never been a fan, otherwise she might've recognized his name. Apparently Cole Donovan had been a big deal a few years back, a star third baseman on track to break some sort of home-run record for the season. She had to scan down a few links to find out why he'd quit in the middle of the season, with that record and a promising career on the line.

Lauren's heart dropped as she read the archived article. His wife had indeed died. Mary Donovan had dropped dead in the grocery store, victim of a heart defect she'd been born with but had never been aware of. A chill ran down Lauren's arms. Here one moment; gone the next. It was the sort of thing no one could possibly be prepared for. There was no one to blame, no drunk driver or misdiagnosis or missed treatment. Just…poof. The young mother of three had been twenty-nine at the time; so had Cole. They'd been high-school sweethearts.

Cole had walked away from baseball after his wife died, giving up a lucrative career for his family. He could've pawned the kids off on relatives, she supposed, or hired a nanny and kept playing, but no. He'd left a promising career to take care of his children, to be a full-time parent.

Lauren felt about an inch tall. She felt like the wicked witch, maybe the Grinch. Perhaps an ogre. All green monsters, she noted. She'd never looked good in certain yellowy shades of green, and she certainly wouldn't look good if she *were* green. Wicked witches were never a nice teal or sea foam. No, they were pea-soup green. Not her color at all.

She'd gone storming over there with that muddy baseball and her indignation, when that family had been through enough heartache for a lifetime. She checked the dates; it had been five years since Mary Donovan had died. The little one—Justin—must've been a baby at the time.

And she'd lost it over a broken window and a little noise. Talk about putting things in perspective!

She left her office a little sorry she'd looked Cole Donovan up online. There were some things that were better left unknown, unspoken, undone. But once those things were out of the box, it was simply too late to stuff them back in.

Lauren's mother and grandmother had trained her well. As she went into the kitchen and took the leftover lasagna from the refrigerator, she decided to make her new neighbors a nice meal as a peace offering. Lasagna and peach cobbler. Not the vegetable lasagna she preferred, but a nice, hearty lasagna with lots of beef. It was possible the children next door didn't get enough protein. Most kids didn't, since they were usually drawn to junk food. At least, that's what everything she saw and read led her to believe. There were no children in her everyday life, no nieces or nephews, no little ones she saw regularly. Several of her friends had young children, but though she heard details of their lives, that didn't mean Lauren saw them more than once or twice a year. Girlfriend lunches and the occasional margarita were not exactly child-friendly gatherings.

Whether the Donovan children got enough protein or not, everyone liked lasagna, and her grandmother's peach cobbler was to die for. That should suffice as a "sorry I made an ass out of myself" offering.

While the vegetable lasagna was warming in the microwave, Lauren poured herself a glass of iced tea. She straightened the other single-serving-size containers of lasagna on the second shelf of the fridge. Like the cabinets in her kitchen, everything in the refrigerator had a place. The fridge and everything inside it was sparkling clean, and the bottled water was lined up neatly between the skim milk and the pitcher of tea she'd made last night.

Her entire house was like the fridge. Everything had a place; disorder was not allowed. She wasn't OCD, not by any means, but she liked everything to be clean, and if there were specific places for items then those items might as well be in those places. That made perfect sense to her.

Lauren ate her lunch at the kitchen nook, overlooking her well-kept backyard. As she ate she mentally went over her schedule for the rest of the day. The edits, thirty minutes on the treadmill, then a shower. Dinner with Gran and Miss Patsy at six, and after that she'd stop by the grocery store. Tomorrow after she finished the edits and dropped them off at FedEx, she'd make the lasagna and peach cobbler.

At the moment the neighboring backyard was as quiet as her own, and she had her schedule set for the next two days. All was well. For now.

The kids had been quiet for a good half hour or so. They must really be feeling guilty about that broken window. Whatever the reason for the rare moment of silence, Cole would take it. He made a couple of phone calls—including one to a glass company to arrange for the neighbor's window to be repaired—and then he sat in front of the computer. Hank had used the family computer last, and it was still on his favorite site for games. This particular favorite was a Dad-approved site, as Cole insisted they all be. He checked the history, to make sure none of the kids had wandered too far astray. While he tried to watch them when they were using the computer, it was impossible to keep an eye on the kids 24/7. One child, maybe, but three? He was constantly being pulled in all directions. It wasn't that he didn't trust the kids, but these days you couldn't be too careful. There were a lot of weirdos out there, and children were trusting by nature.

Finding no offenders in the computer history, Cole went to Google and typed in his neighbor's name. Lauren Russell. He wasn't sure what he was looking for, exactly, but these days it made sense to check up on the people who came to your door. No matter how cute they were. The kids were unerringly trusting; he was not.

Even though he'd gone into the search with no expectations, he was surprised by what he found. First of all, the picture of Lauren that was at the top of the first page of her website was not at all flattering. Her hair had been pulled back tight, entirely out of her face, and she wore one of those fake picture-smiles, like she was literally saying *cheese*. Was that a turtleneck? Did they even make those anymore? She hadn't been wearing enough makeup when the photo had been taken, and the harsh lights had washed her out. But it was her.

He liked her better mad and in her pajamas, hair in a sloppy ponytail with bangs and escaping strands falling into her face, and eyes flashing. She looked better in natural light, with no makeup at all and fury coloring her face with a natural blush.

If he hadn't been looking for her specifically, he never would've found this site. It was all recipes and decorating and table etiquette. In the Donovan house they ate a lot of fish sticks and spaghetti out of a can, their decorations were almost all made by the kids—they'd outgrown the limited space on the fridge door long ago and had moved on to the walls—and proper etiquette at the table meant you didn't stand on it while anyone else was eating.

When they'd been living in Birmingham, Janet had provided a lot of their meals. She'd dropped by every weekend to stock the freezer with casseroles and home-made soup and chili. But they hadn't relied on her en-tirely. Cole refused to let himself rely on anyone for anything. He could find his way around the kitchen, and for the past year Meredith had been learning to cook. He'd done his best to help her, but talk about the blind leading the blind…

A couple days a week Meredith insisted on making supper. Alone. She saw herself as the woman of the house, and like it or not, she was. Cole didn't want her to spend her youth taking care of her brothers—and him—and he did his best to make sure she was just a child for a while longer. But it wouldn't hurt her to learn to pre-pare a meal or two. She was already a whiz at making coffee. Maybe because all the kids had learned that their dad wasn't fit company until after he'd had his caffeine fix, and it made the morning much easier if the coffee was ready when he rolled out of bed.

Lauren Russell's website was mind-boggling and more than a little amusing. Apparently his cute neigh-bor was some kind of Southern Martha Stewart wan-nabe. She made Easter-egg dye out of onion skins and created elaborate handmade valentines for her friends and family. She'd posted recipes and detailed instruc-tions for making fried chicken, biscuits and cornbread, as well as a multitude of fried vegetables. There were recipes for making candy bars, of all things, and home-made ice-cream treats—things easily purchased at the store, so why would anyone bother? Lauren didn't leave out the health-conscious among her readers. There were also recipes for about a hundred ways to cook a chicken breast without frying it, and plenty of methods for cooking veggies without any fat.

Not that he could get his crew to eat a vegetable, except for the household staple french fries. Maybe corn on the cob, if they were feeling adventurous.

Cole closed the website and shut down the web browser. It didn't matter how cute his neighbor—or any other woman—might be. It wasn't that he was still in love with Mary, five years after her death. It wasn't as if he compared every woman he met to his late wife, or idealized her after she was gone, or pined for what they'd had. No, he simply had no time for a woman.

He *had* dated since Mary had died. After she'd been gone a couple of years, well-meaning friends had tried time and again to set him up with women they thought were suitable. He'd dated, leaving the kids with Janet or a babysitter for a couple of hours, but something always went wrong. He had no patience for airheads, no matter how pretty they were. Some of his friends seemed to think "hot" was enough. It wasn't. And no matter how he'd tried, he hadn't been able to entirely leave his home life behind. Babysitters called. Meredith called. While his dates droned on about shoes or movies or—heaven forbid—baseball, his mind had always been elsewhere.

During one memorable emergency trip home, Justin had thrown up on airhead number two. Or had it been airhead number three? During another, Hank had wiped a glob of jelly from his face with the hem of a silk dress. While his date had been wearing it. Cole had found it kind of funny. His date had not. None of the other dates had gone any better, and it hadn't taken long for him to just give up.

Maybe when his children were grown he could take

some time for himself, if he didn't completely forget how to treat a woman, what to do with one. But for now he was all the kids had, and they deserved every bit of him that he had to give. He was already spread too thin, and having a woman in his life would probably stretch him to the breaking point. Like any woman would be satisfied with the little he had to give at this time in his life.

Even though it was going to be a real change, he was looking forward to starting work again. Teaching would be very different from the career he'd left behind, but he liked history, and he loved baseball. He was good with kids—he'd found a healthy reserve of patience in the past five years—and he'd discovered that he was much more adaptable than he'd ever thought he could be. In the past few years he'd searched for a new career he could really enjoy and worked part-time here and there, selling cars—a job he'd hated—and working in a sporting goods store—even worse—and along the way he'd managed to take enough classes to fulfill the requirements for a teaching job.

A full-time teaching job and coaching a high-school baseball team would take up much more time than any of the endeavors he'd undertaken in the past few years. Three kids and a demanding job wouldn't leave him any time at all for a social life that extended beyond putt-putt or a movie with the kids.

Besides, they'd probably have a fit if he started dating again. And heaven forbid he should get serious about a woman! They'd lost their mother. They wouldn't lose their dad, too, not even a small piece of him. It was bad enough that he'd finally taken on such a demanding job. The money he'd saved while he'd been playing combined with Mary's insurance payout and his own ability to manage his investments well had allowed him to limit his time away from home until Justin was old enough to start kindergarten. Come August, the youngest Donovan would be in school. And Cole would be taking on the job of history teacher and baseball coach for the new high school. He could continue to live as they had for several more years—hell, if he was really smart with his money he might never have to work again—but he needed a real job. He needed to refocus his energies and...move on. It was time.

Cole wasn't sure how he'd handle teaching others to play, when he still sometimes longed for the crack of the bat and the thrill of the game. But he'd manage. He'd get the job done. What choice did he have?

The Gardens was an upscale retirement village, with condos, small houses and an apartment building, all arranged like any gated community. There were lots of trees, ample parking, winding sidewalks, several green spaces and a community center. The only differences between this and other communities like it were the personnel, the nurses and administrators who were available at the push of a button, and the ages of the residents. The prices were outrageous, but Gran considered her condo here a worthwhile investment. It didn't look like a retirement home, but it had all the advantages.

Once a week Lauren had supper with Gran and her best friend, Patsy, who lived in one of the houses in the village with her husband of nearly sixty years. They all took turns providing the food, even though they always met at Gran's condo. This week it was Gran's turn to cook, which thrilled Lauren. Not only did she not have to cook, or endure one of Miss Patsy's mystery casseroles, she got to indulge in the food she'd grown up with. Fried green tomatoes; meatloaf; mashed potatoes; cornbread; fried chicken; green beans that had been cooking all day so that they no longer actually resembled green beans at all; squash casserole—an exception to the casserole rule; pot roast that melted in your mouth and desserts that were always out of this world. She didn't know what tonight's menu would be, but it would be wonderful, and the smells and tastes would transport her to her childhood.

Gran's house, a sprawling ranch she hadn't lived in for the past three years, had always been Lauren's inspiration. Rather, it was the vivid memory of that house that inspired her. The food, the beauty, the details that went into making a house a home… Without that influence, she'd probably be working in an office somewhere. It wasn't that her own home had been horrible—far from it—but she was an only child and her parents had both worked full-time. Often more than full-time. Though she was a stickler for good manners and, perversely, loved to entertain, Lauren's mother had hated cooking, laundry, anything domestic. There had been times in her life when Lauren had been positive her mother didn't entirely warm to the idea of child-rearing, either.

Her parents now lived in Washington State, about as far from Huntsville, Alabama, as they could get. A couple of great jobs had called them there, and they loved that part of the country. Lauren talked to them at least once a month, and they usually made it to Huntsville for a yearly visit, often around the holidays. There were frequent emails. Lauren loved her parents, but it had been her grandmother who'd made her house a home, who'd offered time, hearty hugs and homemade cookies.

That hadn't changed.

Patsy was already at Gran's condo when Lauren arrived, and the two older women were chatting as they set the table. For these weekly dinners Gran always used her good china, cloth napkins, polished silverware and crystal glasses for the decaffeinated iced tea. Life was too short, she said, not to use the best of everything at every opportunity. The smells from the kitchen were tantalizing, and Lauren couldn't help but smile as she walked in and called out a friendly "Hello."

The two ladies, like the table, were at their best. Both of them were white-haired and tastefully made-up, and tonight they both wore colorful summer dresses. Miss Patsy was thinner than Gran, a couple of inches taller, and was never seen out and about without enough jewelry to outfit three women.

Gran was more of a minimalist when it came to jewelry. She still wore her wedding band, and tonight she also wore small pearl earrings. Her hair was cut very short and spiked around her head, while Miss Patsy had pulled her long hair up into a bun, as usual.

Not wanting to be underdressed, Lauren had worn a lavender sundress and white sandals, tiny diamond studs in her ears and her hair down instead of in its usual ponytail.

There were hugs all around, then the three women carried dishes from the kitchen to the dining room table. Beyond the table the curtains at the doors, which opened onto a small patio, were pulled back to offer a relaxing view of a perfectly well-kept outdoor space with a wrought-iron table and chairs, hanging tomato plants, potted herbs and flowers. Past the patio a community green space was deserted and perfectly manicured. No kids at all. Lauren couldn't help but wonder how old one had to be to move here….

After they sat in their usual places, and Gran began by passing the meatloaf, Miss Patsy asked Lauren if she'd had a nice day. That was all it took for Lauren to tell the older ladies about the day's frustrations. The noise, the broken window, the man next door. She even told them how she'd stormed out of the house in her pajamas and bunny slippers, which gave everyone—even her—a good laugh. In hindsight it *was* pretty funny. After she'd told them how a repairman had shown up within a couple of hours to fix the broken window, she mentioned what she'd found online about her neighbor.

Gran carefully put down her fork and stared at Lauren as she finished her story. She wasn't smiling, not that Lauren's neighbor's history was much to smile about. When Lauren finished sharing what she knew, Gran leaned forward just a little bit.

"Is this neighbor's name Whiplash Donovan?"

Lauren was surprised. She hadn't mentioned the man's name because it wasn't important. It wasn't as if he would ever meet these two ladies. "Donovan is the last name, but he didn't introduce himself as Whiplash. His first name is Cole."

Gran waved that detail off, literally, with a sweep of her hand. "That's him, has to be! I can't believe it, Whiplash Donovan living right next door to my granddaughter. This is so exciting!"

"Whiplash?" Lauren asked suspiciously.

"He could hit the ball so far and fast, you'd get whiplash trying to keep an eye on it. You know your grandfather was a huge fan of the Atlanta team."

"Of course."

"Well, I was never as fanatical about baseball as he was, but I did follow the game. What choice did I have when he was always watching it on television or listening to the games on the radio? Even after he passed I watched when I could." She gave a small, sad smile. "It made me feel closer to him, as if we were still rooting for the team together even though he was gone."

Pops had been gone four years, and this was a detail of Gran's life Lauren had never known. Sure, she remembered Pops watching sports on television, and wearing those team T-shirts and ball caps, but it wasn't a passion grandfather and granddaughter had shared. They'd gardened together, played games, made homemade birthday cards, assembled endless puzzles....

Gran shook off her melancholy, again with a literal wave of her hand. "Donovan was one of your grandfather's favorites. He so wanted to see that record broken. When Whiplash's wife died and he walked away he took a lot of heat. Many of the fans were very upset with him. A lot of them simply didn't understand." Her chin came up. "But I did. Donovan put his family first—before fame, before money. Baseball players spend so much time on the road, there's no way he'd be able to raise his children and continue to play. He made a choice, and I never for a moment doubted that it was the right one. You have to admire a man who has his priorities in order that way."

Lauren almost grimaced. She didn't have to admire her neighbor. She just had to deliver a peace-offering food and get out of the way.

Getting out of the way was what *she* did best.

Lauren's grandmother reached for a second helping of fried okra. "So, tell me, is he still gorgeous?"

"Gran!" Lauren said, trying to put a hint of shock and disapproval in her voice. Anything to avoid answering with a resounding *yes*.

The older women laughed, and Lauren took a long, slow bite of meatloaf. She chewed deliberately, but eventually she had to swallow. Gran and Miss Patsy were still looking at her. Waiting.

"Fine, yes, he's a handsome man. Some women might consider him gorgeous, I suppose, but he's not my type at all."

"Since when is tall, dark and handsome not your type?" Miss Patsy asked.

Lauren hesitated, and the older women did her the favor of changing the subject. They began to discuss recipes. Normally recipes were one of Lauren's favorite subjects, but her mind was still on Cole Donovan. Just a little. No, that wasn't right. Her mind was on men—or rather, the lack of one in her life.

She was happily single, for the time being. Her attempt at building her life around a man had failed miserably, and she was in no hurry to repeat that mistake. Of course she'd been too young to even think about marriage when she'd allowed hormones to override her common sense, and Billy had been a self-centered jerk. Looking back she could only be relieved that their two-year engagement had ended before she'd actually become his wife. At the same time, she was still annoyed that all the hours she'd spent planning her wedding had been wasted. There had been a couple of other romantic mistakes, misjudgments on her part, but neither of the other mistakes had gone so far.

These days Lauren worked so hard there were no hours to waste, no spare time to sit back and ponder the few failures in her life. Whenever Billy crossed her mind—which wasn't often—he didn't stay there long. He just flitted through like a pesky mosquito, not at all worthy of her attention. The details of the wedding reception she'd planned, however, stayed crisp and clear. Maybe one day the right man would come along and she'd be able to pull out her three-ring binder and start again.

Then again, who had time for men? She didn't. One day, in the foggy, indistinct future, she'd work a man into her busy life. But not anytime soon. There were only so many hours in the day, after all. Where would she pencil romance into her schedule?

If she ever did decide to pencil romance into her schedule, she wouldn't consider a man who had three uncontrollable children. No matter how tall, dark and handsome he might be....

Chapter Three

Cole was surprised to find his neighbor at the door.
Again. He answered her cautiously friendly hello with a
sigh and a "What have they done now?"

Lauren smiled, and as she did he noticed that she held
a very large wicker basket covered with a red-and-white-
checkered towel that looked as if it had never been used
to mop up spilled grape juice or ketchup. She looked
more than a little like Little Red Riding Hood, and he
wanted to eat her up. Did that make him the Big Bad
Wolf?

She lifted the basket a couple of inches. "I've brought
a little something to welcome you to the neighborhood,
and to thank you for getting the window taken care of
so quickly."

What choice had he had? His kids had done the
damage, and he couldn't very well have left Lauren's
house vulnerable overnight. Not that this neighborhood

seemed to be unsafe. It was just common sense. Still, he supposed it would be rude to send her and her basket away, so he stepped back and invited her inside.

She hadn't seemed at all interested in getting to know him yesterday, when he'd made a fumbling attempt at being neighborly. Maybe something had changed her mind. Then again, maybe she was just more sociable when she was wearing a bra.

Her eyes scanned the living room, and he knew very well what she saw. The laundry he'd been folding on the couch, the half-finished puzzle on the coffee table, the toys Justin had been playing with and left scattered about. If he'd known she was coming he would've picked up a bit, but since she'd dropped by unannounced she'd have to take what she got.

She shifted the basket a bit, and Cole realized it must be heavy. Belatedly, he reached out and took it from her.

"Lasagna and peach cobbler," she said. "The cobbler can sit out for a while, but the lasagna needs to go in the refrigerator." She gave him quick instructions on how to heat it up for supper, then backed toward the door.

"Wait one minute," Cole said, and he turned toward the back of the house and called the kids' names, one at a time. They came running, smiling and laughing, their usual boisterous selves, but when they saw Lauren they skidded to a stop and their smiles died.

"We didn't do anything!" Justin said indignantly.

"Yeah," Hank agreed. "We've been playing video games and Meredith is reading some stupid book."

Meredith didn't say anything, but her eyes narrowed suspiciously.

Cole let them stew for a minute, then said, "Even though you broke Ms. Russell's window and stomped all over her garden, she's brought you supper. Lasagna and peach cobbler. What do you say?"

"I hate lasagna!" Justin said vehemently. "Yuck!"

Hank shuffled his feet and looked at the floor, and Meredith rolled her eyes in that maddening way young girls had. Twelve years old, and he could already see the woman she was going to become. Soon. That vision scared the crap out of him. He wasn't ready for her to grow up, wasn't ready for boyfriends and dates and short skirts and makeup. But like it or not, those things were coming.

"I was going to make chicken fingers for supper," Meredith said.

Like frozen chicken strips could hold a candle to homemade lasagna—an observation he didn't dare make out loud. "The chicken fingers can wait for another day. I want you all to thank Ms. Russell." He gave them a glare his neighbor couldn't see, since his back was to her. It was a rarely used glare that told the kids he was serious. He'd spoiled them for too long; he'd indulged them, trying to make up for the fact that he was all they had. Just last year he'd realized that he'd done that, and he was trying to undo the damage. It was a slow process.

Meredith was the first to speak. "Thank you, Ms. Russell." Her chin was lifted a touch too high, which made her appear defiant even though her words were proper enough. Her eyes were anything but friendly.

Hank was antsy. The middle child was never still, unless he was sleeping. "I like lasagna," he said, taking his eyes off the floor to peek up at their neighbor and give her a gentle, oddly charming, mostly toothless smile. "And I'm really tired of Meredith's chicken fingers. Thanks."

Justin, the stubborn one, sighed. "Thank you, Ms.

Russell. For the peach cobbler." The youngest—who would live on chicken strips and honey mustard if given the option—was doing his best not to look directly at his father.

"Why don't y'all call me Miss Lauren," their neighbor said. "After all, I imagine we'll be seeing a lot of each other." She looked directly at Justin. "I'm very sorry to hear that you don't like lasagna. Tell me, what do you like? Just in case I cook for you again, I should know."

Justin wasn't shy about answering. "I like chicken fingers, hot dogs and Pop Tarts and chocolate chip cookies and ice cream." He lifted a stubby little finger. "But not butter-pecan ice cream. Yuck. That's worse than lasagna."

Lauren worked to suppress a smile. Her lips firmed as she resisted, but Cole could see the laughter in her eyes. It was a good—and oddly enticing—look for her. "I'll keep that in mind."

Cole dismissed the kids and they returned to their activities, leaving him alone with Lauren—and the food. She took a step back, toward the door. It was almost as if she was trying not to look directly at him.

"Thank you again," he said. "You really didn't have to, but we'll enjoy it."

She nodded, and still her eyes were everywhere but on him. Had he done something to piss her off? He couldn't think of anything he might've done to make her nervous, but she was definitely uncomfortable. Out of her element. She'd been fine when he'd answered the door, okay when the kids had been with them, but now that they were alone again it was like she couldn't wait to get away.

"You can just drop the pans off on the porch when

you're finished with them," she said. "No rush. I have more than enough cookware."

Cole peeked beneath the warm cloth that covered the food. Sure enough, the food had been prepared and delivered in heavy glass dishes instead of disposable aluminum foil. No wonder the basket weighed so much!

When he returned his gaze to Lauren, he found her no longer avoiding him. In fact, she stared right at him and for a moment, a long, lingering, uncomfortable moment, she looked as if she were completely and totally lost and confused. He recognized the pained expression on her pretty face because he saw it in the mirror almost every day.

It took all of Lauren's discipline not to run home and slam the door behind her. She walked with purpose, almost positive that someone was watching her through a window or from the front porch. Tempted as she was, she didn't run and she didn't look back.

She should've just let things go. If she hadn't decided that the family next door could use a good meal and she needed to make amends, she might not have suffered that moment of clarity. She might've simply resigned herself to the increased neighborhood noise and looked forward to school starting in a few weeks. Once school began she'd have several quiet hours every day.

But for a moment, a long, horrifying moment, she had suffered. Her life was perfect. She loved her job. She loved her house. She had friends and family, though in her small family only Gran lived close enough to see on a regular basis. Lauren never *ever* missed having a man in her life. She didn't have time for a man, didn't want one, didn't miss the messy complications of a romantic relationship. She remembered too well what it had felt like to lose what she'd thought was love, to have the rug pulled out from under her. One day she'd meet a man and fall in love, though next time she intended to be more careful, to be cautious and wait until her career was more well established and then…only then…

A man with three kids was not in her plan. Not only was the time not right, she had no intention of taking on an entire family. Perhaps one day she'd have a child of her own. One, when the time was right. Preferably a little girl, but a son would be acceptable. Not that she planned to rush into anything. She wasn't yet thirty. There was plenty of time to find the right man, wait a while to make sure she wasn't mistaken this time around, and only then, perhaps, a child.

Her life was carefully ordered, and though she'd only admitted so to a few close friends, she had a wish list for the perfect man. Among the requirements were no jocks and no kids. Jocks were often self-centered and since she wasn't at all interested in sports that would be a problem right off the bat. Stepchildren were always a complication. Why ask for trouble?

But she'd watched Cole Donovan as he'd spoken to his children, and her heart had done a decided flip. She'd felt a flutter in her chest. She'd also felt an unexpected flutter a good bit lower. Why was it that a totally unsuitable man who obviously loved his children made her biological clock kick into gear as if it had been jump-started with an electric jolt?

The broad shoulders, big hands and blue eyes hadn't helped matters at all. The way his jeans fit and the fascinating muscles in his forearms had been an unwanted distraction. She'd noticed that he'd recently shaved, and the sharp line of his jaw was more than a little interesting. She'd very much wanted to reach out and touch him, just lay one finger on a muscle or that nice jaw to see how warm he was, how hard.

Not only that, the way Justin had looked into her eyes as he'd made it very clear that he didn't like lasagna had grabbed her heart and made her fight off an inappropriate smile. Hank was absolutely charming, and Meredith was a beautiful girl with vulnerability too easily seen, in spite of her attempt at cold dismissal.

His house was a mess, his kids—charming though they might occasionally be—were uncontrollable, and the disruption of having this family next door was ruining Lauren's once neatly organized life.

But she couldn't deny that they possessed something she didn't. There had been so much love in the room that it had washed over her like a tidal wave. She hadn't expected that strong emotion, hadn't wanted it, and she certainly didn't want to be a part of it.

Who was she kidding? She would never be a part of anything like what she'd discovered at the house next door. It wasn't in her plan, didn't fit into her life, and any strange compulsion she had to cook for Justin and touch Cole Donovan had to be squelched. Now.

They hadn't had a meal like this one since they'd moved away from Birmingham and Janet's frequent offerings. Even though Cole had told her time and time again that it wasn't necessary for her to cook for them, he'd looked forward to the meals his sister-in-law had prepared for them. He'd tried to learn, and he had mastered a few basics, but he wasn't a very good cook. Meredith was going to surpass him in the cooking department in no time.

Though Justin had insisted that he didn't like lasagna, after watching his sister and brother dive into theirs he'd taken a hesitant bite. Now he was relishing his food, just as Hank and Meredith were. The frozen stuff he'd tasted a time or two couldn't hold a candle to this.

Hank scraped the last of what was on his plate onto his fork, shoved it into his mouth, and before he swallowed he said, "I think you should date her, Dad."

Cole automatically reminded his middle child not to talk with food in his mouth, and then he added, "I don't date."

"What's a date?" Justin asked.

Meredith answered, "It's when a boy and a girl, or a man and a woman, go out to eat and to a movie. Sometimes they might dance, or go bowling or something." She kept her eyes on her plate.

Hank added, "And then they *kiss*."

"I want to go on a date," Justin said. "But without the kissing. Yuck. Maybe Miss Lauren would take me to the new movie with the talking hamsters and then we could get ice cream. Would that be a good date?"

Meredith took a deep breath. "You're too young for Miss Lauren," she said bitterly. "She wants to date *Dad,* which is why she brought over lasagna and dessert and stared at him like he was one of the Jonas brothers, and do you really think this food was intended for *us?* No, she wants to show off what a good cook she is, and how pretty she is, and if we hadn't been here she probably would've jumped all over Dad and kissed him..."

"Meredith," Cole snapped. "That's enough."

Hank didn't help matters by throwing in a series of smacking sounds. Sounds that ended abruptly when Cole gave him a narrow-eyed glare.

Meredith stared at her plate, but didn't entirely give up the fight. "First we move away from Aunt Janet and all our friends, and now we have *Miss Lauren* next door trying to change *everything*. I'll bet if Justin threw up on her she'd run away crying just like that other woman you dated."

Cole started to chastise his daughter again, and then he saw the lone tear running down her cheek. "That was a long time ago, Mer. I don't date anymore. Who has the time?" And to be honest, the memory of those few dates was enough to warn him away from trying again too soon. Being a full-time dad and trying to have a social life that didn't include his kids didn't mix.

"Nothing's going to change," he said evenly. "I know the house is different, and I'm starting a new job, and you're going to have to make all new friends here in Huntsville, but when it comes to this family…" He knew what Meredith feared, had seen it before. Of the three kids, she was the only one who remembered their mother. Hank and Justin had been too young, but Meredith had been seven. She remembered her mother. Worse, she remembered the pain of losing her mother.

"Nothing and no one will ever come between the four of us. We're a family, and that can't be changed."

"We're the Four Musketeers!" Hank said, emphasizing the importance of this designation by standing on his chair and lifting his fork high, as if it were a sword.

Great. Another fantasy that called for a cape.

"We don't need Miss Lauren," Meredith whispered. "We don't need anyone."

"No," Cole said, his heart sinking unexpectedly. He didn't want to live the rest of his life alone, and he sure as hell didn't enjoy living like a monk. There was something special about Lauren Russell, something that spoke to him in a way no woman had in a very long time. He barely knew her, but since she'd come to his door fuming mad and still in her pajamas, he'd found himself thinking about her more than he should. She was cute, she was smart, she could cook, she had a really nice ass. She made him smile. What man wouldn't think about her? But it wasn't enough. This was his life, for now.

"We don't need anyone." He ordered Hank to sit and added, "Four Musketeers is enough."

Chapter Four

Lauren had lived in her house for three years now, and she never missed the neighborhood Fourth of July cook-out. She'd missed the Christmas party once, thanks to a nasty cold she hadn't wished to share with her neighbors, and she skipped as many of the annual homeowner's association meetings as was possible, but she truly looked forward to the annual cookout.

Her potato salad and homemade cookies were always a hit, and it wasn't as though she got to see her neighbors on a regular basis. Everyone led busy lives; they were constantly on the go. If not for the occasional get-together, she wouldn't know her neighbors at all.

This year Cole Donovan was the newest arrival on the block, so he was the center of attention. Most of the men and several of the women knew very well who he was. More of them followed baseball than Lauren had imagined. They hadn't needed to look up *Whiplash* to find out who he was. No, they'd known him on sight.

He stood in the center of a tight circle of people and answered questions, now and then glancing toward the pool where his kids swam with other neighborhood children. There were lots of children in the neighborhood, but until the Donovans had moved in none of them had been so close by, or so loud. Most of the children who were of an age to be boisterous were in some kind of day care, since so many of them came from two-income families. Lauren couldn't help but wonder if she'd now be tuned in to every distant scream and peal of laughter.

She'd been talking recipes with several of the women from the neighborhood while the men all gathered in a knot with Cole at the center. As she had since arriving, Lauren tried not to look at Cole, but she'd seen enough to know that he'd been initially uncomfortable with the attention, though that discomfort was fading as he relaxed and got to know the other men. Lauren smiled and laughed and contributed to the conversation in this part of the large yard. Talk was currently on the evils and benefits of carbs in the diet. All the while, she did her best to act as if she and Cole had never even met. Not that she had to bother. He didn't pay her the least bit of attention. His neglect stung more than she was willing to admit, even though she knew it was for the best.

She had *not* chosen the white shorts and simple white sandals and brand-new turquoise tank with him in mind, though she had instinctively passed over the denim shorts that sagged in the butt and the oversize T-shirt she sometimes wore when she worked in the garden for something more attractive. She'd used more mousse and hairspray than usual, and her hair was down, instead of up in the ponytail that would've been more appropriate for such a hot day. But that had nothing to do with the fact that her neighbor was going to be here. Nothing at all.

Some of the men peeled away from the circle to tend the grills, while Juliet Smith and a couple of her closest friends scurried off to the kitchen to make a few last-minute arrangements. Children of all shapes and sizes ran and laughed and splashed in the pool. Without looking, Lauren could pick out the screams of the Donovan children. They were the loudest, and they were strangely and disturbingly familiar.

Summer Schuler, who lived several doors down on the opposite side of the street, sidled up to Lauren and smiled as she leaned in very close. "Your new neighbor is a hunk and a half."

"Is he?" Lauren said coolly. "I hadn't noticed."

Summer laughed, then took a long swig of sweet iced tea from her red plastic cup. "You're very together, Lauren, but you're not blind. And you're a terrible liar to boot. Of course you've noticed. He's single, you're single…."

"He has three children whose only operating speed is full blast…." Lauren added.

Summer laughed again and placed a friendly hand on Lauren's arm. "No man is perfect."

And didn't Lauren know that well enough….

Summer lowered her voice. "I know he doesn't exactly fit all the requirements on your list, but he *is* healthy. And I'm sure he has a wonderful sense of humor."

"He's a jock, he has three kids and he's too tall."

Summer's eyebrows shot up, and not for the first time Lauren had the thought that Summer was improperly named. She had black hair, black eyebrows, dark brown eyes. She didn't look at all like a Summer. "You've added a height requirement?"

"He should be no more than five foot ten. Five-eleven, tops."

"Why?"

"I shouldn't get a crick in my neck every time I talk face-to-face with a man who's a part of my life."

"Girl, you have gone off the deep end. You'd throw a man over for a couple of inches?" Summer bit her lower lip. "Let me rephrase that. It's not like Donovan is freakishly tall, or anything. He's *very* nicely proportioned."

Didn't she know it....

"Invest in a pair of *really* high heels," Summer suggested with a grin.

Lauren's initial thought had been a stepladder, but heels would be more practical. She hadn't worn *really* high heels in years, but she wondered...

Summer continued while Lauren's mind was on shoe shopping. "You need to toss that list. Finding a man isn't like making a cake. There's no recipe for a husband, no list of necessary ingredients."

Lauren started a bit, jerked out of her shoe-related thoughts. Husband? Who'd said anything about a *husband?*

The piercing scream that followed the thought caused Lauren's gut to turn over. She—and everyone else present—turned toward the scream, which was followed by a moment of horrifying silence.

All the children who stood by the pool were very still, for a change. Those in the water treaded in place. One child was down, there at the side of the pool near the steps. Down and completely still. The scream had been Meredith's.

Cole broke away from the group of men and ran. Others were soon right behind him. Lauren drifted in that direction, though she was certain Cole Donovan didn't want her help. There were more than a dozen adults present, and judging by the way he'd ignored her today, not even so much as nodding his head in her direction or waving halfheartedly or making eye contact, he'd prefer assistance from any neighbor here before he called on her. Besides, most of the adults here had children, or grandchildren, and surely they'd been through disasters like this one before. They'd know what to do. They were much better equipped than she was to help out.

And still, Lauren moved forward. There were too many people in the way, but she had to know who was down. She elbowed her way past the hefty man who'd moved into the two-story at the end of the street last year and ducked around a surly teenager dressed all in black. Her eyes soon found Hank and Meredith in the crowd, so the one who was hurt was Justin, the little one. The one who didn't like lasagna—who didn't like *her*.

Cole squatted down, examined his youngest son, then whipped off his T-shirt and pressed it against Justin's temple. He scooped up his son and stood in one smooth motion. Blood ran down one side of the little boy's face, in spite of the makeshift bandage, but he was conscious and talking. Lauren couldn't hear what Justin was saying, but she noted that while he had begun to cry he was not hysterical.

His father was another matter. Cole had gone pale. The hands that held his son were shaking. Subtly, but she saw the tremble even from a distance. A couple of people tried to help, but Cole practically bit their heads off as he headed out of the yard at a fast clip, his long legs carrying him away from the party. Meredith and Hank followed. Meredith was crying, too, and she explained in a trembling voice that she'd reminded Justin not to run but he hadn't listened. Again, someone asked if they could help and Cole said no. He *barked* no. They were going to the hospital for the stitches Justin obviously needed.

T. J. Smith offered to drive, but Cole shook him off with an expression that cut everyone out, that built a barrier around him and his family and left no room for intruders.

Lauren stood completely still for a moment. She didn't need to get involved. Cole didn't want her—or anyone else—to intrude. Justin was conscious, and head wounds did bleed a lot. The child needed stitches, but he'd be fine. He hadn't lost consciousness, which was a good sign. Right? That was all true, but dammit, there was no way she could let Cole get in the car and drive, not in his condition.

She turned to Summer. "I have to go." Lauren didn't give her friend a chance to respond, she just turned and ran, cutting around the other side of the house and across the street to intercept Cole and his crew.

It was a simple gash, bleeding heavily but not life threatening. So why was his heart beating so hard that he couldn't see straight? The sight of all that blood on Justin's head and face made Cole's stomach turn. A part of the T-shirt he'd pressed to the wound was already soaked through. He couldn't bear it if anything happened to his son. He couldn't live with himself if it turned out Janet was right and he was incapable of raising these three kids alone.

If she found out what had happened, would she try to take the kids away from him? He sometimes suspected that she wanted to, and he knew she'd been angry that he'd moved two hours away, taking all she had left of her sister with him. She hadn't made a secret of her displeasure.

His worse fear was that Janet might be right, that he might not be enough for his family.

He threw open the door to the minivan and carefully deposited Justin on the backseat. He didn't want to let go of the kid, didn't want to leave Justin—a ball of fire who was currently pale and bloody and not at all himself—alone. The door on the other side opened and Meredith jumped in. Cole reached into his pants pocket and grabbed his keys, glad they were in his pocket as usual and not sitting on the dresser or hanging on a key rack where he'd have to retrieve them. Nothing could slow him down, nothing could stand between him and help for his son.

Cole had just swung open the driver's door when a sharp *'Wait'* made him freeze in his tracks. His neighbor Lauren ran to the van. Without asking if he wanted or needed help she started issuing orders. "Meredith, you and Hank run inside and throw on dry clothes. Grab a clean shirt for your father. The hospital keeps the air at full blast in the summertime, and y'all will catch a cold if you go in wearing your swimsuits." As they ran for the front door, which Cole had left unlocked since they were going to be right across the street, Lauren yelled after them. "And bring a clean hand towel and a blanket for Justin."

Justin lifted his head and glared at Lauren. It looked to Cole as if the bleeding had already slowed. "I knew you wanted to date my dad. You're not going to kiss him, are you?"

Lauren looked a little surprised—her eyebrows lifted slightly, and her lips thinned—but she responded calmly.

"First of all, a trip to the emergency room isn't a date, and secondly, I don't date." She didn't mention the kiss.

"Why not?" Justin asked.

Yeah, Cole thought. *Why not?*

"I'm a very busy woman," Lauren said. "I have no time for dating."

"Oh," Justin said. He looked more than a little relieved, and surely Lauren noted the fact. "Dad doesn't date, either."

Just a few minutes later, Meredith and Hank ran out of the house. They were both dressed in khaki shorts and plain T-shirts, and Meredith carried a towel, a clean T-shirt for her dad and a well-worn blanket.

"I locked the door," Meredith called as she ran for the backseat and her little brother.

Lauren took charge without missing a beat. She took the towel from Meredith, peeled back the bloody T-shirt and placed the towel against Justin's wound, pressing down with one hand while with the other she snatched away Cole's keys without even glancing his way. Sneaky woman.

"You can't possibly drive," she said. "You're shaking like a leaf."

Cole wanted to argue that he was perfectly capable of driving, but he didn't. She was right.

"Besides, they're doing construction on Governor's Drive, and I know a shortcut to the E.R."

Cole climbed into the backseat with Justin and Hank, and Meredith took the front seat, beside Lauren. He pulled on the clean T-shirt before repositioning Justin so he could hold him as he put pressure on the wound. Cole was grateful to be able to hold on to his son while someone else drove them to the E.R., but at the same time a little warning bell went off in his head.

He *could* do this alone. He didn't need anyone but his children. And to become dependent on his pretty neighbor at this point in his life would be foolish beyond belief.

Lauren shivered. Knowing how cool the E.R. would be, she should've grabbed a sweater. Her toes were cold. Her arms were cold. At the same time, she knew if she'd run inside her house to collect anything, Cole would've taken off without her.

Without a shirt. Was it wrong of her to have taken note of how amazing he looked without a shirt? Sculpted muscles, wide shoulders, slightly hairy chest, not even a hint of a pot belly. This was a crisis, and *all* of her attention really should've been on the injured child. And to be fair, she'd only given a shirtless Cole Donovan a small bit of her attention. Just enough to note that he must still work out, because muscles like that did *not* come from folding laundry and eating chicken fingers. Just enough to be surprised that he had a tattoo on his shoulder—a small baseball with flames shooting out behind it, as if it were flying past a particularly nice muscle.

Cole and Justin had been taken back a while ago, leaving Lauren in the waiting room with a sullen Meredith and a scared Hank. Meredith actually leaned away from Lauren, and probably would've taken another seat if there had been one available. On a holiday weekend the E.R. was packed, and the only empty chair was next to a dubious-looking character. Lauren was relieved that she ranked above a constantly mumbling man with a scraggly beard and a nasty rash.

Hank was another story entirely. He leaned into Lauren, resting his head on her arm, taking her hand and holding on. Somehow he managed to hang on without ever being entirely still. He hadn't said much, but his attitude toward her was decidedly warmer than his sister's.

Eventually he lifted his head and looked up at Lauren with the biggest blue eyes she'd ever seen. He had his father's eyes. In fact, Hank and his younger brother were both little carbon copies of their dad. And he whispered, "Justin's not going to die, is he?"

Lauren's heart broke for the child. "Oh, no, honey. Justin is going to be just fine." She should've said something before now, should've soothed the child's fears hours ago, but she hadn't even considered that they'd be worried the injury was more serious than it was. Deadly serious. "He'll have a boo-boo on his head, and he might have a headache for a while, but he's going to be just fine."

Meredith scoffed and muttered, "Boo-boo?"

Lauren ignored her.

"My mother is dead," Hank said. "I don't remember her, but Dad shows me pictures and tells me stories about her."

Lauren felt as if a brick had settled in her chest. She didn't know what to say, what to do to soothe a child who knew more about death than he should. "I know," she whispered.

"Dad told us not to run around the pool," Hank said, relaxing visibly. "But one of the other kids started chasing Justin, and he just…"

"She doesn't *care,* Hank," Meredith said coolly. "Don't talk her ear off."

It would be easiest just to ignore Meredith and settle back into silence. But these kids and their father were going to be her neighbors for a long while. It would be easiest if they could find a way to get along.

Lauren didn't let go of Hank's hand, but she turned toward Meredith and gave the young girl her full attention. Meredith must look like her mother, because she didn't look much like Cole at all. The nose, maybe a bit through the mouth. But she had blond hair and dark brown eyes, and a heart-shaped face that was almost pixielike. She was almost as tall as Lauren. And right now there was so much anger on that pretty face. "I do care," Lauren said softly.

"You're just trying to impress my dad." Meredith turned her head so she was no longer looking at Lauren. "He's famous, and you don't have a husband or a boyfriend, and if you're nice to us it's just because you want to impress him."

"To be honest, Meredith, your dad *used* to be famous, I don't want or need a husband or a boyfriend, and I'm nice to you because you're my neighbor. I don't go out of my way to impress anyone. Good manners and a willingness to help should be extended to everyone." Okay, so she was channeling her grandmother on that last one. That didn't mean it wasn't true.

"There are baseball cards with his picture on them," Meredith whispered.

"I don't collect baseball cards. I really don't care for the sport much at all. Truthfully, I find baseball to be slow and boring."

"You swear," Meredith said sullenly.

"What am I swearing to?"

"That you're not being nice just to get your hands on my dad."

Lauren sighed. True, Cole Donovan was the best-looking man she'd seen in a long time, even when he forgot to shave. Something about him caused an instinctive physical reaction that she worked very hard to resist.

Good heavens, she was no longer seventeen and unable to control her raging hormones! She could probably write off any physical reaction to him to her ticking biological clock, and the fact that, well, it *had* been a while. But while he might be single, he was not unencumbered. In fact, he was the most *encumbered* man she'd ever met.

"I swear. And if you don't mind a bit of advice from another woman…you'll be dating before you know it and I have to tell you, you really can't go out there thinking you can or should become someone you're not in order to catch a man. You should always, *always* be yourself, because you don't want a boy to like you for being someone you're not." This was not her forte. "You don't want to catch a man at all, you want to *find* the right man. Finding and catching are very different, if you think about it. Be yourself, like yourself, and run as fast as you possibly can from any boy who wants you to change. Does that make any sense?"

The expression on Meredith's face softened considerably. "Kinda."

"You want a boyfriend who will like you for who you are."

"Dad says I'm not allowed to have a boyfriend. Ever."

Lauren smiled. "I'm sure he doesn't mean it. How old are you?"

"Twelve. Twelve and a half. I'm really *almost* thirteen."

"You're a little young now for a boyfriend, but the day will come."

Meredith squirmed a bit. She shifted more toward Lauren, just as Hank decided to put his head on Lauren's lap and close his eyes. Finally, he was still.

"You said you don't date," Meredith said softly. "Why not?"

Lauren didn't want to explain to the young girl that she had a bad track record, that she no longer trusted her own instincts where men were concerned, that she was afraid of the pain that could—*would*—follow a bad romance. "My career is very important to me," she said. "I really don't have time for dating. There's more to life than…dating."

For a long moment they sat there in silence. Hank soon fell asleep, and his breathing became deep and even. Meredith relaxed visibly, her entire body unwinding and her expression softening.

After a while, Meredith said, "Since we're talking about girl stuff, do you think that, you know, maybe you could teach me how to use makeup? I mean, one day, if you have the time and aren't doing anything."

"You have such a beautiful face, you don't need…" Lauren stopped when she recognized her grandmother coming through again. "If your father agrees, I don't see why we can't have a session or two on the proper application of makeup. The trick is to learn to apply it so lightly no one will be able to tell you're wearing makeup at all. You should look like you, only better."

For the first time, Lauren saw Meredith smile. That was it, that was what she had of her father. Her smile. Something about it caught Lauren's heart and held on tight. Meredith leaned against Lauren's arm and closed her eyes. Hank slept on, oblivious to his surroundings. And Lauren was no longer chilled.

"Maybe you can show me how to make that lasagna, too," Meredith said softly. "It was really good."

"You're very young to be cooking," Lauren said. "At your age, all I could make was oatmeal cookies and peas and asparagus casserole."

"Well, Dad's not a very good cook. I try to help out, when I can."

Lauren tried to picture Cole in the kitchen. It wasn't easy. Nothing about him screamed *domestic*. "That's very admirable, Meredith."

The young girl grasped Lauren's arm and relaxed. Her eyes drifted closed. That's how they were positioned when Cole and Justin returned to the waiting room. Cole remained pale but was no longer shaking, and Justin had a large bandage on his head but otherwise appeared to be fine. For a moment, Lauren's eyes met Cole's. She felt a connection to her core, and it was so strong it actually jolted her. He stopped in his tracks, stared into her eyes and almost pulled back, as if he'd felt the same thing.

Attraction. An awareness of one another. A physical response and an instinctive awareness of…possibility.

And absolutely no chance that whatever they felt would actually work in the real world.

Lauren relaxed as she turned onto her street and saw the welcoming light of her front porch ahead. It had been a very long, very *strange* day. She wanted a cup of hot tea, a warm shower, soft pajamas and a good night's sleep.

She pulled the van into the Donovan driveway. All was quiet, since the kids had all dozed off on the way home, and Cole hadn't said a word since they'd pulled out of the hospital parking lot.

"Thanks," he said softly as she shut off the engine. "I don't know what we would have done without your help."

"No problem." She wanted to run for home—tea, shower, pajamas, bed—but as she stepped out of the van and the kids roused, Hank called out.

"Miss Lauren, will you tuck me in?" His voice was

sleepy; he'd probably drift back into dreamland the moment his head hit the pillow.

"Miss Lauren's done enough," Cole said, his voice perhaps a touch sharp. Maybe that was just exhaustion she heard.

"Please," Hank said, drawing the word out to the end of a breath. There was so much heart in his voice, Lauren couldn't say no. She told herself it would be a short delay.

"I'd be happy to tuck you in," she said, helping the little boy from the backseat as Cole carried Justin to the front door and unlocked it. Meredith yawned as she made her way to the door. As Lauren and Hank walked in that direction, Hank took her hand. His hand was incredibly small, so soft and trusting.

Meredith yawned again and said good-night, and Justin roused just long enough to ask if he could sleep with his dad tonight. Cole agreed, and carried his youngest son toward the master bedroom.

Hank turned on the light to his bedroom, which was messy but clean. Action figures lined the shelves and the dresser, and an open toy chest held an array of water guns, a couple of plastic dragons and balls in every size and color. A watercolor of some sort of mythical beast had been framed and hung above the bed. Most of the dirty clothes had made it into the hamper, and the bed was made. It was not made well, but there had been a valiant attempt.

"I think you're awesome," Hank said sleepily as he opened a drawer and pulled out a pair of mismatched pajamas. "You should have some kids of your own, and then I'd have someone else to play with."

"You have a brother and a sister to play with."

"Yeah, but they don't always want to play what I want to play. Meredith likes girl stuff."

"Well," Lauren said, "she *is* a girl."

Hank started stripping off his clothes and throwing them toward the hamper. Lauren turned her back, offering him the privacy he obviously didn't care about.

"Don't you like kids?" Hank asked.

"Of course I do."

"I thought so. You'd make a really good mom."

Lauren's heart broke a little, for the child who'd lost his own mother. "Maybe one day," she said.

She heard the mattress creak, and turned as Hank was crawling under the covers. "Don't you need to brush your teeth?"

"Nope," he said decisively. "Around here we only do the minimum."

"Excuse me?"

"The minimum. Once a day is the minimum."

"No." Lauren sat on the edge of the bed and straightened the covers around Hank's neck. "After every meal is the minimum."

"No way," Hank said softly, his eyes already closing.

"Yes way."

"I don't have many teeth to brush anyway," Hank said, and then he was gone, asleep with a single breath and the comfort of his own bed.

Lauren finished the job of tucking him in, then left the room with unnecessary caution. She could've been singing at the top of her lungs and Hank wouldn't have heard a thing. She turned off the light, pulled the door partway closed, and took a deep breath. Tea, shower, pajamas…

Lauren turned around and literally ran into Cole Donovan's chest. It wasn't fair; he even smelled good.

She mumbled an apology and stepped back. He didn't move at all.

"Hungry?" he asked.

Tea, shower, pajamas, bed. It was a great plan, right? She looked up, caught those incredible blue eyes and mentally prepared a polite *Thanks, but no thanks.* But the word that came out of her mouth was "Starving."

Chapter Five

Feeding Lauren was the least he could do. She'd rounded up some peanut butter crackers and juice for the kids at the hospital, thanks to an array of vending machines, but Cole was pretty sure his cute neighbor wasn't a crackers-and-juice kind of woman. He hadn't been able to eat, not with Justin bleeding all over the place, and if she was half as hungry as he was, she'd be happy with cardboard and tepid water.

Cole opened the fridge and leaned in, studying the contents for something quick and tasty. Lauren came up beside him and leaned in, too, and he was strikingly aware of how close she was. For a moment, just a moment, he could barely breathe.

"There's leftover lasagna," he said, peeking beneath the foil covering the dish.

"No," Lauren said decisively. "That looks like just enough for a meal for four. You should save that for supper tomorrow." She reached in and touched the lid of a plastic container. "What's this?"

"Tuna salad."

"When was it made?"

"Don't you trust me?" He turned his head and smiled at her.

She responded with a smile of her own and a very soft, "Humor me."

"It's left over from yesterday's lunch."

"Tuna salad it is."

Cole grabbed the container and they both backed away. Lauren made herself at home, grabbing a loaf of bread off the counter and checking a couple of cabinets for glasses. "I'm just going to have water," she said. "You?"

"The same." It was that or apple juice or fruit punch, since it was too late for coffee. He needed to sleep tonight.

Without talking they made sandwiches and glasses of ice water. It didn't take long. He grabbed a bag of potato chips and tossed them onto the center of the kitchen table. When Lauren started to sit, Cole stopped her with a raised hand and a sharp, "Not there!"

Lauren stopped, looked up at him and smiled wickedly. "Why not? Is this seat saved?"

He found himself smiling again. "That's Justin's chair. You're very likely to sit in grape jelly or pancake syrup. I haven't checked today, but it's possible."

Lauren looked down, studied the chair, declared it all clear and sat. He took the seat directly across from her, and they both took a few bites before they said another word. Sharing a quiet, late-night meal was strangely comfortable, even though he barely knew Lauren Russell.

Considering her profession, he'd half expected her to

turn up her nose at tuna sandwiches, chips and water, but she ate her meal as if it were as fine as her lasagna. Hunger would do that to a person, he knew.

"I have to thank you again," he said. "Sorry to say, I'm a complete wuss when it comes to any crisis that involves that much blood."

"That's completely understandable," Lauren said. "It was alarming for me, and I'm not a parent. Yet," she added.

His few dates in the past several years had all been disasters, but then, the women had been all wrong. He had a feeling Lauren could be all *right,* but did he dare to pursue the spark he couldn't deny? His determination to wait aside, was there something here worth pursuing? Maybe so. The coward in him told him to eat in silence and then tell her good-night. A part of himself that had been buried for years wanted more. "Have you ever been married?"

Lauren shook her head and grabbed another chip. "I was engaged once, but it didn't work out. Just as well," she added in a lowered voice.

Cole tried to imagine what kind of an idiot would let a woman like Lauren slip through his fingers. Maybe she'd kicked the fiancé to the curb—that made more sense.

He was exhausted and so was she. He felt drained, spent...and not in a good way. And right now he was perfectly happy to sit here and look at Lauren, for a while. Her skin was perfect and he had to make an effort not to reach out and take her hand to see if it felt as soft as it looked. Her hair looked as if it had been touched with sunshine, and her eyes were lively and smart. They didn't miss much.

Did they miss where his mind had taken him?

Yeah, as if he'd make a move on a woman at the end of a day like this one.

He had no spare time, and his recent history with dating was not encouraging, but he wondered if Lauren Russell could—maybe—be more than a helpful neighbor.

"I looked you up on Google," he confessed. "After you came to the door that first day."

She tilted her head and looked him in the eye. "You did?"

"Yeah. No wonder the food you brought over was so good. You're an expert in the kitchen."

She took a small bite of her sandwich and seemed to consider her glass of water while she chewed. "Not an expert, exactly," she said after she'd swallowed. "There's a constant learning curve. I've never mastered cooking on a grill, and I don't think I'll ever make a white cake as perfect as my grandmother's."

"If I can be blunt, you need a new publicity photo for your website. You're much prettier in person."

She blushed, a little. "I had a different photo up at first, but I kept getting email from men in foreign countries. And one in California. I was asked out on several dates, which would've required me to buy a plane ticket, either for myself or for the man who was doing the asking, and I even got two very passionate marriage proposals. If someone wants to stalk me it should be for my recipes, not for…well, whatever."

"So the turtleneck and the slightly insane smile…"

"Very much on purpose."

Lauren lifted her sandwich, set it back down, and looked him squarely in the eye. "And since you've been honest I should tell you…I looked you up, too, that same day. Whiplash."

He laughed lightly, even though he knew very well what Lauren would've found in the simplest search. She knew it all. His career, losing Mary, leaving the game... He usually hated knowing his life was out there for anyone and everyone to find and study and pick apart, but he decided he didn't mind that Lauren knew. "Nobody's called me Whiplash for a very long time."

"My grandmother does. She was a big fan." She left it at that, didn't go into detail about what she'd found or ask questions about the decisions he'd made. After a moment, she smiled. "You know, we were probably looking each other up at the same time."

"Welcome to the big wide world of the internet."

What were the odds that he'd buy a house next door to a woman like this one? There were pretty women everywhere, and there were more than enough single women out there. Lauren was different. He was at ease with her; he could be himself. Even though he knew it was unwise...he wanted more.

She rose and started to clean the table, but he stopped her, standing and placing a hand over hers. "You've done enough today. More than enough. I'll clean up."

He didn't move his hand; she didn't jerk away. In fact, she lifted her head and looked him in the eye for a moment that went on too long. That gaze fed him as surely as the food and water had.

Bad idea.

He snatched his hand away, and Lauren took a step back. She blushed again and turned her head to the side. "I have to get home. You must be exhausted and ready for bed."

It wasn't his imagination that she almost choked on the word *bed*.

"I'll walk you to your door," he said.

She shook her head and walked out of the kitchen with purpose in her step. "That's not necessary."

"But…"

"Really, Cole, it's not that far."

She seemed insistent—anxious to get away—so he compromised. "I'll watch from the porch until you get inside, then."

She nodded, said good-night and headed for home. There was just enough light from his front porch, and hers, for him to watch the sway of those hips as she all but ran for home.

Tea, shower…then what? Somehow her very clear and easy plans for the evening had been torn apart when Cole had asked her if she was hungry. Lauren slammed the door behind her and leaned against it. She closed her eyes, took a deep breath and recited her list of requirements for a serious relationship. She noted all the requirements that Cole Donovan did not meet. She made herself remember the chaos that had first driven her to knock on his door.… And honestly, did she really think it would be a good idea to get involved with a man who had *three* children?

Nothing and no one could blow a hole in her neat schedule and reasonable plans the way Cole Donovan could.

But then she remembered the way she'd felt when Cole touched her hand; how nice it had been to sit across the table from him late at night, talking as if they'd known one another forever. Laughing, confessing…it had felt right and natural. And to be fair, the noise from next door didn't bother her the way it once had. Cole's children had a charm of their own, a devastating charm obviously inherited from their father.

Cole was a little rough around the edges, not at *all* her type, but just being in the same room with him gave her the shivers.

Lauren had thought herself immune to a man's charms, more practical than she'd been in her younger years. She'd thought that by this time in her life she would be capable of separating cold, hard facts from the effects of hormones.

Apparently not.

Cole lay in bed, wide-awake long after he'd watched Lauren walk home. Justin slept on beside him, breathing deep and easy. There was no concussion, nothing more than a bad cut in a place that bled like there was no tomorrow. A good cleaning, a couple of stitches, a cherry lollipop, and Justin had been right as rain. The days when a lollipop could cure all ills were long gone for Cole. His head was still spinning; his stomach had been in knots since he'd heard Meredith scream.

He hadn't been lying when he'd told Lauren he didn't handle crises very well. Not where his kids were concerned.

The world wasn't a safe place, not for anyone. Least of all for a child. At the same time, he couldn't wrap his kids in cotton and hover over them 24/7. That wasn't any way to live. Not for him and not for them. Knowing that didn't keep Cole from worrying. He knew too well how fragile life could be. He knew too well how quickly a man could go from being on top of the world to wondering how he was going to make it through tomorrow.

He wondered if he'd feel any differently if his mother was alive and close by. She'd died three years before Mary, and since Cole had never known his father and had no siblings, that part of his family had died with

her. He still missed her; always would. Mary's parents
lived in Florida, and if their health allowed they made
a couple trips a year up this way. Ted was in a wheel-
chair and Debra hadn't been in good health for as long
as Cole had known her. They weren't—couldn't be—the
kind of grandparents the kids could rely on for stability,
for caretaking. The kids loved their grandparents, and
Ted and Debra loved their grandkids dearly. But when it
came down to the nitty-gritty, all his children had was
an aunt who was more overprotective than he was and
him. They would always have him.

As his brain began to unwind, the picture of Lauren
Russell sitting in the E.R. with a couple of his kids
wrapped around her popped into his head. He could see
her walking away, making the short trip from his front
door to her own with that nice, feminine sway in her
hips. She was trouble of the worst kind, and he'd known
it the first time he laid eyes on her. He didn't think, like
his kids did, that she was "after" him in any way. If anything, she was as wary of him as he was of her. To think
of her as trouble wasn't exactly right. She just had the
potential to be trouble, if he allowed it.

After Mary's death, women had come out of the
woodwork hoping to take her place. It had made him so
angry that they'd thought his wife, the mother of his children, the woman he'd loved since he was sixteen, could
be so easily and quickly replaced. It hadn't helped matters at all that many of them had been groupies, women
who wanted nothing more than to be a major leaguer's
wife. None of them had loved his children; none of them
had even known them. Hell, they hadn't known him,
either. It was no wonder he'd withdrawn so completely
from the opposite sex.

Lauren was trouble because she was different. There

were prettier women in the world, there were women who didn't look at him as if they half expected him to take their heads off. He was sure there were women who could cook as well as she did—though he hadn't ever met them—and many of them filled out their tank tops more generously than she did.

So why was he lying in bed awake after midnight, thinking about her? Why was the image of her holding his kids in the E.R. permanently implanted in his brain? Why had he felt such relief, such comfort, just to share a sandwich with her at the end of a very bad day?

Why did he have the urge to get up, go to the window and look out to see if any of her lights were still on?

Cole went to sleep thinking that he really needed to stay away from Lauren Russell, but in spite of his determination to keep his distance, he dreamed of her. And his dreams were most definitely of the X-rated variety.

Meredith turned over, punched her pillow and fought back new tears. She was so stupid! For a little while she'd actually believed that Lauren Russell might be a friend, a woman who could help with girly things. Not a replacement for her mother, but…something different.

But she'd been right all along. Miss Lauren was just using her—Justin and Hank, too—to get to their dad. And Meredith was horrified that the schemer's plan might be working.

They'd pulled into the driveway so late, the rest of the neighborhood had been sleeping. Miss Lauren had called her friend Summer as they'd left the hospital, to let her know that Justin was okay. Summer was supposed to spread the word through the neighborhood.

Miss Lauren had acted like she was so relieved, like she actually *cared* about Justin, but Meredith knew better. She'd seen the truth when she'd gotten up for a drink of water and had spied her dad and Miss Lauren saying good-night. Neither of them had said anything mushy, and they hadn't kissed or even shaken hands, but Meredith wasn't blind.

Her dad had never looked at a woman that way, as if everything else had ceased to exist, as if the world had stopped and there was no room in it for anyone but the two of them. There was a new look in his eyes, something she'd never seen before. It hadn't lasted very long, but Meredith knew what that look meant. It was, like, from a movie. The next step would've been for them to run toward one another and kiss. With tongue. Yuck.

If they got married, what then? No woman wanted someone else's kids underfoot all the time. Miss Lauren would want babies of her own, brats who would take the place of the old kids. Meredith knew how this worked. She had two close friends in Birmingham whose parents were divorced and remarried, so she'd heard the horror stories about stepmothers and half brothers and sisters. Maybe she and her brothers would get sent off to boarding school, or worse. Maybe her dad would send them to Birmingham to live with Aunt Janet so he could have a new life with a new wife and new kids.

Maybe it was a lot to take out of one quick, mushy look, but it all came together in Meredith's head and she could see where this was leading. There was only one thing to do, only one thing she *could* do. She was going to have to put a stop to this before it went any further.

Cole woke to the smell of coffee. He'd thought the kids would sleep late, but apparently Meredith was up, at least. He opened one eye and found his daughter standing by the bed, steaming mug in hand. Justin slept on, with his pillow tossed to the floor and his head halfway under the covers. His breathing was deep and even.

Meredith kept her voice low. "I thought you might be in a bad mood this morning, so I decided to bring your coffee to you so you'd, you know, feel better."

Cole swung his legs over the side of the bed. He'd gotten accustomed to the pajamas he'd once refused to wear. As the sole parent responding to all late-night calls, they'd become a necessary addition to his wardrobe even though he'd once believed that real men didn't wear pajamas. "Thanks, Mer. Justin's accident did put a damper on the evening." He took the coffee, cradled the mug, sipped.

Meredith's eyes widened. "I wasn't talking about the accident."

Cole glanced up. "What, then?" Was there something going on he didn't know about? Another disaster looming?

"I thought you might be in a bad mood about Miss Lauren."

The name alone was enough to make him perk up. "What about her?"

"You like her."

He made a point of not lying to his kids, even when he knew they wouldn't like the truth. "Maybe a little."

Meredith shuffled her feet, looked down at the floor, then cast her eyes to his. "Last night when y'all were talking, she did tell you that she has a boyfriend, didn't she?"

"She does?" Why was he surprised? Women like Lauren didn't stay single for long. If ever.

"Two of them. One travels a lot, so sometimes she dates the other one when he's out of town. She said something about keeping all her options open."

Had he misread the occasional interested look Lauren had cast his way, the spark of interest he'd noticed last night? No, he was pretty sure he hadn't. At his kitchen table she'd seemed friendly enough; more than friendly. Talk about wishful thinking! Though she'd said she didn't "date," if the woman had two boyfriends, maybe she wasn't opposed to taking on a third. Huh. He never would've taken Lauren Russell for a man-eater.

"How did you end up talking about her boyfriends?"

"She had to call one of them to cancel. She told him she was stuck in the hospital but she'd see him later. That's why I figured she'd mention it to you, since she was probably rushing off to meet him."

The word that caught Cole's attention was *stuck*. Dammit, he hadn't asked Lauren to come along. She'd insisted. She'd snatched the car keys out of his hand! Had Boyfriend One or Boyfriend Two come over last night, had one of them been there while Cole had watched her sashay home? Had she made some sucker wait while she shared a sandwich with her new neighbor or had she run home, changed clothes and gone out to meet him somewhere?

If she'd had plans, why had she insisted on going to the hospital with him? Why had she made herself at home in his kitchen as if she had no other place to be? Like he was going to try to figure out how a woman like that thought.

He took a deep breath, exhaled, then took a long drink of coffee, enjoying the taste before he spoke. "She can have a hundred boyfriends, for all I care. Miss Lauren is just a nice neighbor, that's all."

"You don't want to, like, date her?"

Not anymore…"Sugar, how many times do I have to

tell you. I don't have time for dating." And even if he did, he didn't share. Not where women were concerned.

"I'm going to make eggs for breakfast," Meredith insisted, her voice lighter and brighter with the subject of Lauren behind them. "How do you want yours?"

It didn't matter how he answered, he was going to get scrambled and burned. And he'd eat every bite. "You pick." Cole drank a swig of coffee and stood. "I'm going to get a shower, then I'll be ready for breakfast."

"Dad!" Meredith called as he walked toward the hallway.

Cole turned and his heart almost broke. Meredith was so serious, so earnest. "We don't need her," she said.

"I know that."

"We don't need anyone."

He winked. "You've got that right." But inside, he felt a tiny sense of loss he couldn't ignore. What on earth had made him think, for even an instant, that he could afford to get involved with a woman at this point in his life? His life was not his own, and it wouldn't be for several more years.

Lauren had stopped by the drugstore and picked up a few teenage-appropriate cosmetics. A light blush, a natural lipstick, a brown mascara. She'd never had a sister to play dress-up with, had never really learned much about the application of makeup except by trial and error. So she'd bought a teen magazine that had tips on applying makeup.

She shouldn't be so excited. She definitely shouldn't wonder if she was excited about working with Meredith or about seeing Cole again.

Lauren was crossing the yard, heading for the Donovans' front door, when Meredith stepped out of that door and onto the front porch with a spring in her step. The young girl sprinted across the lawn, a surprisingly determined expression on her pretty face.

"Hi," Lauren called in a bright voice. She lifted the drugstore bag high. "I picked up a few things for us to experiment with. Is this a good time?"

Meredith glanced back toward her house. "Not really. Dad is expecting one of his girlfriends tonight, and we're trying to get the house clean. I saw you headed this way, that's why I came out to meet you. He is such a bear when we don't do things the way he tells us to. You really *don't* want to interrupt him when he's like this."

Lauren frowned. She hadn't seen that side of him. And *girlfriends? Plural?* She shouldn't be surprised, but she was. She was also oddly disappointed. "I didn't know your dad had girlfriends."

Meredith nodded her head. "Lots. Women pretty much fall all over him. Tiffany? The woman who's coming over tonight? She's gorgeous. And she makes the best lasagna I've ever tasted." Her brown eyes widened. "Not that your lasagna wasn't good, too."

Lauren's spine straightened. Maybe this Tiffany was prettier than she was, but better lasagna? Impossible. "Well, we'll do it another time." She offered the bag of cosmetics to Meredith. "You can go ahead and take this, if you'd like."

The young girl shook her head while she looked at the drugstore bag as if it might have a snake in it. "No, thanks. I'll...I'll call you when I have a chance to, you know, play."

Lauren had never before gotten the "Don't call me, I'll call you" brush-off from a twelve-year-old, but she supposed there was a first time for everything. "Sure," she said as she took a step back. "I'll talk to you later."

Meredith turned and ran back to her house, loping gracefully on coltish legs. Lauren spun around and headed toward her own front door. It was just as well, she supposed, that matters had been halted before they went too far. She didn't want to get involved with a man who had girlfriend*s*. She really didn't want or need a man at all! Good-looking or not, she didn't need a complication like Cole Donovan in her life.

It wasn't like they had anything in common. In fact, if she'd ever met a man who wasn't right for her, it was Cole.

Lauren stored the cosmetics she'd bought for Meredith under the sink in the hall bathroom, then made her way to the kitchen. She'd put a lot of thought into decorating each and every room of her house, but it was the kitchen where she felt most at home. It was the kitchen she turned to when she needed soothing. She put the kettle on the stove and snagged her favorite porcelain teacup, chose a decaffeinated tea bag from the wide variety in the pantry and waited for the water to boil. Some people boiled water in the microwave, she knew, but Lauren had never been a fan of the microwave. She had one, because these days it was a requirement in any kitchen, but she didn't use hers often. When she was in a hurry she'd use it to warm up leftovers, but otherwise... It seemed a little like cheating.

Cole Donovan probably didn't even own a teakettle, and likely wouldn't know what to do with one if it showed up in his kitchen. She imagined his microwave saw lots of use. Something else to hold against him.

Lauren sat at the breakfast nook with her tea and cradled the warm cup in both hands. It was soothing, the way the smell of fresh baking bread or the scent of vanilla was soothing. It made her angry that she felt the

need to be soothed simply because Cole Donovan hadn't
turned out to be exactly as he'd initially seemed.

She wasn't looking for more in her life. She didn't
need more. Her life was near perfect, her career proceed-
ing exactly as planned. But as she sat there she still felt,
inexplicably, as if she'd lost something.

Chapter Six

Somehow the noise from the neighbor's backyard wasn't as distracting as it had once been. Just a few weeks ago the screams and laughter and thumps had dragged Lauren completely out of the zone she needed to be in to work. Maybe she was just used to the commotion, and had relegated it to another part of her brain. As long as they didn't break another window…

She was almost finished with her article about squash recipes, which included a story about Sunday dinner at her grandmother's house. Newspaper sales were down, but the paper she wrote for maintained a healthy circulation, their website was popular, and the ads on her own website added to her income. If the book she'd written was a success, another would follow in two or three years and she'd be in great shape, financially. Maybe she'd never be rich, but she could make a very nice living doing what she loved. More than anything, she wanted to be self-sufficient. She didn't ever want to have to depend on a man—or her family—to take care of her. She'd take care of herself, thank you very much.

Maybe one day she'd meet a man who wasn't a snake, one who would accept that she had a career she intended to nurture, that she was a little old-fashioned, that she wanted things in her home and her life to be a certain way and while she was willing to compromise she *wasn't* willing to change for any man. Was it too much to ask that a man not drink out of the milk carton, that he put his socks in the hamper and for goodness' sake put the toilet seat down when he was finished?

Her list of requirements changed and morphed as she grew older. No jocks, no kids, a height of less than six feet tall—wait, that was now five foot ten—neatness, a sense of humor. Good strong genes, an awareness of his own health—she could not abide a man who lived on cheese doodles and beer—and they really should be sexually compatible. It wasn't enough to know what went where; she wanted fireworks in the bedroom. She wanted a man who could blow the top of her head off.

Nearly thirty years old, and she'd had two serious relationships and one that *could've* been serious if it had lasted more than six months. None of them had come even close to fulfilling all her requirements. She was always disappointed. Did she expect too much? No, she didn't think so. Compromise was a part of life, but when it came to the all-important choice of a life mate, compromise was not a good idea. She'd tried that, hadn't she? It was like a recipe and though there was room for experimentation, using the best ingredients gave the best results.

No one had ever come close to blowing the top of her head off.

The current train of thought was *not* helping her to finish her article.

Lauren had to consider the possibility that she'd never meet the right man, that she was too demanding, too difficult, too set in her ways to make room for any man in her life. She hadn't relaxed her standards in recent years. In fact, the list of requirements was growing longer, not shorter. Perhaps she should just settle on remaining unwed and devoting herself to her career. It wasn't like she was lonely. She had friends, family, coworkers she didn't see often, since she did most of her work at home. All she was really missing by not having a man in her life was sex.

Yes, she missed sex, but she wasn't willing to sleep with just any man to satisfy that particular itch.

Naturally, thinking of sex took her mind directly to Cole Donovan. In fact her mind whipped in that direction entirely, and her hands quit moving over the keyboard. She could not think of squash casserole and hold the image of her neighbor naked in her mind at the same time. Not that she had the actual memory to hold on to, but her imagination was quite vivid, and she *had* seen him shirtless. Once. The way his jeans fit gave her a very good idea of the shape of his butt, the strong thighs, the narrow hips. Those memories gave her more than enough to build on, a solid base upon which to expand. The resulting imagining was enough to take her mind off squash and Gran's Sunday suppers.

It was true enough that she didn't have time for a romantic relationship, and goodness knew Cole had his hands full with…life. He already had girlfriends, plural, and she was not one to put herself in a position where she had to compete for a man. But at the same time, it would be a shame to ignore what they obviously felt. Her mind took a huge and unexpected leap. Was it possible that they could be neighbors with benefits?

Lauren took a deep breath, dismissed the thought from her mind, and did her best to return to the subject of squash casseroles. What was wrong with her? Cole Donovan had a series of girlfriends, and she wasn't about to try to compete with the gorgeous Tiffany. Or any of the others. If he wanted benefits—and what man didn't—he didn't have to turn to her. He had options. Besides, even though her mind had taken that unexpected leap, Lauren wasn't the type of woman to get involved in casual sexual relationships. Never had been. Honestly, without love, why bother?

Not that Cole was interested. Even though there had been a moment—okay, more than one moment—when their eyes had caught and she'd felt a wash of something unexpected and exciting, Cole hadn't come over or called since Justin's accident almost a week ago. He'd left the lasagna and cobbler dishes on the front porch and departed without even ringing the bell. She'd just found them sitting there, scrubbed clean and waiting for her to discover them when she went out for the mail. He'd walked into the backyard to talk to the kids a couple of days ago, while she'd been working in the garden, and he hadn't even called out a neighborly hello. She'd peeked at him out of the corner of her eye, but all his attention had been on his children. Which was as it should be, she supposed, but still, was a wave of his hand in her direction too much to ask for?

He wouldn't even look at her, much less…

Just as well. Cole probably never put the seat down, and she was almost positive he was the kind of man who drank out of the carton. He failed miserably in regards to several very important details on her list—in fact, he was the antithesis of her list! His life and hers were so different, they were so entirely incompatible, that it was foolish of her to sit here and imagine him naked.

She tried to turn her thoughts to squash, again, but her mind continued to wander.

Sadly, she'd really hoped to catch a glimpse of Tiffany, or one of the others, just to see for herself what Cole Donovan's type was. She expected big hair and big boobs. She'd seen nothing. Maybe he waited until his kids had gone to bed before he had his women over. It was the least he could do, in her opinion. Unfortunately that meant such visits were also made past *her* bedtime.

Lauren almost decided she should probably— maybe—let Gran set her up with the grandson of one of her friends at the retirement home, maybe the divorced lawyer, Buddy Whatshisname…. Fortunately, she wasn't yet desperate enough to allow herself to be set up by her grandmother.

The operative word being *yet*.

Lauren was momentarily distracted by a particularly piercing scream from next door. Not only did she not jump out of her skin, she didn't even bother to go to the window and look outside to see what had happened. Already she could distinguish the screams of pain from the screams of delight, even though there was little difference in pitch and volume. That scream had been one of joy. Hank, if she was hearing correctly. The one child of the three who actually liked her.

Yet another reason to keep her distance from Cole Donovan. His life was complicated. Nothing and no one would ever come before those kids, and she could only admire him for that. Still, she was very aware that there was no room in his life for her. Not even as a neighbor with benefits.

Her life wasn't entirely bereft, socially. Tomorrow night she was having dinner at Summer's house, just a little something to make up for the fact that Lauren had missed the neighborhood barbecue because she'd run off to help Cole when Justin had been hurt. Summer had two girls and a full-time job, so they didn't get many chances to really talk.

Lauren never went to anyone's home for a meal empty-handed. She'd told Summer that she'd provide the dessert. Chocolate cake, maybe. Or banana pudding. Maybe she'd make another peach cobbler. Maybe all three.

Once this article was off she'd need something to do, something that required all of her brain cells in order to keep her mind off Cole Donovan. Her grandmother's recipe for double-chocolate triple-layer fudge cake would require a trip to the grocery store and hours in the kitchen. Just what she needed—a high-calorie distraction.

Cole wasn't looking forward to dinner at Tim Schuler's house, but Tim was on the school board, and as a new employee it would probably be unwise to refuse. He'd already turned down two previous invitations. Since Tim's wife had arranged for a babysitter who came with stellar recommendations—to Meredith's horror, since she thought herself too old for a babysitter—Cole could find no reason to refuse this time around.

It was a mild night, and the Schulers lived just a few houses down. Cole took his time, not hurrying but enjoying the quiet walk, the moment of peace. It wasn't yet dark, but the sun had set and the neighborhood was still.

He smiled. Maybe the neighborhood was quiet because his kids were inside for the night.

He glanced at Lauren's perfect little house as he passed by. There were no soccer nets or trampolines in her yard, no toys cluttering her porch. The mature trees in the front yard looked as if they'd been painted on canvas, they were so perfect. No blemish marred the trunks of those trees, no split or dying limbs hung dangerously overhead. There were no brown leaves on any of her plants, no dead or wilting roses on the bushes out front. She probably went out early in the morning while the rest of the neighborhood was asleep and pruned everything so no brown spots would ruin the pretty picture, so no damaged leaves or blooms would dare to mar the perfection of the pink and red roses. Her picture-perfect home came complete with everything but a white picket fence.

So, what were her boyfriends like? Were they as perfect as her lawn and her neat little house? He'd kept an eye out for them, out of curiosity, but hadn't seen anyone coming or going. Maybe she met up with her gentlemen callers at their places. He could not imagine Lauren opting for a seedy hotel.

He felt like kind of a heel. After Lauren had driven him to the hospital, he should've done something to thank her. He'd thanked her that night, but it didn't feel like enough. If he cooked, he might offer something along the lines of her lasagna and cobbler. At the very least, a phone call or even a thank-you note. She probably would've done all three if the situation had been reversed. Even if she did have boyfriends out the wazoo, it would've been the right thing to do.

But he realized to his core that to encourage any sort of relationship with Lauren Russell would be stupid.

He liked her too much, she made him lie in bed imagining intriguing possibilities. How soft was her skin? How would her lips taste? Was she a tiger in bed, or was sex for her as neatly arranged as the rest of her life? He wanted to know. He really, *really* wanted to know.

If Lauren had any idea where his mind took him when he thought of her, she'd probably move.

The truth of the matter was, these days there weren't many young, pretty women out there looking to hook up with a man who had three children, a man who always put his kids first, who frankly had no time for a romantic relationship. In the old days, when he'd still been more Whiplash than Cole, it had been another story, not that any one of those predatory women had done anything for him.

The series of bad dates he'd endured a couple of years ago had convinced him that he was on his own, for the time being.

Still, just watching Lauren pick tomatoes or weed her herb garden made his mind turn in that direction. She had a nice ass, a totally feminine way of walking, of turning her head or lifting her hand. And when he'd walked into the E.R. waiting room and seen her sitting there with one child's head on her lap and another holding on to her arm…impossible thoughts had sprung into his mind. It would really be best if he and Lauren never saw one another beyond a distant wave across their yards.

Tim Schuler's house was bigger than Cole's. It was two stories, had a double garage, and the yard and house were perfectly maintained. Cole rang the doorbell, wondering if beyond the front door there was a touch of chaos as there was in his own home. After all, the Schulers had two kids, little girls about the same age as Justin and Hank. Cole hoped fervently that at some point he'd have to step over a doll or a coloring book or *something*. He was feeling inadequate enough these days, and to have perfection constantly thrown in his face didn't help matters at all.

Tim answered the door with a smile, and his youngest perched on his shoulders. Cole couldn't help but grin. The little girl had her hands tangled in her daddy's hair. She wore a Dora nightgown that had seen better days—it reminded Cole of the much-loved Ninja Turtles shirt Justin had worn until it was two sizes too small—and her hair was pulled up in a ponytail.

"Come on in," Tim said, stepping back to allow Cole to enter. "You're right on time. The girls have the table set and the food is just out of the oven."

The girls? His wife and oldest daughter, Cole assumed. He lifted the bottles of wine in his hand. "I wasn't sure what you were having, so I brought both red and white."

"Great! Set the bottles on the dining room table while I put this munchkin to bed."

The munchkin protested, then laughed as her father swung her off his shoulders and carried her up the stairs.

With great relief, Cole stepped over a stuffed animal as he made his way into the dining room, where an oval, highly polished walnut table was neatly set. For four.

Before he even had the chance to wonder who, besides Tim and his wife Summer, would be there for dinner, Lauren walked into the dining room from the door that opened into the kitchen. She backed into the room with a casserole dish in her hands. It wasn't just her hair and her way of moving that he recognized. He'd know that ass anywhere. Lauren said something to the woman in the kitchen, laughed, then turned.

She stopped dead in her tracks when she saw him standing there. Her smile didn't fade away, it died a quick and certain death. A woman with manners, she recovered quickly, though the smile did not return. "So, *you're* Tim's friend who's joining us for dinner." Lauren cut a glance toward the kitchen door as she placed the casserole dish on the table, where it joined several others. She leaned slightly across the table, apparently unaware that the new position offered a very nice view of the swell of her breasts as the dark blue top she wore sagged a bit. "I must warn you," she whispered. "I'm almost positive that we've been set up."

Set up was a nice way to put it. *Ambushed* was more accurate.

Lauren's smile returned, but it wasn't a real smile. This one was practiced and false. It was *very* polite, and more than a little scary. "Sorry about this. I suppose they don't know about Tiffany."

"Who?"

Lauren's eyebrows rose slightly. Was that surprise or disapproval? Maybe both. "Meredith told me all about her, so there's no reason to be shy. Besides, your love life is of no concern to me." Though she tried to remain cool, a blush colored her cheeks.

The pieces fell together, too easily. He should've known…. "Indulge me. Who's Tiffany?"

"Your girlfriend, the gorgeous one who makes better lasagna than I do."

Cole wasn't blind, and he knew Lauren well enough to read the shifting expressions on her face. She was more upset about the lasagna competition than the gorgeous bit. "Forgetting Tiffany for a moment, why would your friend set you up when you have at least two other fellas?"

"What are you talking about?"

Cole crossed his arms over his chest and took a deep, stilling breath. He was so tempted to turn around and run home to confront his daughter…but he didn't. He had to be sure. "You didn't postpone a date with one of your boyfriends from the E.R. waiting room?"

"Of course not! I don't even have a…" Her expression changed, shifting from politely distant to surprised to annoyed as she figured out what was going on. "Oh. There's no Tiffany?"

Cole shook his head, then a memory jolted him. "Actually, there is a Tiffany. We had one date a couple of years ago. I dropped a bowling ball on her foot. Then I got a call from the babysitter because she said Justin had a fever. Tiffany insisted on coming along, said she could help, but she gave it up pretty quickly when I handed her Justin so I could pay the sitter and he leaned down and blew his nose on her shoulder. I made the mistake of laughing. She didn't think it was funny. At all." He shook his head. "I can't believe Mer remembered that name." He hadn't, not right away.

"I should've known," Lauren said softly. "*No one* makes better lasagna than I do."

Cole smiled widely. Lauren smiled back, and this time it was a real smile, with heart and joy and…something real he could not define. It was still a bad idea, he still didn't have the time for romance. But he was relieved to his core to know that Lauren Russell wasn't juggling a couple of low-life boyfriends. She was available. Now the question became…was he?

Lauren knew she should be very annoyed with Summer for not warning her that Cole was going to be joining them for dinner, and furious with Meredith for spinning a tale about nonexistent girlfriends and boyfriends. But the evening had been so pleasant she couldn't carry a grudge. Even if Summer did catch Lauren's eye now and then and literally waggle her eyebrows. Dinner had been delicious and the conversation had been pleasant, once the truth had come out.

They'd talked about movies, kids, baseball, the coming school year, Lauren's column, Summer's job at the doctor's office, Cole's new job at the brand-new high school, and Tim's latest conference. Summer filled Cole in on the teachers at the elementary school, and they talked about carpooling. The hours had flown by, and Summer hadn't been too horribly obvious with her attempt at matchmaking.

Why was it that married women had this compulsion to make sure that everyone they knew was a part of a couple? Were they so ecstatically happy that they wanted to share their joy with the world, or was it the simple matter of misery loving company?

Lauren couldn't even be angry that Summer had suggested Cole walk her home, since it was dark. *Dark* was a bit of a stretch. Not only was there a full moon in a cloudless sky, there were street lamps, and every porch along the way was well lit. But it wasn't as if they weren't headed in the same direction, anyway.

"Sorry," Lauren said as they walked slowly down the quiet street. Cole's natural stride was much longer than hers, but he'd shortened it for their walk home. After ten on a weeknight, her neighbors were in for the evening. Some were probably already asleep, others were crashed in their recliners watching television or reading. Those with older children might be trying to get them to bed. "Summer means well."

If she were home she'd be reading, maybe just getting

ready to turn off the lights and get to sleep. She was an early riser, and to be honest…there was no reason for her to stay up late. But tonight, she was in no hurry to get to bed. She was definitely in no hurry to leave Cole's company.

"I won't hold it against her," Cole said, more relaxed than she'd ever seen him. Maybe it was because he was on his own, without the kids for the first time in a long while. Maybe it was the two glasses of wine. She'd held herself to one, since wine went straight to her head and she really didn't want to make a fool of herself in front of Cole. Though she still wasn't sure why she cared so much. "Any anger I felt was entirely washed away by the chocolate cake."

Lauren smiled and skipped. Once. "So, what they say is true. The way to a man's heart really is through his stomach." The moment the words were out of her mouth, she wished she'd phrased that differently. She had no business thinking about Cole Donovan's heart.

He didn't seem to mind, though. "If that was true, you'd have men following you around like you were the pied piper. If Hank ever gets his hands on a piece of that cake, he'll be more in love with you than he already is." The natural smile Cole had worn for most of the evening died. "My middle child really is very fond of you. He talks about you all the time. After the trip to the hospital he wanted to take you a plate of Oreos as a way to thank you for going with us, and for tucking him in."

"I love Oreos."

"Hank intended to pass them off as homemade."

Lauren laughed because she could see the scenario in her mind so well.

"I'm afraid Hank might have a crush on you," Cole

said, his voice low and easy, with only a touch of concern coloring it.

"I'm sure he'll find himself a more appropriate girlfriend once school starts. Some little girl is going to think him quite the catch." She took a deep breath of fragrant summer air. Was that magnolia? Perhaps, though it was a bit late for magnolias. Some fragrant bloom made the night air sweet, and though she'd normally be compelled to find out what it was, at the moment she just accepted the pleasant scent without question. "I'm just glad someone in your household likes me," Lauren teased, thinking of Justin and Meredith, and their obvious fear that Lauren was out to steal their dad away.

"I'm sorry about Meredith," Cole said. "I don't know what she was thinking."

"I do." Lauren wanted to be angry with the girl, but she couldn't. "In her own way, she was trying to protect you."

"From you?" Cole sounded incredulous, as if he didn't get that at all.

Lauren got it. She'd seen it very clearly when Meredith had been so relieved to hear that Lauren didn't date. "I think so. Maybe she doesn't think I'm good enough for you. Maybe no woman will ever be good enough for her dad."

"She had no right, and no reason. She'll be punished."

"Yeah, *that'll* make her like me," Lauren murmured.

They shuffled along, in no hurry as they enjoyed the cool night air. And the company. Lauren usually walked with purpose no matter where she was headed. In the grocery store, on the street, when she was visiting Gran. She didn't lollygag. Ever. But she didn't want this stroll with Cole to end too soon.

Walking with him, talking, finding comfort in the

company of a man she barely knew, it was unexpectedly and deeply pleasurable. Like the sweet scent from an unidentified blossom, she didn't question why. She simply accepted the gift.

"I like you," he said bluntly and a touch reluctantly. "The problem is, I think I like you too much. My very perceptive daughter must've seen that, somehow."

They were directly in front of Lauren's driveway when he made the confession. It was time for her to turn, to say good-night and go inside. Alone. As always. But instead she stopped, and Cole turned to face her.

No man had ever affected her this way with a simple look. She could so easily fall into him, throw away her husband recipe and melt into his hard, too-tall body.

"I don't have time for this," he said, his voice lowered, deep and so sexy Lauren felt like it was a tangible thing that crept across her skin and warmed her to her core. That voice, and the way he looked at her, made her squirm—and not in a bad way.

"Don't have time for what?" she asked. Conversations in the dark? Confessions? Her?

"It's been a very long time since I wanted anything for myself," he said, taking a step closer. "It's a bad idea. My life is complicated, I have a new job coming up, my kids... I'm all they have, and they always come first, but..."

"But what?" Lauren whispered.

"I'm very, very glad to find out that you're not juggling two rich, handsome, gullible boyfriends. I shouldn't care, but I do."

Cole was looking at her mouth; Lauren held her breath, waiting, anticipating. Was he going to kiss her, or was he going to turn around and walk away? He said he didn't have time to take anything for himself, but this,

this could be just for him. No, for *them*. Checklists be damned, she'd be a fool to walk away from whatever this was that she felt.

This man had come out of the blue and blindsided her, and she wasn't sure what she thought about that. But she did know she wanted him to kiss her. She wanted it more than she'd ever wanted anything.

He hesitated. This was the point where he'd either turn away or keep moving toward her. *Don't stop,* she thought. *Don't come this close and turn away.* She wondered if she could find the strength to reach out and stop him if he decided to turn and head for home.

She didn't have to find out. Cole took her face in his hands and held her steady. He looked into her eyes, and she was very grateful that there was more than enough light to see him by. Cole Donovan was the kind of man women dreamed of. Handsome, oozing testosterone… tall. She could learn to live with tall, if she had to. If she got involved with Cole, really, truly involved, he'd ruin her for anyone else. Lauren recognized that in the split second before his lips met hers. And she didn't care. She wanted, very badly, to be ruined.

His lips were soft, but not too soft. Warm, firm, decisive, and yet there was a touch of hesitance in the way he kissed her.

The hesitance didn't last long. His hands moved to the back of her head, and he deepened the kiss. He didn't touch her anywhere else, he didn't grope or press his body to her, but it was the sexiest, most arousing kiss Lauren had ever experienced. She felt their connection to her toes. It was in the top of her head, her gut, between her legs. She responded with her own hint of hesitation, but like his it didn't last. This was a kiss to get lost in. She placed her hands at his waist because she needed to hold on to something solid to ground her, to keep her from flying off the ground.

Every doubt she'd had about Cole Donovan went out the window while his lips were locked to hers. He wasn't entirely a jock. He was really more of an *ex*-jock. She could get used to the kids, and at least one of them liked her. She could even get used to craning her head back to get a good look—or a proper lip-lock. High heels and a stepladder would take care of that problem. It was ridiculous to have a list of requirements for a man. She mentally shredded the list and tossed the strips into the air.

She felt cocooned, sheltered, connected to the pit of her soul…and damn, it felt good.

Cole ended the kiss, which was a good thing since Lauren was incapable of denying herself more. He left her breathless and turned on, and if he asked her if he could come inside her house she'd drag him there. She had to bite back an offer of coffee, when she had no intention of drinking coffee this late and she didn't have any decaf in the house.

But he didn't ask, and neither did she. He said goodnight and, with his big hands on her shoulders, turned her toward her own front door. She went, knowing it was for the best. She hoped he didn't notice her stumble halfway down the driveway as she reached into the pocket of her capris for her house key. At the front door, key in hand, she turned around. He hadn't moved; he watched her very closely.

"Good night," she whispered, knowing she was much too far away for him to hear. When she was inside the house she locked the door and then went to the window beside it to look out. Cole still hadn't moved. He just stood there, watching her house. Watching her watch him. Just as she was about to go to the door and invite him inside—should she even bother with the pretense of offering coffee?—he turned and continued on to his house.

So much for keeping her distance. So much for being happily single. So much for her very carefully laid-out life plan. Lauren had never in her life wanted anything as much as she wanted Cole Donovan.

Chapter Seven

Cole woke to the smell of coffee, but today Meredith wasn't standing by his bedside, trying to stave off a bad mood with caffeine delivery before his feet hit the floor. Not that caffeine was going to save her.

He'd been tempted to wake his daughter last night, after he'd dismissed the babysitter. But he'd been so angry, and he really didn't want to confront Meredith while he was mad. He needed time to think, to play the conversation he needed to have with her in his head again and again.

This morning he was still annoyed, but more than annoyed he was worried. Why would Meredith spin tales to keep him and Lauren apart? What had she seen that made her think it was necessary to interfere? He was pretty sure this was a new development. During his brief stint of bad dates, Meredith hadn't said a word. The kids had met several of the women he'd dated, since something had almost always gone wrong and he'd ended up making those disastrous emergency trips home. His dates always offered to accompany him, because they thought they could help, or they wanted to meet the kids, or maybe because they thought he'd ask them to stay the night. Hell, maybe they were just curious about what they'd be getting into if there was a second and third and fourth date.

Looking back, he had to wonder if the "accidents" that had occurred once he'd arrived home had been accidental at all. Could Justin upchuck on command? Unlikely, but maybe not impossible. Had all the spills, stumbles and unfortunate incidents with snot and vomit and grape jelly been…planned?

If that was the case, he'd been blind. It had never occurred to him that what had happened had been anything more than bad luck. A sign from the universe that he didn't need to be trying to add a woman to his already hectic schedule. Had he been wrong to devote everything of himself to the kids? Maybe he'd given them a skewed vision of how things were supposed to be. Maybe it was all his fault that Meredith felt the need to lie to put an end to a relationship that hadn't even started before last night.

That kiss had definitely been the start of something.

Whatever happened next, he needed to take things slow. His impulsive days were behind him. He was older…maybe even wiser.…

Cole rolled out of bed and headed for the kitchen, where he found Meredith laying out the bowls and measuring cups she used when she made pancakes. Her pancakes were worse than the burned eggs—gummy on the inside, black on the outside—but the only way she'd learn was by trial and error. She was in very big trouble, but he wasn't going to tell her that she was a lousy cook. Meredith was *twelve*. She was supposed to be a lousy cook. It was kind of amazing that she could cook at all.

Cole headed straight for the coffeepot. His favorite mug was sitting beside it, so he didn't even have to reach into the cupboard to get his caffeine fix going. "Where are the boys?"

"Still sleeping," Meredith said, her back to him. "Kayla, the babysitter we didn't need since I'm perfectly capable of taking care of the house and the boys for a few hours, let them stay up too late playing video games."

He took a long swig of coffee and answered with a hum from deep in his throat.

"How was dinner?" she asked.

"Dinner was great."

"So, Mrs. Schuler is a good cook? What did she make? We had macaroni and cheese, and I made those frozen biscuits…"

"Lauren was there."

It wasn't his imagination that Meredith paled, but by golly she didn't miss a beat. "Really? Did she have one of her boyfriends with her?"

"No." Cole shook his head, cradled his coffee cup, looked into the dark liquid for a moment before lifting his head to stare at his daughter. "The mysterious boyfriends were elsewhere. They were probably out with *Tiffany*."

That stopped her, for a moment. Meredith's chin came up, her eyes flashed. Thank goodness she didn't try to deny what she'd done. "I was just trying to help. We don't need her, Dad. She's just going to get in the way. Hank already likes her, so how bad is he going to feel when she decides she doesn't want anything to do with someone else's brats?" The words came fast and furious, crisp and frantic.

"You're getting a little ahead of yourself, Mer. We haven't even gone on a date yet."

"Yet? Yet! You mean you *are* going to date her?"

Cole kept his cool. "Maybe. I haven't asked, so I'm not sure she'd even say yes."

Meredith's chin trembled. "She'll say yes. And then she'll ruin *everything*."

Cole set his mug on the counter and crossed the room to take his daughter into his arms. He hugged her, and she let loose one sad sob. "We don't need her, Dad. I can learn to make lasagna. And peach cobbler and anything else you want."

He'd thought he'd been doing the right thing, devoting himself to his family, shutting out everyone else, putting his life on hold to be a full-time dad. But it wasn't natural for him to not have a life of his own, and he'd never before considered what that might've been doing to the kids all along. He wanted them all to have good, full lives. He wanted them to grow into well-rounded adults. And for the past five years, he hadn't been setting a very good example.

"First of all, no one is ever going to come between the four of us. We're family, and family comes first." Cole wanted Lauren, he liked her, but he didn't think for a minute that what he felt was anything more than physical attraction. She was pretty, sweet and unattached— hell, she was right next door so he was sure to see her damn near every day, and he'd been without a woman for…well, too damn long. He wanted her, but he didn't need her. He couldn't allow himself to *need* her. The way Meredith was talking, you'd think he was going to invite Lauren to move in. "Second, we're just talking about a date or two. Maybe. We might go out to dinner and find out we don't have a thing in common." If past history was any indication…

But he didn't think that would be the case with Lauren. Last night they'd ended up talking as if they'd known one another for years. There had even been a moment or two during dinner when he'd almost forgotten that Tim and Summer were at the table. He felt a natural comfort with Lauren, an ease he'd enjoyed.

"Really?" There was so much hope in Meredith's voice, Cole's heart broke a little. She'd lost so much in her life, and she was obviously frightened that she was now going to lose him.

"I tell you what. I'll wait a while before I ask Lauren out." He'd already decided he needed to take things slowly with Lauren, anyway. Odds were they'd never work out, so why give Meredith a reason to obsess about something that would probably never happen?

"Will you really wait?" Meredith whispered.

"A little while, if it'll make you feel better." So much for his recent decision to move forward, to take a chance that he could have a personal life. Cole couldn't bring himself to purposely hurt his kids to get something he wanted.

He wondered if Lauren would still be available if he waited. Probably not. He'd been thinking slow, but *how* slow? Maybe Lauren didn't have two or more men on a leash, maybe she wasn't juggling boyfriends who hopped in and out of her bed. But that didn't mean she was going to wait forever. Hell, she might not even wait a couple of months until Meredith got used to the idea of her father dating again.

But he'd made more than one sacrifice for his kids, and one more wasn't going to matter. At least, that's what he told himself as he stood there. Inside, he was a little bit afraid it mattered very much.

Two Tuesdays a month, The Gardens hosted a dance in the community center. The music was from the thirties and forties, standards that had survived all these years. The dance started at four in the afternoon and ran until a little after six. The men were seriously outnumbered by the women, and everyone wore their best, from Sunday frocks to sparkling cocktail dresses. Lauren couldn't remember the last time she'd seen so many women in honest-to-goodness pantyhose.

Now and then Lauren accompanied her grandmother—sometimes with Miss Patsy, sometimes without—to the dance. Not that Gran ever danced, but she did enjoy the social aspect of the gathering. There was always punch and finger foods, and folding chairs lined the walls so anyone who wanted to could sit.

Tonight Miss Patsy and her husband were staying in, because their son and daughter-in-law were in town and Miss Patsy was preparing a selection of mystery casseroles. Lauren and Gran sat side-by-side, punch cups in their hands. They talked and watched the couples dance. One couple in particular was quite good, as if they'd taken lessons and were showing off. Another couple, the one Lauren kept her eyes on, were not quite so good, but they looked at one another with such love she couldn't turn away.

A boulder settled in her gut. A matching knot formed in her throat. A feeling akin to terror washed over her. No one would ever love her that way. Maybe she simply wasn't lovable. After Cole had kissed her she'd been certain she'd hear from him the next day, or that she'd find him on her doorstep one morning very soon. Something.

Anything! Instead he was ignoring her all over again. Not even a phone call.

She'd enjoyed the kiss, it had made her head spin, but maybe it hadn't been as spectacular from where he'd been standing.

"What's on your mind?" Gran asked. She leaned forward and waved her hand in front of Lauren's face.

"What?"

Gran leaned back. "You haven't heard a word I've said."

"Sorry," Lauren said. "My mind is wandering."

"Whiplash?"

Lauren sighed. "His name is Cole, and…" She started to say no, but she couldn't make herself lie to her grandmother. "Maybe. How did you know?"

"I know you too well, and the expression on your face screams *man trouble*."

Was she so easy to read? How embarrassing.

The DJ put on a new song. "Someone To Watch Over Me." It was an unfortunate choice. The song only made Lauren feel more inadequate. She had no one to watch over her. At this rate she probably never would. Great, time for a pity party.

"Okay, he kissed me, just a little," Lauren said, her voice low and quick, "and I thought he'd call but he didn't and now I'm wondering what I did wrong. Did I do something wrong?" She didn't give her grandmother a chance to answer. "It's not like I go around kissing just any man, but it seemed right at the time and it was so nice. At least, I thought it was nice. Maybe he was horrified or embarrassed or…something." Maybe he thought she was too easy, or not easy enough. Maybe he thought she was too *short*.

"Did you call him?" Gran asked, her voice slow and calm as always.

"No! Of course not. The man should always be the one to call."

Gran tsked. "I swear, Lauren, sometimes I think you're more old-fashioned than I am. In this day and age, do you really think a woman should sit around and wait for a man to call if she's interested?"

Well, yeah. "If he's interested, he'll call, right? Isn't that the way it works? What if I do the calling and he... he..."

"Rejects you?"

"Yes." That was it. Lauren didn't like rejection. No one did. Why on earth would she just throw herself out there and all but beg for it?

"At least then you'd stop worrying about it. You do have a tendency to obsess, you know, to worry yourself into a stew when worrying doesn't do you a bit of good. It's a quality you've had since you were three. What do you have to lose? You're not three anymore. Take the bull by the horns!" Gran suggested forcefully. "More rightly, take the man by the...well, whatever you wish to take him by."

"Gran!" Lauren couldn't help but laugh. "You've been watching too much daytime television."

"See those two?" Gran pointed at the couple Lauren had been watching earlier, the two who looked to be ninety plus and hopelessly in love. "There are a lot more women in this place than there are men, and single men? You can count them on one hand. When John moved in, Pearl set her sights on him from the get-go. She took him an apple pie. She offered to mend the hem of his trousers when she noticed that some stitches had come loose. The next thing you know, they're staying at her place more than his. They're getting married next month."

"I just assumed they'd been married fifty years or more," Lauren said.

"No, that's new love."

Great. Ninety-year-old women had better luck in the romance department than she did. "Are you trying to tell me that it's never too late? That maybe when I'm eighty I'll find a man who loves me?" The pity party continued....

"No. I'm advising you to take Whiplash an apple pie and mend his trousers and see what happens. In this day and age there's no reason to sit around waiting for a man to make the first move."

Lauren didn't tell her grandmother that Cole's daughter had tried to interfere before there had been anything to interfere with. She didn't admit that she was terrified that this man she was attracted to had three kids—and two of them didn't like her. She didn't confess that when she looked realistically at the situation she saw more obstacles than potential...but that she wanted desperately to try anyway.

Audrey Walker, social director for The Gardens, joined them, taking the vacant seat by Lauren. She wouldn't stay long. Audrey was like a hummingbird, never still, always busy, always planning something. Audrey and Lauren had attended the same high school. They hadn't been close friends then—they'd run in different circles—but that connection gave them a bond. It was the "I knew you when" bond. Back in high school Audrey had been a cheerleader and an honest-to-goodness beauty queen. She probably had a collection of tiaras and sashes on display in her apartment—or else tucked in a special box stored in a closet.

Everyone had thought Audrey would jet out of town after graduation and become a model or a movie star. Instead she'd married her high school sweetheart and stayed right here in Huntsville. The marriage hadn't lasted very long—no one seemed to know exactly why it had ended so abruptly—but even after it was over Audrey had stayed. She'd been working at The Gardens for the past three years.

Audrey seemed to love her job here. She liked the people, and they liked her.

After they'd exchanged pleasantries, Audrey said, "I'm thinking of putting together a big Labor Day picnic, complete with a big band and an outdoor dance floor.

"You should bring your friend."

Lauren felt her spine stiffen. "What friend?"

"The baseball player. Well, coach, I guess that's what he is these days. Bring him! We always need a few extra able-bodied dancers."

Audrey was called away, and she left in a shot. Yeah, hummingbird fit her perfectly. Lauren turned to her grandmother. Before she could say a word, Gran said, "Patsy must've said something. I would certainly never gossip about my own granddaughter. Or anyone else."

Like gossip wasn't one of the favorite pastimes around here....

"Oh, look, there's Mildred. I need to get that white-chocolate oatmeal cookie recipe from her." Like that, Gran was off the chair and moving at a nice clip across the dance floor.

Coward.

Sitting there alone, Lauren had a moment to think. How badly did she want to see where this thing with Cole might lead? Was she really going to sit around and wait for him to make the next move? What if he didn't?

Lauren had to make a decision, here and now. Was she willing and capable of taking that next step herself?

"Drink this," Hank said in a low, serious voice as he handed over the plastic cup with SpongeBob on one side.

Cole looked down, his eyebrows rising as he studied the unappetizing green liquid. When Hank got into full wizard mode, no one was safe. Fortunately all the ingredients for this potion came from the kitchen, and Cole was careful to keep all cleaners and bug spray out of reach, so the potions weren't toxic. He hoped. "What's this supposed to do?"

"I can't tell you. If you know what's supposed to happen then it won't be a good experiment."

His seven-year-old mad scientist. Since these potions always arrived when Cole was in a bad mood, he knew very well what they were supposed to do. But he played the game, pretending not to understand what the concoctions were for. If he ever got one that actually tasted good he'd pretend to get happy. So far that hadn't happened.

Cole downed the liquid in one long gulp. It tasted of lime fruit punch, salt, watermelon and last night's leftover green beans, which the kids had hardly touched. He should've known this was coming when he'd heard the blender whirring away. He placed the cup on the coffee table in front of the couch, where he'd been sitting with a notebook making workout plans for his new baseball team, smacked his lips and gave what he hoped was a sincere enough "Ahh, good stuff."

As usual, Hank stared at Cole as he waited for the potion to take effect. His eyes narrowed and he leaned closer. Closer. Now and then, after downing a gulp of blended leftovers, Cole would cluck like a chicken, or pretend to fall asleep very quickly, or cross his eyes. If he really wanted Hank to outgrow the wizard phase, he should probably stop playing along. It was time to start, he supposed. This potion elicited no reaction.

Before Cole could get back to his game plan, the doorbell rang. Hank—wearing his sorcerer's cape and waving a magic wand—spun around and ran to answer, leaping dramatically over a small fire truck Justin had left on the floor. Not for the first time, Cole wished fervently that his son would outgrow this particular phase. If it went on much longer, he was going to get his ass kicked at his new school. He needed to start doing his part to take the fun out of the game. No more clucking, no more crossed eyes.

Cole tossed his notebook onto the table next to the empty SpongeBob cup and stood, since whoever was at the door was likely looking for him. The kids had been inside all morning, so it couldn't be another broken window. Could it?

Hank opened the door with a flourish of his cape and wand and, sure enough, Lauren stood there. She was fully dressed. White capris, pink tank, bra. No bunny slippers. No muddy baseball and no basket of food. She looked so good he wanted to eat her up.

She smiled when she saw him, and instinctively, he returned the smile. How could he not? "Come on in. Is everything all right?"

"Everything's fine." Lauren stepped into the room. She was obviously nervous, but damn, she looked good. "I just came over to issue an invitation."

It was likely not the kind of invitation that immediately came to his mind.

"I'd like to invite you and your family over for supper tonight. Do you have plans?"

"No," Cole answered quickly. "What's the occasion?"

"Does there have to be an occasion?" She looked up, caught his eye, and he was immediately taken back to the kiss.

It had been easy to relegate Lauren to the back of his mind when he hadn't seen her face-to-face, but when she was standing in front of him the memory of her—her mouth, the softness of her body, the way she tasted, the sweet smell of her skin—it all came rushing back. He didn't want to wait a couple of months before he asked her on a date. He didn't want to waste a single day. *Slow* was a bad idea....

Besides, this wasn't a date, it was an invitation for the entire family. It was a neighborly invitation, that was all. *Yeah, right.*

"What time?"

"Six, if that's okay with you." Her smile widened, and he felt like a teenager, bewitched by a woman for the first time.

"Six it is."

She rose up on her toes, dropped down again. Was she nervous? "Don't you even want to know what we're having?"

"Don't care," Cole said honestly.

"See y'all at six, then." Lauren backed away slowly. Cole moved forward, caught up with her near the door. He couldn't kiss her again, not with the kids watching, but he inhaled deeply and her scent filled his lungs.

"I can't wait."

Once she was on the porch, Lauren spun and walked away. Cole watched her, enjoying the sway of her hips, the gentle, feminine shape of her body. Most of all, he enjoyed the way she glanced back.

He barely knew the woman, and already he was in too deep.

He closed the door and returned to the couch, scooping up his notebook and plopping down. It took a moment for him to realize that Hank was jumping up and down, waving his wand. "It worked! My magic potion worked!"

Cole glanced at the cup on the coffee table. Crap. "It did?" he asked, as if he was ignorant of the potion's purpose. "What did it do?"

"My magic potion made you smile. It made you happy. It's an ungrumpy potion, and it worked! Finally." His smile faded. "I have to go write down the ingredients before I forget." With that he turned, cape whipping around his thin body, and he ran for his bedroom.

Hank would never understand that it had been Lauren who made his dad happy, so that potion would probably become a regular part of his diet. At least until Hank outgrew this wizard kick.

Lauren, a woman he barely knew, made him happy. She made him smile. Shouldn't these kids see their dad happy now and then? Meredith wasn't going to like it, but dammit, he had to give this a shot.

Meredith sulked openly as she picked at her chicken and rice. She didn't care who knew that she was unhappy! Justin and Hank were traitors, chatting away as if nothing was wrong, eating everything on their plates like they hadn't been fed a good meal in months, smiling at Lauren Russell as if she were…as if she were their mother.

She wasn't. No one would ever take the place of their mother.

It was bad enough that Hank had been taken in by Miss Lauren from the beginning. Now Justin was going over to the dark side.

Dad had taken her aside this afternoon and told her,

in a very serious voice, that while he didn't want to upset her, he didn't want to wait much longer before he asked Lauren out on a date. Then she got the spiel about how no one would ever take the place of her mother, and no one would come between the four of them, but that the time had come to move on. Blah, blah, blah. Move on! Meredith didn't *want* to move on, and she didn't see why her dad wanted things to change.

Miss Lauren's kitchen wasn't anything like theirs. The shape of the room was the same, but her appliances looked newer. Everything matched. The plates and the glasses and the cloth napkins, the tablecloth. It all looked like something out of a magazine, the ones at the grocery store checkout. There was a low, clear vase of fresh flowers at the center of the table. Even that matched everything else, as if Miss Lauren only grew flowers that matched her decor.

Where did Miss Lauren keep her stuff? There was nothing cluttering the counter, no dirty dishes in the sink, no pictures on the fridge. The only things on her counter were a carefully arranged bowl of fruit and a tall, perfect chocolate cake Hank had been eyeing since they'd walked into the room.

Meredith was not unaware of the fact that her father looked at Miss Lauren the way Hank looked at the cake. He smiled a lot. She smiled back. It was totally disgusting.

This had to be taken care of before the situation got completely out of hand.

Meredith knew what Lauren saw in her dad. For an old guy, Cole Donovan was handsome. He didn't have a pot belly and he still had all his hair. His picture was on a baseball card, for goodness' sake! Meredith remembered going to baseball games, hearing fans scream her father's name, getting caught up in the excitement when he got a hit or made a great play on the field. She could still hear them chanting "Whip-*lash!* Whip-*lash!* Whip-*lash!*"

But Meredith had to wonder, what did her dad see in Miss Lauren? She wasn't the prettiest woman in the world. In fact, she was kind of flat-chested and ordinary. She wasn't at all funny. She didn't bat her eyelashes at him in adoration. It had to be her cooking. Meredith picked at a piece of celery in the chicken and rice, then she poked her fork at the homemade roll. If she could learn to cook just as well as Miss Lauren, they wouldn't need her at all.

While the two adults at the table were looking at one another with totally disgusting gooey eyes, Meredith reached out and knocked over Justin's milk. Since he hadn't drunk much, the milk splattered and quickly soaked the tablecloth. It pooled around the vase.

"Hey!" Justin shouted, turning an accusing glare to his sister. "Why did you do that?"

"Do what?" Meredith said sweetly, as Miss Lauren jumped up and ran for the paper towels. She'd have a fit over some spilled milk, she'd get angry that her meticulous order had been disrupted, and then everyone would see what she was really like.

It had worked before.

"You knocked over my milk!" Justin shouted.

Meredith shook her head. "It's okay, Justin, I know you didn't mean to make a mess. Accidents happen."

Miss Lauren—who was definitely annoyed and more than a little flustered—started sopping up the milk with a clump of paper towels. Dad helped. Too bad there was a tablecloth to slow the flow. If the glass had fallen over on a bare table the milk would be running onto the floor by now. That would make a real mess and Miss Lauren would be freaking out. Then Dad would see what a basket case she really was.

To Meredith's dismay, Miss Lauren didn't yell at Justin. Her annoyance faded quickly, and soon she was smiling again. She even laughed. "Justin, honey, Meredith's right. Haven't you ever heard that you shouldn't cry over spilled milk?"

"But I didn't spill..." Justin began.

"Justin's very clumsy," Meredith interrupted. "He's always dropping stuff or losing things, or spilling his milk." She glanced around the very neat kitchen. "Everywhere he goes, he makes a big mess."

The youngest Donovan child gave Meredith a narrow-eyed glare that made him look like a very small version of their dad. "I do not."

Hank, who hadn't even stopped eating, said, "I think I need to make a big batch of my ungrumpy potion."

"How about chocolate cake instead?" Miss Lauren suggested. "In my experience, no one can eat cake and remain grumpy."

The thought of chocolate cake soothed even Justin, who had been falsely accused. "I think I'll need two pieces to get ungrumped."

Miss Lauren laughed. Dad laughed. And Meredith had the sinking feeling that she was losing this battle.

And losing this battle would mean losing her father.

The boys were in the backyard, chasing fireflies. Cole could see them through the window. Lauren was cleaning up. He'd offered to help but she'd refused, so he stood at the end of the counter and watched her.

Meredith, refusing to leave them alone, sat at the clean kitchen table leafing through several cookbooks.

Lauren was a good woman, a *rare* woman. Chemistry was one thing, but when he felt that chemistry with a woman he actually liked…wouldn't it be foolish to walk away? Maybe they'd get involved and he'd find out that she wasn't all she appeared to be. Maybe they'd tire of one another quickly. Maybe whatever he felt wouldn't last. But damn, he wanted to find out.

He tried to remind himself to take things slowly, but he had a sinking feeling that spectacular plan was going to fly out the window.

The dishwasher was running, and she had the milk-soaked linens in the washing machine. Other dishes were stacked in the sink and the few things she wanted to wash by hand—good lord, why would anyone go to that trouble—had been washed and set aside to dry.

He should go. He didn't want to go.

"Mer, would you collect the boys and get them in?" he said. "If they don't start getting baths now they'll be midnight getting to bed."

"But I really wanted to look through these…"

"Take them with you," Lauren said, smiling at the sullen girl. "I've probably got two hundred cookbooks. Any kind of cuisine you want to try, I can get you started."

Meredith stood, snatched up the books and stalked toward the back door. She didn't say thanks, she didn't even look back. The door slammed behind her, and they heard her calling her brothers' names at the top of her lungs.

Cole looked at Meredith. "Sorry."

She shook her head gently. "No need to apologize. Twelve is a difficult age, as I remember."

"She spilled the milk on purpose, then tried to blame it on Justin."

"I know," she whispered.

They were neighbors who hadn't known one another nearly long enough to explain away the electricity in the room. They had all the time in the world, and yet it felt as if every minute that passed was a minute wasted. He'd said *slow,* he'd planned *slow.* But this…it was anything but slow.

"If we…do this, it'll happen again. And worse." Might as well lay it all out on the table, let Lauren know what she was in for.

She didn't pretend not to know what he was talking about. "I suspect that's true."

Cole moved closer to Lauren. She stood there, waiting for him, tilting her head up to catch his eye. His arms wrapped around her, so easily. She leaned into him and it felt incredible. Amazing. He could stand here for hours, just like this.

He nuzzled Lauren's neck and breathed deeply. Her scent filled him. She leaned into him, fitting against him as if they'd been made for one another. Height difference aside, the way they fit together was very right. He liked it. She sighed, took a long, deep breath. His body responded to hers and he realized he could *not* stand here for hours just like this.

"I'm going to ask you out on a date," he whispered.

Lauren hummed deep in her throat, then she whispered, "It's about time."

"I'm a little afraid, though."

"Why?"

"I haven't dated in a while, but the last few were…"

"Interesting?"

"Disasters."

She laughed and turned her head. Their lips brushed, met, settled together for a kiss that rocked him to the core. Slow? Uh-uh. Whatever this was, wherever it was going, it was powerful and would not be set aside. Lauren's lips moved gently, testing him, teasing.

She took her lips from his and whispered, "Let's not overthink this. If we do we might end up talking ourselves out of something good."

Was she getting in his head now, or did she have the same nagging doubts he did? "You don't strike me as a 'go with the flow' kinda girl."

"I'm usually not. For you I'll make an exception." She tilted her head, touched her lips to his.

Before the kiss had a chance to grow into more, a sharp crash from next door—too close—interrupted. Hank screamed at his sister. Something about a broken jar of fireflies, as far as he could tell.

"I have to go," he said, reluctantly stepping away. Lauren nodded, crossed her arms across her midsection and leaned against the sink. "If you ask me on a date," she said, "I think I'll say yes and take my chances."

If he hadn't already been a goner, that would've done it.

Chapter Eight

Lauren had just finished putting away the second load of dishes out of the dishwasher when a tap at the back door made her jump. Seeing Cole standing there beyond the square window, illuminated by the back porch light, made her smile. Inside her heart did a strange flip, and her gut tightened.

She could so easily fall in love with him.

She unlocked and opened the back door. "Is everything all right?"

"The kids are asleep." His voice was low, as if they were nearby and he was afraid he'd wake them if he spoke too loudly.

"Good."

He didn't make a move, not to come inside, not to tell her why he'd come back.

"Did you forget something?" she asked. Yes, she had to look *up,* but it wasn't so bad. She was content to just stare at him, to take in every feature, to soak it all in while she could. Perfect nose, stunning eyes, sharp, masculine, recently shaven jawline. And oh, the body… Maybe she should take Summer's advice and invest in some very high heels, just for moments like this one. What would he think if she met him at the door wearing those high heels? And nothing else? "Yeah." His response was almost a growl, a low rumble that Lauren felt to her bones. "I forgot what it felt like to want something so much I hurt."

Lauren's gut clenched. Her heart did something funny and she could barely catch her breath. The timing and the situation were far from ideal. She hadn't known Cole nearly long enough to feel so strongly about him. His kids were a complication; at least one of them hated her.

But she knew what he meant when he talked about wanting something so badly it hurt. She was also ready and willing to take her own advice and stop overthinking. For the first time in a long while, she wanted to jump without a parachute. Cole made her feel like she could fly.

Lauren stepped back and Cole entered her kitchen. She didn't even try to fool herself about why he was here. She didn't offer coffee or cake, didn't pretend that he was here for conversation or to borrow a cup of sugar. More important, she didn't suffer a single second thought.

"What about the kids?"

Cole kicked the door shut, never taking his eyes off her as he reached into his back pocket and pulled out the receiving end of a baby monitor. "The other half of this is in the hallway. If anyone gets up, I'll know it."

Lauren grinned. "You still have a baby monitor?"

"I use it when one of the kids is sick and I want to know if they wake up in the night."

"Handy," Lauren whispered.

"Yes, it is."

Cole pulled her to him, crushed her body against his and kissed her. Not like the first kiss, which had been tentative and almost sweet. Not like their kiss earlier this evening, which had been interrupted too soon. This was a devouring kiss, a sexual kiss, the beginning of something wonderful. There wasn't a hint of hesitation in the way he held her, in the way his mouth claimed hers.

He held her body against his so she could feel his erection pressing against her. He wasn't shy, didn't try to hide what he wanted. His tongue thrust into her mouth, and her knees started to go weak. She was such a pushover where Cole was concerned....

If he made love to her she was definitely going to fall hard. If they took the next step—who was she kidding, there was no *if* here, no *if* in his kiss or in her response—she was going to be in over her head, drowning. Lost. She'd sworn to herself that she'd never again build her life around a man, and here he was, a man she could very easily give up everything to, and for.

No *if.* It was nice, to simply give up and give in, to surrender to what she'd felt all along. The kiss went on and on, and as it did her world got smaller and smaller. There was nothing but his mouth and hers, the warmth and strength of his arms, the way her body thrummed.

Cole's fingers, warm and strong, slipped just beneath her waistband. Her heart took a leap, the deep tremble that had begun when she'd seen him standing at her back door intensified. He easily unfastened the button there with a flick of his thumb. Inside, everything melted. Lauren was a goner. She wanted him here and now. On the table, on the floor, against the counter…she didn't care where, as long as it happened *now.*

But a part of her, the cautious part that made sure every segment of her day was planned from beginning to end, insisted that she clear the air. He had to understand where she was coming from. Whatever they felt, it was just some freaky physical attraction. Hormones. Pheromones. She wasn't out to trap him, the way his kids— Meredith, at least—seemed to think she was. For now, at least, she just wanted him in her bed. Neighbors with benefits.

Because if it was all about the physical and nothing more, he couldn't break her heart.

"This is just sex, right?" she whispered hoarsely.

Cole's answer was somewhere between a grunt and a moan. It sounded affirmative to her. That was good enough.

She unfastened the snap at his waistband and slowly lowered the strained zipper of his jeans. That was all it took for him to groan again and lift her off her feet. Lauren wrapped her legs around his waist, bringing them closer together, positioning herself so near to what she craved. They stood like that for a minute, so close but not yet close enough. Another minute and she'd happily have him on the kitchen floor.

"Bedroom," Cole growled, and Lauren responded by pointing toward the hallway. He carried her there, kissing her throat, her mouth, her earlobe. When they reached the doorway to her bedroom, where a soft night-light lit the way, he glanced toward the bed and moaned. "You've got to be kidding me. Is this a test?"

Lauren turned her head to see what he was talking about, then smiled when she imagined how the neatly made bed with the mountain of carefully arranged pillows would look to him. "They're just pillows."

"A lot of pillows." He placed her on her feet near the

bedside. "Please tell me they don't have to be removed carefully and stacked in a certain order or color coded or…"

Lauren turned, grabbed the edge of the comforter, and yanked up hard. Pillows went flying, this way and that. Up, across, onto the floor and to the end of the bed. Another shake, and they were all scattered on the floor. She turned to face him again and smiled up. "All better?"

Cole smiled as he removed her top, pulling it over her head with more than a hint of impatience. He flicked the hook and eye at her spine with nimble fingers and removed her bra, slipping the straps down her arms and tossing the confining garment to the floor. Then he reached back and released her hair from its ponytail, running his fingers through the loosened strands. Slowly, with no more indication of impatience. He even took a moment to rake his thumb across her cheek as if he were literally savoring the feel of her.

He very gently tilted her head to the side, then leaned down to lay his mouth on her throat, there on the curve where shoulder turned to neck. At the same time he cupped one breast in his palm and brushed a thumb over a very sensitive nipple. Lauren shuddered, and suddenly she was the impatient one. She placed her hands on Cole's waist, held on so she wouldn't melt to the floor. What was he waiting for? She'd never before been a real fan of the quickie, but then again she'd never been so ready for a man that her entire body trembled in anticipation. Tonight quick would be just fine.

Once again his fingers slipped beneath the waistband of her capris, but this time he pushed them down along with her panties. Thank goodness! She stepped out, and stood before him completely naked, bared to her soul.

Even though she was anxious, Lauren took a deep

breath and attempted to grasp some control. After all, a moment like this one should be savored. She didn't gobble down her dessert, she never read the last page of a mystery to see whodunit before she'd read the entire book, and there was no reason to rush now. Cole wasn't going anywhere; neither was she. It wasn't just the destination she was concerned with, it was the ride. And, oh, what a ride this was.

Even though she was normally a modest person, Lauren wasn't about to dive beneath the covers and hide, not when Cole was still fully dressed—unzipped jeans aside—and she wanted nothing more than to touch his bare skin. Besides, the gentle illumination from the night-light was soft enough to be flattering, and he looked at her as if he very much liked what he saw. She pushed his T-shirt up, her fingers relishing the warmth of his skin on her fingertips. Cole was so hard, he was muscled and tough in a way she would never be, and even though he was obviously as anxious as she was, he allowed her to take her time. He allowed her to trail her fingers softly over his chest, to lean in and lay her lips there as she pushed the shirt up and over his head. He stepped out of his shoes as she pushed his jeans down and off. The sight of him naked made her insides quiver.

He was gorgeous and hard and ready…and hers….

Reality intruded like a splash of ice water. "Oh, tell me you came prepared." When she'd thought about not overthinking, that hadn't meant they shouldn't think *at all*.

His voice was raspy as he responded, "Do I not *look* prepared?"

She smiled, touched him, leaned in so her breasts rested against him. He was so warm. Almost hot. "A condom, Cole. Please tell me…"

He squatted and reached into the back pocket of his jeans, pulling out three wrapped condoms. A baby monitor and a three-pack. He was most certainly prepared.

With the condoms in hand he lifted Lauren off her feet and gently tossed her onto the bed, where she bounced softly. He followed, hovering above her, spreading her legs with his knee, pushing her farther back on the bed. He leaned down and kissed her throat, sucking, sending her into overdrive, and then with a grunt he moved away to separate one condom from the others—tossing the remaining two to the bedside table, where they landed beside the baby monitor she hadn't even noticed him placing there.

He covered himself quickly, then returned to the position above her, close but not close enough. "It's been a long time for me."

"For me, too."

He grinned. "I just don't want you to have...unrealistic expectations." Again he kissed her throat, then lowered his warm mouth to her nipples.

Lauren almost came off the bed. Maybe she didn't have much to brag about in the chest department, but her nipples were very sensitive. If he sucked there too hard she was going to be finished before they began.

She reached down, wrapped her fingers around him and guided him to her. He didn't need any more encouragement. He took his mouth from her nipple, slid up her body, and—with a little guidance from her—pushed slowly and completely inside her trembling body.

The slow didn't last, which was good because she didn't want or need slow right now. She wanted power, force, quick thrusts to bring her quickly to the edge, and over. She came with a moan from deep inside her throat, and Cole came with her. Fast but powerful. Too soon, but also just right.

He blew the top of her head off.

If unwanted thoughts of love teased her muddled brain, for a moment, that was why.

It had never occurred to him that three condoms might not be enough. Cole had actually thought he was being overly optimistic to bring so many. After all, it wasn't like he could spend the night. The baby monitor would get him by for a short while, but eventually he'd need to go home, to his own bed. And no matter how much he wanted to, he couldn't ask Lauren to come home with him.

The fact that he had condoms at all had taken some planning. Talk about optimism. Slipping them into the cart at the drugstore had been an impulse, one he was very glad he'd listened to.

He'd been in Lauren's bed for hours, longer than he'd planned, longer than he should've been. But every time he'd thought about leaving, one thing had led to another and he'd gotten sidetracked. Seriously and completely sidetracked.

"Where did you come from?" Lauren whispered as she settled against his side and cuddled there.

He ignored the question, since he knew it wasn't literal—and he didn't have a proper answer to the real meaning of the question. She'd blindsided him. Had he done the same to her?

After five long years, he felt like he was coming out of a fog, shaking off the dust. Where the hell had *she* come from?

If he'd thought all they had was sex, the warning bells in his head wouldn't be going off. If he believed for one minute that their attraction was strictly physical, his satisfaction wouldn't be tempered with a healthy dose of caution.

Lauren had been upfront about what this was to her. Just sex, she'd said. She didn't need anything more from this new relationship than he did. His life would be so much easier if he could make himself believe that.

"I need to go," he said, but he didn't move.

"I know." She didn't move, either. Not a muscle.

"I might've come prepared, but apparently I wasn't prepared enough for you."

Lauren laughed, her breath warm against his side, her body shaking slightly. He loved her body. It was soft and giving and tight. She gave and took with total abandon, and made love with no holds barred.

Dangerous woman, this one.

He ran his hand along her hip, never tiring of the feel of her soft skin. He kissed her throat, loving the way she smelled and tasted. This woman could so easily become an addiction. Now that he knew what she felt like, smelled like, how could he not have her? Every day wouldn't be often enough. And dammit, this wasn't just sex. There was something more here, something special.

He pushed his hand between her thighs, teased her with his fingers until she gasped and asked for more. He was so tempted to take a chance. Just one chance... But he knew better. As much as he wanted to be inside her again, he couldn't. So he made her come with his hands and his mouth, watching her, amazed by her response. She called his name.

Cole dragged himself out of Lauren's bed. The single night-light was enough for him to see by as he grabbed his clothes and began to dress. He wasn't in any hurry.

A part of him really wanted to say to hell with it and fall back into bed and stay there all night.

But he didn't. As he dressed he wondered if Lauren was a luxury he could afford. He also wondered if he dared to give her up when he'd just found her. Even as ordered and freakishly organized as she was, he had a feeling slow was not her thing when it came to romance. If not for the kids he wouldn't care for it himself, but he didn't dare bring a woman into their lives when losing her would hurt them more than it would hurt him.

Very nicely exhausted, Lauren grabbed her pillow, sighed, asked him to lock the door when he left, and then she drifted off to sleep. By the time he was completely dressed she was breathing evenly and deeply. He was so tempted to just crawl back into that bed and hold her for a while longer.

But he didn't. Cole grabbed the baby monitor and walked out of the room, wondering if this was a one-time thing or if Lauren Russell was about to become a very important part of his life. He didn't see how they could handle anything in-between.

He left her house by the back door, locking it behind him as she'd asked him to. At this time of night the neighborhood was quiet. There was the occasional chirp of insects, the rustle of leaves as a pleasant breeze kicked up…and that was it. No voices, no laughter, no crying or screams or demands.

When he reached his own back door he stood there for a moment, back to the wall, eyes on the darkness. He drank in the quiet the same way he'd drunk in Lauren, with relish, with relief and with more than a little guilt.

His days were usually hectic from start to finish. Hank liked to stay up late; Meredith was awake at the crack of dawn, with Justin not far behind her. Cole didn't have any time to himself, not even half an hour to enjoy his coffee in silence. A short shower was usually the only quiet time he got, during a normal day.

The rare quiet moments had been the best part of working and going to school in the past few years. Fifteen minutes alone in the car; half an hour in front of a computer; five minutes in a break room with a cup of coffee. But since school had let out and he'd become a full-time dad, moving to Huntsville, he hadn't even had that. Parenting was a stressful job, and being a single parent should come with battle pay. He was pretty sure he was going to end up with post-traumatic stress syndrome.

His poor mother. She'd been a single parent, and he hadn't always been the best kid in the world. He wished he could apologize to her, tell her he understood now. What sacrifices had she made for him? Was he the reason she'd never remarried? God, he hoped not.

"Sorry, Mom," he whispered to the night, wondering if she could hear, hoping that she could.

Some days the hectic pace of Cole's life didn t bother him at all. Other days he wondered if he'd done the right thing, if he would've been better off letting Janet raise his kids while he continued to play ball. The money certainly would've been better. His life would've been centered around the sport he loved instead of around the kids.

But the truth was, he loved his kids more than he loved baseball. What decent father wouldn't? They'd needed him; they still did. That didn't mean he didn't sometimes wonder what his life would be like if he'd made other decisions five years ago.

The kids were older, he was about to start a new job. It was time he gave serious thought to a life for himself. Maybe Lauren would be a part of that life; maybe she was just a temporary player in his transition. But whatever part she might play…Cole had a feeling his life was about to take a serious shift, far beyond a new job, a new house, a new town and getting the last of the kids in school.

But he didn't know if that shift was a good thing or if it would only lead to trouble. Trouble for him and, more important, for his children.

Cole closed his eyes; he took a deep breath and let it out slowly. Morning would come too soon, and with morning would come his usual hectic pace. But tomorrow would be different from every other hectic day, he knew it to the pit of his soul. Even if he only had a couple hours of sleep to go on, even if he didn't have a moment of the day to himself…his life had just taken a sharp turn. No matter what happened, there would be no turning back.

Talk about an effective ungrumpy potion…

Chapter Nine

Lauren found herself humming as she cleaned the kitchen after preparing and eating her poached egg and whole-wheat toast. She'd never felt so good after a *very* short night's sleep.

Even more than—okay, perhaps as much as—the physical satisfaction that still hummed through her body, she found herself surprisingly content. She'd tried to convince herself what she and Cole had was nothing deeper than sex, but her mind wasn't behaving this morning. Maybe Cole Donovan would turn out to be the one, maybe he wouldn't. Maybe his visits would become a regular thing. Maybe not. Lauren was a woman with a plan. Always. She didn't like anyone or anything to throw a monkey wrench into her schedule. But Cole was such a nice monkey wrench, she decided she should adjust accordingly.

Go with the flow had sounded great in the heat of the moment, but it was so *not* her style.

One night together, and she was already wondering where they would go next. Just sex sounded great, in theory; it was such a clean, simple plan. But could she stick to it?

Everything else was very much on track. The book would be out in a few months. Her career was certainly headed in the right direction. Fall was right around the corner, and with it would come cooler weather, college football and pumpkin recipes. Her mind took a turn, veering away from career. She wondered if Cole could dance, if he would attend The Gardens' Labor Day event as her—wait for it—date.

It wasn't long before she heard the now-familiar sounds of the Donovan children at play. Instead of being annoyed, she found herself smiling. There was joy in those screams. Children playing outside on a beautiful summer day was a happy part of life. She'd been so closeted in her own little world, so isolated, that she'd forgotten that. As a child she'd been known to romp herself, after all. On a morning where her body hummed in contentment, all was right with the world.

There had been a short-lived but hard rain around dawn that morning, so the ground in her garden would be soft. Perfect for pulling weeds.

After changing into proper gardening clothes—an old pair of shorts, older tennis shoes, thick gloves and a soft T-shirt—Lauren stepped through the kitchen door and into her backyard to pull a few of those weeds and maybe pick some bell peppers and tomatoes, if she deemed them ready upon closer inspection. She couldn't help but glance into the Donovan yard. Just the boys were out this morning. The water hose had already been put to use. Since the ground had been soaked to begin with, their play left puddles and muddy patches here and there. Hank took a running jump at one of those puddles, landed on his backside and slid. Justin copied his older brother, and they both laughed. The kids were so caught up in their games they didn't even see her. Meredith wasn't playing with her brothers this morning. Of course, she was a little old to be jumping into mud puddles for the hell of it. Cole was nowhere to be found. Maybe he was sleeping late. The man really should be completely exhausted. And wasn't that lovely.

Lauren sat down beside her bell pepper plants and started to gently but firmly pull the few weeds there out by the root. The ground was so soft, the sometimes difficult chore was easy. Her house was always immaculately clean, she took great care with her own hygiene and clothing…but she loved digging in her garden. She loved the feel of her fingers in the dirt, even if she did wear gloves to keep the dirt from getting packed under her fingernails. As she weeded the garden she cast occasional glances toward the house next door. Checking on the kids, she told herself, even though her gaze very often cut to the back door and she wondered if Cole would appear there.

She had the strangest urge to walk to that back door, knock, and ask if Cole could come out to play….

It wasn't long before Justin saw her. He elbowed his brother in the side and they both ran toward her. The way they ran was unexpectedly beautiful, their little legs pumping, their heads held high. And they smiled. At her.

"Good morning," she said.

"Whatcha doin'?" Justin asked as he skidded to a stop just a couple of feet away.

"Pulling weeds." Lauren demonstrated, grabbing

a pesky weed at the base and pulling so it came up smoothly, root and all.

Hank looked at the small pile of weeds Lauren had already pulled. "Hey, are any of those poisonous?"

Surprised, Lauren looked him in the eye. "No, but they're not meant for eating, either. Why do you ask?"

"Just wondering," he said.

It was Justin who explained. "Hank makes magic potions. Sometimes they even work."

"Magic potions," Lauren responded, hiding her amusement. Judging by the expression on Hank's face, the potions were serious business, not something to be made light of. "You know, that's very much like cooking. You have to have a recipe and all the right ingredients, and it takes just the right touch to produce the desired results. Maybe one day you'll be a great chef."

Hank looked horrified. "Uh-uh. Cooking is only for *girls.*"

"No, cooking is not only for girls. Some of the best chefs in the world are men."

"Not in our family," Justin said, his voice sounding strangely grown-up, at the moment.

Lauren smiled. It sounded like Cole could use some help in the kitchen.

When the back door to the Donovan house opened the movement caught her eye. Cole stepped outside. He was looking for the boys and had found her. Man, had he ever found her. He looked straight at her, unsmiling, big and strong and sexy as she'd ever imagined a man could be. In blue jeans and a very plain shirt, he looked... delicious. How could she not look at him and think about last night?

She was thinking, quite vividly, about last night

when something cool and sticky smacked her in the jaw and neck.

Justin stood at the other end of one of her bell pepper plants, one of the younger ones she'd planted so she'd have a continuous crop of peppers until the first freeze. The cool and sticky sensation was a muddy root ball. Mud ran down her neck, under her shirt, into her bra. She had a little bit of it on her lower lip. She tried to dislodge the mud on her lip, but ended up tasting it.

Justin smiled. "I'm helping, see? I didn't mean to hit you in the face, but it's a really big weed."

Hank—realizing exactly what his brother had done—laughed so hard he fell to the ground. Cole was running in her direction at full speed, and for the first time since she'd gotten out of bed this morning, Lauren wondered what the hell she might be getting herself into.

Great. Just great. He begins to think that maybe he can actually have a life of his own, and then he's reminded why that's not nearly as easy as it sounds.

"I'm so sorry," Cole said. Sorry wasn't enough, but it was all he had at the moment. One cheek, one side of Lauren's neck and a good portion of her shirt were splattered with mud. Justin was at the one end of a plant. The other end was still dripping mud on Lauren—though the worst of the damage had already been done. "Justin, put that down." He glared at his middle child. "Hank, stop laughing." When Hank didn't immediately do as he'd been told, Cole added, "Now."

Hank pressed his lips together and fought the laughter. Justin finally dropped the plant to the ground.

"Y'all go get cleaned up. Hose off before you go inside." They were both muddy from head to toe.

As they ran off, Hank started laughing again.

Cole dropped to his haunches and reached out to wipe his fingers across Lauren's face, scraping mud away from her mouth. "I'm sorry."

Lauren had been so calm last night, when milk had run across her table, when Meredith had been purposely unfriendly. She'd handled the kids so well. Now, however, she was apparently at a loss for words. She sputtered, trying to dislodge the last bit of mud from her lip. Being whacked in the face with a root ball wasn't quite the same as cleaning up spilled milk.

Opposites attracted, he'd heard. But realistically, did he and Lauren have even a ghost of a chance? Her life was so well-ordered; his was constant chaos. Mud stains weren't an everyday part of her life; he lived with them daily.

She had only herself to consider; he came with a ready-made family. Any woman who took him on would get the kids as part of the package. Looking at Lauren now, he figured she'd just realized she'd be getting the short end of the stick in that deal.

He wouldn't be doing her any favors if he tried to make her a part of his life.

"Hey, Dad, get out of the way!"

Cole turned. Hank and Justin stood a few feet away—as far as the hose from the back of the house would reach. Justin still held the nozzle in his hand. They were both dripping wet, but most of the mud had been washed away. "That's good enough," he said. "Y'all head in…"

Before he could finish, Justin lifted the nozzle and pulled the trigger, sending a stream of water directly into Lauren's face. She was unprepared as water went up her nose and into her mouth and down her T-shirt. Cole threw himself into the path of the stream of water, taking the burst to the chest. He was grateful that the kids hadn't been able to get any closer. If the water pressure had been any stronger, they might've knocked Lauren to the ground.

"Stop it!" he shouted.

The spray of water died to a trickle. Justin said, "I was just trying to wash the mud off Miss Lauren." Hank laughed. Meredith opened the back door and stood there for a moment before she figured out what had happened, and then she started laughing, too.

Last night he'd thought he and Lauren were at the beginning of something potentially big. It had just been washed away in a sea of mud and water from the hose. She wouldn't ever want to see him again, he figured. No matter how great the sex was...no matter how great she looked even now, sitting on the ground with her T-shirt soaked and her hair plastered to her head.

The boys ran for the house, realizing they needed to escape while they still could.

Lauren looked shell-shocked. She sat there on the ground, soaked to the skin, eyes wide. And then she looked at him and he saw the terror. No, terror was too strong a word. What he saw there, in those warm hazel eyes, was the sad acceptance of the truth.

"This is my life," he said. "Not every day, and it's not always mud and water. Sometimes it's gum and spaghetti. Apple juice and permanent marker. If you're looking for neat and orderly, that's not me."

"I know," she said, her first words since he'd come out here to rescue her.

"Do you still want to give it a try?" he asked. "I won't blame you if you run for the hills, tell me never to darken your door again, kick my ass to the curb...." It wasn't what he wanted, but why should he expect anything more?

Cole really, really wanted Lauren to tell him to quit overthinking, like she had last night. He wanted her to shake off the mud, laugh, tell him it was no big deal. She didn't.

"I can't make a decision right now," she said. "I just… can't."

He was tempted to make the decision for her, to tell her they were finished. Finished before they'd even started. But he couldn't make himself say the words. He wasn't what she needed, the odds that they could make it work were slim, but he didn't want to let her go. Not so soon, not after last night.

Last night she'd helped him to discover that even though he'd dedicated himself to his children, he was still a man—still a person—and he wanted more from life. He'd walked away from her with so much hope in his heart. He'd left her house looking at the future as more than being Dad, coach, teacher. Was all that gone now? So soon?

She stood slowly, shaking off water and mud and maybe even her anger. Cole tried to help, but she waved him off. Not a good sign. He watched as she stalked to the back door of her immaculate house. As bad as things were, he enjoyed watching her stalk away. Those hips, the way she held her head, those legs…

At the back door Lauren turned to face him. He half expected her to tell him that she never wanted to see him or any of his offspring again. Instead she said, "Lunch. Noon. Be here on time and *come alone*."

Lauren wasn't sure exactly what she'd say to Cole when he arrived for lunch, so after she'd showered and washed her hair and thrown away her muddy clothes— there was no saving them, she was certain—she directed

her attention to the meal. Chicken salad on a bed of let-
tuce, assorted crackers, fresh fruit and homemade rolls.
The rolls were a concession for Cole, since crackers
would've been enough for her. Since the rest of the meal
was pretty much chick food, she decided the least she
could do was throw him a roll or two. For dessert there
was key lime pie. A pitcher of fresh tea was cooling in
the fridge.

She'd put on a cool sundress, and had spent a good
five minutes trying to decide between a pair of high heels
she hadn't worn in years and flat sandals. In the end the
sandals won. The heels might send the wrong message.
To her, if not to Cole.

She liked him so much. More than she'd liked any
man for a very long time. Last night had been wonderful from beginning to end. But she wasn't sure she was
ready to take on those kids! Yes, they were occasionally
adorable, but they were also occasionally hellacious. She
wanted children of her own, one day, but judging by what
she'd seen of the Donovan children, did she really want
her kids to have Cole's DNA?

Lauren set the table, using dark green luncheon plates
and her green-plaid cotton napkins, which were perfect
for a casual lunch. She was really getting ahead of herself, thinking about babies and DNA when she didn't
even know if she and Cole would ever have a normal
date, much less a lasting relationship.

He arrived right on time. Like her he'd showered—he
smelled of soap and coffee—and had changed into clean
khakis and a button-up shirt. He was on his best behavior, but what about his children? The question before her
was simple, she realized as she watched him closely.

Was he worth it?

"I grounded the kids," he said.

Lauren found herself smiling. "Hello to you, too."

He smiled, and when he did her heart leaped. No, wait, that was not her heart. What leaped inside her was a good bit lower.

"Hello. I grounded the kids," he said again. "Are you okay?"

"I'm fine. I don't suppose a little mud ever hurt anyone." And as she said the words, she believed them to be true. She was making a mountain out of a molehill.

Maybe. When they were alone it was so easy to relegate all their potential future problems to the back of her mind. Didn't she need to know that they had a future before she let the problems that might come their way eclipse everything else?

Lauren walked to Cole, wrapped her arms around his waist and looked up. She loved his eyes, so blue and intense they took her breath away. She loved the feel of her body against his, in a way she'd never known was possible. He was solid and warm and even though he was a mile taller than she was, somehow they were just right for one another.

"I've been thinking about this situation," she said.

"Me, too. If you're going to dump me, do it fast and get it over with." He looked a little worried about that possibility.

"Are you mine to dump?"

"Like it or not, I believe I am." He didn't sound as happy about that as she might've liked, but at the same time she understood.

"I'm not going to dump you," she said.

"But? I hear a *but* there."

"But we need a list. We need some rules, Cole."

Was that a growl from deep in his throat? "I'm not very good with rules."

"I've noticed that."

"But for you, I'm willing to try."

She smiled at him, let the frustration of her encounter with a mud ball slip away. Rules. A list. This was her comfort zone. "Okay, first of all…"

"But not yet."

Cole leaned down and placed his mouth against hers. The sensation, the power of that kiss took her breath away. Every cell of her body responded, and they stood in her kitchen and kissed, rules unset, list unwritten. In the back of her mind a little voice whispered, *This isn't settled, and you know it.* But her body and his were more forceful in insisting that, for now, that little detail didn't matter.

Lunch was done. Cole had kissed her silly, and eaten lunch at her kitchen table without taking his eyes off her, and then he'd kissed her some more. They'd never gotten around to her list. The list could wait. She'd sat on his lap at the kitchen table for a while. There had been no rush, no frantic need, just…touching. Learning one another. Kissing and teasing and more kissing. The way he touched her was enough to make her forget every list she'd ever written. And the ones she hadn't written yet, well, they were supremely unimportant.

Hank had come over to fetch his dad too soon. They'd heard little feet approaching and had moved apart just as the back door swung open. There was another emergency at the Donovan household. Cole had left, once he was assured blood and fire were not involved. She wondered if he'd be back later, when the kids were asleep. Baby monitor and all.

Difficulties aside, was this it? Was he the one? She hadn't been looking for a man, hadn't even wanted a relationship at this time of her life. And yet, here he was. Could she love Cole or was this all just testosterone and estrogen meeting in a perfect storm of hormones?

The jarring ring of the phone yanked Lauren out of her daydream. She checked the caller ID; it was her editor. Hilary never called just to chat. Was something wrong?

"Hello?"

"Oh, my God, you won't believe it." Hilary Casale was a veteran at the publishing house. She'd always been cool as a cucumber, distant, even. Lauren had never heard so much as a hint of excitement in her voice. Until now.

"Won't believe what?" Lauren asked. Something was wrong, she just knew it. Her contentment flew out the window. She should've known it wouldn't last.

"I got the call this morning, but there were details to be settled before I called you with the news… This is going to change everything…. You are the luckiest new author I have ever…" Hilary was breathless and damn near incoherent.

But she'd said *lucky,* and that had to be good. Right? "Please tell me what's going on."

Hilary took a deep, stilling breath Lauren could hear through the phone lines, then she began again. "I got a phone call from a producer who heard about your book from an associate of mine. Edward Mandel is putting together a reality show where up-and-coming cooks compete for their own show on one of the food networks. I don't remember which one, but that doesn't matter. He checked out your website and he liked what he saw. He wants you."

"He wants me for what?"

Hilary laughed. "He wants you to be one of the contestants. Shooting starts in six weeks. You'll be marketed as the Southern homemaker, the one who uses lots of butter and talks with a deep accent, you can do that, right? I mean, you have kind of an accent but it's not particularly deep. Think *Designing Women* accent. Can you pull that off?"

Lauren's mind was oddly blank. She was having trouble processing this offer that had come out of nowhere. "I suppose, but…"

"There is no *but,* Lauren. This is the opportunity of a lifetime. Whatever Mandel wants, you deliver. The show will put your book on the *Times* list. Win or lose, your career will be made." Hilary's voice became increasingly faster and louder. "Why aren't you screaming? Why aren't you laughing and jumping up and down? Well, I can't know that you're not jumping up and down, but you don't even sound excited!"

The offer—interesting as it sounded—had stunned her. It instantly turned Lauren's neat plans for the coming months upside down. Sex, rules, lists, more sex, maybe a real date… "Where will this show be filmed?"

"Here in New York! We'll do dinner when you come in. Once the show starts I think you'll be pretty tied up, so…"

"I need to think about this."

Hilary's response was a long moment of dead silence. Finally she said, "What is there to think about?"

Cole. "My grandmother. I can't leave.…"

"Hire someone. You'll be making enough from the show, and it'll only last a few weeks. Six, I think. Maybe ten. Well, unless you win and they want to start your new show right away, but face it, that's a long shot. The reality show itself is the payoff. Edward wants to meet with you, as soon as possible. Oh, and a word of warning—

don't call him Eddie. Apparently it's a thing with him. This weekend? Would that work for you?"

Lauren felt as if her stomach was tied up in knots. Why couldn't she have enjoyed her contentment a little while longer? "I need to think about this. I'll call you back."

Though it was horribly rude, and not at all like her, Lauren hung up before Hilary could offer more arguments about how this was the chance of a lifetime.

One chance of a lifetime was a lot to take in. Two in less than twenty-four hours made her head spin.

The emergency that had called him away from Lauren hadn't been an emergency at all, but a laundry issue. Meredith's way of bringing him home. Maybe it was just as well, because he'd been minutes from making love to Lauren on her kitchen table. And he needed to make another trip to the drugstore before that happened.

They still had that list to put together. He'd never been good at lists. Or rules. Or plans. Why make them when something always got in the way? But if a list of rules was what Lauren wanted, he'd try. Cole was pouring another cup of coffee when the phone rang. He groaned when he saw Janet's number on the caller ID. He was tempted to let it ring, but if he did she'd just call his cell, and then she'd start texting, and before noon she'd send out the National Guard looking for him. Better to just get it over with.

"Good afternoon, Janet," he answered, knowing it would be her and not her workaholic husband on the line.

"Good afternoon." Her voice was cool, as it had been since he'd told her they were moving to Huntsville, months ago. "How are the kids?"

"They're fine. Do you want to talk to them? They're

in their rooms." Still grounded, not that he intended to tell Janet that much. "Give me a minute and I'll…"

"That's not necessary. Listen, Cole, I'd like to come visit this weekend. Do you mind?" She didn't give him a chance to respond. "Saturday would be best. I can call you when I'm on the way."

So much for "asking" if he minded. "We'll be here."

Janet asked about the kids and how they were adjusting to their new home, talked for a moment about her own two girls, who were in college now, and then the conversation was over. When the phone was back on the charger Cole glanced around the living room. He wasn't an idiot. Janet was coming by to see if her niece and nephews were being properly taken care of, if they could get along without her right around the corner. He had to prove to her that all was well.

Even if it wasn't.

He called all the kids into the living room for a powwow. When they were lined up on the sofa, he said, "Aunt Janet is coming on Saturday." They remained stoic. They loved their aunt, but they knew very well how she was. Demanding, critical…overprotective to the point of smothering. And it was a regular part of any visit that she inspect their rooms. "We're going to show her that everything here is hunky-dory."

"What's that?" Justin asked.

"Great. Wonderful. Perfect."

"That means I have to clean my room, doesn't it?" Hank asked solemnly.

"Yes, it does." He looked at Meredith. "And we're going to feed our guest. Start planning a menu. Something simple and easy, but no frozen chicken nuggets. I can talk to Lauren. Maybe she'll have some ideas…"

"No!" Meredith snapped. "I can handle preparing a

meal for Aunt Janet without any help from the woman next door." She shook her hair in an undeniably defiant gesture.

"Fine. I'll leave it to you. The house will be clean, you three will be clean and dressed in clothes that match—" he caught Hank's eye for that one "—and we will convince Aunt Janet that we don't need any help." He'd never get Janet out of their hair, and besides, that wasn't what he wanted. The kids deserved to have something of their mother's family in their lives on a regular basis, and Janet deserved to have this connection with her sister. What he *did* want was for her to quit implying—and sometimes outright saying—that he was an incompetent parent, that he couldn't handle his family alone.

Knockout night with Lauren aside, best lunch ever in his rear mirror, he *was* alone. He couldn't let what he wanted become more important than what his kids needed. Not ever. And at the end of the day, he couldn't allow himself to need anyone. Not Janet. Not even Lauren.

Hilary was merciless. She called until Lauren finally agreed to meet with the producer who'd chosen her for his show. She still hadn't decided if she wanted to participate or not—no matter what a fabulous opportunity Hilary thought it would be. Judging by what little she'd seen of reality shows, they'd probably make her construct a meal in thirty minutes using only Spam, orange Jell-O and dried beans. They'd probably make her race for spices, or ask her to turn a box of dried mac and cheese into a meal fit for a king. That was so *not* her.

The producer, Edward "don't call him Eddie" Mandel, was flying in on Saturday. Lauren had been surprised that he hadn't asked her to come to him, but Hilary said they'd be shooting footage of all the contestants at home, so he wanted to check out her surroundings.

She spent all afternoon planning what she'd feed Mandel. Planning a meal—what to serve, which plates and glasses to use, what kind of dessert she should prepare—calmed her. She needed to be calm for her brain to work. Did she want this? She did not expect she'd enjoy the show, if she decided to move forward with it, and she didn't want to win. As much as she wanted a career, television was not in her plans; she wasn't what one would call a TV-personality type. She was too quiet, too reserved. She'd make a terrible game-show contestant, because if she won a million dollars she'd probably just smile, clap her hands gently a couple of times and mouth a single, quiet "Yay."

But if the reality show would really increase the sales of her book the way Hilary said it would, shouldn't she at least give it a try? It wasn't like she'd be moving to New York permanently.

Would Cole be waiting for her when she got home or would he have moved on to another woman by that time?

A warning bell went off in her head. She barely knew the man. Yes, she was attracted to him; yes, she liked him; yes, he was great in bed. But should she be planning her life around a man just because he made her feel good? Just because when he kissed her she forgot everything else? How often had she let herself depend on a man in the past? Three. How many times had she been disappointed?

Three.

Why should she consider even for a moment that Cole would be any different?

Last night she'd been so sure that they were at the beginning of something grand—lunch had been beyond wonderful—but she couldn't entirely dismiss this morning's debacle. Great sex and soul-searing kisses did not a relationship make. She was wild about Cole, in a way she'd never expected to be. He'd come out of nowhere and turned her neat plans upside down. He was a wonderful father—his kids were occasionally wild, but he loved them so much she had to give him points for that—a good neighbor, a great lover.

But could she really trust him?

Cole stared at the phone longer than he should've. He was never indecisive. He made mistakes, everyone did, but he made his mistakes rushing forward like a bull in a china shop. The kids were outside, the washer and the dryer were both running, breakfast dishes were in the dishwasher. Finally he lifted the receiver and dialed the number he'd memorized. It rang four times, then he got a recording.

Like he was going to leave Lauren a message when he wasn't entirely sure what he'd say if he got her on the other end of the line. *Thank you? What are you doing tonight? Are you as confused as I am?*

No, even if he was confused, he'd never admit it.

He could ask her to help get the house and the kids ready for Saturday's visit, but they weren't at that place in their relationship, and hell, might never be. Could you call a couple of conversations, one night of great sex and one out-of-control make-out session a relationship? He did, but what about Lauren? Besides, Meredith would have a fit if he indicated in any way that she was incapable of handling the duties of the woman of the house on her own.

He wasn't about to leave a stuttering message on Lauren's answering machine. He'd try her later.

The screams from the backyard went silent; that got Cole's attention. As much as he sometimes longed for it, silence in this household was rarely a sign of anything good. He could only hope there was no blood, and no broken windows. He walked away from the phone, toward the kitchen door and the backyard.

Before he opened the door he saw the reason for the silence. He watched the foursome through the window set in the door, smiling as Hank and Justin leaned over a plate Lauren held in both hands, the offering held out and down for their inspection. Meredith hung back, but even she eyed whatever was on the plate their neighbor proffered.

Cole was content to just watch Lauren for a few minutes. She'd changed clothes again. Now she wore denim shorts that showed off great legs; a white tank that hugged her curves, such as they were; white sandals. Brave of her to wear white after what had happened this morning. Her hair was pulled up in a ponytail, and his gut tightened as he imagined loosening her hair and letting it down again. Her smile was infectious. Hank and Justin were grinning ear to ear as they each choose a huge cookie from the plate. Even Meredith relaxed a bit as she chose one for herself.

Lauren glanced toward the house, saw him standing there, watching, and the smile changed.

Cole opened the door and walked outside. The kids were devouring their cookies, which were the size of softballs and bursting with chocolate chips. "So, you're going to feed my kids sugar and then go home?" he said, smiling at Lauren.

"No, I thought I'd stick around and study the results." She held the plate toward him. "You, too. A new recipe.

I thought I'd experiment on y'all before I use it in a column."

"She can experiment on me any day, Dad," Hank said enthusiastically. "These cookies are awesome."

Barely glancing down, Cole grabbed a cookie for himself. The offerings were arranged on a heavy green platter with pink flowers painted around the edge. "Good lord, woman, don't you own a paper plate?"

"I don't like paper plates," she responded.

"Why not?"

"They're not pretty."

"I wouldn't have survived the past few years without paper plates." If he could only find a way to get the kids in disposable clothes, he'd have it made....

The cookie was awesome, just as Hank said it was. He wasn't surprised. Lauren didn't do anything in half measures.

Justin, now as charmed by Miss Lauren as his brother had been from first sight, reached up and snagged Lauren's wrist. She looked down at him. "Do you want another cookie?"

"Later. Jump on the trampoline with me!"

Lauren shook her head. "Thank you, but I'll have to decline."

"Huh?"

Her smile widened. "No, thank you."

"But...it's *fun*." Justin's argument was simple and heartfelt.

"I've never been on a trampoline before. I'm afraid I'd fall off and hurt myself."

"You've never been on a trampoline, not in your whole life?" Hank was clearly horrified.

Again, Lauren shook her head.

"That's sad," Justin said sincerely.

"If she doesn't want to get on the trampoline, leave her alone," Meredith said, her voice cool. She wasn't looking out for Lauren's well-being, Cole knew. She wanted their neighbor to go home ASAP.

"Oh, I don't know," Cole said casually. He took a bite of the cookie. It melted in his mouth. "It doesn't seem right that Miss Lauren has never been on a trampoline." They worked in concert, Cole taking the plate of cookies, Justin taking her hand, Hank leading the way. Only Meredith hung back, uncertain. Unhappy. Looking every bit the sullen almost-teenager. He still wasn't sure what to do about that, but walking away from something promising didn't seem to be the way for any of them.

Lauren argued halfheartedly as Justin all but dragged her to the trampoline. "I wouldn't even know what to do."

"You just jump," Hank said. "It's easy!"

Justin added, "Dad tells us that when he says *jump* we're supposed to ask how high, but he never actually tells us to jump so I don't know why he says that."

Lauren glanced over her shoulder, caught his eye and laughed.

She was a good sport; he shouldn't have expected anything else. She kicked off her shoes and got onto the trampoline, taking careful steps as she worked her way to the center. The boys yelled, "Jump! Jump!"

Lauren took a very small jump, looked at Cole, and asked, "How high?"

And then she put everything she had into a motion that threw her high into the air. She laughed, and screamed… and yes, she jiggled nicely, here and there.

The boys laughed. Even Meredith smiled, as she walked closer to snag another cookie from the platter. To be honest, Cole had never expected to watch Lauren let loose this way. Then again, he hadn't really expected last night, either. And when he'd gone to her house for lunch he certainly hadn't expected her to all but devour him in her perfect kitchen.

He couldn't help but wonder, as he watched her, what next? Just when he was certain his life held no more surprises, here it came. Here *she* came.

Surprise.

Chapter Ten

Where Lauren was concerned, things were happening too fast. His plan to take things slowly hadn't lasted long at all. Cole understood that he couldn't afford to jump into a relationship with both feet. There was too much at stake, too many ways things could go wrong. She had to understand that, too, but neither of them seemed interested in taking it slowly.

Summer Schuler invited the kids to go to the movies with her and her bunch, then out for pizza afterward. They'd all met at the barbecue—before the disaster and the trip to the E.R.—and the kids had played together a time or two since then, since summer days were long and there was a trampoline in the Donovan backyard. The boys jumped on the offer, tempted by the movie and totally sold by the pizza, but Meredith hesitated. In the end it was the movie that pulled her in.

Considering the way the day had begun, with Lauren

getting a face full of mud and a spritz with the hose, he should've made them stay home, properly grounded. But a little time at Lauren's *without* a baby monitor might not be a bad thing. As they were getting ready to leave, Justin's face fell. His eyes got big and sad, his lower lip quivered. "Dad will be here all alone."

Cole had to work not to smile. To Justin, being left at home alone would be traumatic. For Cole—for any child-rearing adult who found him or herself with a few precious hours of alone time—it was a rare gift.

"I'll be fine," he said solemnly. "There's a movie I want to watch on TV, then I'll eat some supper and work on the plans for my history class."

"We won't be too late," Justin said, forcing a bright smile.

"I can stay…" Meredith began, but Cole stopped her.

"I'm sure Mrs. Schuler will appreciate your help with the little kids."

Meredith agreed with a nod of her head. Her favorite actor was in the movie, and she was anxious to see him on the big screen.

Cole had to wonder if Summer Schuler had invited his kids along in order to give him and Lauren some time alone. How much had Lauren told her friend? Anything? This could be simply another attempt at blatant matchmaking. Summer and Lauren might've planned this together. It could also be just what it seemed to be, an invitation to the movies for a couple of neighborhood children. There was no reason to read anything more into it.

Last night he'd gone to Lauren's house with a baby monitor and a few condoms. This afternoon he hadn't been able to keep his hands off her. They'd started something, something unexpected and powerful, but still, he was going to look like a complete ass if he knocked on her door expecting…well, anything. He couldn't just run next door whenever he got an itch he wanted Lauren to scratch, whenever it was convenient.

Could he?

No, she deserved better than to be convenient. But it had been so long since he'd had a woman in his life, he wasn't sure what came next. All he knew was that he could still remember how Lauren felt, how she tasted, how she moaned… He was getting hard just thinking about her.

Summer collected the kids and they left in a rush, piling into the Schuler van and taking off, kids waving wildly. Cole, standing in the doorway, waved back. After they rounded the corner he turned his attention to the house next door, staring at the front porch and the inviting door there.

He didn't know what Lauren was to him, not yet. He had no idea what he might be to her. But the idea of just sitting here alone while she was right next door—also alone—made his brain itch. What did he have to lose by making a move?

Nothing. *Everything.*

Lauren had changed her upcoming Saturday menu plan five times. She wanted to impress the producer, even if she wasn't sure she wanted to be on his reality show. She was a professional. Impressing people with good food and Southern hospitality was what she did best. It was her job.

Should the meal be simple and hearty, or elegant? She didn't know the man who was coming to her house, so she should be sensitive to food preferences. No seafood, pork or red meat. Chicken, then. That narrowed her choices considerably.

She was flipping through her recipe cards, searching for a proper chicken recipe, when the doorbell rang. The mail had already run and she wasn't expecting a package. That left limited possibilities. A child selling something she didn't want or need, which was unlikely since school hadn't started yet and it wasn't Girl Scout cookie season; someone trying to convert her to their religion; a neighbor with a petition; or Cole. At the front door, this time?

Lauren thought about straightening her hair as she walked slowly to the door, but then she restrained herself. There was no reason for her to make an effort to look her best for a man who had already seen her in spectacular disarray. Mad sex did nothing for her hairstyle or makeup. Nothing good, anyway.

She peeked through the security viewer, saw the man she'd pretty much expected to be there, then sighed long and too loud. He really had come out of nowhere, and she didn't have any idea what would happen next. To find out, she'd have to open the door. In spite of the fact that he'd muddied up her plans, she very much wanted to know what might come next.

Cole Donovan stood there, smile on his face, an anonymous-looking and large brown bag in his grasp. "Do you like Chinese?"

"Sure." She looked behind him. "Where are the kids?"

"Out for the evening with the Schuler family."

She still hadn't invited him in, and she wasn't sure that she should. Cole was a complication, and even though they were amazingly compatible—at least in one way— she didn't want to be taken for granted. She didn't want him to think of her as the easy and overly eager next-door neighbor. "There's enough food in that bag for many more than two."

"I wasn't sure what you liked. Besides, it's not like leftovers go to waste in my house."

Lauren had a very bad feeling that she could fall in love with Cole Donovan with very little encouragement. She was already halfway there, and that was bad. Very bad. He wasn't falling in love with her; it was too soon, and besides, he had his hands full with his children. She was just a distraction, nothing more. She'd been an idiot to think they could be neighbors with benefits. Heaven above, she could see it so clearly. He'd be perfectly happy with a relationship that was strictly physical. In spite of herself, in spite of the fact that she'd been the one to insist that all they had was sex, she wanted more. She wanted everything.

But he was her neighbor, and no matter where this went they were going to have to find a way to get along.

She still hadn't finished her list regarding his children. She'd gotten as far as *no mud* and *stay out of my garden* before setting it aside.

"Chinese, yes," she said. "Sex, no." She felt a hot flush rise on her cheeks. "Just in case that was what you had in mind. We really need to talk first." She felt like she was cutting off her nose to spite her face, considering how much she wanted him, but there was so much unsaid, so much still to do…and she still hadn't told him about the television deal. Would he be happy for her or annoyed that she was leaving? Would he even care?

"Seduction by fried rice." He smiled. Maybe there was a little disappointment in his expression, but he didn't run away, taking his fried rice with him. "I'll be happy for the company."

Lauren stepped back and let him into her house. He

knew the way to the kitchen, and walked ahead of her, unerringly headed in that direction. She couldn't help but stare at his butt—just a little. It was a nice butt, tight and perfectly shaped in those snug jeans. And out of those jeans, as well. She remembered. How could she forget? Maybe she'd made a mistake. Maybe she should've sent him away. But where was the danger in a shared meal and a little conversation?

There was none. No danger at all.

He and Lauren had talked before, but not like this. Alone, kidless, no pressure, no timetable. There was sexual tension but it wasn't like before, when he'd been about to burst with wanting her. This was more like a slow simmer. It wasn't that he didn't want to sleep with her again. He did. Maybe one day he would. But she'd made it very clear—not tonight.

Strangely enough, he didn't mind all that much, even though he'd stopped at the drugstore when he'd gone out for Chinese. If it was right, in time it would happen again. And again.

They got to know one another a little better over shrimp and broccoli and honey chicken. And fried rice. The two of them barely made a dent in what he'd bought, but that was okay. He hadn't been lying when he'd said leftovers didn't have a chance in his house.

He loved Lauren's kitchen. It was always clean, always in perfect order. It always smelled good, like lingering cinnamon or vanilla. And she was usually in it.

They'd covered the basics. Childhoods, schools, most embarrassing moments, favorite foods, movies, books. He'd been a little surprised to find out that she'd been a bit of a nerd in high school. She'd played clarinet in the band, had belonged to the Future Homemakers Club—

that wasn't a surprise at all—and she'd volunteered in the library. Naturally she'd been a straight-A student. If they'd gone to the same high school, would he even have noticed her? He'd been the star baseball player who did just enough to get by in class. He hadn't done clubs at all.

After a while he'd even talked about baseball, a little. He didn't do much of that these days. What was there to say? Playing baseball was a part of his past; he wasn't big on reliving the past, but he didn't mind talking to Lauren about it. She was curious without being *too* interested.

Leaning back in her chair, Lauren took a deep breath and looked him in the eye. "So tell me, are you ever sorry?"

"Sorry about what?" He shoved back his empty plate. There was no way he could eat another bite.

The easy expression Lauren had worn all evening was gone, replaced by uncertainty and tension. And that was how he realized the true meaning of her question.

"Do I regret giving up baseball to raise my kids?"

She shook her head, making her thick ponytail dance. "I have no business asking that. It's just, when you talked about playing baseball your face lit up. Leaving was a huge sacrifice, and you know very well that not everyone would've made the decision you did."

He hadn't talked to anyone about this in a very long time, and he had never been completely honest. He'd never been open. Publicly, he made sure everyone knew he'd never suffered a moment's regret. Privately, it was another story.

"There were times when I was certain I'd made a terrible mistake. Usually when the flu was making a rampant run through the house and one kid had thrown up in the hall and the other one hadn't made it out of the bed.

Or when Justin would cry for no reason, screaming for hours, and I couldn't comfort him. When Hank decided he could fly and jumped off the top bunk and broke his arm, and when Meredith needed her first bra." He caught Lauren's eye and held it. "I suspect you're the kind of woman who never feels inadequate, but there have been times, many times, when I felt like a completely useless parent. Baseball is easier."

"Almost everyone feels inadequate at one time or another," she said. And then she smiled. "And then there are those who *should* feel inadequate but never do."

"I've met a few of those." The mood had lightened, which was fine with him. He didn't want this conversation to turn maudlin.

"You know, that's one of the things I like about you," she said casually.

He got a weird flutter when she admitted that she liked him. But his voice was cool as he said, "What's that?"

She leaned toward him, smiling but serious. "Whatever you do, you throw yourself into it wholeheartedly. Baseball, raising your kids, now teaching and being a coach. You have a 'damn the torpedoes, full speed ahead' attitude about everything you do."

He wondered if somewhere in that pretty head she was thinking, *Even me.*

Lauren looked at him with a decidedly serious gleam in her eye. "I think you're the best father I've ever met, and your children are very lucky to have you. They're not perfect, you're not perfect, but they love you so much, and you love them. That's what makes a family work. I envy you that. It's what I want, one day. Babies, a house filled with love, hell, even the flu when it runs around."

She smiled. She could smile because she hadn't had to endure the flu. It wasn't quaint; it was war.

Cole tried to picture Lauren as a part of his family, and as much as he wanted to, he couldn't make it work. Sure, he didn't know her as well as he should, all things considered, so he shouldn't even let his mind wander in that direction. His home, his family, was in a constant state of chaos. Lauren was the exact opposite of chaos. She was order, precision. His kids would eat her alive, given half a chance.

There was a part of him that really wanted to try her there, to put her in the middle of his family and see how she fit in. Sometimes a square peg *could* fit in a round hole. It just took a little effort.

But her casual mention of babies had raised a red flag. He didn't want more kids, not ever. No more babies, no more late nights and stomach flu and babies who cried for no reason.

No more being left behind to handle it all on his own.

Thankfully, she changed the subject. "I've had something interesting come up this week."

Cole bit back his immediate response about what he'd had come up lately. Instead he relaxed and asked, "What's that?"

She told him about a phone call from her editor, an opportunity…New York. A producer was coming to her house on Saturday to check her out, to see if she was worthy of his show. Like anyone in his right mind would find Lauren unworthy of anything.

Why had she waited so long to tell him about the offer? Did she think he would be angry? Or was he not important enough to get the news right away?

Even though he'd already decided that Lauren could never be a part of his family, that she didn't fit in at all, that what they wanted was never going to be the same, his heart sank a little. If she went to New York it wouldn't be for a few weeks, as she said it would be. No, she'd get caught up in television shows and book tours and she'd never come home. It pissed him off, more than a little, but he also realized that he didn't have any right to hold her back. He'd had his shot at the big time and had chosen to walk away. Lauren should have her shot. He shouldn't let what he wanted from her get in the way.

Lauren jumped up and snatched both plates from the table, carrying them to the sink. Rising from the table slowly, Cole was right behind her. What did he have to lose? Nothing. Everything. Time was flying past and this moment would never come again. When he bent down and placed his mouth on her neck, which was exposed thanks to her ponytail, she jumped and dropped one of the plates. It landed with a clatter, but didn't break.

"I told you," she said without turning to face him, "no sex." Her hands gripped the edge of the sink.

"This isn't sex," he whispered. His hands rested at her waist and he moved the kiss to the top of her spine. She shuddered as his lips lingered there. She tasted so good, sweet and salty. She always smelled of something good. Cookies. She smelled like cookies.

Lauren's body unwound and she sagged against him. "It's just a kiss," he whispered, his breath brushing against her skin. "Tell me to stop, and I will."

She didn't tell him to stop.

He loved the smell of her, the warmth of her skin, the brush of her soft hair. He loved the way he could feel her surrender, as her body relaxed and her breath changed. Yes, no matter how wrong she was for him, no matter how she didn't fit, he could so easily imagine making this an everyday pleasure. Stealing a kiss at the sink. Seducing her.

But he couldn't give her everything she wanted, and she was going to be gone before he knew it. Gone to New York, or wherever her career took her. Gone, moving on to a man who could give her what she wanted. Babies. Chaos. Maybe he couldn't keep her, but for now she was his. Tonight, maybe tomorrow—she was his for just a little while longer.

She turned slowly, placed her arms around his neck and swayed into him. "Well, dammit, Cole, if you're going to *just kiss* me, you might as well do it right."

Chapter Eleven

Lauren sighed. She was so blasted *easy*, where Cole was concerned. One kiss on her neck and she turned into room-temperature butter. Soft, yielding. Yes, she was definitely melting.

When he'd come to the door she'd said no sex, and at the time she'd meant it. She needed time to think, and she didn't think clearly when he was kissing her. When he was inside her she didn't think at all. He wasn't really going for it like he could have. He didn't slip his hand into her waistband or up her shirt. He didn't slide that hand between her legs and stroke. If he'd made a bold move she would've stopped him—probably, maybe— and that would be the end of that. But he just kissed her, which was the absolute worst thing he could do if she had any hope at all of stopping before things went too far, because the longer his mouth was on her the further gone she was.

It was nice, to just kiss, to think of nothing but his mouth on hers, to enjoy the pleasure of lip to lip. The kiss deepened, and so did her response.

Lauren began to wonder when Cole's hand was going to wander, when he was going to touch her where she needed to be touched. Her body pounded with that wonder, shook and demanded and all but screamed.

One last, rational thought flitted through her brain. She'd probably be leaving in a few weeks, and it wasn't like she met a man who could do this to her on a regular basis. No, men like Cole were few and far between. No wonder she was halfway in love with him.

Maybe a little more than halfway, to be completely honest.

Since she'd been the one to set the "no sex" boundary this evening, it was only fair that she be the one to make the next move. She slipped her hands beneath Cole's shirt, raking her fingers along his hard chest and then bringing them back down to unfasten his jeans.

"I thought you said..." he whispered hoarsely, his mouth brushing against hers.

She stopped him with her hand down his pants and a kiss, then she whispered, "It's a woman's prerogative to change her mind. Didn't you know that?"

"No argument here." His voice was a growl, and from that moment he didn't waste any time shucking her capris down and off, spreading her legs, grabbing a condom from his back pocket. Then she was propped on the edge of the sink and he stood between her legs and he was inside her. He was warm and hard and as lost in physical sensation as she was. There was nothing in the world but the way they came together, the drive that brought them to this place, the sheer pleasure they created.

She'd never known her body could respond this way,

that sensations could be so intense and demanding and pleasurable. She'd never known that she could be so driven, so out of control. Lauren Russell was never out of control, but with Cole inside her she felt as if she were on the verge of losing everything she believed herself to be and flying off the face of the planet. Only he held her grounded.

He pounded into her hard, and she met him thrust for thrust, driven. Searching. She locked her mouth to his while their bodies moved, swiped her tongue into his mouth as if she could swallow him whole.

She didn't want it to end, but it had to end. And the end was amazing.

He held her, for a while. They were both gasping for breath, holding on to one another as if they'd never let go. Maybe both of them knowing they were going to have to, sooner or later.

Cole placed her back on her feet, moving slowly, still so close he was a part of her. They were both sweating and panting, but like him...she didn't want to move away. She didn't want this moment to end because it was so fine. Was she supposed to walk away from this? Away from him?

Lauren had sworn she'd never become the kind of woman who built her life around a man, but at the moment she couldn't imagine leaving, not now, not when there were so many possibilities right here in her own backyard.

She laid her lips on his throat, tasted the salty sweat there. "Maybe I won't go to New York after all," she whispered.

Cole slept like a baby after getting back to his own bed, and woke to the smell of coffee. Unfortunately an unwelcome realization soon wiggled into his brain and stole the blissful, ignorant satiation he'd wallowed in all night.

Last night he and Lauren had gotten closer, closer than he'd ever thought to be with a woman again. Sex was fine; sex was great. He liked sex. But last night, as out of control as it had been at one point, had taken them well beyond a simple sexual relationship. It was complicated, and the last thing he needed in his life was another complication.

He liked Lauren a lot, and yes, there had been moments when he'd daydreamed about maybe making her a part of this family. Slowly, of course. Cautiously. But there was a reason he always drew back, realizing in his gut that it would never work. The truth of the matter was, they didn't want the same things in the years to come. He didn't want any more babies. Ever. He had three and that was enough. No more changing diapers, teething and sleepless nights. He was thrilled that Justin was starting school and that part of his life was behind him. Lauren was made for motherhood. She'd actually said the words last night. One day…babies of her own… She probably dreamed of carrying those babies, decorating nurseries, making her own organic baby food and knitting booties. She didn't know that in all those pictures of the sweet baby nestled contently in a mother's arms, the infant had to be drugged. That was the way of things in his house, anyway. Babies spit up and pulled hair and grabbed at earrings…. The pictures lied.

Not only that, he knew a little bit about how women thought. Lauren was ambitious, but would she turn down a great opportunity because he was here and they'd started something? Maybe her statement about not going to New York had been nothing but an afterglow slip-up and she'd realized the error of her ways the moment the words had left her mouth. Surely by this morning she was thinking clearly. But what if she wasn't? He didn't want to stand in her way, didn't want to be the reason she turned her back on a great opportunity. And what if she did just that, said no to the television show, and then this budding relationship fell apart? She'd blame him. Forever. One of them would have to move.

"I'm an idiot," he muttered as he walked toward the kitchen. As tempting as Lauren was, the last thing he needed was a woman to turn his life upside down. No, his life was already pretty much upside down, but hers... This thing they'd started could tear her neat world apart. He'd been conflicted about her from the start, but last night she'd said the word that would, eventually, tear them apart.

Babies.

She hadn't said that word in such a way to indicate that she was trying to get pregnant now, heaven forbid, but the look in her eyes, the softness in her voice... Babies were definitely in her future plans. And Lauren was a woman who made sure her plans came true.

Baby was probably on a list somewhere.

Cole leaned against the counter and sipped at his coffee. He imagined the worst, the very worst, that could happen if he didn't put on the brakes. Lauren would send the New York producer packing—for him—and they'd continue to have sex on a regular basis. For a while everything would be fine. Hell, it would be great. He'd be careful, he always was, but one day that protection would fail and she'd turn up pregnant. Or else they'd get caught up in the heat of the moment and decide it wasn't the right time of the month for her to conceive and they'd be wrong. Or maybe she'd just put *conceive* on one of her lists, and it would happen. She'd be thrilled; he'd be terrified.

He'd marry her, of course he would—she deserved that much—and then there would be another baby. Cole's heart sank, settled in his gut like a boulder. If he was really going to let his mind wander to the worst of all possibilities, he might as well go all the way. What if something happened to her? A bad heart, a drunk driver...the possibilities were endless, but the result would be the same. He'd be left alone again, with *four* kids this time, another baby he couldn't take care of, another child to catch the flu when it made the rounds. He couldn't go there again, couldn't even imagine it.

He'd always known that he might one day marry again, that when the kids were older he'd find the time for a romantic relationship. But he'd never really considered the possibility that he'd fall deeply in love again and have to risk the pain of loss that could come with it.

"Dad?" Meredith said, and it sounded like it wasn't the first time she'd spoken to him.

"What is it?" He tried to give his daughter his full attention.

"Saturday lunch. Remember, you told me to cook for Aunt Janet?"

"I know I did, but on second thought, maybe it would be better if we pick something up..."

Meredith stomped one foot. "No! I want to show Aunt Janet that I can handle this without her help, that I'm capable of being the woman of the house and she doesn't need to worry about us."

Janet was always going to worry, but if it made Meredith feel more confident, then why not? "Okay, Mer, if that's what you want."

"It is." She looked and sounded determined. "I'm

going to try some new recipes, a tuna casserole and an apple cobbler. I'll make a shopping list this afternoon."

"Sure thing." Cole's mind went back to the more immediate concern. He needed to end things with Lauren, he needed to…set her free. Get out of her way. It was going to hurt a lot more than he'd ever imagined it might.

"You have lost your mind." Lauren stared at her reflection in the mirror. "You let a man kiss you out of your pants *and* your common sense." She'd started out last night determined to prove that she wasn't easy and had ended it being just that. Not just easy, but eager. And the really bad thing was, she didn't regret it. Not at all.

Her body still hummed, and she couldn't stop smiling. If any of her friends had done what she'd done, and had been foolish enough to share everything about an evening like the one she'd had with Cole, they'd get the speech about caution, about building a solid base of friendship before things progressed to the next level. They'd probably get a lecture about insisting on no sex and then folding like a house of cards. Unfortunately, when Cole looked at her with those blue eyes, when he touched her, caution was the last thing on her mind.

This wasn't like her, not at all. She wasn't impulsive, she didn't take chances, she didn't plan her days—much less her career—around a man she'd only known for a few weeks! And yet that was exactly what she was doing. Cole Donovan was a dangerous man… With a kiss and a touch of his hand, she forgot who she was.

Yes, definitely dangerous.

She was falling in love with Cole, and things had happened so quickly she didn't have even a glimmer of hope that he might feel the same way. It was too soon.

Lauren managed to fill the morning with a shower, a

check of her email, writing out a few bills, and a review of her menu for Saturday. The producer—don't-call-him-Eddie Mandel—and a cameraman were flying in, their plane scheduled to land around one-thirty. Lauren would serve them a late lunch, the cameraman would take a few pictures of her house and check the lighting, and she and Mandel would talk. Lauren wasn't sure about all this. Hilary made it sound like it was a done deal, and why would they fly down a cameraman if it wasn't? It was wasteful to spend that kind of money if they weren't sure.

But was *she* sure? Did she really want to leave town just when things were getting interesting with Cole?

Tonight she'd be having dinner at Gran's. She'd have to share the news about the possibility of the reality show with Gran and Miss Patsy, but there was no way she'd share anything about Cole. Her grandmother was an old-fashioned woman, and she'd be shocked, absolutely shocked, to know how far things had gone. And so quickly. Lauren was more than a little shocked herself.

When Gran had suggested that Lauren offer an apple pie and a bit of seamstress work, she certainly hadn't imagined *this*.

Lauren walked past the hall bathroom and caught her reflection in that mirror. She made a face at herself, stuck out her tongue. And then she smiled. Okay, maybe she was kind of an idiot where Cole was concerned, but at the moment she was a very happy idiot.

Cole waited until he saw Lauren walk out of her house, headed for the backyard and a few ripe tomatoes. Hank and Justin were kicking a soccer ball, and Meredith was sitting at the kitchen table, studiously intent on writing out a detailed grocery list. God only knew what Saturday lunch would bring.

He smiled at Lauren as he walked into her backyard, but the smile was strained, not his best, so he let it fade away. Better to have this conversation here, out in the open. Behind closed doors she was much too tempting. Behind closed doors, with this unsaid, they'd end up in bed again. He called a casual hello, and her head popped up. She'd been distracted, hadn't even realized he was there.

That wasn't like her.

But she caught his eye and smiled, glanced past him to the boys and returned his greeting.

When he was close, he lowered his voice and said, "I had a thought this morning." No need to drag this out any more than was necessary.

"What kind of thought?" Lauren asked softly. What he wanted to do was take her in his arms and kiss her, then tell her she looked beautiful. He wanted to tell her that he'd awakened that morning thinking of her. But instead he said, "The kind of thought that tells me we need to put on the brakes."

Lauren paled, just a little. She hadn't expected that. Another woman might've cried or thrown accusations. He had a feeling Lauren never made a scene, not even in her own backyard. "Things *have* been happening very fast." Her voice was so controlled, so tight, he thought it might crack.

"They have. Too fast for me," he said, working to keep his voice casual. "I like you, you're hot. Really hot. But let's face it, our lives don't mesh."

She glared at him, and he read the unspoken censure there. *Hot? That's what I am to you?*

"I suppose they don't," she agreed reluctantly.

"Your life is so ordered, so controlled. Mine is anything but."

"I suppose that's true." She looked over his shoulder, not at anything in particular just...not at him.

No matter where they went from here, he didn't want Lauren to think that he'd throw her over for such a small, insignificant reason. The fact that his life was chaos and her days were filled with schedules and checklists and order wasn't enough to keep them apart. "You want kids," he said.

She shifted her gaze so she was looking at him. "Not now, but yes. One day."

She'd said as much last night. Lauren wanted kids of her own, a home, a family. She wanted babies and everything that came with them. "I don't," he said sharply. "Not now, not ever. Three is enough for me. I gave up everything to take care of my children and I don't regret it, but I don't have anything left to give. I've been selfishly thinking that maybe you and I..." He couldn't make himself say it. "But the truth is, we don't want the same things, not where it's important. The sex is great, don't get me wrong, but that's all it is for me." She shouldn't find fault with that. Hadn't she said the same thing herself?

That was a cop-out. In the past couple of days *everything* had changed.

Lauren looked confused, for a moment, and then she just looked hurt. "You're telling me your heart is completely full and there's no room in it for anyone else."

Put that way it sounded harsh, but basically, that was the truth. And it was much simpler than letting her know that he couldn't bear to love and lose again. A clean break was best, even if it was going to hurt for a while. "Yes."

Her face flushed, as it did when she was angry or embarrassed. She blushed so easily. She started looking around him again, then glanced down, as if there was something of interest growing around the tomatoes. "I guess it's a good thing I found this out now."

"That's what I was thinking."

Her chin came up. Maybe her eyes were a little bright, but to her credit she didn't cry. She didn't call him a bastard, either, or kick at his shin. Nope, Lauren Russell did not make a scene. Ever. "By the way, I've decided to go to New York, if the producer wants me. It'll be a big change, but it's also a great opportunity."

"Good," he said, his heart sinking more than it should. He fought for a smile. "You'll be famous and I can say I knew you when."

She just nodded, collected her tomatoes a bit more roughly than usual and turned toward her kitchen door. Cole tried to tell himself that it was best this way, that it was a good thing they'd come to their senses before it was too late.

A part of him knew it was already too late, at least for him. He was going to miss her. Not just the sex, but her smile, her laugh, the way she looked at him and gave him her complete attention, as if in that moment nothing and no one else existed.

But there was no going back. It was time for him to return to his life, and time for Lauren to get on with hers.

Lauren had never been so on edge during a dinner at Gran's. The two older women knew something was wrong. How could they not? Her hands shook; she dropped her fork onto her plate and it clattered so loudly she jumped out of her skin.

Finally, Gran set her own fork aside and looked Lauren in the eye. "What's going on with you?"

Lauren took a deep breath. She couldn't tell her grandmother that her love affair with Cole had gone wrong, that she'd slept with him and fallen in love and he'd dumped her while she was picking tomatoes. "A producer from New York is coming to my house on Saturday. I think they want me for some reality cooking show."

"That sounds wonderful!" Miss Patsy said.

Gran smiled. "It does. How exciting! I don't understand why you look like the world is coming to an end."

Because it is…. "I don't know how long I'll be gone," Lauren said, her voice quick and sharp. "Maybe weeks, maybe months! What if you need me? Forget it, I don't know what I was thinking. I can't just get on a plane and leave you here not knowing when I'll be back."

"You most certainly can," Gran said, unsmiling. "Do I look like an old woman who can't take care of herself? Do I look like I'm on my last legs and can't be left alone for a while?"

"Of course not, but…but what about my column?"

"You can either stockpile a few columns or take a leave of absence. I'm sure your job will be waiting for you when you return," Miss Patsy said. "My goodness, you'll come home a celebrity!"

Gran stared, her dark eyes boring into Lauren's. "That's not it. You know your job is secure, and you know I'll be fine. Is it Whiplash? Are you worried about leaving him behind?"

"Gran!" Lauren could feel heat in her cheeks. "Don't be silly. I barely know the man."

"Did you take him an apple pie?"

"No." Chocolate cake, cookies, peach cobbler…but no pie. "He's really not my type, Gran."

Gran looked disappointed. She screwed up her mouth and made a gentle harrumphing noise. "All I can say is, you'd better not turn down a chance for something like this because of me. I'll be fine."

"I know you will." Lauren started at her plate. "I'm just…scared."

"Of what?" Miss Patsy asked.

Failure, success…walking away from something she'd thought—wrongly, as it turned out—could be wonderful. "The unknown," she answered.

"*Life* is unknown," Gran said. "Go for it, girl. Go for what you want and grab it."

It was great advice. The problem was, at the moment Lauren had no earthly idea what she really wanted to grab.

Chapter Twelve

With one eye open and the other closed, Cole stared into the thick, green potion. This was his third serving of the day, and the budding wizard was becoming concerned because his ungrumpy potion didn't seem to be working.

He couldn't tell the kid that no potion was going to cure him, not today. Not tomorrow. One day, maybe.

But he drank. Tried a wide smile.

"Eww," Justin said. The youngest peeked around Hank's cape. "That's kind of a scary smile."

"My potion has gone wrong," Hank said solemnly. "Maybe I'm losing my magical powers."

He could only hope…. "It does happen, you know."

He sent the boys off to brush their teeth, ignoring Hank's nightly argument that he'd already done the minimum required for the day, and collapsed back on the couch. After they went to bed he'd do another load of laundry, maybe rearrange a couple of cabinets in the kitchen. He didn't feel much like sleeping.

Meredith plopped down on the chair facing the couch and glared at him. "What did she do?"

"What?"

"Don't treat me like a kid, Dad. You're sad and angry and…and weird. It was *her,* I know it. She said something or did something mean and now you're…"

He didn't play games; he knew who "her" was. "Lauren didn't do anything to me," Cole said.

"But you're dating her, aren't you? Last night, while we were at the movies, you went over there and she did something. I know something's wrong! I knew from the beginning that she was going to be trouble."

In her own way, Meredith was as protective of him as he was of her. "Lauren didn't do anything. I told her I didn't think we should see each other anymore."

It wasn't his imagination that relief washed over Meredith's face. "You don't seem very happy about it."

"I'm not," he said. He could be honest with his kids without going overboard and telling them anything they didn't need to know. "But it's for the best."

Meredith took a deep breath and seemed to relax even more. Her shoulders, her hands… She unwound from the inside out.

"You don't like Lauren at all," he asked. "Why?"

The tension came back in a flash. "Because we don't need anyone else in this family. The four of us are enough. Anyone else would be…weird."

Cole managed a real smile. "Is that why you sabotaged my dates a few years back?" The boys were too young to remember, but Meredith was another matter.

She looked away. "It wasn't sabotage, exactly. It was more like a…test. They all failed miserably."

"How the hell did you get Justin to throw up on command?"

Meredith leaned forward in her chair. "Okay, that was just a lucky break. I'd planned to spill juice down the front of her dress, and Hank was supposed to blow his nose on the hem of her dress. But Justin got sick and that was *perfect*."

"No more, okay?" Cole said, working hard to keep a straight face. "Y'all are too old for that now, and one day I might want to date again."

"Please, none of those women like before."

"I'll do my best. And I don't see anything happening for a good long while." No, first he'd have to get over Lauren.

He'd never expected it would come to this, that after just two days he'd feel as if he'd lost something important.

Lauren decided to keep it simple, for the producer and cameraman's meal. Chicken and rice, a three-bean salad, homemade rolls and chocolate cake. She'd cooked and puttered around the house for the past two days, since she and Cole had spoken in her garden. She hadn't seen or spoken to him since, because honestly, what was there to say?

She'd seen the boys outside and heard all about the movie, and even though she shouldn't have—she didn't need to be deepening any of her ties with the family next door—she'd made them cookies.

Gran and Miss Patsy had both been very encouraging about her opportunity. After she'd told them about it they'd gone on and on about how wonderful it was, what a great success she was going to be. Eventually they had her on board. It wasn't like she was moving to New York to stay. If she was chosen for the reality show she'd just be there a few weeks, maybe a couple of months. If she was lucky. With most of these shows someone went home every week. Lauren didn't expect to win, but she didn't want to be the first one to go home, either. That would be embarrassing.

Besides, she felt a deep and undeniable need to get away, to escape her latest romantic mistake. She wasn't sure she could bear watching Cole come and go, listening to the screams of the children she'd begun to like so much. Not until she'd had some time to wash away the memory of what they'd almost had.

Almost. In truth they'd had nothing but sex, just as she'd wanted from the beginning, just as she'd planned. Here she was all but grieving because she'd lost something important and Cole was just sorry to have lost something *hot.* Had she been born with a built-in radar that directed her to the most shallow males available? It certainly seemed that way.

Her guests wouldn't be here for a couple of hours. She'd offered to collect them from the airport, but Mandel had told her that he was renting a car. After he and the cameraman visited with her they were driving to Memphis to meet another potential contestant. How many were being considered? How many would be chosen? Lauren's competitive side emerged. At first she'd gone back and forth about whether or not she wanted this job. Now she just wanted to escape. But if the show didn't happen for her, *she* wanted to be the one to turn it down. Not the other way around.

The table was set. She'd decided they'd eat in the rarely used dining room instead of the more comfortable kitchen. The cake was sitting on the buffet, pretty as a picture. The chicken and rice was warming in the oven, and the bean salad was in the fridge. She'd made the rolls early this morning. They just needed to be warmed. Some sliced tomatoes would be a nice addition to the meal. Lauren stepped into the backyard, her eyes on a couple of big, ripe tomatoes.

A sound—a sob—from next door caught her attention, and she turned her head.

Meredith stood by the kitchen door, her back against the wall, her head down. She was crying as if her heart had been broken.

Lauren stopped. Meredith had made it clear that she didn't like her. The lie about Tiffany had proved that, as well as the cutting glances which weren't at all subtle. Cole had kicked her to the curb after a couple nights of mind-blowing sex that she'd thought had been the start of something and he'd thought had been a grand old time. The family next door was not her concern.

But Meredith was just a child, and she sounded so distraught. Lauren took a deep breath and turned toward the Donovan backyard. Hank and Justin weren't in the yard at the moment. The trampoline and soccer net were untended. She had to step around a soccer ball and an action figure—with one arm he was the perfect match for the one-legged Barbie on the front porch—in order to reach the small patio.

"Meredith, what's wrong?"

The young girl was surprised. She'd been so lost in her misery she hadn't heard Lauren's approach. Her head snapped up, revealing red eyes, a wet and blotchy face and a very runny nose.

"Like you care," Meredith muttered.

It would've been very easy to take the hint, turn around and mind her own business. But honestly, she had never seen anyone look so miserable. "If I didn't care, I wouldn't be here. Is something wrong?" Her heart leaped. "Is someone hurt?"

Meredith shook her head. "It's nothing like that. I'm cooking for my aunt, and she'll be here any minute. It was going to be such a nice meal, and I got up really early to get started, but...but...something must be wrong with the oven. I burned the tuna casserole *and* the apple cobbler, and the rolls are black on the bottom, and the peas stuck to the bottom of the pot. The whole kitchen stinks of burned peas! It's too late to start anything else, and Aunt Janet is just going to freak because she'll think we can't get by without her."

"What does your father say?"

"I haven't told him. He and the boys are straightening up the porch and their rooms. Aunt Janet will inspect them. She always inspects *everything.* Dad told the boys to clean their rooms, but they just shoved stuff in the closet. He wasn't very happy about that so now he's telling them exactly what to do. He's going to be so mad when he finds out I ruined lunch. I can't do *anything* right!"

Lauren laid a hand on Meredith's shoulder, wondering if the gesture would be rejected with a shrug. It wasn't. "Your father will not be angry with you. He loves you very much, and I'm sure he'll understand and appreciate the effort you put into your plans. Plans don't always work out the way we want them to, but the attempt was admirable."

Meredith nodded her head as if she understood. She was still upset, but less so. "I did try. Dad will be disappointed, but he won't yell at me or anything. He'll say it was a valiant effort—he says that all the time when I mess up—and then he'll take care of it. I need to go tell him what happened so he can run out and pick up some chicken." Meredith sighed. Her thin body seemed to shudder a bit. "I guess Aunt Janet is right when she says we're helpless without her."

The girl turned to go inside, but Lauren impulsively stopped her with a hand and a word. "Wait." Meredith turned to look up at Lauren, though she was just a little bit shorter. With those long legs she'd soon be taller than Lauren, beautiful and coltish and perhaps one day even elegant. But today she was just a child. "I have an idea."

When Meredith had found the burned, stinky mess of what was supposed to be lunch in the oven, a thousand thoughts had gone through her head. Panic, anger, horror, a sense of total failure. She'd figured lunch was a lost cause and they'd end up eating fried chicken out of a bucket. She'd never expected this.

She followed Miss Lauren's instructions, hiding the burned food—because it wouldn't do for it to be discovered in the trash—and setting the dining room table with the good china. Dad called the delicate rose-rimmed plates "Mom's good dishes" and they were never touched, much less used. They *always* ate off paper plates. But Miss Lauren insisted, and at the moment Meredith would do anything their neighbor asked of her. Anything at all.

Miss Lauren didn't have to do this. She didn't have to do anything! She could've ignored the crying fit Meredith had been having on the back porch. If the situation had been reversed, that's what she would've done.

All Miss Lauren had asked was that they keep Dad out of the kitchen. Meredith had brought Hank and Justin in on the plan to help with that. Now and then, as they worked in the kitchen, Miss Lauren would hear a noise and glance toward the doorway. She looked like she was ready to bolt if Dad showed up.

She looked—and acted—like she really cared, and that made Meredith feel about an inch tall.

They opened the windows and sprayed air freshener to kill the odor of burned food. It worked, though Meredith could still detect a hint of burned peas. When that was done, and the ruined food was hidden, Miss Lauren ran next door. She literally *ran,* because time was short. Meredith followed, out of their kitchen door, across the yard, to Miss Lauren's kitchen.

Which smelled heavenly, as always.

Miss Lauren grabbed a matching pair of oven mitts that didn't have a single burned mark or food stain on them, and took a big dish from the oven.

"There's a covered dish in the fridge," she instructed without looking back. "Grab it. We'll come back for the rest."

Meredith carried the dish very carefully, half-afraid she'd drop it on the way home. She didn't. Miss Lauren made her check to see that the dining room was clear before she went in and placed the dish on the center of the table. She frowned at the table. "You need flowers," she said, as if the absence of a centerpiece was a serious infraction.

"We don't have any flowers," Meredith said. "Just weeds."

Miss Lauren smiled. "I have a garden full." She studied the wrinkled tablecloth—who had time to iron?—and frowned. "There's no time to take care of that tablecloth, but I do have a particular rose that matches that stripe perfectly." She nodded. "It'll do."

They ran back and forth, carrying food, collecting flowers and a vase. Hank looked in a couple of times, and ran interference when Dad got too close to the kitchen.

When everything was done, Miss Lauren studied the

results and smiled widely, happy with what they'd done even if the tablecloth was wrinkled.

Meredith took a deep breath, looked at her neighbor and asked plainly, "Why did you do all this?"

Miss Lauren stared dead-straight-on at her, not waving the question off as if it meant nothing, not brushing the query away. It *did* mean something, and they both knew it. "You were in trouble, I helped. It's as simple as that. I'm sure you would've done the same for me."

"But…" Meredith was about to say she wouldn't have, she would've laughed if she'd found out Miss Lauren was in a bind. Was she a bad person? Why was she so anxious to think the worst of a woman who had only been nice to her?

She didn't get to continue the conversation. From the front of the house, a car door slammed. Justin yelled, "She's here!" and Dad's voice followed.

At the sound of that voice Miss Lauren twitched, and then she said she had to go. She hurried from the dining room, and then out the kitchen door, making a hasty escape.

Cole led Janet into the dining room, not certain exactly what to expect. Meredith had all but ordered him to stay out of the kitchen, and he'd done as she asked. This seemed to be so important to her, he wanted to give her the chance to succeed on her own. He'd told her to holler if she needed help and she hadn't, so everything must've gone well.

Maybe tuna casserole wasn't fancy, but it should do the trick. Her apple cobbler called for canned apples, but shoot, that's the kind of recipe he'd pick if he were cooking. Not everyone wanted to spend their lives in the kitchen, like…

Cole stopped in the doorway when he saw the table. He recognized the chicken and rice, remembered the fancy ceramic dish it was in from the night Lauren had invited them all over for supper. The rolls were not the ones he'd bought at the grocery store, they were much larger, almost certainly homemade, and he sure as hell hadn't bought the ingredients for the bean salad in the sparkling glass dish.

Sliced tomatoes. He didn't have a tomato garden.

Good lord, were those the plates that had to be washed *by hand?*

But he said nothing. Meredith was beaming. He hadn't seen her this happy in a long time. The boys grinned, obviously in on keeping the secret. None of his kids possessed much of a poker face—which was a good thing.

Janet was obviously impressed. "Meredith, this looks wonderful!"

Hank piped up. "Wait till you see the chocolate cake we're having for dessert!" His smile was wide and gap-toothed and full of joy.

The chocolate cake sealed the deal. Lauren had made this meal. Every bite of it. Now was not the time to ask the kids what the hell had happened.

Justin climbed into his chair, closed his eyes, pressed his palms together and said, "Give us this day our daily chicken…"

Lauren rushed around the kitchen, trying to make the best of what she could find in the fridge and the freezer. Maybe the plane from New York would be late. Maybe her guests had been delayed in Atlanta. Everyone got delayed in Atlanta.

She had three individual servings of frozen vegetable lasagna, and she could put together a very nice tray of cheese, tomatoes, olives and carrot sticks. She was a whiz with a knife, and in short order managed to turn the simple foods into a work of art. Flowers, spirals, butterflies. Impressive, if she did say so herself.

There wasn't time to make another batch of rolls, but she did have the makings of corn bread in the pantry. Corn bread and lasagna. Her grandmother would be horrified. But, Lauren would do what she had to do. It was worth any sacrifice. She'd never forget the expression on Meredith's face as they'd surveyed the finished product on the Donovan dining room table.

So what if Cole had dumped her less than twenty-four hours after they'd had sex in the kitchen? So what if he had turned out to be a jerk like all the rest? Meredith was just a child, and she shouldn't have to pay for her father's sins. They were still going to be neighbors, after all. The trip to New York wouldn't last all that long. By the time she came home she'd be well over Cole Donovan.

She didn't have time to dwell on Cole at the moment. She had a meal to plan and put together at the very last minute. So far so good, but dessert was a problem. She had the ingredients for several acceptable dishes, but time was short. Maybe she should just tell the producer that she was on a diet and could not bear the temptation. Yeah, like lasagna and corn bread were diet foods.

Lauren made her way through the kitchen like a woman on a mission, searching for something sweet that she could put together quickly. A bag of chocolate chips inspired her, and she rounded up the rest of the ingredients for chocolate-chip bar cookies.

And as she prepared the batter, she wondered how things were going at the Donovan house. She tried to think only of Meredith and the boys, but like it or not her mind ended up on Cole. He'd realize the meal had come from her kitchen. She only hoped he could keep a secret and wouldn't spoil Meredith's day.

She didn't worry too much about that. He'd turned out to be a terrible and much too short-lived boyfriend, but he was a fabulous father.

"You must give me the recipe for the chicken and rice," Janet said.

Cole almost choked. How was Meredith going to handle that one?

His daughter just smiled, calm as could be. She looked almost smug—and so much like her mother. "All the recipes are online." She rattled off the URL for Lauren's website. Nice cover.

After everyone had oohed and ahhed over the chocolate cake, and they'd discussed the weather and the new house and the neighborhood in general, Janet asked the kids if they'd like to spend the next week with her. Cole wasn't shocked by the offer; Janet had pulled him aside as they'd headed in for lunch and asked if he minded. He'd reluctantly agreed—if the kids wanted to go. They could see their friends, Janet offered to take them shopping for school clothes, and they could visit their old stomping grounds. The boys jumped on the offer, but Meredith declined. Janet didn't push, and for that Cole was grateful.

He was constantly bemoaning the lack of alone time, but that didn't mean he wanted to kids to be away for a whole week. Five or ten minutes here and there would suffice. So many times he had to remind himself that he was all they had, but the real truth was, they were all he had.

Janet offered to help with the dishes, but Cole wouldn't let her. Not only would she wonder about the lack of dirty pots and pans in the kitchen, he wanted a word with his daughter. Alone. He sent the boys off to pack, and asked Janet if she'd help them. She wandered off to do just that.

When he and Meredith were alone, looking out of the window over the kitchen sink—he could just see the edge of Lauren's garden—he said simply, "Explain."

Meredith ran to the oven and opened it. Inside were two pans and one pot, all three showing evidence of severe overcooking. "The burned rolls are in the garbage can," she said, "but Miss Lauren said if we put it all in the trash Aunt Janet might find it. I guess we could've taken it all to her house, but there just wasn't time. Maybe she just doesn't allow burned stuff in her kitchen, I don't know, but I…"

"Lauren," he said, relying again on a single, lowly spoken, meaningful word to get his point across.

Meredith nodded. "I was upset, and she offered to help." Her brown eyes got wide. "Maybe I was wrong about her, Dad. Maybe she's not a bad person out to get you. She didn't have to help me, but she did. The dishes and the flowers were her idea, too, and didn't the table look nice? But yeah, it's the food that's the best. Talk about a lifesaver! It's just lucky Miss Lauren had all this food sitting around."

They'd just eaten a meal intended for her producer, he was certain. He did feel a little guilty, but if anyone could put together a decent meal in a hurry it was Lauren Russell.

"Maybe you should date her again, Dad," Meredith said brightly. Was this the same girl who'd made up fictional love interests to keep them apart? Who'd argued that Lauren was a conniving woman out to steal him away? "I think you still like her. You do like her, don't you? She likes you, I can tell. Did you break up with her because of me? I hope not. I was…I was wrong."

Cole leaned against the sink and crossed his arms over his chest. Yeah, he liked Lauren—for all the good it was going to do either of them. She needed a different life from the one he could offer, and worse, he had seen in her the power for more pain than he could bear to face again in this lifetime. No need to tell Meredith all of that, because there was another, simpler answer. "Lauren is going to New York."

Meredith's face fell. "What?"

"That chicken and rice and chocolate cake were intended for the producer of some reality show who's coming this afternoon to talk to her." Might as well be blunt. "It would be a waste of time for me to date her, a waste of my time and hers. She's going to go to New York, become a famous chef, get her own television show and never come back."

Meredith's lower lip trembled. Her dark eyes shone with unshed tears. All she said was "Oh."

"I tell you what," Cole said, trying to make his voice sound light even though he felt anything but inside. "While the boys are in Birmingham we'll scour Lauren's website and learn to make a few of those recipes ourselves. What do you say?" What better way to convince Meredith—and himself—that they didn't need their neighbor?

Meredith had been right all along. They didn't need anyone else.

"Okay," Meredith said, but she didn't sound very enthusiastic about the idea.

Cole turned, looked out the window again. He was so tempted to go next door, to thank Lauren for helping… to ask her to forgive him and stay. He could see it in his mind, so clearly. He'd touch her face; she'd look at him with those green eyes that could make him feel as though there was no one else in the world. *I'm sorry. Stay.*

But he remained at the window. She deserved this chance; she deserved the life she wanted with a man who could give it to her without reservation.

She deserved someone besides him.

Chapter Thirteen

Naturally, her guests were not delayed in Atlanta. If anything, they were a few minutes early. Lauren plastered on a smile and answered the door. It was easy to tell who was who. The man directly before her was older than the one who stood to the rear. Edward Mandel was completely bald, carried a leather briefcase that appeared to be brand-new, and wore a suit that looked as though it had been made for him.

The younger man behind him had long blond hair caught in a ponytail, and he carried a camera.

She offered Mandel her hand, they shook and took care of unnecessary introductions, and then she invited the two men into her home, greeting the second man—he'd introduced himself simply as Ben—with a handshake.

Lauren's heart was still pounding and there was a sheen of sweat on her neck. She dearly hated rushing around at the last minute, but this time it couldn't be helped. Besides, it wasn't like the meal she'd prepared was a bad one. It was just different. And sadly, it was not her best.

The cookies were in the oven, filling the house with that unmistakable, welcoming scent. The warmed lasagna was on top of the stove and the artfully arranged platter of vegetables and cheese sat on a counter nearby.

Mandel glanced around her house as she led them inside. "What's the humidity like around here?" he snapped. "It's absolutely sweltering out there. I can't believe people live in this heat on purpose."

He would've been more comfortable without the expensive suit jacket, but she didn't tell him so. "It has been a particularly hot summer," Lauren said sweetly. Perhaps Mandel was not a good traveler. Maybe he was just having a bad day. "Would you like me to crank up the air-conditioning for you?"

"No, no, I'm fine, honey. Don't want to be any trouble." He looked her up and down critically, his eyes lingering on her chest for a moment. Was that dismay she read on his face? "What would you think about dyeing your hair red, honey? We already have a blonde. Redheads are popular, you should really be a redhead. With your coloring you could pull it off. And what about a padded bra? You do have a padded bra, don't you? We need to rev up your image right out of the gate. We want people to love you. On these shows you have to be either loved or hated or else you're out in the first couple of weeks."

"Those are interesting suggestions, and we can discuss them later. Are you hungry?" she asked. "Or would you like to talk before we eat?"

"I'm starving," Ben said.

The producer barely glanced at the younger man. "Let's talk first. Ben will live if he has to wait awhile before he eats."

Okay, so Edward "don't call me Eddie" Mandel was rude. Maybe he was jealous because Ben had so much hair and he didn't have a lick. That didn't mean working for him would be a horrible experience. Besides, it would be temporary. *If* he wanted her, and *if* she took the job, it would just last a few weeks. Unless she won and he was the producer of her show…a problem she'd handle if and when it came to that.

Lauren showed her guests into the living room and they sat. She was just about to offer iced tea when the doorbell rang. She excused herself, determined to get rid of whoever it was in a hurry.

She was surprised to see Justin standing on her doorstep.

"Thanks for the cake," he said, glancing toward his house. "Meredith didn't tell Aunt Janet you made it, but we knew. We all knew. No one makes chocolate cake like you do."

"It will remain our little secret," Lauren said. "Now, I have to go because I have—"

"And I wanted to say goodbye," he interrupted. "Me and Hank are going to Birmingham with Aunt Janet so we can see our friends."

"Hank and I," Lauren corrected gently.

"You're going to Birmingham with us?" Justin's eyes got big.

Lauren smiled. "No."

"I didn't think so. Meredith said you're going to New York, and I was afraid you wouldn't be here when I got back from Birmingham, and then I couldn't thank you for the cake. That's good manners, right? Thanking you for the cake?" His eyes were so wide, so innocent...so like his father's.

"Yes, it is. Now, I'm very sorry but I have to go. I have guests."

"But..." Justin looked back toward his house again. "Can I have a hug? In case you're not here when I get back."

"Sure." Lauren stepped onto the porch and Justin launched himself up into her arms. He held on tight, even lifted his skinny legs off the ground and wrapped them around her. She struggled to hold on to him without tipping forward, even laughed as he kissed her on the cheek.

"You're a good neighbor, Miss Lauren," Justin said enthusiastically. "I hope you don't go to New York. I hope you're here when I get home. I promise not to break any more windows, and I'll be very careful with big, muddy weeds from now on. Promise."

An unexpected knot of emotion inside her caught and swelled. There was something incredibly special about holding a child, something powerful about the complete trust they revealed when they hugged and just let go that could not be ignored.

"We'll see, Justin."

Hank came out of the Donovan front door and waved. "Come on, Justin, we have to finish packing!"

"Okay!" Justin's response rang in Lauren's ears—literally, since his mouth was at her earlobe—before he disentangled himself and dropped to the porch. He grinned and waved as he ran for home.

A horrible thought grabbed at Lauren. Escape had seemed like such a good idea, for a while, but if she did go to New York, if everything fell into place for her, career-wise, and she made a new home there...she was going to miss the Donovan kids. Noise, accidents, mud, broken windows and all, she would miss them. And yes, she was going to miss their father, horribly. Even if he was a rat.

And he *was* a rat, making her love him and then deciding she wasn't worth the trouble. She closed the door on Justin and returned to the living room. Would she mind going red? Maybe it wouldn't be too bad. And she could endure a padded bra for a few weeks. As she reached the doorway she asked, "Would y'all like some iced tea?"

Mandel pointed a finger at her. "Y'all. That's good. Use it whenever you can, honey. Maybe you can play up the accent when you're on air. Viewers eat that up, for some reason I don't get. Love for the hillbillies, I guess."

Ben worked to contain a smile, but didn't do a very good job of it. He looked almost apologetic, even though he'd done nothing he needed to apologize for. "I'd love a glass of tea."

Lauren turned toward the kitchen and took a single step, but an odor stopped her in her tracks. Something was burning. In the next instance she noticed the smoke, and right on cue the smoke alarm started screaming.

She ran to the kitchen, and to the stove. Black smoke poured out of the oven, filling the room. She turned it off, checking the settings as she did so. The oven was set to broil, and she knew darn well she hadn't left it that way. With a heavy oven mitt on her hand she rescued the bar cookies. Or tried to. They were beyond saving. The smoke alarm was shrill, but she ignored it for now, turning all her attention to the food.

The bar cookies that should be golden brown were black on top, completely burned. As the smoke began to clear she looked around the stovetop for the cornbread and lasagna. They were both gone. With a sinking heart she glanced into the oven one more time, and there they were, on the shelf below the one the pan of cookies had been sitting upon. The lasagna had been dumped on top of the cornbread, and they, too were burned.

She turned, looking for her veggie and cheese tray. The tray was there, but it was empty, wiped clean.

The back door was very slightly ajar.

Had she really just been thinking that she'd *miss* the Donovan children? Had a hug really made her have second thoughts about pursuing this great opportunity?

Before she could give in to her impulse and run into the backyard screaming their names, Mandel walked into the kitchen. "What the hell is this?" He waved his hand in front of his nose, wrinkled that nose and headed straight for the smoke alarm to silence the scream of warning. Then he turned his attention to the stove. "Please tell me this isn't supposed to be the meal that shows off your culinary skills."

"Nope," Ben called from the dining room. "It's in here."

Lauren could hear the humor in his voice, and she cringed. What was waiting for her in the dining room? She followed Mandel, and when they reached the dining room and she saw what was waiting for them, she felt as if she might faint. She went light-headed for a moment, and the edges of her vision turned gray.

The table was still nicely set as she'd left it, with cloth napkins and her good china and crystal and silver, but the food sitting in the middle of the table was *not* hers. A burned tuna casserole; an equally burned apple cobbler; a pan of blackened peas, still in the dented pot, the odor wafting into the air and fighting with the scent of roses. She only knew what was in the casserole and cobbler because Meredith had told her as they'd hidden the dishes in the oven in the Donovan kitchen. It took her a moment to recognize the fourth dish. All the cheese and veggies she'd sculpted into attractive shapes had been scraped into a large bowl, stirred well, and then, apparently, it had all been lightly microwaved.

Mandel sighed. "You're cute, you say y'all, you haven't said you won't dye your hair red and strap on some fake boobs, but honey, you have to be able to actually cook to be in this competition."

"I can cook." Lauren followed the two men to the front door. "This is…this is… I can explain."

Ben was already walking toward the rental car, but Mandel turned to look Lauren in the eye. "Don't feel bad, honey. Some people don't perform well under pressure. Reality TV isn't for you." With that he turned and walked away.

Lauren sputtered for a minute, and then she yelled after the obnoxious man. "Don't call me honey, *Eddie!*" She slammed the door, clenched her fists, and then pounded on the closed door once. And again.

Why would they do this to her? Obviously Justin had been a distraction while Meredith and Hank did the damage. And she'd thought he was being so sweet! She'd been suckered in by a hug and a wide grin. She should've known. Again she wondered, *why?* She'd done all she could to help Meredith, and this was the thanks she got.

As much as she didn't want to face Cole ever again, she wasn't about to stand here and let this infraction go.

The kids were up to something. True, the boys were busy packing and making plans for the week, and they were excited about seeing their friends. But there was something else going on. They'd been in and out of the house while he and Janet had made plans for the week. They'd been whispering, sneaking around.

They were in cahoots.

They were all back inside now, the boys gathering together their favorite video games and their bathing suits while Janet tried to convince Meredith to come along, too. Cole wasn't sure what he'd do with himself if they all decided to go with Janet. With Lauren out of the picture and all the kids gone, he wouldn't know what to do with himself.

Maybe he didn't know how to be alone anymore. That was a scary thought.

When the doorbell rang, he jumped. What now? When he found Lauren on the front porch he was momentarily blindsided. She could do that to him with a glance, steal his breath, his brain, everything he had left of a soul. She wasn't holding a muddy baseball or an offering of food, but judging by the expression on her face the coming conversation was more along the lines of "baseball" than "lasagna."

His eyes met hers, and he saw her hesitation. Some of the wind went out of her sails; some of the heat there cooled. Her voice was definitely cool when she said, "May I speak to your children?"

The whispering. The cahoots. "What have they done?"

"I'd really prefer to take this up with them, if you don't mind."

Cole turned and yelled, calling the kids to the front door. They came, along with Janet. When they saw Lauren standing there, they were chagrined—but not surprised. Three heads dropped; they all stared at the carpet.

Lauren walked into the house. She ignored him; she ignored Janet. Her attention was entirely on the children. "Why?" she asked softly. It was the kind of *why* that could break a man's heart, if he listened closely for the pain within it.

Meredith's shoulders rounded, as if she were trying to shrink into herself. Hank shuffled his feet and continued to stare at the carpet. It was Justin who bravely lifted his head and stepped forward. "We're not going to let some stinky old television man take you away."

"Yeah," Hank said softly. "You don't belong in New York, you belong here. We figured if they thought you'd made the tuna casserole and burned the peas they wouldn't want you for their stupid show."

"Oh, no," Cole whispered. "What have you three done?"

Meredith, the oldest, the one who really should've known better, hadn't said a word. Cole stepped closer, took her chin in his hand and forced her to look at him. He was angry, he was curious, but the tears and the sorrow in his daughter's eyes softened it all.

"I know what I did was wrong, but I don't want her to go. None of us do. You don't want her to leave, do you, Dad?" A couple of fat tears ran down her cheeks.

Janet stepped forward. "Cole, leave the girl alone. Can't you see she's upset?"

Cole raised a stilling finger in Janet's direction. She didn't like it, but she understood and she backed away.

Meredith spoke to her aunt. "It was Miss Lauren who made lunch today, not me. I tried to cook, but I messed it all up. I burned everything because I was trying to do too much at once."

Janet raised a hand to her heart. "Oh, thank God."

Cole's eyebrows shot up.

"She's twelve!" Janet explained. "She shouldn't be a better cook than me. Not yet, anyway."

Meredith looked at Cole again. "You didn't answer, Dad. Don't you want Lauren to stay?"

"It doesn't matter what I want," he snapped. "You can't meddle in people's lives this way." He turned to Lauren, who no longer looked spitting mad. She looked as confused as he felt. "I'm so sorry. I'll call the producer, I'll explain what happened…"

"Don't bother," Lauren said. "The jerk asked me to dye my hair red and play up my Southern accent." She twisted her lips a little. "Among other things. And he kept calling me honey. I had almost decided to turn down his offer, anyway. Life's too short to work with jerks who want you to deny who you are."

"But it's such a great opportunity…"

"Life is full of great opportunities. The trick is knowing which one to grab and which one to wave at as it passes by." She gave the kids a smile. "Don't think you three won't have to make this up to me. When you get home from your visit to Birmingham I'll expect you all to help me weed my garden."

"I can do that!" Justin said enthusiastically.

"Yes, well, we'll have instructions on how to do the job properly. And you'll be raking leaves, also, when the time comes," Lauren added.

"I can make a potion and mail it to the man who was mean to you," Hank said. "Do you want me to turn him into a frog or just make all his hair fall out?"

"Someone beat you to the punch on that one," Lauren said. "And you'd still have to help me in the yard, anyway."

"I'm sorry," Meredith said. "I just…really didn't want you to leave. I've been so mean to you and you were just nice to me and…and…if you leave I won't have a chance to make it up to you, not *ever,* and…" She snif-

fled, started to cry, and Lauren pushed her way past Cole
and wrapped her arms around Meredith.

"It's all right," she said. "I'm not mad at you. How
could I be mad at you? Yes, what you did was wrong,
but you've apologized and I can't ask for anything else.
Your heart was in the right place. It always has been.
We'll talk about it later, when you're not so upset." She
wiped away a tear with her thumb.

Cole didn't miss the little squeeze Meredith gave
Lauren, or, as she moved away, the enthusiasm of Hank's
hug, or the way Lauren braced herself for Justin's hug,
which came complete with his feet flying off the floor
while his little arms held on for dear life.

Then she said goodbye and left the house without
saying a word to him, or to Janet.

Cole turned to his sister-in-law, half-expecting a ton
of sharp, unpleasant questions about this woman who
had obviously wormed her way into the family in a very
short time. How much did she see? "Well, that was odd,"
Janet said, and then she smiled. "Very interesting. I have
a feeling that woman's a keeper."

"She's just a neighbor, Janet," Cole said halfheartedly.

"Yeah, right," she said dryly, "that's why she worked
so hard not to so much as glance in your direction." She
turned to the kids. "Let's finish packing and get on the
road!"

Cole was surprised when, not half an hour later, Meredith came out of her bedroom carrying her pink suit-
case. The one she used for sleepovers.

"Mer," he said, "I'm not mad. You don't have to run
off with Aunt Janet."

"I know," Meredith said. "But I emailed Hayley and
she said we could spend some time together this week,
so if you don't mind…"

"Of course I don't mind."

"Besides, while we're gone you can ask Lauren out on a date."

"Not a good idea."

"Why not? You won't have to worry about a babysitter while we're gone, and she said she's not going to New York."

He missed them already. Not that he would ruin Meredith's week with her friends because he'd be lonely. "I'll sleep late and plan my classes and watch movies. Who needs a date?" He winked at Meredith as Janet walked by and answered.

"You do. In the worst way."

Cole had always thought that Janet had made herself a big part of their lives because she was controlling. He'd always imagined she'd have a fit if he ever started dating again. No woman could ever take the place of her sister, could ever be mother to their children. And a woman he was serious about? Forget it. Talk about full-out war.

"I don't need…" he began.

Janet smiled at Meredith and asked her if she'd go pack up a piece of leftover chocolate cake for Uncle Fred, and as soon as Meredith was gone Janet's smile vanished. She hissed at him. "Do you really think you're doing these kids a favor by not having a life of your own? Do you really think it's healthy for them to watch you bury yourself in being a parent until there's nothing left for you?"

Cole felt his insides coil. Even though he'd had similar thoughts lately, this was *his* problem. *His* life. "Janet, this is none of your…"

"None of my business, yeah, I know," she snapped. "But the children are my business because they're Mary's kids, her *babies*. I realize that I sometimes get too involved, and I also know you tried to get a teaching job in Birmingham and it just didn't work out. If I've been difficult, it's because I miss the kids. Darn it, Cole, I even miss *you* now and then. In the end we want the same thing. We want the kids to be all right, we want them to be happy." She wrinkled her nose. "They're going to grow up with a very warped sense of what an adult's life is supposed to be like if you don't get off the stick and start living again. Now, I don't know this Lauren at all. She's pretty, she's a good cook, the kids obviously adore her...but that's not enough. But if you really like her..."

"The timing is wrong. The kids need me full-time."

Janet sighed; she did that a lot. "I knew a guy once, a friend of Fred's. He was in sorta the same situation, only his wife ran away with some other man, leaving him with a couple of children who were very young at the time. He did exactly what you're doing. He devoted his life to his children, turning down a couple of interesting romantic opportunities. There was one woman, I'm certain he loved her, but he let her go. The kids grew up, the guy grew old alone, the woman he loved moved on...and he died of a broken heart. Alone. No one came to his funeral but the kids, because he didn't have a life beyond being a father."

Janet stared beyond Cole's shoulder. She was such a bad liar.

"Next you'll tell me the woman he loved danced on his grave wearing a red dress."

Her lips pursed and she blushed. "Okay, so I made it up. But it could happen. That man could be you, Cole. Mary would not have wanted this for you, any more than you would've wanted it for her if the situation was reversed."

The conversation was cut short when Meredith returned, Hank and Justin on her heels. They were ready to go.

Cole got kisses and hugs all around, then stood on the porch and watched as the kids threw their suitcases into the trunk. Janet opened the door to the backseat, but the kids skirted around her and ran to Cole. More hugs, he figured. They hadn't been apart for this long in…well, forever.

But they stopped short of hugging distance. It was Hank who spoke, Hank who lifted his chin, stared into Cole's eyes and said in a very serious voice, "We did our part, now it's your turn."

"My turn to do what?"

"Make her like you," Justin said.

Meredith looked toward Lauren's house. "Take her to a movie that's not a cartoon. No talking animals, either." She pinned dark eyes on Cole's face. "And if you take her out to eat, don't go anywhere that has a happy meal."

Cole smiled; dating advice from his twelve-year-old daughter.

Hank leaned in close and revealed the secret location of his magic wand and the supersecret ingredients for his ungrumpy potion. Just in case. And then he whispered, with the weight of the world in his young voice, "Go get her, Dad."

Chapter Fourteen

Lauren went home, closed and locked the door behind her, and went straight to her office. There was a huge mess in the kitchen to take care of, and it wasn't something she could let sit for very long. It would take days to get the stench of burned food out of her house! She didn't bother to turn on her computer; she just sat in the chair at her desk, took a deep breath and cried.

She didn't cry about some stupid show she'd never been sure she wanted, anyway, and she certainly wasn't crying about the mess in her kitchen and dining room. No, she cried because her heart was broken for what had been lost. Cole, yes, but it was more than that. She'd been studiously avoiding falling in love for years, after her disastrous engagement had ended, because she didn't want to deal with a broken heart. She didn't want to give any man that power over her, not ever again. And now here she was, her heart broken not by one man but by an entire family.

They weren't hers; they had never been hers.

She didn't cry for very long. What was the point? Lauren wiped away her tears, blew her nose and lost herself in disposing of the inedible food the Donovan children had placed on her table, as well as the burned food from her own oven. Meredith had probably been the one to turn on the broiler. The child, learning to cook, had probably made that mistake at some point and knew what the result would be. The veggies and cheese in the microwave...that was Hank, she just knew it. It hadn't taken them a full two minutes to destroy the meal she'd planned for Mandel and the cameraman, Ben, he with the long hair and no last name.

Lauren knew she should eat something, but even though she hadn't eaten for hours she wasn't hungry. The thought of eating made her stomach turn. She tried to blame her lack of appetite on the disgusting food she had to dispose of, but she knew in her heart that her inability to eat went much deeper.

It didn't take very long to get the kitchen and dining room in order. She should be furious with the kids, but knowing why they'd done what they'd done she couldn't manage to rouse any real anger. Maybe she didn't belong in that family, maybe she and Cole had nothing left...but they'd come so close to something special, it broke her heart to know it was over.

While Lauren was taking out the garbage, she heard car doors slamming. Sounded like it was coming from the Donovan house. Aunt Janet, she supposed, heading home to Birmingham. Were the boys really going with her? For all she knew that had been a tale from beginning to end, something to give Justin an excuse to come to her front door and distract her. Then again, that was a lot of slamming doors for one woman.

After that all was quiet. Lauren half expected the ring of the doorbell, or a knock on the door, or a ball bouncing against the side of her house or rolling off the roof. But everything was perfectly quiet, just the way she liked it.

Go get her, Dad. Good advice. Too bad Cole didn't have a clue how to get that done.

Looking back, Cole could see that he had panicked when he'd told Lauren they couldn't see each other anymore. He'd convinced himself it was for her own good, that they didn't want the same things, that she would be better off without him. But what two people *did* want exactly the same things from life?

The truth was he loved her, and it terrified him. With love there was also pain that came out of left field and smacked you to the ground. With love came loss. One minute everything was fine and the next someone had yanked the rug out from under you and you were face-down, stunned, heartbroken. That kind of pain could really knock the wind out of you. He couldn't allow himself to fall in love again, to take the chance that he'd lose...

But the sad truth was, he *had* lost love. He'd not only lost Lauren, he'd purposely given her up. Hell, he'd thrown her away. He'd yanked away what they'd found so unexpectedly, and then the kids had ruined her chance at becoming a cooking star. Together, they'd effectively ruined her life.

Cole sat on the couch, propped his feet on the coffee table, and wallowed in the silence. Without the normal chaos of his life, there were no distractions to take his mind off all the mistakes he'd made. He couldn't use his kids as excuses for everything he'd done wrong.

Yeah, *go get her* was not so simple. From where he was sitting, it looked damn near impossible.

Lauren was up at the crack of dawn on Sunday, after grabbing just a few hours of sleep. Why was it that when she wanted most to escape into dreamless sleep, she couldn't manage? Her sleep had been fitful; her dreams disturbing.

So she cooked. Cooking calmed her the way cigarettes or booze or chocolate soothed others. She found great solace in creaming butter and whipping eggs, in taking a few simple ingredients and turning them into something mouthwatering. The scent of bread or cookies or cake baking had the power to wipe out the stench of everything else. Or at least move it to the back of her mind instead of the forefront.

Gradually her heart rate returned to normal, and she was able to think of things besides Cole Donovan. She didn't want to get out—she was in full cocoon mode—so she had to satisfy herself with the ingredients she had on hand. Butter, flour, cocoa, eggs, sugar, buttermilk… all the basics.

Since she wasn't in a time crunch, as she had been yesterday, she was able to make whatever suited her. Another chocolate cake, buttermilk biscuits, gingerbread cookies which were round instead of gingerbreadman shaped, since it was nowhere near Christmas and she didn't want any kind of man in her kitchen at the moment. Not even a sweet one. There was no way she could eat all this food. She'd make a trip to The Gardens this afternoon. The common area was always a busy place on the weekends, as family gathered to visit. Someone would eat what she'd prepared.

Oh, lemon bars…

The ring of the phone pulled her out of her zone. She half expected it to be Hilary, checking to see how things had gone with the producer. Lauren had thought about her editor last night, but since she didn't have Hilary's home phone number there was no point in worrying about it just yet. Monday morning would be soon enough to let Hilary know that she'd blown a great opportunity. She didn't think her editor would care that she hadn't blown it all on her own.

She glanced at the caller ID. Not Hilary, after all. She glared at Cole Donovan's name. "Just when I stop thinking about you, you have to call and remind me that you're right next door." She stuck out her tongue and turned away from the phone. Eventually the answering machine picked up. He didn't leave a message.

Lauren returned to her newest project. Lemon bars.

A few minutes later the phone rang again. Lauren checked the ID and sure enough, it was Cole again.

Or maybe one of the kids. Maybe they hadn't all gone to Birmingham. Justin had said he and Hank were going, so that meant Meredith was at home. Lauren reached for the phone. What if something was wrong? She stopped herself with her hand on the receiver. "I'm not 9-1-1," she whispered. But she didn't walk away. She didn't drop her hand. This time when the answering machine came on, Cole's voice sounded through the speaker.

"Pick up, Lauren, I know you're there."

He sounded annoyed, but not panicked. If someone had been hurt his voice would've been different. She did not lift the receiver.

"If you don't pick up right now, I'm coming over…"

Lauren snatched up the phone. The last thing she needed was for Cole to come to her door when she was in such a state. Eventually she'd get over him. She might even convince herself that he was right and she was better off without him. But she wasn't there yet.

"What do you want?" Maybe her voice was sharper than usual, maybe she sounded a bit like a shrew, but Cole had basically ruined her life, so she didn't feel as if she had to be polite when he called.

"I want you to get ready for company."

Lauren didn't want to see Cole again, not so soon. She certainly didn't want him in her house, in her *kitchen*. But here he was…and what he'd done had stunned her.

"They'll be here this afternoon," he said calmly.

"How?" Lauren asked. "How did this happen?"

"You'd mentioned his name and I remembered it, so I made some phone calls."

Made some phone calls. He made it sound so easy! "Why on earth would you do this? I told you I didn't want it, I don't need it, and the guy is a world-class jerk."

Cole leaned against her counter, so close to where they'd made love for the last time, and looked at her with piercing blue eyes she'd once loved. It had happened so fast! In love, out of love…

She narrowed her eyes and glared at him. "Are you trying to get rid of me? You think this will be easier if I'm in New York and you're here?"

"No," Cole said decisively. "*Hell,* no. If you decide you don't want to be a reality show contestant you can tell the jerk so. But you won't lose this opportunity because my kids interfered. If you decide to wave at it as it passes by, that will be entirely your choice." He waved his hand for effect.

"I don't know why he'd change his mind," Lauren muttered.

Cole folded his arms across his chest, kicked out one foot and crossed his ankles. So casual; so cool. "I explained to him what the kids did, that's all. He seems to think what happened is cute, and will make a nice intro for you, a good hook."

"Better than red hair, a pronounced Southern accent and a padded bra?"

At that, Cole looked surprised. "Seriously?"

"Sadly, yes."

"Then he's a bigger idiot than I am." Cole pushed away from the counter.

She wasn't ready to discuss how and why Cole was an idiot. "He's not going to want to film the kids, is he?" Her heart jumped a little at the idea of someone like Mandel taking advantage of the children, plastering their faces on television for all the world to see, making fun of them, taking away their privacy…

"They're all out of town for the week, staying with Janet for a few days, so we don't have to worry about that now. It won't be a problem."

"Good." Maybe some kids dreamed of being on television, but something inside her didn't like the idea at all.

"I talked to Mandel on his cell. He'll be here in an hour or so," Cole said. "Charm the guy, feed him cake and biscuits, and then you decide. *You,* Lauren, not him."

It was what she'd wanted all along, wasn't it? To make the choice herself. To be the captain of her own fate.

As if she actually had any control over her life! She could make plans, she could write neat little lists, she could even convince herself that she was in control. But then someone like Cole—and his kids—came along to shred all her neat little lists to pieces.

And she'd liked it. She'd loved it.

She loved it, still.

"What if I'm not sure I want to leave?" Lauren asked. "What if I'd rather stay here and…and see what happens next?"

"Don't turn down the deal on my account," Cole said.

Lauren's heart dropped. He was only helping her out because he felt guilty about what the kids had done, not because he cared for her. But before she could allow her heart to sink entirely into her stomach he added, "I'll be here when you get home."

Cole walked toward the back door. "If you'll have me. Can I call you later to see how it went?" he asked.

"No," she whispered.

He nodded, accepting her answer without argument.

"I think you should come over after they leave," she said softly. "We need to talk."

He looked back at her, smiled and nodded. "We definitely need to talk."

Was she fooling herself, thinking she saw a glimmer of hope in his eyes? Hope very much like her own; hope that her personal reality was about to take a serious shift.

Chapter Fifteen

Edward Mandel and his cameraman, Ben, were obviously hesitant when they walked through Lauren's front door. Maybe they weren't sure what they'd find here today. After yesterday's fiasco they had good cause to be cautious. One good inhalation of breath and they both smiled. There was nothing like the smell of fresh baked goods to improve anyone's mood.

"I don't usually do this, hon—Ms. Russell, but your neighbor was most insistent." Mandel smiled. "And I have to admit, it's a great story. We can use it."

Lauren just smiled. Half the time she didn't know how to respond to the obnoxious producer. "Please, call me Lauren. It's well past lunchtime, but can I get you something to eat?"

"That's why we're here." Ben winked at her.

"The woman in Memphis has been signed on, but there's no reason we can't have two Southern belles on the show," Mandel said, trying to sound practical and accommodating, she supposed. He held up one gnarled finger. "But she's called dibs on the red hair and she doesn't need a padded bra, so we'll just have to play up the Southern thing for you. We can make it work."

Lauren led them into the kitchen. She hadn't bothered preparing the dining room today. There was no freshly cut centerpiece, no fancy place settings. Just her warm kitchen, a pitcher of very sweet iced tea, and a counter lined with baked goods. Ben headed straight for the cake. Edward was drawn to the lemon bars. A stack of crystal dessert plates sat at the end of the counter, along with silverware and neatly folded linen napkins. Both men grabbed a plate and started taking samples, small portions of everything she had prepared. They sat at her kitchen table facing one another, a pitcher of tea and two glasses between them. Lauren stepped forward to pour them each a glass, but she didn't join them. She stood by, in case they needed anything that wasn't within reach.

For a few minutes there was silence. The only sounds were smacking, slurping and the occasional low moan of pleasure. Lauren got a great deal of pleasure herself from watching the men, the beatific expressions on their faces, the way they each found their favorites and dug in.

Mandel had cleaned his plate and gone back for more when he looked her in the eye. "You're in. Everything here is to die for, you're pretty enough, we'll use the story about the neighbor kids trying to sabotage you so you wouldn't leave.... I swear, I think you could win it all. I wasn't sure before this, but there's just something about your story that people will buy into. And it's not like you can't cook. Are the kids cute? Please tell me they're cute." He plopped back down in his chair, his plate refilled.

"Adorable," Lauren said sincerely.

"When can we start shooting? Maybe we can record a few scenes today. Ben, you've had enough to eat. Check the lighting in the kitchen…"

"No, thank you," Lauren said, with a slight smile blooming on her face.

"You don't want to use the kids?" Mandel sounded horrified. "But it's such a great hook. We don't have to show their faces, if that's what you're worried about, but…"

"You misunderstand, Mr. Mandel. I'm saying no to the whole thing. I don't want to appear on your show."

He looked stunned. Even Ben—who continued to eat and did not rise to start checking the lighting in her kitchen—was surprised. "*Everyone* wants to be on television," Mandel said.

"It's a lovely offer and I thank you for thinking of me, but I'm afraid the timing is very bad," Lauren said.

"What do you mean the timing is bad?" Mandel stood, indignant. Lauren didn't feel the need to point out that there were biscuit crumbs on his silk tie and a smudge of chocolate icing on his chin. "This is the opportunity of a lifetime, and if you don't take it you'll be sorry."

"I don't think I will." At least, she was hopeful that there would be no regrets. "You see, I have a choice. I can fly to New York, appear on your show, and if I'm lucky I'll be able to teach other people how to cook and decorate and entertain and make a house a home. Or I can stay here and practice what I preach."

Mandel sighed, sat down, took a long swig of iced tea that was so sweet it could make your teeth rattle. "If you change your mind…"

"I won't."

"Why on earth did you invite us back if you didn't

want the gig?" He shrugged, trying to appear nonchalant. "Not that I care. There are hundreds of people dying for a spot on my show. *Thousands,* even."

"I didn't invite you back," Lauren said. "It was my neighbor who called. I merely showed you a bit of Southern hospitality once you were here." And proved to them, in the process, that she *could* cook. "It was the least I could do."

Perhaps Mandel was annoyed, but he finished what was on his plate before he stood, reaching into a breast pocket inside his jacket to withdraw a business card and toss it onto the kitchen table. "Just in case you change your mind," he said. "I plan to have the cast set by the end of the week, so don't drag your feet."

Lauren didn't suffer a moment's doubt. She wouldn't be calling.

Ben grabbed a couple of biscuits for the road, winked at her again and followed Mandel out the door.

Instead of calling Cole—as if he wouldn't hear and/ or see Mandel leaving in his noisy rental car—Lauren walked next door. She left by way of her front door before Mandel reached the corner. She walked across the grass with purpose in her step, her destination straight ahead. In a matter of seconds she stood on the front porch and rang the bell. They'd cleaned up a bit. There were no more mangled dolls, no more muddy balls. She glanced up at the spot where she'd hang a fern, given the chance.

Cole opened the door quickly. Yeah, he'd been watching and waiting. They stood there for a moment, and she had to look up to meet his gaze.

"When do you leave?" he asked, his voice low and serious.

"I don't," Lauren said. "I turned the offer down."

She smiled. "The producer was quite surprised. May I come in?"

"Sure." Cole back away from the door and Lauren walked inside. "Why did you decide not to go?"

"My assessment of Mr. Mandel is no better today than it was yesterday. I have no desire to participate in competitions that will likely have me preparing meals with one hand tied behind my back, or eating bugs in order to get my hands on a stick of butter, or…I don't know, setting a proper table with a ball of twine, a stack of paper plates and a sheet of construction paper. That's not who I am."

Cole didn't smile, even though her examples had been purposely extreme. "Whatever the reason, I'm glad you're not going."

"Then why on earth did you track Mandel down and insist that he give me another shot?"

Cole glanced around the quiet room, even though they were all alone. Maybe he didn't want to look at her as he answered. Maybe he was afraid she'd see too much in his eyes. "Because if this is an opportunity you don't want, it has to be in your control to turn it down."

Lauren sighed. "Complete control is highly overrated."

He looked at her then. "Not something I ever expected to hear you say."

"Not something I ever expected to say." Lauren smiled a little. "There's another reason I turned down the chance to go to New York."

"And that is?" he prodded when she hesitated.

"I don't want to wave at you as you pass by, Cole. I want to grab you, literally and figuratively. I want to hold on to you through thick and thin, through mud and magic potions and maybe even long discussions—one day—about babies." She held her breath. There it was. She'd laid her heart on the line, she'd even presented him with his worst fear. Babies. Cole could either let himself be grabbed or he could turn away. If she was right about him... Oh, she so hoped she was right....

He moved toward her, cautiously, giving her a chance to back away. She didn't.

"I was wrong," he said.

She could see so much in his eyes, and if she was reading those eyes correctly this day was going to end very nicely. "Details, please? What precisely were you wrong about?" She tried to hold her ground, but it was hard not to melt when Cole was this close to her.

"When I told you it was done between us, I was wrong. I was scared and I panicked."

She just hummed under her breath. "Say it again."

"I was scared?"

She shook her head.

"I was wrong."

"Yes, that's it."

Cole reached out and touched her hair, pushing away one wayward strand. She reached up and placed two fingertips on his jaw. He was so warm and wonderfully solid.

"I haven't been in love for a very long time and when it came at me out of nowhere, I lost it. I said it was all about babies, and to be honest that really is a scary thought for me. But that's not why I ran. You got too close and I panicked." He stood so close she could feel the heat rolling off his body. "I don't want to lose you, Lauren."

Love.

"Do you drink out of the milk carton?" she asked.

"Daily," he admitted.

"Throw your socks on the floor?"

"I have been known to miss the hamper, on occasion."

"Do you leave the toilet seat up?"

"Now and then." He grimaced. "If this is a test I must be failing miserably."

"No test," Lauren said. "I'm just mentally revising a list."

"A list?"

"How tall are you, exactly?"

"Six-two."

Lauren sighed. "Might as well just shred my list, I suppose." She lifted her arms and draped them around Cole's neck. "Or buy a stepladder and some high-heeled shoes." Truth be told, she hadn't given that particular list much thought lately. There were other, more important things to consider. Like laughing, and learning to jump on a trampoline, and hugging kids who embraced with all they had...and falling in love with a man who turned her perfectly organized house into a home. "What are you doing this evening?" she asked.

Cole pulled her closer, dipped his head to place his cheek close to hers. "I don't know, what am I doing this evening?"

"You can help me deliver what's left of the food I prepared today to my grandmother's retirement village."

He grumbled. "Not exactly what I had in mind. We have the house to ourselves and you want me to go to an old folks' home to deliver cookies?"

"Gran's anxious to meet you." Lauren closed her eyes and took a deep breath. She loved the way Cole smelled, loved what his closeness did to her. "And I'm anxious for you to meet her. Gran's important to me. She's my rock. She's...me in fifty years, so I'm hoping you'll like her."

"If she's that much like you then I'm sure I'll love her.

Maybe not as much as I love you…" He stopped, seeming to choke on the words.

It was the second time in a matter of minutes that the word *love* had come out of his mouth. Unplanned, spontaneous. She liked it; she liked it a lot.

"I love you, too," she whispered.

Cole grinned, tipped Lauren's head back and kissed her. Maybe they didn't have every detail of their lives planned; maybe some of the years to come were going to be messy and difficult and chaotic. But there was one detail about which she had no doubt.

She was home.

* * * * *

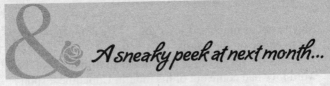

A sneaky peek at next month...

Cherish

ROMANCE TO MELT THE HEART EVERY TIME

My wish list for next month's titles...

In stores from 20th April 2012:

☐ The Cop, the Puppy and Me – Cara Colter

& Courtney's Baby Plan – Allison Leigh

☐ Daddy on Her Doorstep – Lilian Darcy

& Courting His Favourite Nurse – Lynne Marshall

In stores from 4th May 2012:

☐ The Cattle King's Bride – Margaret Way

& The Last Real Cowboy – Donna Alward

☐ Taming the Lost Prince – Raye Morgan

& Inherited: Expectant Cinderella – Myrna Mackenzie

Available at WHSmith, Tesco, Asda, Eason, Amazon and Apple

Just can't wait?

Visit us Online

You can buy our books online a month before they hit the shops! **www.millsandboon.co.uk**

0412/

MILLS & BOON® Book Club

2 Free Books!

Join the Mills & Boon Book Club

Want to read more **Cherish**™ books? We're offering you **2 more** absolutely **FREE!**

We'll also treat you to these fabulous extras:

- Books up to 2 months ahead of shops
- FREE home delivery
- Bonus books with our special rewards scheme
- Exclusive offers and much more!

Get your free books now!

Visit us Online

Find out more at
www.millsandboon.co.uk/freebookoffer

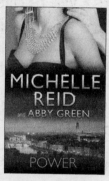

Have Your Say

You've just finished your book.
So what did you think?

We'd love to hear your thoughts on our
'Have your say' online panel
www.millsandboon.co.uk/haveyoursay

- Easy to use
- Short questionnaire
- Chance to win Mills & Boon® goodies

Visit us Online

Tell us what you thought of this book now at
www.millsandboon.co.uk/haveyoursay